Distant Danger

THE 1988 MYSTERY WRITERS OF AMERICA ANTHOLOGY

EDITED BY
Janwillem van de Wetering

WYNWOOD™ Press
New York, New York

Library of Congress Cataloging-in-Publication Data
Distant danger.
   1. Detective and mystery stories, American.
I. Van de Wetering, Janwillem.
II. Mystery Writers of America.
PS648.D4D57 1988   813'.0872'08   88-10709
ISBN 0-8007-7201-6

Copyright © 1988 by Mystery Writers of America
Introduction copyright © 1988 by Janwillem van de Wetering
Published by WYNWOOD™ Press
New York , New York
Printed in the United States of America

Contents

Introduction

Exotic crime—that was the idea we had when we (Mystery Writers of America's big bananas, fellow author Joyce Harrington and I) began making moves to put this volume together—but then a suspicion nudged me, whispering that maybe all crime is exotic.

Crime is that which is not done within the moral structure of our tribe. Crime is the—to others—hopefully invisible shadowside where we romp and revel behind strange and evil masks, inspired and cheered by demons of our own making.

So any crime story would do?

No, we needed distant danger. Exotic associates with faraway.

No American stories?

To me America is faraway, even though I live in the USA, for the place is enormous, and mostly distant to my structure, filled with body comforts. Besides, I got here late. As I played editor I could lean on my colleagues and they gracefully gave way a little, so we did include just a few gripping tales from nooks and crannies in "all them other states," as my nontraveling Maine neighbor would have it.

US city life was left out as, my coeditors claimed, blood and gore in the asphalt alleys would be old hat to most readers.

Islands were in, so was Outer Space, a dump in Africa, a ghoulish dead-end foreign little port, an artist's studio in Kyoto, downtown Hong Kong, and windswept rocks in the old country, down a memory lane spanning many generations.

Almost two hundred stories were submitted and we shivered, blushed, ohh-and-ahhed, looked over our shoulders, gasped, rushed in fear or dawdled in fascination, harrumphed shyly, grinned inanely, jumped up and down, through all and sundry.

Meanwhile, taking a minute off from hard work to please the audience and heaven, I thought I found another common denominator, competing with the exotic flavor we were so diligently looking for.

It seemed that, in each and every account of trouble that took its turn, my own conscience was tested, and I judged, rather than style, quality, plot, pace, or whatever other literary aspect an anthologer should be concerned with, the human predicament each author was holding up for shots, and the role *I* would have played had the author deemed me interesting enough to star in his or her ruminations.

Egocentric? No, please . . . I mean the *I* that also represents *you*, our targeted respected reader.

How would I behave? How would I cope with each fascinatingly presented set of good and evil? How would *I* choose?

Biographers of Freud and Jung came up with a similar fact: Both scientists, while reaching far into the human shadow, kept stacks of thrillers at their bedsides. They were both asked why, and they both said, "Oh, just to see how the choice might go."

I see another buoy bobbing on the surface of a lifelong enquiry: the *test stories* contemporary psychologists come up with, which are designed to determine the "level of conscience" of candidates competing to fill important positions.

I recall an example designed by Lawrence Kohlberg of Harvard: A man is told his wife is dying. She can recover if he provides an expensive medicine. The man is poor so he steals the drug. How about that?

Candidates who claim that theft is wrong because parents/police/peers say so are classified low.

Candidates who would steal to "please Jesus/Buddha/Ayatollah" fare little better.

The real good guy is the individualist who steals because he wants to save a beloved party. Love-for-others gains straight As, provided activity is prompted by a self that refers to no others.

A foolproof way to kick good guys up, bad guys down?

Wouldn't that be nice? A real good guy becomes police chief of a wicked city, a real bad guy replaces a test-animal to boldly strike out noplace/faraway, in some useful machine, of course, that relays back data, for science serves humanity.

How high or, goodness forbids, low, would we be rated ourselves?

Rather than submit to white-coated scientists who would analyze us in public, we might come up with some method that can safely be applied within the privacy of our own homes, where we can grade the ego's conscience, that unique set of self-determined values, these private proper principles which allow us to sink just so deep (rise just so high?) and no further. Or do we merely react along ways in which boss/advertiser/politician sets us up?

I wouldn't dare to outguess you, but my educators told me I was like water "flowing down the easiest way," or I was that subject to temptation that "a wet finger glued me down."

Really?

No!

Horrified by this harsh verdict, I desperately sought to restore a smashed image. Reality was too rough, so I preferred to test myself under the widest variety of theoretical circumstances. Faced by a limited imagination, I freely borrowed the fantasy of others.

By reading this book you may be doing that too, and if so, so what?

After all, calamities are statistically fairly scarce. If they were not, perhaps we wouldn't be around to have this dialogue.

The bad guys aren't knocking on my door today urging participation in some neighbor-hurting scheme, but we can have someone gifted imagine such an event, get him to write it down, then partake of that person's creation, then wonder whether we would buy the devil's spiel.

Okay, we would not. But now suppose: This is Nazi Germany 1938, or Chile 1987. An easy Yes will result in all sorts of personal favors, and if we're really sly nobody would ever know, although they'd be nicely envious of our new Mercedes.

Another test case has writer/reader identify with a jock/spaceman under duress, but with the solace of a charming female android human-look-alike programmed into a multidimensional cassette—some simple switch pressing and there she is, all ours, to—oh wow, oh wow.

The other guy abuses the magic that cost you/me the hard-won spoils of a previous trip to hell. Revenge?

In yet another example we live with and on alien smelly garbage. This is worse than Job's dungpile, but there's some chance of leaving the soggy stench for good. It might mean downgrading some ideals, but what ideals could you/I possibly have left?

Doubly tested, for exoticism and intimate self-justification, our selection now shows up. We do hope you may find it useful, for mentioned and maybe many other ends.

JANWILLEM VAN DE WETERING

Distant Danger

EDWARD D. HOCH

The Vultures of Malabar

In Bombay they don't always bury or cremate their dead," Simon Ark said as our plane passed over the sprawling harbor city on India's west coast and came in for a perfect landing at Santa Cruz Airport. "Bodies are sometimes left to be devoured by vultures."

"You can't be serious!" I protested. Visions of corpses in the streets filled my mind. Simon had persuaded me to accompany him to Bombay with the promise that we'd be meeting some of the leaders of India's thriving film industry. Now it seemed more likely we'd be fighting off vultures on their way to an evening meal.

"It's quite true," Simon insisted as our plane taxied to a stop at the ramp. "The Parsis, who came here from Persia, are followers of the Zoroastrian religion. Their religious beliefs forbid both burial and cremation because they defile the sacred elements of earth, fire, and water."

"But *vultures*, Simon?"

"You'll be meeting some of the Parsi community tomorrow, my friend. You can judge for yourself."

We traveled from the airport through the crowded streets of Bombay to the Taj Mahal Intercontinental Hotel, where I'd reserved adjoining rooms for us in the modern wing. It was a great old structure dating from 1903, and somehow it made me think of the years of British rule in India—the benevolent Raj which had faded away with

15

the twilight of empire. I left Simon at the door to his room and wondered once again what I was doing there.

Come to Bombay and meet the movie people, Simon had said, and it had sounded fine at the time. Neptune Books was looking for someone to write an authoritative volume on the Indian film industry for a series of cinema books I was editing. It was an opportunity to do some work while spending a week with Simon. I saw him all too rarely these days, especially since my wife Shelly had taken an active dislike to him.

"The man is an anachronism," she'd insisted one night over dinner. "He claims to be two thousand years old, but he doesn't have to act so much like he's living in the past! This is the twentieth century—almost the twenty-first! We care about inflation and energy and nuclear war, not about confronting the devil or seeking out ghosts or finding a unicorn! If the devil is still around, he probably wears a suit and tie and holds down a nine-to-five job in New York."

"Not in publishing, I hope." I'd learned to take Shelly's occasional outbursts calmly, especially on the subject of Simon Ark.

But in spite of Shelly's outbursts, or partly because of them, here I was in Bombay with Simon, gazing out the hotel window at a world I'd never seen before. A hot dry April breeze blew in off the sea. I knew what had brought me to Bombay, but I still didn't know what had brought Simon Ark here.

After a good night's rest to recover from jet lag, Simon and I boarded a black-and-yellow taxi at the stand outside the hotel. "What are those men doing?" I asked the driver as we pulled away from the curb, pointing to a pair of brightly turbaned natives who seemed to be peering into the ears of passers-by.

The driver, who spoke the careful English of India under the British Empire, explained. "They are kan-saf wallas—professional ear-cleaners. For about six cents in your money they will gently remove wax from the ear, using a small silver spoon, warm mustard oil, and wisps of cotton."

"I guess I've seen everything now," I said.

But Simon was more interested in our destination than in the ear-cleaners. "We'll be meeting with members of the Sanjan family. They are very active in the Bombay film industry, and I believe they'll be of great help to you."

"And to you, Simon? You didn't fly halfway around the world for your health. What is it here you seek?"

"I always seek the same thing, my friend, though it comes in different guises."

"The devil? Evil?"

"Perhaps only human greed. One never knows."

I'd expected the taxi to take us to one of the film studios or perhaps to the Pali Hill region, where many of the top stars had luxurious homes, but the cab circled Back Bay along the main promenade of Marine Drive and approached the wealthy area of high-rise apartments that was Malabar Hill. When I questioned Simon he merely smiled and said, "No movie stars today. That will come later. The Sanjan family are the backers, the moneyed people. They live here."

We took the elevator to the tenth floor. "Welcome, welcome," an elderly man said, opening an apartment door and beckoning us inside.

Simon introduced me and told him of my interest in a book about the Indian film industry. "This is Dilip Sanjan. He knows more about films than any other man in Bombay."

Sanjan was short and vigorous, though I guessed his age to be well into the seventies. He looked toward the living room and a woman came forward. "My wife, Reba," he said. She seemed no more than forty, and her beauty was striking. I was not at all surprised when he added, "Reba was a star in several pictures before we married."

While Reba brought us refreshments Sanjan and Simon settled down to talk. "Simon and I knew each other fifty years ago," the Indian told me. "When this present trouble arose, he was the only person I could turn to. He is an expert on Satanic rites."

I grinned at Simon and asked, "Did he look the same fifty years ago, Mr. Sanjan?"

"The same, yes. A bit older, if anything. What is the secret of your longevity, Simon?"

"Vitamins," Simon replied with a smile. "But let us get to the matter at hand. You have an unusual problem, Dilip." As he spoke, Simon's eyes followed Reba while she moved to open a sliding glass door onto the balcony.

"As I told you on the telephone, my old friend, it concerns the *dakhmas*."

"Explain them to my friend here."

Sanjan turned to me. "We are Parsis, followers of Zoroaster the prophet. Clustered at the top of Malabar Hill are seven circular enclosures, walled but roofless, where our dead are left to be devoured by vultures. These are called *dakhmas,* or towers of silence. There is a double door in the wall of each tower through which a team of four professional pallbearers, clad all in white, carries the body of the deceased. The towers are kept locked and no one else may enter them. The body is laid out naked on a circular stone platform about thirty yards in diameter. The platform slopes gently toward a central pit, and at a later date the pallbearers return to push any remaining bones into the pit."

"Simon told me about the custom," I admitted, repressing a shudder. It was their religion, after all. "Are there still many vultures in Bombay?"

"Enough. We have our reform element, of course, who claim the vulture population is declining and the dead should be cremated. But I can tell you, when a fresh corpse is carried into the *dakhmas* there are usually several dozen of the birds in attendance."

"You speak from personal experience?"

Simon Ark interrupted. "Dilip is a hereditary pall-bearer."

The old man bowed slightly in acknowledgment. "As were my father and grandfather before me." He turned his attention to Simon. "The custom has not changed since we talked of it some fifty years ago, Simon. But now something new and troublesome has occurred. Someone is entering the towers for an unauthorized purpose."

"You told me that much on the telephone," Simon said. "But how is this possible? Have the door locks been tampered with?"

"No, they have not. But remember that the seven walled enclosures are open to the sky, and hidden by dense vegetation which grows quite close to the walls. The walls are over twenty feet high, but a person could reach the top by climbing a nearby tree, then lower himself inside on a rope. A rope was found hanging from one of the branches."

"What about the vultures?" I asked.

"They do not bother the living."

Simon leaned forward. "How do you know of this intruder?"

"One of the pallbearers, Vija Rau, went to a *dakhma* a few days ago to push bones into the central pit. He surprised a man inside—a man bent over studying the bones as if he were looking for something significant. He leaped upon Vija, stabbed him in the side, and escaped through the open door."

"Is Vija alive?"

"Yes. He is recovering in hospital."

"I will want to speak with him," Simon said. "What other evidence is there of—"

He was interrupted by a sudden gasp from Reba. She dashed across the room to the balcony, and I caught just a glimpse of a great black-winged bird poised on the railing, then it was gone. Reba let out a shriek. We ran to her side and followed her horrified gaze to the floor of the balcony.

What was lying there I didn't recognize at first. And then I realized that the great black vulture, startled by Reba, had dropped the thing from its beak as it flew away. It was a human finger.

At the hospital Simon and I waited to see the wounded Vija Rau. I had still not fully recovered from the incident on the Sanjans' balcony, but Simon was inclined to take it in stride. "After all, the vultures are only behaving in their natural manner. No human or animal can ever be criticized for that. The Parsis place the bodies on the *dakhmas* to be devoured, and the vultures do their job. If one occasionally leaves the dinner table with a piece of its meal, who are we to criticize? Dilip tells me this sort of thing has happened before, and I'm sure it will happen again."

"I hope I'm gone from here when it does."

We were admitted to Rau's hospital room.

The Indian was a young man with a ready smile. He sat up in bed to greet us, though his left side still seemed to pain him a bit. "Dilip Sanjan told me you would come," he said, extending a hand. "I will be out of here in a few days. It was a foolish thing."

"A knife wound is never foolish," Simon told him. "The man might have killed you."

"I was so startled to find him in the *dakhma* that I inadvertently blocked his exit. I don't think he meant to harm me—only to escape."

"The doctor says the wound could have been fatal," Simon persisted. "Did you recognize the man?"

"Not by name, but he looked familiar. It was so unreal— as if I were seeing a film."

"Had you ever encountered an intruder there before?"

"Certainly not! The *dakhmas* are sacred places!"

"And there was nothing of value on the bodies?"

The wounded man shook his head. "They are laid out naked for the vultures. No clothing, no jewelry. In the case of Indu, I personally prepared his body, removing his ring and emptying his pockets after the body was delivered to us. He had a few trinkets—a little silver spoon, some gold coins—nothing more."

"And nothing remains in the *dakhmas* but bones?"

"Nothing."

"Who was this Indu person?" Simon asked.

"Indu Sanjan, a younger cousin. There is much intermarriage, and most Parsis are somehow related. Indu did odd jobs for Dilip's son, Dom Sanjan, at the film studio, but they were not especially close."

"Is the Sanjan studio successful?"

Vija Rau shrugged. "It is small."

"What did Indu die of?"

"An auto accident. He was struck by a hit-and-run driver while crossing the street near the Taj Mahal Hotel."

A nurse arrived to cut short our visit, and we said goodbye as she led us out.

"Did you learn anything?" I asked Simon as we reached the street.

"Not a great deal, my friend. It seems likely that Indu Sanjan was murdered by the hit-and-run driver, but that doesn't explain what someone wanted with his bones."

"You think it was for some sort of devil worship?"

Simon merely smiled. "Never invoke the bizarre until you have exhausted the mundane, my friend."

We went next to call on a film distributor who handled the output of Sanjan's studio. His name was Rudyard Chambers, and his traditional British bearing showed little trace of the Indian mother who Simon assured me had borne him. "Simon Ark," he said, repeating the name. "Yes, Dilip has mentioned you."

"I come as a friend of his," Simon assured him. "I am carrying out an investigation on his behalf. But you must realize there are some questions more easily asked an outsider."

"Of course."

"What can you tell me about Dilip's film-making operations?"

"You must realize first of all that Dilip Sanjan is something of an outsider here. The Bombay film industry is almost exclusively Hindu. So much so, in fact, that production of a new motion picture often starts with a sacred Hindu fire ceremony on the set. Sanjan's Parsi community is Zoroastrian, of course, not Hindu—an entirely different religion in a country where religion is still very important. The Parsis have excelled in ship-building, commerce, and industry, but there are few of them in the film business. Sanjan's little studio is unique."

"Has there ever been a hint of anything outside the law?"

"Never, to my knowledge. His pictures are small but quite respectable. He employs mainly actors from his own community though he also sometimes hires Hindus."

Simon seemed satisfied with the information, though I couldn't see that it was leading us anywhere. Chambers saw us to the door and promised to help us in any way he could.

It was late afternoon when we returned to the hotel, and I was startled to see Reba Sanjan waiting for us in the lobby. Her face was drawn and anxious, and my first thought was that something had happened to her husband. But it was not Sanjan she had come about.

"Vija Rau was stabbed to death in his hospital bed!" she told us, so excitably we could barely catch the words. "An hour after you visited him!"

Simon Ark reached out to steady her. "Do they know who did it?"

"No—someone must have slipped past the nurse's desk!"

"Did your husband send you here?"

She nodded. "He blames himself. He says Vija would still be alive if he hadn't summoned you."

Simon took a deep breath. "We must visit the tower of silence where Vija was wounded."

"It will be dark soon—There are no lights—"

"In the morning, then. Can you arrange it?"

"Only the hereditary pallbearers may enter the *dakhmas.*"

"I know that." He repeated his question. "Can you arrange it?"

"Only by stealing my husband's key to the locked doors."

"Do it, then, before there are more deaths."

She sighed and nodded. "What time will you be there?"

"Nine o'clock. Meet us at the foot of Malabar Hill."

"That may be difficult. There is a funeral scheduled for that hour."

Simon hesitated.

"Vija Rau's," she reminded him.

We dined at the hotel, in a surprisingly westernized setting with authentic French foods and wines. From down the hall came the familiar sounds of a discotheque. "Western culture is found everywhere," I commented with a wry grin.

Old Sanjan had invited us to a studio party and film screening that evening, but he phoned after dinner to say he'd be unable to attend because of Rau's death. He urged us to go without him, saying his son, Dom, was expecting us.

Simon and I arrived around eight. The party was being held on the elaborate roof garden of the studio office building. One could walk among flowers and trees while commanding a striking view of the city's skyline by night. There were perhaps a hundred people at the party, representing a side of Bombay's culture we hadn't seen before. Many of the women were fashionably dressed in western style, though a few wore traditional saris. Some, in what seemed a compromise, wore saris over low-cut strapless gowns.

One girl in her twenties wore a striking arrangement of gold jewelry that hung from her left earlobe. She asked me, "Are you alone?"

"No, I'm with that gentleman in black."

She eyed Simon critically. "Is he a priest?"

"Of a sort," I sipped my drink. "Are you Hindu or Parsi?"

She giggled and pointed to the red *tika* mark in the center of her forehead. "Hindu. I thought everyone knew that! But there are many Parsis here tonight. They are very successful in the business world. Do you know Dom Sanjan?"

"No, I'm a friend of his father." I told her my name.

"I'm Sushi Mahim. Come along and I'll introduce you to Dom."

Sanjan's son was a tall light-skinned Indian in a grey business suit. He was about my age and he shook my hand vigorously. "I have already met Simon Ark," he said in the perfect English to which I'd become accustomed since our arrival. "I hope you enjoy yourself."

"It's too bad your father couldn't attend."

Dom Sanjan nodded sadly. "Two deaths in the family are a terrible blow. Vija Rau was not really related, but he and my father were hereditary pallbearers together."

"The other dead man, Indu Sanjan, worked for you?"

"Occasionally he did odd jobs at the studio. I told Simon I saw the car hit him. I was the first to reach his body. I tried to apply artificial respiration, but it was too late." He glanced at a younger group with some annoyance, moving us away from the noticably sweet odor of marijuana. "But what brings you to Bombay?"

"I'm the senior editor of a New York publishing house. We're doing a series of books on film around the world and I want to include a volume on the Indian film industry."

"Speak to Sushi here. She is a script girl at the Hindi Studios, the largest in India."

"Is that right?"

"We make nearly two hundred films a year," she answered proudly. "About one-third of India's total output."

"I was thinking Dilip Sanjan might write a book about the Indian film industry."

"But his view is so limited!" she insisted. "He is not Hindu."

"You have a point."

"The Parsis are businessmen, not artists. They barter in diamonds and drillheads—not in dreams."

Simon Ark had moved over to join us. "Very poetic," he told her.

Before she could answer, Dom Sanjan took us both by the arm. "We must go downstairs. Ths screening is about to begin."

Like most Indian films, it lasted nearly three hours. A complicated plot was broken at frequent intervals by singing and dancing, and the audience seemed to enjoy it. Sushi sat between Simon and me, translating in a low voice when she thought it might be necessary. At the evening's end she promised to put me in touch with a woman at her studio about the book.

On the way back to the hotel, around midnight, I commented, "At least I have a line on an author. But the evening contributed nothing toward your investigation, Simon."

"On the contrary, my friend. It may have contributed a bit."

That was all he would say.

We were out early the following morning, eating a quick breakfast and taking one of the black-and-yellow taxis to the foot of Malabar Hill. As we approached, we saw several cars of a funeral procession starting up the winding road.

"Follow along behind," Simon instructed the driver. When we reached the summit we left the taxi and followed a line of white-clad mourners through the dense vegetation. In the lead were four men carrying a sort of stretcher on which the body was covered by a sheet. In their white shoes, white suits, and white caps, they reminded me of ambulance attendants removing an accident victim to the hospital rather than pallbearers carrying the deceased to his final bizarre resting place.

The procession of mourners paused before a high curving wall almost hidden by the bushes and trees. A key was inserted in the lock of the double metal doors and they swung open. A woman wept and moaned as the pallbearers entered the tower with their burden. Overhead I heard the flapping of wings and glanced up to see great black vultures settling onto the rim of the wall.

After a few moments the pallbearers came out with the sheet folded neatly on the stretcher and the procession started back down the hill. But suddenly Reba Sanjan detached herself from the line of mourners and hurried over to us.

"Here is the key," she whispered, producing it from within the folds of her white sari. "Be careful."

"Which tower was Rau in when he was attacked?" Simon asked.

"The next one along, to the right." Then she was gone, hurrying after the others.

We waited until they were out of sight and then went along the path to the next walled enclosure. From the outside it seemed identical with the first one, though I was glad to see no vultures hovering over this one. They were otherwise occupied for the moment.

"What do you expect to find here, Simon?" I asked.

"The person who stabbed Rau was obviously interrupted. If he feared recognition enough to kill Rau at the hospital, he may have been afraid to return here. Perhaps we may still find what he was seeking."

"What is there but bones? Didn't Sanjan summon you

because he believed someone wanted bones for a Satanic rite of some sort?"

"There are easier ways to obtain bones. The evidence here points to something else."

"But the body was naked, Simon! And the vultures eat everything *but* the bones!"

"Let us see, my friend." He fitted the big old key into the lock and turned it. The metal door swung open on squeaky hinges. Simon left the key in the lock and we entered the sacred place.

The morning sun had just cleared the top of the enclosure's far wall, blinding us for an instant with its brilliance. We shielded our eyes and moved slowly around the circular stone platform, carefully avoiding the bone pit at the center. The platform was nearly empty, with only a few scattered bones to serve as reminders of its purpose. I was thankful at least that there was no recent arrival there to greet us. But almost at once, as Simon bent to examine the remaining bones, shadows began to darken the sky.

"Vultures, Simon."

"They think we bring them a repast."

"Aren't they satisfied with the one next door? Let's go!"

"Vultures do not bother the living."

As they swooped low above my head I wasn't so sure. "Maybe they can't tell the difference."

But Simon ignored them and went on with his search. When he'd circled the stone platform he turned his attention to the bone pit itself. The bottom was lined with skulls and bones, probably several feet deep. "You're certainly not going down there, Simon!"

"No, my friend." He glanced at the sky. "But let us wait here a bit."

"For what?"

"Perhaps the sun will do our searching for us."

"The sun?"

"In less than an hour it should be high enough to shine directly into the pit."

"You mean we have to stay here for an hour?"

"Perhaps by that time you'll grow to love the vultures."

"I doubt it."

But we waited. I couldn't imagine what he expected the sun to reveal, but we waited.

"It would not have been too difficult for the mysterious assailant to lower himself on a rope and escape the same way," Simon observed.

"If anyone was crazy enough to want to." I glanced up at the vultures, who had retreated to the top of the wall. "What about the rope the assailant left behind after he stabbed Rau? Is there any clue there?"

"Not according to Dilip Sanjan. It was a common sort of rope, a kind sold everywhere."

I was growing more restless by the minute. "Wouldn't we be better off investigating Rau's murder at the hospital?"

"His murder began here. It only ended at the hospital."

Presently he walked to the edge of the pit to observe the sun's progress on the bleached bones below. "Do you see anything yet?" I asked.

"No," he admitted. "Let us give it five more minutes, until the sun reaches the far side."

"Do you think the intruder might have had a key, like we did?"

"If he had, he wouldn't have needed the rope, would he?"

"I suppose not."

Suddenly Simon gripped my shoulder. "There! Look there!"

I followed his pointing finger, but all I saw was the glimmer of something reflecting the sun. "What is it? A piece of glass?"

Before he could answer, there was a clanging sound behind us. Simon spun around, shouting, "The key!" I dashed to the metal doors, but it was too late. I heard the key turn in the lock.

"Someone's locked us in, Simon!"

"So it seems."

At first we tried shouting and pounding on the doors. Then I boosted Simon up on my shoulders and he attempted to reach the top of the wall. But his groping fingers were several feet short of their goal.

"Can you get a grip?" I asked. Simon felt around, but the old wall was too smooth to provide a hand- or foothold. He came down to the ground again. I settled down beside him. "Who would do this? Rau's killer?"

"No doubt. I should have realized he would return after the funeral to have another search for his treasure."

"What treasure? That bit of glass in the pit?"

"Unless I am mistaken, my friend, that bit of glass is a diamond."

"A diamond! But how did it get here? Sanjan told us the dead were stripped of all clothing and jewelry before being laid out for the vultures."

"And so they are. The diamond—if that's what it is—was inside the body of the dead man."

I stared at him.

"Don't you see, my friend? When Vija Rau told us he surprised his attacker going through the bones of the man Indu, I suspected it had to be because Indu had something inside his body the killer wanted. Last night before the film showing I overhead that young woman Sushi mention that Parsis sometimes dealt in diamonds. That was the first mention of diamonds, but it was enough to give me something to look for."

"What if the vultures have swallowed the diamond—if there was one—or carried it away?"

"Perhaps they have. Indu himself might have swallowed several before he was killed by that car. But I do think at least one of them is down in that bone pit."

"Well, it's nice knowing I'm going to die so close to a diamond," I said.

"You won't die," he assured me.

"No? Then suppose you tell me how we're going to get out of here? We're locked in an enclosure with a solid twenty-foot wall all around, on top of a hill where no one comes and no one could hear if we were to set up a shout. And I'm sure that if we were to fall asleep those vultures would start pecking at us.''

"You're needlessly upset," Simon said. "There are at least three ways out of here if you stop to think about it.''

"I'll settle for one.''

"Very well. Take off your shirt, please, and give it to me.''

"My shirt?'' I exclaimed and did as he said.

"Now give me your cigarette lighter.''

I've virtually stopped smoking but I still carry a lighter. I handed it over and watched as he weighted the shirt with a piece of bone from the platform. Then he flicked the lighter and held the flame to the shirt. It took a moment to catch fire, and another moment before the flames spread, then he handed it quickly to me.

"Your throwing arm is better than mine. Hurl it over the wall. As high as you can.''

"But—''

"Quickly!''

I threw the flaming shirt with its bone weight, and watched it clear the wall.

"Are you trying to burn us up before the vultures get at us?''

"I hope so," he replied seriously. "The vegetation seemed quite dry when we were outside.''

"Do you think it's catching onto anything out there?''

"If it doesn't we'll try again with my shirt.''

But a wisp of smoke soon appeared above the wall, and we could hear the crackling of dry underbrush. "What if no one comes to our rescue, Simon?'' I asked.

"We're perfectly safe in here. The entire hilltop could burn without getting through these walls. But it should bring the fire department before long, and they'll get us out of here. I only hope they're Hindu firemen and not Parsi, or they may not want to enter here.''

Simon was right again. The fire department arrived within twenty minutes. And they were Hindu.

Back at the hotel, I dug another shirt out of my suitcase. "What were the other two ways we could have escaped, Simon?"

"There is no time for that now. We still have a murderer to catch."

"Where do we start looking?"

"I would suggest right in front of this hotel, my friend. It was there that Indu was run down by the car, you'll remember."

"I wonder what he was doing there."

"We know that too, if you will only think about it. He was found with a tiny silver spoon in his pocket, yes?"

"For narcotics?"

"No—for cleaning out ears."

And then I remembered the professional ear-cleaners we'd observed on our arrival, working near the hotel's taxi stand.

We went down to the stand and observed the ear-cleaners for a time. "What do you hope to see, Simon?" I asked.

"Time will tell."

We had used the firemen's ladder to retrieve the diamond from the bone pit at the *dakhma*, and it now rested in Simon's pocket. I knew he was waiting for something or someone, but I couldn't guess what or who. "How do you know it'll happen today?"

"Because he thinks we're still up there, trapped and dying."

"But all I see are passersby having their ears cleaned out."

"An Indian custom, surely. But look at that man there. He's no Indian."

I followed Simon's gaze to a well-dressed man of vaguely Germanic features. The ear-cleaner had pushed

aside his long blond hair to get at the ear. "You're right,
Simon. It does seem odd."

"More than odd. Come on!"

I followed him across the sidewalk and watched in
astonishment as he gripped the hand of the ear-cleaner.
"Call a police officer," he said to me. "Quickly!"

But suddenly a familiar figure had materialized at our
side. It was Sanjan's son, Dom Sanjan. "What's the
trouble here? Can I be of service?"

There was a moment of confusion, with Dom Sanjan
reaching his arm toward Simon. Then I saw Simon
falling, and heard the screech of brakes. I acted faster than
I'd have thought possible, yanking Simon to safety as a
car sped past us.

"Never mind me," Simon ordered. "Don't let him get
away!"

"Who?"

"Dom Sanjan! He's the man behind these murders!"

The events of the next few hours tumbled over one
another. We held Dom Sanjan for the police, and very
quickly they also rounded up the ear-cleaner and the
Germanic customer and the man who'd been driving the
car that almost hit Simon. We were at the police station
near our hotel, telling the authorities what we knew,
when old Dilip Sanjan arrived with his wife.

"What is this, Simon? Did I summon you halfway
around the world to bring disgrace to my family?"

"I am sorry, old friend," Simon told him. "I would have
wished it to be otherwise."

"Dom cannot be involved."

"He is very much involved. Sit down and I will tell
you."

The old man sat, and Simon began to speak, telling it as
he had told the police not an hour earlier. "It was
diamonds, it was all for diamonds. A clever smuggling
operation involving a pipeline from South Africa. The
Germanic-looking man was a South African, one of sev-

eral who smuggled the diamonds out of the mine and into India. Their system was next to foolproof. The South African hid the diamonds in his ears, wearing his hair long to further conceal them. Outside our hotel he visited one of the professional ear-cleaners, who removed the diamonds while doing his cleaning. The diamonds were then passed to Dom Sanjan who, I suspect, sent them to their ultimate destination inside film cans shipped from your company."

"I can't believe that!" Dilip protested.

"Let Simon speak," Reba said, resting her hand on his arm.

"But somehow Indu betrayed the gang and started keeping some diamonds for himself and Dom Sanjan had him run down by a car and killed. The diamonds he was carrying were not found, though, and it was not until after the funeral that your son and his cohorts realized Indu had been in the habit of swallowing the gems after removing them from the ears of the smugglers. So one of the gang was sent to search the *dakhma* for the remains of Indu Sanjan. It was while he was looking for diamonds among Indu's bones that Vija Rau surprised him and was stabbed."

"But why was Rau later killed at the hospital?" Reba asked.

"He told me that seeing the intruder crouched among the bones in the *dakhma* was like viewing a film. It seemed that way, I suspect, because the intruder was a young actor who worked with Dom at the studio. He couldn't risk Rau identifying him later. It was this same man who drove the car that killed Indu and almost hit me today."

"It is a good story," Dilip said. "But what evidence is there to implicate my son?"

"He tried to push me in front of the car today when I caught the diamonds being passed. That is enough evidence for the police. For myself, there is the simple fact: the *dakhma* intruder had to know the diamonds were inside Indu when he died and not simply in his pockets. The only person who could have told him that with assurance was your son Dom, who admitted he was the first to reach Indu's body after the accident. He even told of applying artificial respiration—hardly a wise maneuver after a traffic accident when there could be broken bones and internal injuries. But it helped disguise Dom's real purpose while he searched the dead man for the diamonds. I'm sorry, Dilip, there were other things pointing to your son as well."

"Such as?"

"Rau half remembered his assailant from a film, and Indu worked at the studio for your son. Dom was the most likely link between the men. You or Reba could not have been involved because then the *dakhma* intruder could have used a key instead of a rope to enter the enclosure and search for the diamonds."

Dilip Sanjan had little more to say, and within the hour his son Dom had confessed to the charges, even admitting he'd been the one to lock us in the *dakhma*.

Later, Reba found us alone and said, "You have brought my husband great sadness, but you have brought him truth as well. It is better for him to know the human greed that defiled our dead than to conjure up demons where none existed."

I saw Sushi's friend the following morning and arranged for the book on Indian films. Then Simon and I flew home from Bombay. Shelly met us at the airport—I didn't tell her about the vultures.

HELENE JUAREZ PHIPPS

The Saintmaker's Wife

Except for the hair and beard, the figure of the Standing Christ was finished. Soon the Brothers would come for it and Cayetano would be the proudest santero in all New Mexico. As a maker of many carved, wooden saints, he knew that this one was his triumph. He sighed with pride as he placed his initials on the rough pine base; then in an ornate scroll, he added the year 1852. After that, he set the carved wooden santo on the ledge beside the rounded dome of the open hearth and put aside his paint brushes and his carving tools. His young wife, Meche, brought in his midday meal and she refused to look up at the figure.

"It's too bloody," she said. "His ribs are striped with blood and it makes me sick to look at him."

"You stupid child," Cayetano said, "that was the way it was with Him. The Son of God bled very badly. He bled from His hands, from His back, from His sides, and then, they rubbed the vinegar in to make it pain Him all the more."

"Who told you that?" Meche asked, as she set before him an earthen dish with the tortillas made from blue Indian corn and the beans fried many times and mashed with a wooden spoon to accommodate the old man's teeth.

"I have always known it," Cayetano said. "I have seen Him that way hanging from the cross in many chapels all over New Mexico, in Ranchos, in Truchas, in Chimayo, wherever the Brothers of the Third Order have placed my saints. I have seen Him with blood streaming into His eyes, pouring down His face." He rolled up a tortilla and scooped up a mound of beans. "You ask too many silly questions and you don't know, yet, how to cook beans. These have turned. . . ."

Meche watched the murky trickle of beans sliding sideways from the corners of his mouth. "It's the heat," she said. "They always turn sour in the heat. But if you hadn't been so busy with your Christ figure, we could have gone up into the hills where it is cooler. We could have camped by the side of the running stream and made love in the soft matting of the marsh grasses. Here it is too hot for beans and for love."

"Love . . . ?" asked the old saint-carver. "What is love?" He walked over to the figure that he had just completed. "To work with one's hands is love. To create for our Father is love. To love is to be at one with pain."

"To carve a bloody bulto like your Standing Christ is not my kind of love," Meche replied, shaking her braids with passion. "To work your old fingers to the bone for the brother Penitentes is not love. It is punishment. If you want a wife to make love to, you should take care of your hands. I don't want to feel your rough fingernails and your callouses, and you, all smelling of paint. If you only want to caress hard wood with all its splinters, then why did you take me from my parents? I could have waited for a young man. . . ."

"You have much to learn, chiquita. That is why I brought you up here with me. Only a man can teach you. You learn nothing from a boy."

"You think you will live long enough to teach me

anything?" Meche removed the plate that the old man had wiped clean with the last of the tortilla.

"I intend to," Cayetano said. "I fully intend to."

The thick walls of the adobe cottage held out the heat, but the door creaking open on its heavy pinions forced in a blast of air, warmer than any hearth fire. Meche stood in the low doorway and looked down toward the stream that trickled sullenly across the lower fields.

Four Penitentes from the new morada on the other side of the hill, in their black coats and their white tunics, stood hesitantly before the rude log bridge that spanned the slow-flowing waters, then one by one, stepped cautiously across.

"Here come the old blackbirds now," Meche said, "to collect their Christ for the new chapel. The new morada . . . that's all you and your Penitente brothers think about. Why do you have to work yourselves so hard for a church that believes in beating one's self to a bleeding pulp in order to get to heaven?"

"Surely, Meche, you will be sent straight down to the burning fires," Cayetano gestured to the dirt-packed floor and made her feel as though demons were lurking just below the surface, awaiting her descent. "You think you are so pure, you feel no need to punish yourself in the name of God. But there will come a time when you will want to feel the ecstasy of divine love." The old man picked at a scaly spot on his arm that was sinewed and gnarled like the branch of a weathered oak and removed a length of scab.

"I don't need a whip laced with yucca thorns at my back to achieve God's forgiveness," Meche retorted, her voice sharp with scorn. Then her eyes darted upward to the wall behind her husband which held the lengths of leather and the links of chain that were used in the Penitente rituals. "Nor do I need a beating with metal prongs to leave me bruised and full of sores."

"That's because you women are too weak. It takes a man to repent with vigor."

"Then you must have more to repent. Whip yourself all you want. My penance is standing by and watching you work yourself to death for the Brotherhood."

"You must stop that kind of talk," Cayetano said. And then for a moment, Meche thought that he had forgotten that she was standing there before him. He looked up at the santo on the ledge and murmured, "You will have to cut your hair, Meche. The Standing Christ must have real hair on His head, a tuft for His beard."

Meche put her hands to her waist-length braids. Her heavy brows that met in the center of her long Spanish face lifted upward as though she had just seen the devil. "My hair! Why does He need my hair?"

"Because He is a man. What is a man without hair? I can't give the santo unfinished to the Brothers."

Meche looked at Cayetano. The thick thatch of hair on his head was turning white in stripes running backward from his narrow, ascetic forehead. "Use your own hair," she said, "he's your creation."

Cayetano's eyes darkened with longing and regret. "The Son of God was a young man when He died on the cross. His hair would not have been white, like mine. He had your youth and your strength, and then, for Him, it was all over."

"You've carved saints before this one. Where did you get hair for them?" Meche asked.

"I had a wife before you. Her hair was still black when she died. She asked me to save her hair for the santos. In that way she felt she could live on a little longer. But now . . . there is no more."

"Then she is still alive in your mind. You see her when you go to chapel. The saints in their niches are wearing her hair."

"I have nothing left of her," Cayetano said. "Her memory began to fade when I first laid eyes on you. You are being very foolish to be jealous of the dead. But you are foolish because you are young. You have not had time to weigh your desires and your dreams."

"I have no dreams," Meche said. "Your wife, the one who died, knew you when you were young. What have I to look ahead to?"

"Life. A long life," Cayetano replied.

"Then, you'll have to give me money to go into town to buy beans and corn. We need food to live. And we never have enough. If you would give up your carvings and farm this land, we would be richer. . . ."

"There is no one else in the valley who can carve a saint with soul in his face and the body of a virile man. Why should I ruin my hands with a harrow?"

"Save your hands, then. But it will be up to me to see that we don't starve." Meche picked up the basket with a handle and slipped it over one smooth arm. She had only time to glimpse the aged, troubled face of Cayetano before she was out the door.

"Wait, Meche," he called to her. But she was already halfway to the bridge. He had to run awkwardly, crab-wise, downhill, to catch up with her.

Meche waited impatiently, trying not to show her annoyance for the time it took him to reach her side. Cayetano was breathing heavily as though a stubborn bubble of air was trying to burst forth from his chest. He took some coins from the beaded buckskin sack that he carried at his waist. His hands were trembling. "Here, I want you to have something extra for your market." He handed her another handful of silver, ". . . and more . . . for a skirt. The Brothers are coming to pay me for the santo. You can buy yourself something pretty. I want you to look nice."

Meche took the money from him. "You shouldn't have hurried so," she told him. "I would have waited." She dropped the coins into her basket. "I'll cut my hair for you when I get back."

Near a stand of aspen, she met the Brothers walking single file. As she stepped aside to let them pass, she pulled back her shawl so her white blouse showed and allowed them a glimpse of her brightly bordered skirt before she lifted it high above her knees in order to climb the turnstile bar. She avoided looking back to meet Cayetano's eyes and kept her own on the precarious footpath, her thoughts inside grinding away like the corn being ground to powder on the neighbor's metate.

The road to Santa Cruz was a cowpath of shifting sand dotted with tufts of dried grasses and brittle weeds. The path curved through a deep pine forest. For a while, Meche followed two wild turkeys who stalked on ahead until, shaking their wattles and clucking frantically, the birds skitted off into the brush.

When Meche emerged from the shadows of the trees the shawl felt hot and heavy on her shoulders. She passed, first, the low-lying adobe houses, then clusters of shacks, the outbuildings of the town. The sound of her soft-soled moccasins crushing the dried leaves on the path set the tethered dogs to growl and bark.

When she reached the plaza the sun was at its peak. It was time for the long and awesome siesta beneath the heavy weight of the heat and the hour. There were still a few Indians in blankets seated about the central square. The Spanish-speaking people were resting behind closed doors.

Here and there, a pile of tomatoes on a strip of cotton, a basket of onions on the ground, some earrings of silver, little mounds of herbs dried in bunches—cumin and oregano and thyme—temporarily abandoned by their vendors. On one corner that led off to the narrow side street, a hollowed-out gourd held little buttons of peyote.

A small boy with a taut, mud-grey body and spindly legs tapped her on the shoulder, holding out a few shrivelled buttons in his palm. "A dream, Señorita, buy a dream . . . a handful of dreams," the boy chanted softly. His dark eyes with heavy lids were drooping in the heat.

"Señora," Meche corrected him. "How much?"

"Very little. How much is a dream worth to you?"

"I have no dreams," she said. "How should I know?"

"Please," he went on, tugging at her skirt. "A dream will make you happy."

"Instead of a dream, I want something cool to drink. Show me where...." She followed the boy to an outdoor stand where tamarind juice was being sold by the jarful.

Seated in the shade beneath a ramada covered with branches of pine and yucca stalks, she listened eagerly as the boy told her the gossip of the town. "See there," he said, "coming out now?" He pointed to the church across the square. His eyes grew rounder with the excitement of the revelation.

Meche looked over his head to the little box of a chapel, its mica-whiteness covering the soft adobe contours. A black-robed priest with his scepter raised high was following a coffin. By his side, a man and woman dressed in black sluffed through the dust, and three young boys in tight-fitting suits walked slowly behind them. "No one important," Meche said, "it is such a small procession."

"Her name is Luisa. Luisa Valdez."

"Luisa Valdez? I don't remember her," Meche said.

"You shouldn't. She sinned very badly. No one wants to see her to her grave."

"You can't punish the dead after they are gone," Meche said. "What did she do?"

Three men with rifles in their hands walked by the procession and took cover in the shade of the vigas that overhung the buildings clustered across from the church.

"Her husband found her with his friend, Pelayo. He killed her. He stabbed her twenty-two, maybe twenty-seven times."

"Her own husband?" Meche felt a chill ripple down her spine, the wings of danger fluttering about her. "And the other man? What happened to him?"

"The husband stabbed him only twice. But that was all

he needed. He was not a young man. He died almost at once."

Meche sipped her drink and felt the syrup acrid and cloying in her mouth. "Where is he now? The husband?"

"Valdez? Antonio Valdez?" The boy shrugged his narrow shoulders. "On a roof somewhere? In a barn, perhaps? Hiding behind the tall grasses in a field? ¿Sabe? Everyone in town is looking for him. That is another reason why no one is around to see her to her grave."

"Another drink?" Meche offered.

"No. I have my business. You're sure you don't want one?" He held out a peyote button with a downy center. "It makes you sleep. It makes you dream."

"What have I to dream about?" she said. "Go push your dreams on someone else." She reached out to the boy's thin, dusty arm to try to keep him with her. She had no wish to stay in the town alone. "When did he kill Luisa?"

The boy didn't know exactly. She had been found slashed to bits. In some places, almost cut apart. The sun was dimming and the afternoon was beginning to come to an end. In the distance, storm clouds were gathering above the mesas.

"There was a jovencito from my village. Valdez." Meche rolled the name over her tongue, savoring it. "I think his name was Antonio. I remember him. He was wild ... always running off. ... Yes, I wanted to know that Valdez. But then my parents gave me to my husband. He took me up to the hills. Now we live so far from town, where nothing ever happens." As she talked the boy gathered his peyote buttons and put them inside the lining of his trousers. He was ready to leave her.

The two of them walked out into the square just as the first large drops of rain began to spot the dark red earth.

After the siesta, more people were walking about the town. Nearly every man carried a gun, even the trapper, with six traps on his back, who was gathering up his load of skins from one corner of the plaza. As the rain started to come down with force, two women who had been haggling over prices picked up their skirts and ran for refuge to the arcade that housed the general store and cantina. Following them inside to shelter, Meche spied some bright-colored blankets and skirts that had been brought in by the Indians.

The storetender's wife came out from behind the stacked bolts of calico to help her. Two of the men with guns, and the trapper, brushed past Meche on their way to the bar at the far end of the store. They were talking about the murders.

"Why haven't they caught him yet?" Meche asked the woman. "There are so many of them. This town is so small. There are so few houses. Hardly a tree. . . ."

"The women would hide him," the storetender's wife said. Her earrings jingled as she moved her head. She wore silver beads around a wrinkled neck. "The girl was a fool." The woman looked down at Meche's feet. Meche could see the wide center part that divided her head into two halves. "She left a young man for another three times her age."

Fingering the soft wool woven from the fleece of local sheep, Meche discarded one length of fabric after another, until she found a skirt with stripes of pink and yellow zigzagging against a vibrant blue ground. She held the skirt in front of her and checked its length, then folded it and tied it in a cloth that she had knotted at four corners to form a sack. She twisted it all together into a compact bundle that could fit into her basket. "How old was Luisa?" she asked as she paid the woman for the skirt.

"About your age . . . seventeen? What could she have wanted? The man was so much older . . . but then, he had a little money, a house with furniture, a chair for the priest."

"We have a chair for the priest," Meche said. "But there

must have been something more. The young ones don't
know everything.''

Outside a fork of lightning streaked across the sky.
Meche huddled in the doorway afraid to venture out.
Across the square, in front of the church, the two aspen
were bending beneath the wind and the geraniums on the
ground around them were being crushed by the force of
the rain. The water that ran in the street was the color of
rust, like the earth and the stones.

At the other end of the store was a partition with a
Dutch door that led into the cantina. The upper half of the
door was open and walking over to it, Meche saw the boy
with the peyote buds standing at the bar, drinking from a
heavy mug. She edged over to the opening so that she
could catch his eye. She wanted him to walk with her so
that she would not have to be alone outside with the
thunder.

The men inside, drinking, were talking louder about
Luisa and Antonio. Their voices could be heard above the
pitch of the rain.

Meche pushed open the lower half of the swinging
door. ''Leave her name out of it,'' she cried. ''She can't
answer for herself, anymore.''

''She got what she deserved.'' The trapper who was
standing at the bar picked up his glass and walked
towards her.

''But what will he get?'' Meche asked. ''If she deserved
to die, then he deserves to live.''

''Who knows what they will do to him? I wouldn't want
to be in his shoes. One cut would have been enough.'' The
trapper came closer, holding his unfinished drink in his
hand.

The smell of the strong liquor made Meche's stomach
turn. His big muscles and his dark unkempt beard re-
pelled her. She moved outside toward the edge of the
overhang. The rain blew in on her face, on her hair. Her
heavy braid caught the drops and held them. She tried to
shake off the dampness. She remembered her promise to

Cayetano and looked up at the sky. The black clouds were moving in bunched, grape-like clusters toward the mountains.

The drink was thrust up to her face. She pushed the trapper's arm, holding the glass away from her. Yet, she had to voice her question. "Why wasn't she content with Antonio? Why did she need to go to someone else?"

"Why does anyone?"

"But she was dead. How could he keep on . . . ?" She made a slicing movement with her hand and dropped her basket with the skirt.

The trapper watched while she bent down to pick it up. "What've you got there?"

"A new skirt."

"Girls always want to look pretty for someone besides their husbands. Their husbands don't care."

"Mine does. He is different. He is an artist. He looks for beauty around him. He wants me to look nice."

"He must be a rich man, then. Like Luisa's dead friend." He laughed hoarsely.

"But why did she need another? Wasn't one enough?"

"He found her with an old man. That's why he punished her so. A man older than her father."

"How old was he?" Meche asked.

"About seventy," the boy spoke up.

"No, hijo you have it wrong. He was closer to my age. He was a rich man. He owned three cows, maybe more."

"Maybe all she wanted was milk." The laughter from inside grew coarse and Meche, staring at the water running in the road, finally stepped down into the swirling eddies. Her shoes were instantly dyed rust-red and her legs up to her ankles. She sloshed on through the puddles to high ground beyond the plaza.

Half a dozen men with guns were standing at the far edge of the square, looking up at the clearing sky.

"Someone should climb a tree and look down on the rooftops," the man who appeared to be the leader said, two six-shooters at his waist like waiting copperheads.

"Why?" A boy who looked enough like him to be his
son set his Winchester on the ground. "You want me to
try?"

"He could be up there somewhere, hiding behind the
watchtowers."

"Why should he hide? He only did his duty," Meche
said to the woman from whom she bought some beans
and husks of corn.

"Luisa comes from a big family. Half of those you see
around are her brothers. If he hadn't cut her so many
times they wouldn't feel such anger."

"Perhaps he had too much passion left, and no other
way. . . ." Meche said. There was so much excitement in
the town, she didn't want to leave. So much could
happen and she would miss it all. But the rain had
stopped and she had no more reason to linger. Cayetano
would be waiting for his supper, and her hair. The
Brothers would have to leave without their Christ. The
thought that she had caused them a fruitless journey
made her smile.

She started home slowly, the wet earth sucking at her
shoes. She walked past the lilac-covered walls of the
town and out into the open country. It seemed miles
before she reached the first hilltop with the stark Penitente cross, then the long sloping path to the valley. She
could see that the rains had changed the course of the
creek and she detoured through an apple orchard walled
in by sandstone cliffs, beyond it, a gentle rise studded
with wooden crosses. Just ahead was the pine forest with
the path leading to Cayetano's house. Through the arch of
evergreens, she could barely glimpse the fringe of aspen,
the leaves shimmering, lightly gilded by the late afternoon
sun.

The pine branches were still drooping from the rain
when she entered the deep woods. She pulled her shawl
over her head.

She had only taken a few steps into the shadows when
she heard a muffled cough. Behind a boulder, half-hidden

by chokecherries and rabbit brush, she saw the fringe of a blanket, the silhouette of a leg, white-trousered, revealed by the branches shifting in the wind.

When she walked over to Antonio Valdez he was already past the first minutes of awakening. He was sitting up beneath the branches of yellow pine, with bloodshot eyes looking ahead to the clearing. His black hair was plastered to his scalp. His clothes were stuck to his body.

Meche tried not to breathe too deeply, not to reveal her intense fear of him. "Antonio . . . Antonio Valdez. I know you. I know who you are. Don't be afraid. . . ."

Antonio started up suddenly, and Meche saw him reach for his knife.

"No, no. I will not betray you. Walk a ways with me and I will show you how you can get away."

He was barefoot in his leather sandals. He had no jacket. He dragged a saddle blanket with him as he stood up, still holding his knife, uncertain.

"You could sleep after all that?" Meche asked in a low, calm voice. "I should think you would have been running. You dare not stop here. They are looking for you with guns. I don't blame you for what you did, but you should run."

He was looking at her, unseeing. She wondered if he felt that she was really there. "You must come with me. I promise . . . I will help you."

As she knew he would, he followed.

Where was Antonio Valdez going now? She turned to see him walking by her side. She devoured him with her eyes, this robust, haggard-looking young man who in an ecstasy of impassioned love had carved up the woman he had loved. Could he hear the rapid beating of her heart? They walked side by side through the darkest portion of the forest. Golden leaves of the aspen ahead were fading in the receding light.

Meche stopped and faced her silent companion. "If you stay here, Antonio, I can bring you food. But they will find you. You cannot stay here forever. You must make your way out of these mountains. The whole town is enraged. If you can get down to Santa Fe, you'll be able to catch the stage. . . ." She reached inside her basket and took out a handful of coins. She handed him the remainder of the market money. Then she dropped her shawl from her shoulders. "Let me have your knife."

Hesitantly he took the money from her and then handed her the weapon that he had so recently used to take two lives.

"With my hair and my rebozo over your head and my skirt, you can possibly get far from here without anyone's knowing." Meche dropped to her knees beside a log and motioned for him to cut off the yard-long length of braid.

He shook his head and refused the knife that she held out to him. He stood there, motionless, and watched as she began to cut through the heavy strands of hair. One length she wove around her fingers into a single curl; the remainder she pulled into a formless mound, like a nest. Then she handed him her new skirt and her shawl. "Go on," she urged, "put them on, then I will fix the hair beneath the rebozo. It is your life." She pleaded with him, but he still refused. "They will be looking for a man, not a woman. You will have to pretend for a while. No one will know."

Again he shook his head. "The skirt is new," he said. "You have never worn it. Give me your old one."

Meche recognized the flame of longing in his eyes. He is a man who understands a woman's heart, she said to herself. Inwardly she cursed the girl who had betrayed him. Then, shyly, she undressed and stood naked before him. She turned, and his eyes moved up and down her body.

Antonio fell to his knees and pressed his head against her thighs.

"Oh, no," she said, protesting lightly.

"Oh, si," he said, "si, si, si . . ." like the hissing of
a serpent. And then he did everything to her, she
thought, that he must have done to his wife many times
before he dreamed of killing her. Would he kill her
too, she wondered, as she moved closer to him in a
final embrace. He held her to him and she felt the
thumping of her heart gradually subside, and she began
to shiver from the dampness of the ground and a forming
fear.

He helped her up, then turned away, respectfully, as
they both dressed. Her eyes filled with tears. She had
deceived her husband and she had enjoying doing it, and
she was helping a wife-killer to escape and it was all
wrong. But it was worth it.

Antonio moved to touch her before he left, but she
turned from him and walked quickly to the break in the
aspen. Darkness descended without a twilight. Her feet
took her on ahead until she saw the faint line of smoke
coming from the rounded chimney, then she began to run.

The front door was open. The dampness from the rain
had collected by the stoop and the earth was spongy
underneath her moccasins as Meche walked inside and
stepped down into the small, cell-like room.

The smell of mud and corn and chili came in whiffs
into the house. The thick walls, the close interior,
the low-beamed ceiling were bathed in the odor.
Antonio Valdez and his dead ones could not enjoy that
smell.

"I have to tell you . . ." Meche began.

But Cayetano had fallen asleep before the figure of his
santo. Meche saw that he had added even more blood to
its ribs while he had been waiting for her to return. The
drops of red paint that he had used had dripped onto the
indigo blanket that he had spread out on the floor. The
whip with yucca thorns that had been hanging on the
wall was not in place.

Meche knew that she should awaken him and tell him

that she had returned, but her body was still singing and she wanted to hold onto the feeling of renewal that coursed all through her veins. She wanted to hold it all contained within herself.

Kneeling beside Cayetano, she saw the ancient toes, the nails curling over the tips, chipped and yellowed. He was so old, she thought, she had never considered it so intensely before. So old and wrinkled and coarse and hard. His skin was like that of the desert lizards and the golden horned toads. And she remember the sibilant triumphant call, like that of a young serpent before it shed its skin. Antonio was like that, he would toss off the vicissitudes of life, the deaths and the dangers, and he would grow a second skin.

Meche got up and took the coil of hair that she had saved from her braid and set it at the feet of the Standing Christ, an offering. If Antonio should catch the stage and not be recognized in her dress and shawl, then he too would find a resurrection.

From the flowered leather chest next to the priest's chair, she brought out another blanket and spread it over Cayetano. He stirred under the weight of it and Meche saw that he had the yucca whip in his hand.

He waited until she lay down beside him before he asked her, "What was it you wanted to tell me? I heard you when you came in. I was not asleep." He waited a long time for the answer that did not come. She was grateful that he did not pursue it.

Both of them were lying on their backs because of the hard floor that bruised their hips. They had to suffer this bruise, unless she got up and found another blanket. The beams of the ceiling seemed to be coming closer down on them. The air in the room was smothering.

"I love you, Meche," she heard Cayetano whisper in her ear. "The Christ will look handsome with your dark hair."

The room was whirling. "Yes, I know," she said. She pulled the blanket over her and she could still see Cayetano's toes. As she moved closer to him, she reached over and took the whip from his hand and placed it by her side. She sank heavily back onto the floor and could feel the rough spikes pushing, punishing against her thighs. She had had her dream and it was gone, and she knew that, in the long night ahead, she would never find another. With her hand clenched tightly around the handle of the whip, she fell asleep with her head on her husband's shoulder.

HERBERT RESNICOW

Greater Love
Than This . . .

The first murder in space? Right here on Grubstake's Asteroid Base. I was one of the five people involved. Make that three people. Three people and two other people. Two others who were one other. That's the truth. Sort of.

It happened long ago, just after they made me Base Manager. No, he wasn't convicted; wasn't even tried. It was damn hard to get qualified people out here, then. And he'd been punished enough. Haven't seen him since. He still owes me for a very expensive piece of equipment.

Those days it was like the Old West of two hundred years ago. A prospector would get a grubstake from a merchant—food, equipment, a mule—and go looking for gold. On the Asteroid Belt I give the team the Base, food, equipment and a butterfly, and they go looking for iridium. You can make a lot of credits here if you work hard. Retire in ten years. If you live that long. Some do.

But iridium isn't it. The dream is to find a cluster of asterites: more beautiful than opals, rarer than alexandrites, and a million credits per carat.

A butterfly is a tiny version of the Base, except that its wings are disproportionately large so as to hold all the photovoltaic membrane. The Base has only to hang above the Asteroid Belt; you can watch it unrolling slowly below us, the most beautiful sight in space. The colors—the mass—the majesty—like the wheel of God. I watch it for hours when I can't sleep. But in a butterfly you have no time to watch; a butterfly has to hop at least twelve asteroids per tour to earn its keep, so it needs more juice for its ion engines and to keep the accumulators full. Just in case. So we have two bike generators on a butterfly. The team does a lot of pumping; we keep the wing mass low. Mass is the controlling factor out here.

Because of this, a pair of mature philas makes the best team. They're smaller than men and less likely to go cafard on a tour, the way some philos do. Next is a mature hetero pair. Then, believe it or not, two young female heteros. I had two Chinese teenagers once, broke all production records before their butterfly got holed. They weren't all that strong, but together they weighed one-eighty pounds Earth, which is less than some of my fatslob male prospectors mass all by themselves.

I watch the strength to mass ratio; the bigger the ratio the more foodsticks you can pack into the boat. The more food, the longer the tour and the longer the tour, the more asteroids can be prospected and the more iridium found. And the more chances to find a cluster of asterites.

I hesitated when Mars Base sent me Donald Albert and Bertram Kane. I never take inexperienced hetero males; guaranteed they're going to do something stupid on their first tour. I don't mind losing klutzes, but butterflies are expensive.

But Donald and Bertram were perfect. Tiny, five foot even, one-twenty pounds Earth, with huge muscles, thighs as big as their waists. Both just out of school. I was already counting my cut from the finds of a twenty-four asteroid tour. But what really decided me was . . . other than Bertram being blond, they could have been twins, and the age was exactly right. I looked at them and saw the twins that Marge, God rest her soul, and I had planned to have, would have had if . . . they even looked like her.

Donald and Bertram looked up at me, schoolboys with shining eager faces, visions of hundred-carat asterites glowing in their eyes. "You two are lifelong friends?" I asked.

"Yes, sir," Bertram answered.

"It's a strict rule," I said, "that only one person at a time goes down to a rock. The other stays in the boat with the inner hatch closed."

"Yes, sir," Donald said, lying.

"In the old days," I continued, "when every klutz thought the rocks were paved with asterites, some klutzes got the brilliant idea that they could prospect twice as many rocks if they both went down together. So they would gimmick the hatches. You wouldn't do that, boys, would you?"

"No, sir," they swore, both lying.

"That's good," I said. "Because, before you were born, I was a prospector for nine years, and I know all the tricks. On my butterflies, the inner hatch can't be opened from the inside if the outer hatch is open, and the outer hatch can't be closed if anyone is outside, even if you remove the safety line, so there's no way you can both go out at the same time."

They looked surprised at this. What the hell do they teach them at Mars Base these days? Fingerpainting? "Why, sir?" Bertram asked.

"Because I don't like to lose butterflies," I explained. "Klutzes I can always get more of." They still looked blank. "Space is not quite as safe as Mommy's bosom," I pointed out. I think this sank in a little.

"What if your friend gets hurt outside?" Bertram asked. "How do you get out to help him?" Straight out of the feelies: the brave hero, wearing only a snorkel, vanquishes the bug-eyed monsters, rescues his friend, and saves the world. And gets the girl, of course. Fadeout.

"You don't get out to help him, son. You follow the

regs. Otherwise you're both dead. Fast. You leave your partner hanging on his cable, set the controls for Base, and pedal the bike like crazy. When you get back here, if your partner is still alive, which is very unlikely, we'll try to save him. If you're near the end of your tour, you may have to pump at top speed for ten hours, but that's all you can do."

Once I pedalled back alone, at top speed, for eight hours. That was our last tour. We had decided to retire to Luna Port to have our family because Marge, God rest her soul, wanted to have the twins before she was thirty. We didn't have quite enough credits, and we could have managed, but I wanted to make one more tour so Marge would never have to worry about money again.

Marge, God rest her soul, was down on a nice-looking rock and I was plugged into the feely, resting. Her scream cut into my drowse. I jumped up to get my suit. Somehow she knew; she was always ahead of me. "Don't try it!" she yelled. "Get us back fast; it's our only chance." She cut off the mike; didn't want me to hear her die.

With my wife hanging from a five-hundred meter cable, I got us back. Eight hours. All dead. Including me. I couldn't go out again, not even on a ferry. So they had to make me Base Manager. Now I'm in a position to kill more children. Thank you, God, for the promotion.

Clearly, neither Bertram nor Donald liked the idea of being separated from each other, even by death. Well, if that's what they wanted, the inside of a butterfly is really made for togetherness. "One more thing," I said, "you'll have to use a Simula."

"What's a Simula?" Donald asked. I wondered what else they forgot to teach them at Mars Base. Something trivial, no doubt, which would allow them to turn the Base into a brilliant astronomical display, visible from Earth in daylight.

When we first started prospecting the Asteroids, things weren't as easy as they are now. Or as safe. So we got a lot of crazies applying. Most of these were weeded out at

Mars Base, but a few suicidals got through. These got
their wish, but they took some good people with them.
That's when they started the Psych Profiles. The Profiles
worked for a while, then the butterfly loss rate jumped
again.

They finally figured it out. The danger, the isolation,
the chance to get rich quick, attracted young, single,
hetero males. Lock two of these in a tiny cabin for three
months and they're bound to kill each other. So they
made the Simulas. The technology was there; all they
needed was the necessity. A Simula is a few grams of
molecular circuitry encapsulated in a small black box, a
very expensive piece of equipment with an input plug on
one end and an output receptacle on the other. I keep a
full set on hand for each prospector as well as a level
adjuster, because I never know which of the twenty-four
male or twenty-four female types I may need.

I explained to Bertram and Donald how to use a
Simula. Just set up as for a feely. Put the appropriate
background and atmosphere cubes into the computer.
Plug the computer output into the Simula input. Stick
your own sensor plug into the Simula output slot. Everything that comes out of the computer goes through your
Simula before it comes into your nervous system. Put on
the helmet, cuffs and goggles, and snap on the switch,
and relax. Easy.

What's hard is my part, knowing which Simula type
to give to whom and how to adjust it. There are thirty-two
characteristics I can adjust over an intensity range of
twenty steps, giving 20^32 different combinations for each
male and each female Simula. That's more people than
may ever live in the whole Universe, and I have to pick
the right combination for each prospector out of that
number.

I studied the kids' Profiles for an hour. Tweedledee and
Tweedledum to nine nines. I decided to adjust the levels
to a straight ten intensity across the board in all thirty-two
characteristics. Naturally I gave them each a Type I

Simula; what else do you give Boy Scouts? With almost five billion trillion trillion possible setups, I had to make both Simulas a perfect match. Why not? Given those Profiles, anyone else would have done the same.

I didn't tell the boys their Simulas were identical. I stencilled "Alice" on one in big white letters and "Betsy" on the other. When I adjusted the levels, I put "Alice Adams" into the name input of the first and "Betsy Brown" into the second. I gave the "A" to Donald and the "B" to Bertram and sent them out on their first tour.

No two things are *exactly* the same; at the sub-atomic level there's a little uncertainty at work, which seems to be an integral attribute of matter. Maybe God did it that way so the universe would not be completely predictable, to give us choices: True and False, Good and Evil, Right and Wrong. Thank you, God; with your permission I chose to send Donald and Bertram on a tour with Alice and Betsy, two Type I Simulas who, on a macroscopic level, were exactly alike.

A Simula is a program with a personality. Not in the way a computer is said to have a personality, but a real personality, a human personality. That's what it's designed to be: a person with a personality. To be a companion, a friend, a lover, confidant, spouse—whatever you want, whatever you need to carry you through a tour sane.

Making a Simula is like making a feely, but different. To make, say, a Type III Female Simula, you get two hundred Type III women. Implant an impressor in each one and keep a telemetry crew in range for one year, night and day. Everything the model does is impressed: eating, shopping, talking, making love, going to church, everything. At the end of six months, half the models have dropped out and the other half, in spite of the money, is showing irritation at the loss of privacy. (Type III's are not exhibitionists.) Then they answer questions. For weeks. Impress the words, the blushes, the tiredness, the anger, the charm, everything. Nuances, postures, habits, attitudes. Then free association: dreams, wishes, hopes, fantasies, fears. They play roles: fairy princess, scullery maid, nun, courtesan, heroine, victim, nurse, doctor. They dress in different costumes, wear different hairdos, different makeup. They laugh, cry, become sad, happy, drowsy, alert, sick, healthy, tense, relaxed. All goes into the cubes.

After two years they're paid off. Plenty. The Simula is a very expensive piece of equipment.

The impressions are fed into a very big computer. Anomalies are discarded; the rest is weighted. Everything is blended, melded, traces smoothed out until there is a narrow band, the essence of a Type III Female. This is tested on one hundred Type III men, adjusting, finagling, smoothing, until there is a single fine trace, the quintessence of a Type III Female. Now set the intensity ranges for each of the basic characteristics. Add learning, adjustment, accommodation, a tiny bit of random variation for mood. You couldn't tell her from a real woman. On a feely, at least.

There are twenty-four Male Types and twenty-four Female Types. Two sets of little black boxes. I give one Simula to each of the two one-sex hetero team members. Each according to his kind. I do my best to make a good match. So far, I've done fairly well; maybe I've been off a click in the Simula Profile now and then, but it doesn't seem to matter too much. Still, if you make a perfect match, it's the greatest thing in the world. For everybody concerned, at least.

I made a perfect match for Donald Albert and for Bertram Kane. That I know.

A Simula will do anything you want, within the limits of its personality and capabilities, according to the situation and the atmosphere provided by the feely. Naturally, it must be consistent with the past experience the two of you, you and your Simula, have had together, otherwise you might as well wipe and start over. A Simula learns and changes; it's not static, except when it's turned off. It grows, matures, ages, has moods, and will really love you, if that's what you want. If you're smart, that's what you will want. After all, the two of you were made for each other.

If you want to hop into the pod with your Simula first time out, you might be able to do that, depending on the Type she is. But what for? If that's what you want, put on an X feely. The writer has more imagination than you, the director has more skill, the actor has more talent, and the leading ladies are more beautiful and sexy than your Simula, even if she's a Type XXIV Female. After all, that's what actors are paid for, to put on a good show.

That's not the way to use a Simula. She's real. She may be typical of a certain type of woman, but she's not a fake. She's an amalgam of the characteristics of that kind of woman, personified. There may very well be a real woman with exactly those characteristics. As far as you're concerned, there is one. In the little black box with her name stencilled on the cover. And she's bound to fall in love with you. She's not forced to, as in a feely, but she will, if you don't mess up.

It's best to start slowly, normally, properly, as with a real woman who means something to you, who is important to you. Put in a cube of a park, or a cocktail party, or a dinner-dance or a pick-up bar, whatever your style is. It will all be filtered and modified by the Simula circuitry. She'll be there too. You'll meet casually, accidentally, and you'll like each other. Because you're her type and she's your Type. You'll talk and get to know each other better. Everything you find out about her will increase her desirability in your eyes and your's in her eyes. It was designed that way. Fated.

When you meet again, she'll know you. She'll remember what you said and did. She'll be changed by you and you by her. Like real life. You'll adapt a little and she'll adapt a little. Each time you meet you'll be a little closer, warmer. Just like in real life. That's the whole idea, to make it like real life. To make it *really* real life. You'll be happy and she'll be happy. Because you're made for each other. A perfect match.

You can court, make love, marry, raise a family, have problems, argue, make up, overcome difficulties, get sick, everything. She can even die, if you're together long enough. She is a real person, not only in her life but in your life. She doesn't know she isn't real; she knows she's real. She can prove it to you; you can't prove the opposite to her. After all, who are you arguing with?

Put in the right cube and you can go to Luna Port with her for your honeymoon. Eat breakfast with her before you go down to prospect a rock. The tour becomes a job you go to and your teammate becomes just a guy you work with. If you get mad at him, forget it. After work you can come home to your family and he can go to his. And you'll both come back from the tour alive. And sane. And pushing to go out again.

The prospectors I give Simulas to ask me not to wipe their Simulas during the rest quarter. They look forward to going out again so they can take up their life, their *real* life, exactly where they left off the last time. It *is* real to each one. It is exactly the life he would have had if he had met his dream girl.

It's against regs to let a prospector use his Simula on Base. If I ever let him have her, he'd never go out on a tour again. And I never give a Simula to any member of a pair, married or not. It would break up the union. No living person could ever come up to your Simula.

I've never used a Simula, but I dream of Marge every night.

I gave Donald and Bertram Type I's. You meet a Type I at a Sunday school picnic. Young, blond, sweet, innocent, fresh. Pretty. Slightly plump. She wears practically no makeup. You have to ask her father if you can walk her home from church next Sunday. Perfect for Donald. Perfect for Bertram. One for you and one for you. Except that it's the same one for you, Donald, and for you,

Bertram. Exactly the same, to one part in five billion trillion trillion. More or less.

One box is marked "Alice." That's for Donald. One box is marked "Betsy." That's for Bertram. Switch the names and you couldn't tell them apart. Don't they make a lovely couple? Alice and Donald? Betsy and Bertram? Lovely.

Their butterfly came back in a month.

Oh, God, could one of them be lost already?

I check the meters. Thank God, the mass is still there. No one hanging on a cable. They've both come back.

Maybe one is sick?

I go out to the berth myself. I hook up the airlock and the power and control cables. I go to the console. I flip the switches. The hatch opens.

Bertram comes out. He looks like hell.

He walks over to me slowly. Slowly.

I keep looking at the airlock. Donald doesn't come out.

My eyes ask Bertram. He tells me. Donald is dead.

May God damn the asterites. It happened before and it will happen again, but I never thought it would hit my boys. My cherubim.

Usually it happens with older prospectors. Desperate ones. Those who've lost all hope. They find a big cluster of asterites. One starts thinking. Thinking how much more he'd have if he didn't have to share it with the other. One shift, when the other is down on the rock, he lifts away the butterfly. He swings back to the rock and the bob at the end of the cable smashes against the asteroid.

Two shares go to one. It was an accident, Pop. Honest, Pop. Sure.

I've seen it happen three times.

But Donald's body is not hanging from the line. It's still in the cabin.

What happened, Bertram? How does a man die inside a butterfly?

"I killed him, Pop, that's what happened. I had to. I did what any man must do. I had to kill him."

Your lifelong friend? The other cherub? My beautiful boy? Why?

"I had to kill him, Pop. I had a funny feeling. Something was wrong. Betsy was different. In mid-shift, I went back to the cabin. I found Donald plugged into Betsy. My Betsy. So I killed them both."

My Betsy. Your Alice. Exactly alike to nine nines. It isn't funny, God. It really isn't funny.

JOE GORES

Pahua

Bora Bora rose slowly before them, taking on features. Its irregular volcanic cone, almost black at this distance, thrust up nearly half a mile from the center of the enormous lagoon. It was such a dead calm day that *Te Manu*'s sails flapped idly and Ferro had the auxiliary plunking away even in the open sea.

Jennings came from the doghouse to join him in the cockpit. He was skinny and sandy-haired, a university professor from Los Angeles whose subject, he said, was marine zoology.

"Bora Bora!" he exclaimed, as if he were Captain Cook just discovering it. "Unique Bora Bora, a high island in the process of becoming an atoll!" He flung out a dramatic arm. "It's sinking! Come back enough million years from now and all you'd find would be a circular barrier reef and an empty lagoon where Bora Bora used to be."

"Yeah. Better tell your wife we'll be in soon," said Ferro.

Jennings disappeared below, where Margo was preparing for her grand entrance to Bora Bora. Once, that would have been a joke, but now there were two luxury hotels, daily plane flights from Tahiti, glass-bottomed boats and island tours.

Ferro swung the tiller, pointing *Te Manu*'s prow into Teavanui Pass; the lagoon had harbored American warships during World War II, when the island had been a submarine base. Now, looking down into the six turbulent fathoms under his keel, he saw several black, batlike shapes four feet across, flapping away.

"Oh! What are those things?"

Margo Jennings was on deck. Margo of the sultry, vivid lips, eyes of sin and impossibly blonde hair. A tight blouse and brief shorts accented her body.

"They're rays," said Ferro. "Probably eagle or leopard rays. They like to hang around the reef openings."

Which, he thought as he took *Te Manu* across the enormous breadth of cobalt lagoon, was a hell of an identification to have to make for the wife of a marine zoologist. As they drew up to the newly constructed Bora Bora Hotel dock, half a dozen eager brown boys crowded forward to catch their mooring lines. Ferro switched off, rose and stretched.

"We may as well unload your gear here."

On the seaward side of the ketch, a foot-long menpachi squirrel fish broke water. Sideways. Protruding from its red-hued flank was a pointed metal tip. The fish kept coming, followed by a length of steel spear and then a hand. A man's head broke water. He had black, curly hair and a lean jaw; on flipping up his face mask, he revealed laughing brown eyes and a Grecian profile.

"Hey, dad, you dig fish?"

Ferro said he didn't. A few moments later, the diver appeared on the dock, where Margo was striking a fashion-model pose. The man was in his mid-twenties, lean and hard and wearing a male bikini.

Jennings came aft. "Who is that?"

"A swinger trying to give us fish."

For the next hour, they were busy unloading the mountain of underwater gear that Jennings had chartered Ferro's ketch to bring from Tahiti. The skin diver, whose name was Chuck Payne, helped. Besides the usual underwater camera housings, the wetsuits and scuba gear, there were such items as self-contained underwater flood-lamps, a portable rotary air compressor, several tanks each of oxygen and acetylene and an underwater cutting torch.

"When you splitting for Tahiti, man?" asked Payne casually.

Ferro said shortly, "Tomorrow."

That evening, he ate at a small opensided thatched café where undersized pigs scooted in and out and begged like dogs for table scraps. An island boy strummed a guitar strung like a ukulele, while a brown-skinned, slightly chunky girl sang in the heavy gutturals of the islands. Two gold teeth gleamed as she sang. Finally, she came over to Ferro's table.

"Hey, brudda, me Otera. You da kine feller name Ferro?"

"Sure."

"Matua tell me 'bout boat name *Te Manu*, one feller name Ferro."

Matua Tearea, the Tahitian who usually crewed with Ferro, had stayed in Papeete because the quarters on the laden ketch had been too cramped for four people.

They drank Hinano while the boy, Otera's brother, had *limonade*. He was a short, stocky, well-built fifteen-year-old named Matara, with an unfailing white-toothed grin. He had been out on the reef last night after *urua*—the big horse-eyed jacks which liked the reef turbulence—and had, he said, seen "strange things."

"Strange things, such as what?"

The boy's eyes became bright with excitement. "First, 'way under water, a light—sorta soft-like. Then, between breakers when the water is still, suddenly it boil."

"The water boiled?" Ferro sat up. "You mean like it was hot?"

"Ae. Or mebbe like big *pahua* closing down on something."

Pahua, Ferro knew, was the Tahitian word for the giant *Tridacna* clam, a mollusk which lies hinge-downward in coral reefs and can snap shut on the arm or leg of an unwary diver and drown him. Called a bear's-paw clam in English, because of its shape, the *Tridacna* can weigh half a ton and be two yards across.

One that size, Ferro thought on his way back to *Te Manu*, might possibly cause a swirl in closing that could be mistaken for "boiling" water. But what about the light Matara had seen? The eyes of *pahua*, as the boy believed? Hardly.

Still, there were legends of an immense *pahua* which waited on unknown reefs to swallow up whole ships; and since the inexplicable death of a man named Ernest Dandela, Ferro did not scoff at legends.

The morning dawned beautiful and clear, with the trades clattering the palm fronds and ruffling the placid lagoon. Ferro ate half a banana and used the rest on a drop-line to catch reef fish for breakfast. Soon Otera appeared.

"*Ia orana*," said Ferro, "*maitai oe?*"

"*Aita*. No dam' good." Her face was set and inscrutable. "Matara no come back from reef last night."

"What section was he going to?"

"*Ae*. Same place as other time. *Tau tohora*."

Whale Reef. An odd name, Ferro thought. "Do you want to go look for him?"

She said yes.

The slim outrigger canoe was fifteen feet long, painstakingly hollowed from a single log and fitted with a lateen sail. The outrigger, which rode the water parallel to it like a smaller hull, made it very stable as the sail filled with a strong off-shore wind. Ferro used the huge hand-carved steering paddle as they knifed across the narrow mile of lagoon toward the reef north of Teavanui Pass.

The water, pale when they left shore, turned a deep aquamarine as the bottom dropped away beneath them, and then became a turbulent turquoise as they approached the inner rim of the barrier reef. On top of the reef itself, their outrigger bumped and dragged across coral.

Otera gave a sudden wild cry, arm extended. "*Aue!* Matara!"

Ferro twisted the heavy paddle, bringing the canoe around, at the same time dropping the single canvas sail.

The body was nearly submerged, face down, and when Ferro waded over to it, he found one ankle wedged between the coral heads. The boy's heavy-handled knife was still sheathed in his waistband, and his home-made diving goggles were on his face. Ferro got him under the arms and heaved him into the canoe.

"*Aue!*" Otera said finally. "It was indeed *te pahua.*"

The boy's right forearm was terribly mangled, gouged and torn in a clearly discernible arc on top and bottom as if gripped by huge jaws, or by the ragged clamping edges of a *Tridacna's* giant shell. The bear's-paw. It had killed many divers. But ... Ferro leaned abruptly forward. Imbedded in the mangled flesh were a number of reddish-brown flakes.

It was late afternoon before Ferro finally settled down to a solitary beer at the Bora Bora Hotel bar. The doctor had confirmed death by drowning. But Ferro had identified the reddish flakes, too.

So, then, what really had happened at Whale Reef? Why hadn't he, as island divers have done since time immemorial, smashed away the rim of shell holding his arm with the heavy knife handle?

"I thought you had split this ayem, cat."

Jennings, Margo and the skin diver, Chuck Payne, had just entered the bar.

"I found a dead diver up on the reef today, so I had to stay," said Ferro.

"I dig, man. Guess you'll split tomorrow, huh?"

Ferro eyed him coldly. "I couldn't say."

He ate again that evening at the little café and paused later by Vaitape Pier, where he had *Te Manu* moored. Someone spoke his name. He turned to confront the insignificant figure of Gerald Jennings.

"Where's Margo?" demanded Jennings. The little man's

eyes were haunted, even though he strove to make his question sound casual. "Sorry, Ferro, I didn't mean to sound—I just—I missed Margo at the hotel and thought, perhaps . . ."

He trailed off to turn abruptly away into the darkness. Poor, bloody bastard, Ferro thought as he went aboard the yacht. Fifteen years too old for Margo, much too vulnerable to be married to her. He descended to the narrow, crowded cabin which had been home for nearly four years, and lit one of the gimbelled kerosene lamps. Margo was bad news.

As he turned toward the bunks, eyes still dazzled from the lamp, Margo Jennings came into his arms with a lithe, writhing movement. Her parted lips sought Ferro's urgently. She was nude.

"Darling," the mouth whispered against his, "take me away from here! Tonight! To Tahiti, just the two of us!"

Ferro, remembering popping flash bulbs years before, when he had been in a similar situation in a San Francisco hotel room, stepped back from her embrace and bent to put an ungentle shoulder into her belly. His arm clamped around the backs of her belatedly kicking legs as he came erect with her body over his shoulder.

"You filthy ape, put me down! Put—"

Without apparent effort, Ferro ran up the ladder and out on deck. Without pausing, he gave a mighty heave.

"What are you doing?" she yelped.

Then her bare backside shattered the placid surface of the water with a great splash. Ferro went below, was back on deck with a huge woolly towel, her discarded clothes and a liter of Hinano for himself by the time she had dragged herself aboard. Draining sea water on the deck, with the moonlight silvering her exquisite nude body, she began mouthing an amazing string of obscenities. Finally Ferro tossed her the towel.

"Here, shove this in your mouth. And then get dressed."

"You goddam queer!" she bawled, and stalked off.

On impulse, Ferro cast loose fore and aft, fired up the engine and swung *Te Manu* into the moonlit breadth of lagoon. When he was fifty yards from the dock, a figure appeared to either wave an arm or shake a fist. It could have been Jennings. Ferro kept going, up around the bulge of Farepiti Point into Fanui Bay. The dock, he remembered, was a long, gray cement affair left over from the submarine base, crumbling, but with two huge iron mooring bitts not too badly rusted for Ferro to moor the yacht side-to along the dock.

Below the keel were five fathoms of black, midnight water shelving down quickly to a dozen or more. He stripped and went over the side.

After hyperventilating for a minute or two with the deep, whistling breaths he had learned in the Tuamotu shell beds, he started to dive. Almost immediately, he began pushing himself, counting seconds, trying to make each dive longer and deeper than the last. On the final one, after finding bottom at seventy feet, he counted to two hundred and seventy-six before he broke water with a great splashing lunge.

On deck, he shook himself like a wet dog, the scar under his right arm, where he had torn free from Dandela's spear, still looking thick and lumpy.

As he turned to go below, Jennings came erect on the far side of the doghouse. His nickel-plated thirty-two revolver was pointed at Ferro's chest.

"Look at you!" yelled Jennings, wild-eyed. "Prancing about like a—a stallion! I know that Margo was with you tonight!"

Ferro made one of the yards between them. Slow and easy.

"I saw her on deck!" babbled Jennings. *"Naked!* So I— I went back to the hotel and got *this.* . . ." He waved the revolver and Ferro made another yard. "I got back to the dock too late, so I—"

Ferro twisted to the right like a mongoose dodging a

cobra, and the knife edge of his left hand slammed explosively down on Jennings's wrist. At the same instant, his right hand came up under the pistol, twisting it toward Jennings so the slight man squealed with pain. The thirty-two came free in Ferro's hand. He quickly stepped back a pace to break the pistol so the ejector would jack the bullets out.

"You—you hurt my arm!" whimpered Jennings.

"I ought to bust your head." Ferro was trembling with reaction. "Chain her up if you don't want her whoring around."

He watched the slight, defeated figure disappear into the lacy shadows under the palm trees. Hell, Jennings wouldn't have believed him no matter what he said, anyway! He got out a hammock and strung it between two coco palms well clear of the yacht; he wanted some sleep that night without more unexpected visitors. One thing was certain. He was going to stay in Bora Bora until he found out why someone—sure as hell not Jennings— wanted him off the island. And whether it tied in with a bear's-paw clam that not only could make water boil in a way suggesting escaping air, but also could imbed rusty flakes of metal in human flesh. . . .

When Otera showed up the next morning, he asked her why Whale Reef had been given that name. She told him, and a great deal of it fell into place.

He sent Otera off to get her father and sat down on the cement dock to work through it logically.

A boy out reef-fishing sees something underwater which makes him curious. Being an islander, respecting but not fearing the sea, he dives down to investigate and ends up dead. Only one man seems dubious about the death being merely an accident: Ferro. Solution: get rid of him. Method: a woman. Or, perhaps, a bullet from a jealous husband.

So . . . Jennings probably was a fake zoologist; Margo would be the bait which had brought him into the scheme.

That left the planner of all this—someone who had preceded *Te Manu* to Bora Bora, since Matara had seen the lights and "boiling" water the night before their arrival. Chuck Payne, of course. The swinging skin diver.

But what were they after?

And what, without proof, could Ferro do about Matara's murder?

Otera arrived with her father, a huge, graying man named Taho'o, who had the deep mahogany color of the full-blooded Polynesian and was massively muscled despite his sixty-odd years.

"We will deal with those who killed my son," he said in a deep voice.

"Not until I make sure that it was murder," said Ferro.

The old man finally agreed to wait, so Ferro cast off and ran the yacht down to the southwestern tip of the island where the hotel was built overlooking the lagoon. As he tied up at their dock, he was struck again by all the trappings which have become obligatory for the South Seas luxury hotel. The grass-roofed bar/restaurant with the fabulous view of the lagoon; the individual grass-roofed bungalows costing fifty dollars a day to inhabit.

Ferro went through the last-minute ritual of departure, topping his freshwater and fuel tanks, buying some fresh eggs, and telling the dock boys that he was off for Tahiti. Word of it, he knew, soon would reach Payne. Once outside the reef, he set a course away from Bora Bora until the shadows lengthened and he could put about once again. He negotiated Teavanui Pass by starlight, then went up the western side of the island to a certain anchorage on the northern tip by Tercia Point.

Waiting for him there were Taho'o and Otera in the outrigger canoe.

No moon. Taho'o steering, with minute movements of the heavy paddle; Otera riding the outrigger to keep it down in the water hissing by below their keel; Ferro in wetsuit and flippers, mask pushed up on his forehead and mouthpiece hanging ready around his neck. On his back, twin 71.2-cubic-foot tanks of air with a two-hose, two-stage regulator.

"Here!" shouted Taho'o above the roar.

Ferro went over the side and waded clumsily toward the towering thunder of surf, crouched like a skier to breast the waves. He was atop the reef, a good quarter-mile north of the place where Matara's body had been floating.

A breaker nearly buried him in a welter of foam. As the water sucked back out, he went with it, in a rush, out and then sharply down into the sea, kicking hard to drive himself below the next breaker. He paused to pop his ears, then found a hundred and sixty-five degrees south by east on his luminous-dialled wrist compass: this bearing would keep him parallel to the outer reef face. He stayed at thirty feet, everything as black as if he swam with his eyes shut except for the minute sparkles of plankton which greenly touched his movements with bioluminescence.

Ferro felt a quickening of his pulse; ahead was the soft glow of an underwater lamp. He angled toward it, well prepared for the sight of the great, dim, whalelike shape. A sunken submarine which had struck the reef during a near-hurricane in 1943.

Between him and the light loomed the conning tower, its silhouette already blurred and softened by more than twenty-five years of busy corals, anemones and barnacles. He swam forward. The reef had opened up the forward port side like a sardine tin. The floodlamps shone on the raised hatch cover of the gun-access trunk, just forward of the conning tower and abaft of the deck cannon. The trunk, he knew, was a vertical cylinder six feet high and four in diameter, with a second hatch on its lower end opening into the control room.

Ferro peered over the rim. If the control room still had been airtight when Payne had opened the hatch for the first time, the air would have risen to the surface in a great bubble, making the water seem to boil for the eyes of Matara on the reef above.

Below, in the control room, was an intense, flickering, blue-green light. Someone was using the oxyacetylene torch to cut through the sub's pressure hull to the main ballast tanks. Ferro could imagine Matara, craning forward as he was, staring down. . . . A sudden slam of the heavy hatch cover on his arm, his lessening struggles. . . . The body released into the surf to be pounded to hamburger on the reef, only somehow to be swept on top relatively intact.

Ferro was shoved violently from behind. Already overbalanced, he did a slow tumble into the access trunk. The cover slammed down behind him, leaving only the light of the flickering torch. The diver in the crowded room turned, saw him and apparently realized from something in Ferro's gear that he was an interloper.

Ferro flippered desperately away from the other's attack, from the blue-green tongue whose caress would be fatal; its sixty-three-hundred-degree temperature would turn flesh to blackened char. He slammed painfully into the diving rudder wheels, ducked just as the torch slashed to make red sparks fly as it wiped flame across the drainage manifold. He dove, twisted, went right under the attacker's lethal arm as the hot breath of the torch sliced a tip off his rubber flipper.

But Ferro already was scissoring wildly toward the twin tanks of oxygen and acetylene resting under the main switchboard. Outfitted with single-stage regulators, they fed the torch through five-sixteenths-of-an-inch hoses. If he could cut off the gases at the regulators . . .

His hands twisted the small hand wheels in panic as his back crawled in expectation of deadly flame. A pop. Blessed blackness. The torch was out, harmless, and in that instant, the initiative passed to Ferro. His opponent— Payne, he was sure—probably was good underwater; but Ferro was superb, and knew it. Just a matter of time, now.

It took five minutes. Then Ferro's hand brushed against something that moved. His iron fingers closed and jerked hard, tearing mouthpiece, hose and regulator right off Payne's air tank. There, in the total darkness, he knew Payne was drowning, but he felt no compunction. He waited out the other's dying, macabre dance for air, then felt his way back forward to the gun-access trunk.

The upper hatch had been dogged down from the outside. The man who had pushed him meant to seal them *both* into the sub. Ferro felt a twinge: it had been Jennings, not Payne, who had just drowned. Poor, besotted Jennings, always destined by Payne, as Ferro knew now, to die when his usefulness was ended. Payne probably had goaded him into going after Ferro with the gun in hopes they would kill each other. And now he meant them both to die in the submarine.

Smiling grimly to himself, Ferro worked his way carefully forward, finally to emerge from the forward escape hatch.

It was midnight when he knocked gently on the door of Jennings' bungalow. Chuck Payne threw it open, then turned white. Inside the room, Margo, honeyed hair aswirl around her shoulders as she hastily drew a filmy negligée about her, gaped at him with something like terror.

"*You!* I thought that you . . . Chuck said that you . . . that he . . ."

"Cool it, baby." Payne was trying to recover. To Ferro, he said, "You got nothing on either of us, cat. Nothing at all."

Ferro rested his haunches against the edge of Margo's dressing table. "I don't need anything," he said, "as long as I can stop you from going back to the sub."

Payne thought about it. "You mean that you want in."

"Why not? Say, fifty percent."

"Fifty percent?" Margo shrilled. "We wouldn't give you—"

"Cool it, baby," he said again, almost absently. They must have made a good pair, Ferro thought, even in L.A. where the con was a way of life. They'd have tossed Margo at Jennings, and he just would have started signing checks.

Payne said, "How about a third?"

"A third of what?"

"One hundred thousand bucks! Mercury. Used as ballast on the sub."

"Where did you get that idea?" asked Ferro almost gently.

"I read a book by this crazy diving cat, Bob Marx, who went after the mercury ballast in two German subs sunk during the Second War off Cape Hatteras."

"Did he get the mercury?"

"The U.S. Navy made him quit before he could."

It would have been funny, Ferro thought, if it hadn't been so grotesque. And Jennings had died for it!

He said, "How did you hear about the sub here in Bora Bora?"

"My old man used to talk about it—not that he dug anything about the mercury in it, of course. He was stationed here and was the radio operator who received their last position. Only he forgot to log it in, and when the sub turned up missing, he was afraid of being court-martialled, so he didn't say anything. The Navy just listed it as 'missing in action' without knowing it was right out on the reef."

Ferro nodded. "And the kid you drowned? Why did he have to die?"

Margo's beautifully rounded breast stirred impatiently. She said with scornful impatience, "Because he dove down there and *saw the sub,* of course! Chuck had to stop him before he could tell anyone else that it was there. No grubby native kid was going to foul us up!"

"So I killed the kid. Big deal," said Payne. "So look, man, we did all the planning on this, so a third—that's fair, right? The third Jennings would have gotten."

That was when Ferro started to laugh. It was not a pleasant laugh; in fact, it was rather chilling. "So you killed the boy to keep him from telling anybody that the submarine was there. Do you know what they call that reef where the sub lies?"

"Some silly island name. What does—"

"*Tau tohora*—'Whale Reef' in Tahitian. There's no word in the language for 'submarine' so they used 'whale' instead. Everybody on the island—except maybe the Navy—has known all about the sub since the day it went down in forty-three."

"But the mercury!" cried Margo. "What if someone—"

"Oh, that. There isn't any mercury," said Ferro. "There never was. American subs don't use a permanent ballast material. They use sea water—flood the tanks to get a negative buoyancy and dive, blow out the water with compressed air to get a positive buoyancy and rise. You killed the kid for nothing. For sea water."

He stood up and crossed the room. With the door open, he turned to look back at them, speaking loudly and clearly.

"You shouldn't have killed the boy," he said distinctly.

Payne's face became still, watchful. He did not look nearly so handsome as when Ferro had entered the room.

"You said it yourself, man—you don't have any proof that we did anything."

"*You* said that," Ferro corrected him. "I said I didn't need proof. Neither do they." He gestured out into the tropical darkness. "The kid's relatives, friends, out there somewhere—waiting. You won't make it until morning here, so maybe if you run for it—"

Margo said uncertainly, "You're just trying to scare us."

"Sure I am," said Ferro.

He left, passing through a patch of incredibly fragrant night-blooming jasmine. The air was fresh and cool. On the other side of the thatch-roofed bungalow a tropical night bird called in soft interrogation. Another answered with what sounded to Ferro like a sort of go-ahead note. Something rustled in the bushes by the cabin door. Something big.

Of course, it was just a prowling tomcat in the hedge. And the birds were just birds. Of course.

But walking out along the jetty toward *Te Manu*, Ferro knew that he was damned glad to be leaving for Tahiti in the morning. He remembered that in the old days they always gave captured enemies to the women. And he remembered Otera's stony face when they had found her dead brother on the reef.

LILLIAN DE LA TORRE

The Second Sight of Dr. Sam: Johnson

S ir," said the learned Dr. Sam: Johnson to the Laird of Raasay, "he who meddles with the uncanny, meddles with danger; but none the less for that, 'tis the duty of the philosopher, diligently to enquire into the truth of these matters."

All assented to my learned friend's proposition, none dreaming how soon and how terribly his words were to be verified, and his intrepidity put to the test.

No premonition of events to come disturbed the pleasure with which I saw my learned companion thus complacently domesticated upon the Isle of Raasay. Our long cherished scheam of visiting the Western Islands of Scotland was now a reality; and it was in acknowledgement of the plans of the Laird for exploring the wonders of the isle that the respectable author of the *Dictionary* uttered these words.

As he did so, he gazed with complacency upon his companions by the Laird's fireside; a group of Highland gentlemen, shewing in face and bearing that superiority which consciousness of birth and learning most justifiably supplies. Of the family of MacLeod were the Laird himself, a sensible, polite, and most hospitable gentleman, and his brother, Dr. MacLeod, a civil medical man of good skill. These gentlemen shewed a strong family resemblance, being tall and strongly made, with firm ruddy countenances; genteelly apparelled in sad-coloured suits with clean ruffles.

Their companions in the ingle-nook by the glowing peat fire were two brothers, Angus and Colin MacQueen, sons of the incumbent rector of the parish of Snizoort on Skye. They resembled one another, being lean, light, and active, with bony dark faces; wearing suits of scholarly black, and their own heavy dark hair cut short.

The elder, Mr. Angus MacQueen, was a learned young man, a close observer of the natural phænomena of the island. He filled the trusted post of tutor to Raasay's heir. The younger son, Colin, new returned from the University, had all his elder brother's wide and curious learning, but displayed withal an ill-regulated instability of mind and a hectick behaviour, poorly held in check by respect for Raasay and my learned companion.

Dr. Samuel Johnson's character—nay, his figure and manner, are, I believe, more generally known than those of almost any man, yet it may not be superfluous here to attempt a sketch of him. His person was large, robust, I may say approaching to the gigantick, and grown unwieldy from corpulency. His countenance was naturally of the cast of an antient statue, but somewhat disfigured by the scars of that evil which it was formerly imagined the royal touch would cure. He was now in his sixty-fourth year, and was become a little dull of hearing. His sight had always been somewhat weak, yet so much does mind govern and even supply the deficiency of organs that his perceptions were uncommonly quick and accurate. His head and sometimes also his body shook with a kind of motion like the effect of a palsy; he appeared to be frequently disturbed by cramps or convulsive contractions, of the nature of that distemper called St. Vitus's dance. He wore a full suit of plain brown cloathes with twisted-hair buttons of the same colour, a

large bushy greyish wig, a plain shirt, black worsted
stockings, and silver buckles. He had a loud voice and a
slow deliberate utterance, which no doubt gave some
additional weight to the sterling metal of his conversation. He had a constitutional melancholy the clouds of
which darkened the brightness of his fancy and gave a
gloomy cast to his whole course of thinking; yet, though
grave and awful in his deportment when he thought it
necessary or proper, he frequently indulged himself in
pleasantry and sportive sallies. He was prone to superstition but not to credulity. Though his imagination might
incline him to a belief of the marvellous, his vigorous
reason examined the evidence with jealousy.

Such was my learned friend during our visit to the
Western Islands; and thus it was that on this first evening
of our sojourn on Raasay our talk turned on the topogra-
phy, the antiquities, and especially the superstitions of
the Isle of Raasay.

Dr. Johnson had professed himself eager to enquire into
our Highland phænomenon of second sight.

"Sir," said Angus MacQueen, "I am *resolved* not to
believe it, because it is founded on no principle."

"Then," said Dr. Johnson, "there are many verified
facts that you will not believe. What principle is there
why the lodestone attracts iron? Why an egg produces a
chicken by heat? Why a tree grows upward, when the
natural tendency of all things is downward? Sir, it depends on the degree of evidence you have."

Young Angus MacQueen made no reply. Colin Mac-
Queen rolled his wild dark eyes on the awe-inspiring
figure of my friend as he asked:

"What evidence would satisfy you?"

"Whist, then, Colin," interposed his brother, "let past
things be."

"I knew a MacKenzie," Dr. McLeod said cheerfully,
"who would faint away, and when he revived again he
had visions to tell of. He told me upon one occasion, I
should meet a funeral just at the fork of the road, and the

bearers people I knew, and he named them, too. Well, sir, three weeks after, I did meet a funeral on that very road, and the very bearers he named. Was not that second sight?"

"Sir," said my friend, "what if this man lay a-dying, and your MacKenzie and the whole town knew who his friends would be to carry him to the grave? —Ay, and by the one nearest way to the graveyard?"

"What do you say then to the women of Skye," said the honest Laird, "who stopped me on the road to say that they had heard two *taisks*, and one an English one—"

"What is a *taisk*?" I ventured to enquire. It is the part of a chronicler to omit no opportunity to clarify his record.

"A *taisk*, Mr. Boswell, is the voice of one about to die. Many of us in the Highlands hear *taisks* though we have not the second sight."

"Sir," said Dr. Johnson, "it is easy enough for the women of Skye to say what they heard. Did you hear it?"

"I have not the gift," said the Laird of Raasay, "but returning the same road, I met two funerals, and one was of an Englishwoman."

"Is there none in the Isle of Raasay with the second sight?" enquired my learned friend.

"There is indeed," replied Colin MacQueen in a low voice. "There is an old wife on the other side the island with the second sight. She foresaw my brother's murder."

"How, sir!" exclaimed Dr. Johnson. "Murder! I had no intent to distress you."

"I will tell you the story." Young MacQueen's eyes glittered in the fire-light. "Rory was younger than I, and meddled with the lasses where he had no concern. Old Kirstie comes one night to Angus and me, and falls to weeping, crying out that she has heard Rory's *taisk*, and seen him lying dead with his head broke. Wasn't it so, Angus?"

"It was so," said the young tutor sombrely.

"And did it fall out so?" I enquired.

"So it fell out, for Angus was there and saw it," replied

young Colin, "and if 'twas a grief to us, it broke old Kirstie's heart; for it was her own son killed him. A strapping surly ghillie he was, Black Fergus they called him, and he broke Rory's head for him over the bouman's lass."

"Did the villain suffer for his crime?" enquired Dr. Johnson, profoundly struck by this tale of moral obliquity.

"He did, sir, though we have neither court nor judge upon Raasay since the troubled days of the '45; but rather than be took he flung himself into the sea; and his mother saw him in a dream rising up out of the sea dripping wet, with his face rotted away."

" 'Twould interest me much," said Dr. Johnson, "if I might meet with this aged Sybil."

"Nothing is easier," replied Dr. MacLeod, "for tomorrow I propose to shew you the strange caves of our eastern coast, and the old woman lives hard by. You shall interrogate her to your heart's content."

"Sir," said Dr. Johnson, "I am obliged to you. What is the nature of the caves you mention?"

"They are sea caves," replied Dr. MacLeod, "of great age and extent. No one has ever explored all their ramifications."

"My young friend MacQueen," added the Laird, bowing to Angus, "who is botanist, lapidarian, and antiquary of our island, knows them better than any man; but even he has never penetrated to their depths."

"He fears the Kelpie," said young Colin recklessly.

"The Kelpie?" I echoed.

"A water-demon," said Colin. "He lives in the Kelpie Pool under the Kelpie's Window, and he eats men."

"Such is the belief of the islanders," assented Angus MacQueen. "In their superstition they connect this supernatural being with a certain natural orifice in the cave wall, giving upon a deep pool of the sea."

"The pool is bottomless," struck in Colin, "and under it sits the Kelpie and hates mankind."

"It is impossible," pronounced Dr. Johnson, "by its

very nature, that any depression which contains water should lack a bottom."

"This ones does," muttered Colin.

" 'Tis perfectly true," said Raasay, "that the Kelpie Pool has never been sounded."

"Thus do we see the credulity of ill-instructed men," cried Dr. Johnson, with a glance of fire at young Colin, "who because a thing *has never been done,* conclude illogically that it *cannot be done.*"

"Tomorrow you shall see the Kelpie Pool," said the learned young tutor, "and judge for yourself. I can promise you also some interesting petrifications; and you shall see there a device which I have constructed to measure the rise and fall of the tides."

"I shall be happy to be instructed," replied Dr. Johnson civilly.

"Pray tell me," I enquired, "is the Isle of Raasay rich in fauna?"

"We have blackcock, moor-fowl, plovers, and wild pigeons in abundance," replied Dr. MacLeod.

Johnson: "And of the four-footed kind?"

MacQueen: "We have neither rabbits nor hares, nor was there ever any fox upon the island until recently; but now our birds are hunted, and one sees often the melancholy sight of a little heap of discarded feathers where the brute has supped."

Boswell: "How came a fox to Raasay? By swimming the channel from the mainland?"

MacLeod: "We cannot believe so, for a fox is a bad swimmer. We can only suppose that some person brought it over out of pure malice."

Johnson: "You must set a trap for him."

MacQueen: "I think to do so, for the remains of his hunting betray where he runs."

Boswell: "Now had you but horses on the island, we should give Reynard a run."

This said, by mutual consent we all arose. Dr. Johnson and the Laird strolled off with Mr. Angus MacQueen to behold the stars of these northern latitudes. Dr. MacLeod, yawning, sought his bed; young Colin disappeared from my side like a phantom into the night; and I was left alone to the pleasing task of arranging my notes of the evening's discourse.

The morrow dawned wet and stormy, being one of those Hebridean days of which Dr. Johnson complained that they presented all the inconveniencies of tempest without its sublimities. Our enforced confinement was made pleasant by the learned discourse of the Reverend Donald MacQueen and his no less learned son; till, the storm abating, the younger man left us near sundown, to inspect his sea-gage at the edge of the island. He parted from Dr. Johnson on terms of mutual respect, and promised to bring him some specimens of petrifications.

The night came on with many brilliant stars; and we congratulated ourselves on the prospect of a fair dawn for the promised ramble about the island.

Colin was at my bedside next morning between five and six. I sprung up, and rouzed my venerable companion. Dr. Johnson quickly equipped himself for the expedition, and seized his formidable walking-stick, without which he never stirred while in Scotland. This was a mighty oaken cudgel, knotted and gnarled; equipped with which the doughty philosopher felt himself the equal of any man.

We took a dram and a bit of bread directly. A boy of the name of Stewart was sent with us as our carrier of provisions. We were five in all: Colin MacQueen, Dr. MacLeod, the lad Stewart, Dr. Johnson, and myself.

"Pray sir, where is Mr. Angus MacQueen?" enquired Dr. Johnson.

"Still on the prowl," said his brother carelessly.

"Observing the stars, no doubt," said Dr. MacLeod. "No matter, we shall surely encounter him in our peregrinations."

We walked briskly along; but the country was very

stony at first, and a great many risings and fallings lay in
our way. We had a shot at a flock of plovers sitting. But
mine was harmless. We came first to a pretty large lake,
sunk down comparatively with the land about it. Then to
another; and then we mounted up to the top of Duncaan,
where we sat down, ate cold mutton and bread and
cheese and drank brandy and punch. Then we had a
Highland song from Colin, which Dr. Johnson set about
learning, *Hatyin foam foam eri.* We then walked over a
much better country, very good pasture; saw many moor-
fowl, but could never get near them; descended a hill on
the east side of the island; and so came to a hut by the sea.
It was somewhat circular in shape, the door unfastened.

We called a blessing on the house and entered. At the
far end an old woman was huddled over a peat fire. As we
entered, she dropped the steaming breeks she had been
drying before the glowing peat, and redded up for company by shuffling them hastily under the bedstead.

"Well, Kirstie," Colin MacQueen greeted her, "here's
Dr. Johnson come all the way from London to ask you
about your gift of the second sight."

To our utter astonishment the wizened old creature
dropped to her knees and began to keen in a dreadful
voice, rocking herself to and fro and wringing her hands.

"Come, come, my good creature," said the humane
Doctor, "there's no occasion for such a display, I'm sure,"
and he benevolently insinuated half-a-crown into her
clenched claw-like hand.

The aged Sybil peeped at it briefly, and stowed it away
about her person; but she continued to keen softly, and
presently her words became audible:

"Alas, 'tis no gift, but a curse, to have seen what I have
seen, poor Rory gone, and my own son drowned, and now
this very day—" The keening rose to a wail.

"We are causing too much distress by our enquiries,"
muttered my friend.

But the aged crone caught him by the wrist.

"It is laid on me to tell no less than to see."

"What have you seen today, then?" enquired Dr. Mac-Leod soothingly.

"Come," said Colin roughly, "there is nothing to be gained by lingering."

"*Angus! Angus! Angus!*"

"What of Angus?" asked Dr. Johnson with apprehension.

"I have heard his *taisk!* I have seen him lying broken and dead! He's gone, like Rory, like my own son that's drowned. Ai! Ai!"

"Come away," cried Colin, and flung out at the door. My friends complied, and I followed them, but not before I had bestowed some small charity upon the pathetic aged creature.

Colin led the way, walking heedlessly and fast. My friend and I perforce dropped behind.

"This is most remarkable," said Dr. Johnson. "If we should indeed find that the young man has met with a misfortune—which Heaven forfend—"

"We may speak as eye-witnesses of this often-doubted phænomenon," said I, concluding his statement.

"Nevertheless, sir," pronounced the learned philosopher, "man's intellect has been given him to *guard against credulity*. Let us take care not to fall into an attitude of superstitious belief in the old dame's powers. As yet her allegation is unsupported."

By this time we were come to the cave. It lies in a section of the coast where the cliffs mount up to a threatening height, with a deep sound under, for a reef of jagged rocks some way out takes the pounding of the sea.

Dr. Johnson shewed especial curiosity about the minerals of the island. Ever solicitous for the improvement of human comfort, he enquired whether any coal were known on the island, "for," said he, "coal is commonly to be found in mountainous country, such as we see upon Raasay."

"See," he continued, "this vein of black sand, where otherwise the sand is white."

He gathered a handful; it stained his hand, and he cast it away.

"It is surely powdered coal," concluded my learned friend, punching at the deposit with his sturdy stick.

"Sir," I ventured, "it more nearly resembles charcoal."

"Coal or charcoal, 'tis all one," returned my friend. "Did I live upon Raasay, I should try whether I could find the vein, for there's no fire like a coal fire."

"Come, let us enter the cave," cried Colin MacQueen impatiently.

To my surprise the ghillie who carried our provisions unconditionally refused to enter the cave, alleging it to be haunted; a circumstance which was confirmed to his untutored mind by a strange echo from within, as of footsteps walking, that seemed to sound over the breakers.

"I'll not go in," said the lad stubbornly, " 'tis full of wild-fire these days, and something walks there."

" 'Tis your fox that walks there," observed Dr. Johnson, poking at a pile of feathers hard by the entrance.

"Well, my lad, if you won't come you may e'en stay here," said Colin MacQueen impatiently. "I fear neither fox nor fox-fire, and I'm for the cave. Come, gentlemen."

He led the way up a sloping incline and through a low entrance-way. Dr. Johnson had to stoop his great frame as he crowded through. Within, our footsteps rattled on the pebbly path. Colin carried a torch, which gleamed upon the rising roof and upon the petrifications that hung from it, formed by drops that perpetually distil therefrom. They are like little trees. I broke off some of them.

The cave widened and grew lofty as we progressed. Dr. Johnson was much struck by the absolute silence, broken only by the noise of our advance, which reechoed ahead of us.

I drew Colin's attention to certain places on the floor, where partitions of stone appeared to be human work, shewing indeed the remains of desiccated foliage with which they had once been filled.

"In the days of the pirates," he explained, "this cave

was a place of refuge. These are what is left of the beds. Here," he continued, "the cave divides. The left-hand arm slopes down to the sea, where a wide opening provided shelter for boats and a hiding-place for oars. Half-way down, there is a fresh spring. We take the right-hand turning, gentlemen."

"In times past," contributed Dr. MacLeod as we as-cended the right-hand slope, "the cave sometimes served as a refuge for malefactors; but it invariably proved a trap."

"How so sir?" I asked, "with a fresh spring, escape by sea or land, and the unexplored fastnesses of the cave to lurk in?"

There was a puff of air, and the torch with which Colin was leading the way was suddenly extinguished. At first the blackness was pitchy.

"You may proceed without fear," spoke Colin out of the darkness, "provided you always keep the wall of the cave at your left hand. I will endeavour to restore the light."

"Colin knows this cave as he knows his own house," Dr. MacLeod assured us.

We groped our way forward.

"Thus it was, in darkness on this ascent, that men waited to take or destroy the outlaw," Dr. MacLeod took up his narrative. "Just around this bend we come into light."

He spoke truly, for already a faint ray was diluting the darkness. As we rounded the bend we saw, ahead and close at hand, an irregular opening through which we could glimpse the sky.

"Whoever takes shelter in the innermost recesses of this cave," said Dr. MacLeod, "must pass by that opening whenever thirst drives him down to the spring below. A marksman stationed at the bend can pick him off as he passes against the light."

"That's the Kelpie's Window," said Colin at my elbow. I started, and then in the uncertain light perceived him

where he leaned in a little recess striking a light with flint
and steel.

"Press on," said Colin, "I'll come behind with the
torch."

I own it oppressed me with gloomy thoughts to climb
in the darkness this path where savage and lawless men
of the past had died. My venerable companion is of more
intrepid mould; he and Dr. MacLeod pressed forward
undismayed.

"I was on this path not three months since," pursued
the physician, "when Black Fergus the murderer took
shelter in these caves."

"Did you take him?" enquired Dr. Johnson with interest.

"We did not," said Dr. MacLeod. "We waited here in
the dark, off and on by relays, for three days and three
nights."

"Did not he come down?"

"When he came, he came running; and before we could
take aim, he had flung himself into the sea."

I was powerfully struck by this narration. I seemed to
see the hunted figure, driven by thirst to a watery grave.

We attained the top of this sinister incline, and stood in
the Kelpie's Window, a sheer 100 feet above the black
waters of the Kelpie Pool. Height makes me flinch; I
retreated behind a rock which jutted out beside the
opening.

Dr. Johnson stood firm and viewed the craggy descent
with curiosity. The cliff fell away almost perpendicular,
but much gashed and broken with spires and chimneys of
rock.

"From this point Black Fergus flung himself into the
sea," mused Dr. Johnson. " 'Tis a fearful drop. His body
must have been much battered by those jagged rocks
below."

"We never recovered his body," replied Dr. MacLeod.
"He had sunk before we reached the window, and he rose
no more."

Colin came behind us with the torch alight.

"He must rise to the surface in the evolution of time," said Dr. Johnson. "—What is that at the edge of the Kelpie Pool?"

The physician stared fixedly below.

"It is certainly a body," he pronounced.

" 'Tis Black Fergus," cried I, peeping in my turn.

Colin leaned boldly out to see.

"That is never Black Fergus," he said. "—Good God! 'Tis my brother!"

He turned and plunged down the dusky slope, carrying the torch with him.

"Wait sir!" cried Dr. Johnson.

"I fear he is right," said Dr. MacLeod quietly, "that broad sun-hat is certainly Angus's. I must go to him."

He in his turn ran down the slope, following the diminishing gleam of Colin's torch.

It was indeed the unfortunate young tutor. His grief-stricken brother drew the body gently to land, and we made shift among us to bear it to the mouth of the cave. The terrified ghillie wrung his hands and babbled about the Kelpie; but Dr. MacLeod bade him hold his tongue and run to the big house for bearers.

"Poor lad," said Dr. MacLeod, "those petrifications have been the death of him. He must have over-balanced and fallen from the Kelpie's Window."

"I don't understand it," cried poor Colin. "Angus had no fear of height; he could climb like a cat."

"Nevertheless, he fell from the Kelpie's Window and drowned in the Kelpie Pool," I said with a shudder.

"Not drowned," said the physician, "he was dead when he hit the water. He must have struck his head as he fell; his skull is shattered."

The bearers arriving, we carried the unfortunate young man to his patron's house and laid him down.

This sad occurrence, as may be imagined, cast a pall over Raasay; all retired early, with solemn thoughts of the mutability of human affairs.

The night was advanced when I awoke with a start and was astounded to behold my venerable companion risen from bed and accoutered for walking in his wide brown cloth greatcoat with its bulging pockets, his Hebridean boots, and his cocked hat firmly secured by a scarf. I watched while he stole forth from the chamber, then rose in my turn and made haste to follow.

Lighted by a fine moon, the sturdy philosopher crossed the island at a brisk pace. I caught him up as we neared the opposite coast. As I came up with him he whirled suddenly and threw himself in an attitude of defence, menacing me truculently with his heavy staff.

"Sir, sir!" I expostulated.

"Is it you, you rogue!" exclaimed he, relaxing his pugnacity.

"What means this nocturnal expedition, sir?" I ventured to enquire.

"Only that I have a fancy to interrogate old Kirstie farther about the second sight," responded he.

"You do well," I approved, "for we have had a convincing if tragic exhibition of her powers."

"Have not I warned you against an attitude of credulity?" said the learned Doctor severely. "I must understand more of her powers before I may say I have seen a demonstration of the second sight."

"What more can you ask?" I replied.

By now we were within sight of old Kirstie's hut. Without replying, Dr. Johnson astounded me by striking up an Erse song in a tuneless bellow.

"Sir, sir, this is most unseemly!" I expostulated.

"*Hatyin foam foam eri,*" chanted Dr. Johnson lustily, striding along vigorously.

A boat was drawn up in a cove; Dr. Johnson rapped it smartly with his stick as we passed it. Then with a final triumphant *"Tullishole!"* he thundered resoundingly on the door of the hut.

The little old crone opened for us without any delay, and dropped us a trepidatious curtsey. The close apartment reeked of the remains of the cocky leeky standing at the hearth. We had interrupted breakfast, for a half consumed bowl of the stewed leeks and joints of fowl stood on the rude table.

"So, ma'am," said Dr. Johnson bluntly, "Angus Mac-Queen is dead like his brother."

The old beldame began to wail, but Dr. Johnson most unfeelingly cut her short.

"We found him dead in the Kelpie Pool with his head broke."

"He should never have gone in the cave!" whispered the aged Sybil. "He had my warning!"

"There's Something lives in that cave," said Dr. Johnson solemnly.

"Ay! Ay!"

"There's Something wicked lives in that cave, that comes forth to kill the blackcock by night, and hides in the upper reaches by day."

"Ay!"

"Have you seen it in your visions?"

"Ay, a mortal great ghostie that eats the bones of men. . . . Alas! Alas!" the keening broke forth afresh.

"Then, ma'am," said the intrepid philosopher, "I have a mind to see this ghostie."

Hefting his heavy stick, Dr. Johnson left the hut. The woman burst forth into a clamour of warning, admonition, and entreaty, to which my friend paid little heed. Having bestowed a small gratuity, which served to intermit the old dame's ululations, I hurried after the venerable Doctor.

I caught him up at the cove. The declining moon was bright and clear.

"That is MacQueen's boat," I recognized it. "Who has brought it here?"

My only answer was a touch on the arm.

"Be quiet," said my friend in my ear. "Take this—" he pressed a pistol in my hand, "and when we come to the cave—"

"You will never go into the cave at this hour!" I gasped.

"You need only go as far as the fork. Watch what I do, but take care not to reveal your presence. I have a mind to conjure up the Kelpie."

There was no gainsaying my learned friend. So it was done. I own it was rather a relief than otherwise, after the pitchy blackness of the first ascent, to come in sight of the moonlight streaming through the Kelpie's Window. I shrank gratefully into the shelter of the shoulder of rock where Colin had stood that morning. I thought no shame to breathe a prayer for the intercession of St. Andrew, patron of Scotland.

My lion-hearted friend mounted steadily, till at last I saw him stand in bold relief against the moonlit sky in the ill-omened Kelpie's Window. He stood four-square without shrinking, his cocked hat tied firmly to his head, his heavy stick lost in the voluminous skirts of his greatcoat. What incantation he recited I know not.

Whatever incantation the intrepid initiate recited, it served to raise the Kelpie. There was a slip and slither of stealthy footsteps in the cave above; and then he came down with a rush and rattle of pebbles. I saw his bulk dimly in the half light, with the great club raised; then my friend wheeled nimbly into the shelter of the rock that had served me that morning. At the same time he struck down strongly with his heavy stick, and with a horrible cry the threatening figure overbalanced and tumbled headlong.

I hastened up the slope. At the top, my friend stood motionless and grave. At the foot of the cliff the fallen figure lay horribly still at the pool's edge.

"If he appear to his mother this time," muttered Dr. Johnson, "I'll know that she has the second sight."

"It mazes me," I remarked when once more we sat together at the Laird's fireside, "how in a record of second sight thrice confirmed, you, sir, managed to read the unsupernatural truth."

"Man's power of ratiocination," returned Dr. Johnson, "is his truest second sight."

"Doubtless," remarked Colin MacQueen, "old Kirstie, poor thing, was just as amazed at the learned Doctor's perceptions as we were at hers."

"Pray explain, then, how ratiocination led you to the truth."

"Sir, 'tis my earnest endeavour to instruct myself in your Highland phænomenon of second sight, of whose existence I have heard so much. I repeat, I am willing to be convinced; but of each demonstration I remain a skeptick. I ask: Is second sight possible? and I reply in the affirmative. Of each separate occurrence I then ask: Is *this* second sight? Could not it be something else? I have yet to hear of the case that would not admit of some other explanation. Such was my frame of mind when first I heard of old Kirstie and her feats of second sight."

"She prophesied Rory's death," said Colin.

Johnson: "Nay, sir, she *warned* you of his danger. Her reputation for second sight enabled her to do so without betraying her son. She foresaw what happened, not by second sight, but by her knowledge of her son's murderous frame of mind."

Boswell: "Then her story of her son rising out of the sea before her in the night was a pure invention."

Johnson: "Nay, sir, 'twas pure truth, save for the one detail that he was alive."

MacQueen: "How knew you that?"

Johnson: "Sir, I had concluded before I heard of this second apparition that the first one was a lie. If the second was a lie, it had one of two motives: if her son was dead, to add to her reputation for second sight; if alive, to contribute to his safety by confirming his supposed death. Thus far had ratiocination carried me when we visited her hut and heard her third prophecy. I had no faith in this third apparition, which I took, wrongly, to be a second warning."

Boswell: "Why a warning?"

Johnson: "Because, sir. I saw in the hut that which convinced me that Black Fergus was alive and on the island."

Boswell: "What?"

Johnson: "Why, sir, the great pair of breeks which we caught her drying at the fire, that she quickly hid under the bedstead. Think you that that poor wizened body had been wearing them, even were the women of Raasay given to masculine attire?"

"But with my own eyes I saw him leap into the sea and rise no more," objected Dr. MacLeod.

"You saw him leap," returned Dr. Johnson. "I saw when I stood in the Kelpie's Window how a strong and intrepid swimmer could leap outward and take no harm, for the Kelpie Pool is deep and calm, and for his life a man can swim a long stretch under water. Had you looked along the cliffs instead of down into the pool, Dr. MacLeod, you might have seen his head breaking water, like a seal's, to breathe. So it was that he came dripping to his mother out of the sea by night, and she comforted him, and hid him in the cave, and they plotted how he should reappear disguised when the nine-days' wonder had died down."

"Did ratiocinating on a single pair of sodden breeches tell you all this?" I rallied my learned friend.

"Not so," replied Dr. Johnson. "I concluded only to keep a sharp eye for signs of where she had hidden him. By the cave I saw the remains of his hunting—we have scotched your fox, Dr. MacLeod—and the charcoal of his fire ground into the sand; and in the cave we saw the fern he had couched on. From Dr. MacLeod I learned of the fresh spring and the chambers above; and I saw the Kelpie's Window and the pool below. Then we found the unfortunate young Angus, and the thing was certain. I knew at once how he had met his death."

"Why? Why did Black Fergus wish to harm him?" burst forth Colin MacQueen bitterly.

"Your brother ventured into the cave, torch in hand, to

fetch those specimens of petrifications he promised me. There he came face to face with his brother's murderer, and knew him. So much is certain. I think he fled, and was struck down from behind."

"How came he in the Kelpie Pool, then?"

"Ratiocination tells me," replied Dr. Johnson, smiling slightly, "that guilt and terror obscured the man's reason. Instead of hiding the body where it might never have been found, he endeavoured to simulate an accident, by flinging the body from the Kelpie's Window. He then swam or waded by night to his mother's hut and implored her to facilitate his flight. There he lay hid while the old beldame dried his garments."

"Was he, then, in the very house when the old woman 'prophesied' Angus's death?"

"Was he elsewhere, without his breeches?" countered Dr. Johnson. "When I saw Angus lying murdered, I knew who had done it, I knew what he must do next. I resolved to stop his flight."

"Why you? Why single-handed?"

"Since the '45, there is no law on Raasay, save what is brought from the mainland. I, an Englishman, a stranger, might most safely take justice upon myself. By night, I returned to the hut."

"How dared you seek him out on his own ground?"

"I preferred to face him on ground I had chosen. By the ostentatiousness of my arrival I gave such warning as drove him from the hut to his hiding-place in the cave. Mr. Boswell will confess that though I am scarce fit for Italian opera, my rendition of an Erse song has a peculiar carrying power. For the same purpose I thundered, sir,—" turning to Colin, "upon your boat, which the murderer had stolen and beached, ready for his flight. Having thus assured the murderer's presence in the cave, I entered in search of him."

"Good heavens, sir!" cried Colin impetuously, "to venture thus into the lair of a wild beast, and hope to surprize him ere he can surprize you!'

"I had no such hope," replied my intrepid friend. "He was sure to perceive me and attack me first. I permitted him to do so, only choosing my ground with some care."

"The Kelpie's Window hardly seems like favourable ground."

"On the contrary," replied Dr. Johnson. "If I was to bait my own trap, I had to have visibility, a quality provided in the whole cave only by the Kelpie's Window. There also shelter is provided, as Mr. Boswell found."

"Do you mean to say, sir," cried Dr. MacLeod, "that you stood in that orifice, contemplating such a declivity, and permitted a desperate murderer to creep up on you in the dark?"

"I expected him; I detected his approach; I was able to evade him at the crucial moment. That he fell from the Kelpie's Window was no part of my plan, for I had counted on taking him with my pistol."

"Sir, sir," I cried, "you took a grave risk thus staking your life on your hearing."

"Nor did I so," replied Dr. Johnson, half smiling. "You forget that Black Fergus had been supping on cocky leeky. It takes neither ratiocination nor second sight, sir, to detect the proximity of your pervasive Scottish leek!"

WALTER SATTERTHWAIT
The Smoke People

P alm trees *whicked* past the open windows. Ahead, and rapidly approaching, were the beach road and the sea wall; beyond lay a tawny stretch of sand and the blue, glittering expanse of Indian Ocean, a few faraway dhows with shark-fin sails loafing across it. Constable Kobari began to slow the Toyota Land Cruiser—as though trying to persuade the stop sign at the corner that he might break precedent and actually obey the traffic laws.

Abruptly, he released the clutch, floored the gas pedal, and wrenched at the steering wheel. Tires wailing, lurching on its stiff suspension, the Toyota spun to the right and sprinted south, skidding and skittering. Kobari cackled once, delighted, worked up through the gears with wicked relish, then turned and grinned at Sergeant Andrew Mbutu.

Andrew, who had many times witnessed Kobari's impersonation of Steve McQueen, was not impressed. "One day," he said in Swahili, "you'll kill us both."

"It's the reflexes, sergeant," explained Kobari seriously. "The reflexes and the timing. If both are good, you need never worry."

"And what of the tires?" asked Andrew. "Suppose one had burst just then."

Kobari considered this for a moment. At last he said, "In that case, the car would've gone over the sea wall." He grinned. "And we would both be dead."

Andrew nodded. "Splendid."

"But the tires didn't burst," said Kobari easily, and returned to lancing his Maserati down the straight at Monte Carlo.

He was young yet, still lived in a world where every betrayal was an astonishment. Hopeless, really, talking to him.

Tarmac humming beneath them, they raced along the road. To their left the ocean, impossibly blue as always, and today impossibly flat; to their right palm trees and thorn bushes in the sandy brick-red soil. They drove past the Salim Ginnery, past the Protestant church. Past a dusty Asian shop crouched beneath drooping ragged palms. Past the walled compounds of the wealthy Europeans—glimpses through wrought iron gates of gardens, carnations and chrysanthemums, trellises slung with bougainvillea and jasmine and rose.

"They are Giriyama, aren't they, sergeant," said Kobari.

"What?" Andrew turned to him. "Who?" Thinking of those cool complacent estates: no Giriyama there, certainly, except as servants.

"The Smoke People," Kobari said.

Andrew frowned, annoyed. He was himself a Giriyama tribesman. Kobari was a Kikuyu. Like every important civil servant in the government, like nearly every member of the constabulary. Like fat Sergeant Oto, for example, who was handling the dispatcher's chores today. Andrew could picture him receiving the report. Thoughtfully puffing out his puffy cheeks, "One of the Smoke People, is it. We'll put Mbutu on that—his sort, after all. And mucking about in all that offal, maybe that'll bring him down a peg or two."

But no smirk lurked within Kobari's question; the constable was guileless. Rather irritatingly so at the moment, when Andrew would have quite enjoyed a target for his spleen.

"Yes," Andrew told him simply.

Kobari nodded. "They live there all their lives?"

Andrew sighed; no getting away from it. He had become, by tribal right, the constabulary's resident expert on Smoke People. "Some have," he said. "But their lives seldom last long. Isn't this the turnoff?"

At their destination, two kilometers farther on, a grey Citroën 2-CV, weathered and dented, had been pulled over to the side of the dirt road beneath an acacia tree. Standing beside the car, holding a handkerchief to his face, looking uncomfortable in his limp black suit, and extraordinarily out of place against a backdrop of trees and shrubbery, was Dr. Murmajee, the Township's pathologist.

Kobari swept past the Citroën and brought the Toyota to an elaborate stop. Andrew opened the door and stepped out, wincing at the awful stench from the garbage dump. The smell, bad enough for the last few hundred feet in the Land Cruiser, was here truly appalling: scorched hair and fiber; putrescence, long advanced, both animal and vegetable.

Murmajee approached, switching the handkerchief to his left hand, holding out his right. "Beastly, isn't it, sergeant?" he said, and daubed his shiny forehead with the white cloth. "Disease, yes, and death, of course, we deal with those often enough, oh my yes, but this . . ." He shook his head, made a delicate little shiver.

"Yes," agreed Andrew. Breathing through his mouth but damned if he'd stick a nappy up his nose. "Have you examined the body?"

"Oh, but I only just got here, you see," said Murmajee. He pressed the handkerchief lightly to his face. "And I thought I would wait, you see, for the proper authorities. Yourself, and, yes of course, the good constable."

Wants a bit of moral support, thought Andrew. Anywhere else, he'd be prodding the corpse already, humming and cooing, mama tickling a babe. Well, fair enough; who could blame him?

Andrew stepped around the Citroën and walked to the rim of the pit. It was perhaps seventy-five meters long, forty wide, twenty deep. Low rambling piles of black, unidentifiable rubble lined its floor, some still slowly smoldering; oily smoke drifted among them, rose here and there in thin grey streamers. The place was desolate, bleak and blasted.

Gehenna, Andrew thought, remembering the stories of the mission priests.

To his left, wide enough for the trucks that each day delivered the Township's refuse, a track sloped down into the murk and reek.

He turned to Dr. Murmajee. "You are coming, doctor?"

Murmajee's round shoulders rose and sank in a slow sigh. Behind him, Constable Kobari had found a handkerchief of his own, had tied it across his lower face. A desperado planning to ambush the stagecoach to Dodge City.

Andrew started off along the track. Sand rustled beneath his heavy police brogues; gravel scuttled, clicking, down the incline.

From the track's end, at the bottom, a narrow path ran along the side of the pit, skirting the mounds of smoking rubbish. Down here, some of this stuff was recognizable: caved-in oil drums, a heap of rotting vegetable slops, empty food tins large and small, collapsed cardboard boxes, plastic bleach containers. The smell was much worse now; the air was thick, unmoving, congealed. Andrew stepped cautiously, careful not to stumble, fall: perhaps prick or slash himself on some barb of rusted metal. Teeming no doubt with tetanus and a million other, likely nastier, microbes.

A sudden movement to his right. A piebald dog, skin sucked flat against its ribs, tail curled between its legs, slunk off through the smoke. A dog would be a necessity down here, yes, certainly: for the rats.

At the far end of the pit sat two small huts, thrown together of uneven sections of corrugated iron, bits of planking and cardboard, lengths of rope and twine. And before the huts, waiting, their faces blank and impassive, stood the Smoke People.

The man wore a stained and tattered khaki shirt, a pair of black britches that came down only to his calves, a pair of yellow plastic sandals several sizes too large. The two women, their heads shaven, wore *kangas*, lengths of printed cotton tied above their breasts and falling to below their knees. One of the women, the younger, a girl really, had a child supported on her hip by a sling draped from her shoulders.

Andrew nodded to the group. "I am Sergeant Mbutu," he said in precise Swahili. "There has been a death reported?"

Neither of the women spoke. But the man nodded listlessly toward the nearer of the two huts. "He is in there."

Andrew turned to Kobari. "Get their names. Find out what happened." Then, with Murmajee beside him, he walked over to the hut. The entranceway was low; even Andrew was forced to crouch as he went in. An odor of unwashed bodies, sour, fetid.

Light came through an opening cut in the iron wall. Showed a single small room, a bare dirt floor. On Andrew's right, a shallow depression in the earth, holding some charred chunks of wood, a drift of ash. Beside it, a small pot, handle-less; a paper sack of cornmeal, for porridge; a whisky bottle half-filled with water; a small jar of white powder—salt or sugar. On Andrew's left was a bare mattress, battered and rent. The body, dressed only in cotton short pants, lay atop it.

Dr. Murmajee, handkerchief still against his face, shuffled to the mattress, lowered his thick body onto his haunches. As he busied himself, Andrew looked about the room.

Nothing much else to see. Clean enough, despite the

rankness of the air. But barren: no other furniture, no decoration, no color, nothing.

"Humm," announced Dr. Murmajee.

Andrew turned. "Yes?"

Murmajee was nodding. "I believe, yes I think it quite likely, that the body was moved after death."

"I can see that, doctor," said Andrew patiently. "People seldom die with their hands carefully folded across their chests."

"Just so," said Murmajee into his handkerchief. "Indeed."

Andrew squatted down beside him and slipped a hand beneath the dead man's shoulder, gingerly, avoiding the flesh. He felt the mattress. Damp. "And they have washed him, as well."

Murmajee turned to him. "It is their custom, however; is it not?"

"Yes, but illegal until after we have finished an investigation. How long has he been dead?"

"Oh my. Not for so very long, no. Rigor is only beginning." He tapped blunt fingers against the cheek. "Here, you see, in the muscles of the face. With this heat, I should say, oh, two hours? Perhaps three?"

Ten o'clock now. So between seven and eight this morning.

"And the cause of death?"

As he studied the dead man, Murmajee's eyes narrowed thoughtfully above the handkerchief. "No obvious wounds or contusions. He looks healthy enough—quite surprisingly so, wouldn't you say? In his middle thirties, possibly. Oh my. Difficult." He turned to Andrew. "Cardiac arrest?"

"That is a description, doctor," Andrew pointed out, "and not an explanation."

"Yes," agreed Murmajee sadly. "I suppose an autopsy might tell us more. Will there be one?" Without any real enthusiasm; he preferred opening up Europeans.

"The C.I.D. will decide." Andrew stood. "You can say nothing about the possible cause?"

"Well . . . there *are* certain indications, you see. Pallor. Pupillary contraction. I might, yes, in different circumstances, I might very well suspect the use of drugs."

"Drugs?" said Andrew, surprised. "An overdose?"

Murmajee giggled. "Absurd, of course. The local Africans don't much care for that sort of thing—as you well know, yes, of course. And a chap like this, well, where would he obtain them, isn't it? I only say, mind you now, that I *might* suspect."

"Narcotics?" Andrew asked.

"One of those, perhaps, yes. One of the barbiturates, perhaps. Sometimes one can determine, you see, by the condition of the body. Regurgitation, convulsions. But washed like this, and rearranged, oh my, no, no." He shook his head unhappily. "Stomach contents. I'm very much afraid, are the only way."

Andrew nodded. "Thank you, doctor. You may go now."

Murmajee rose to his feet with a small grunt, bobbed his head at Andrew, and waddled out the door.

Outside, Kobari stood with his notebook open, still sporting his bandit's bandana. The three Smoke People hadn't moved. From Kobari, Andrew learned that the man was Simon Ngio; that the older woman was his wife, Martha; that the young girl with the child was Esther Ogoyo, wife to the dead man, Mathew.

Ngio had told Kobari that Esther Ogoyo awoke that morning at eight thirty and discovered that her husband was dead. She woke up Ngio and his wife, told them, and Ngio walked to the beach road, to one of the European houses, and reported the death.

Ignoring for the moment the women, who still stood silent and immobile, watching him, Andrew stepped over to Simon Ngio. The man was in his fifties, a few inches taller than Andrew, exceedingly thin, all bone and ligament and taut skin. His eyes, vacant and dull, were rimmed with red. Not from grief, Andrew knew; from *tembo*, palm wine: he recognized its morning-after fumes, spiky with acetone, on the man's breath.

Andrew said, "You were a good friend, of course, to the dead man."

Ngio nodded quickly. "Very good," he said, and his eyes slipped away. He had only two teeth, blackened stumps on his lower gum.

"You have lived here for how long?"

"Eight years."

Eight years of living in swill. How did they manage it? "And the dead man?"

"Four years." Ngio's glance kept sliding this way and that as he answered. Nervous. Guilty of something, surely; but not necessarily of murder. Of living, perhaps.

Andrew asked him, "What time in the morning do you usually awake?"

"At dawn," he said, and then his eyes darted, panicky, to his wife, a few feet away. As though he realized suddenly a danger in the admission. With a flicker of interest, Andrew looked at the woman, saw that she was following this carefully, her eyes watchful in the pinched, wrinkled face.

"And at what time," Andrew asked Ngio, "did you awake today?"

"Halfway through the third hour." Eight thirty. "When the woman came to tell me of her husband." He blinked, looked away. A poor liar.

"He was drinking last night," snapped Ngio's wife. Coming to the rescue. Her voice was rasping, serrated like a knife. "He always sleeps later when he drinks."

"True," Ngio said, and grinned with transparent, ridiculous relief. "I drank much *tembo* last night."

Andrew nodded. "Was Mathew Agoyo also drinking last night?"

"Oh yes. We were good friends, we always shared our *tembo*."

"Did he share with you his *dawa*?" Medicine, drugs.

"Dawa?" Eyes shifting rapidly, concerned. "What *dawa?"*

Ngio's wife spoke: "Mathew had no *dawa."*

Andrew glanced at her. Sly old witch.

He looked at the young girl, the wife of the dead man. She was staring off, seemingly indifferent. Shock? Simple stupidity? Retarded, possibly. Awfully young to be trapped down here, without friends or other family, without hope.

The baby was awake now, gazing at Andrew. As indifferent, apparently, as its mother. Indifference, down here, would be a valuable habit to cultivate. Big brown eyes, clear skin. Anywhere else, he might grow up to be a healthy child. . . . Doomed, of course. Not the constabulary's problem, no.

He turned to Ngio. The man repeated his wife's words: "Mathew had no *dawa."*

Very imaginative.

Drugs of some kind, yes. And knowing it, these three had got together and concocted this fantasy. Eight thirty in the morning: nonsense. Andrew knew that the trucks began arriving at dawn, rumbling and creaking, engines groaning. No one could sleep through that.

But what drugs, and from where? These wretches, all together, hadn't enough money to buy aspirin, let alone narcotics. Every penny cadged would go for food, to supplement the scraps the Township let them cull from the garbage heaps, in exchange for tending the fires. Or for cheap *tembo,* to help them bridge one foul day to the next.

Found some pills or something amid the chicken bones and the soup tins? Possible, yes. But which one of them had found it? How had the man died? Accident, suicide? Murder? If the latter, Andrew would put his money on the old woman, the only one with enough cunning, or, for that matter, enough energy.

If not murder, why the lies?

He turned to Constable Kobari, said in English, "You

watch these two for a few moments. I want to talk to the
girl."

Kobari nodded, adjusted the top of his bandana with a
casual curled finger. Really fancies that thing. Throw
down the strongbox, marshall, or I'll fill you full of lead.

"Mrs. Ogoyo?" he said to the young woman. "Would
you please step away with me for a moment?"

Mrs. Ngio edged closer to the girl. "Have you no pity?
Her husband died only a few short hours ago." She
turned to the girl with a theatrical look of concern.

"Oh," said Andrew, rather pleased. "How do you know
he died only a few hours ago? From what I understood,
you knew only that he died sometime during the night."

Her eyes narrowed. "You *polisi*. Always trying to trick
people up, trying to fool them. Well, you can't fool me.
We may be poor, but we're decent and honest. We have a
right to be left alone in our grief. A few hours, I said, and
naturally I meant that the hours of the nighttime were
only a few hours past." Carried away by her own performance, she located a pocket of indignation, and chal-
lenged him: "What *else* could I mean?"

Turning from Andrew, she put her arm around the
young woman, squeezed her, clucked and muttered. The
young woman seemed oblivious still. Then Mrs. Ngio,
with an impressive display of wrath, nostrils distended,
faced Andrew again. "Can't you see she suffers? Why do
you plague her?"

Andrew was entertained: the hag doesn't trust the girl
with this story any more than she trusts her husband.

He smiled pleasantly. "It will be very brief, I assure
you."

Briefer than he intended. For just then he heard behind
him a familiar voice. "Good *Lord*, Mbutu, what have you
dragged us into now?"

Cadet Inspector Moi of the Criminal Investigation Di-
rectorate possessed a famous closetful of safari suits, each
a subtly different pastel shade. Today's selection was
lavender, and he held a handkerchief of matching hue to

his nose, covering his rakish goatee, also famous, as he circled round a clutter of rusted food tins. Behind him was his sergeant, Hadrubal Inye.

"Ghastly," said Moi, his face puckered with distaste. "This is altogether too much, you know. Calling us out on something like this."

Andrew said, "It was not I who called C.I.D. And, as you know, to do so is standard procedure in the event of sudden death."

" 'Course I know it, man. What do you take me for? But I saw that Indian fellow up top, the local chopper, and he tells me this is a simple case of cardiac arrest. Open and shut." Moi had spent a year on an exchange program at Scotland Yard, where he had learned how to select a tailor and how to speak, and to think, like Inspector Lestrade.

Andrew said, "There are several disturbing indications here. . . ."

"Disturbing?" said Moi. "Hah. What astounds me is that *all* this rabble"—he nodded to the Smoke People— "haven't been disturbed to death. *Look* at this place, will you?" He shuddered. "Well, to business, eh? Where's the bag of bones?"

Andrew indicated the small hut.

Moi turned to his sergeant. "You trot inside, Inye, there's a good lad. Check to see if the Indian missed any knives or hatchets in the body, eh? Ha ha."

When Moi's back was turned, Inye rolled his eyes heavenward for Andrew's benefit.

"Now, Mbutu," said Moi. "Suppose you come fill me in, hmmm?" He stepped several paces away, carefully avoiding a greasy strip of automobile tire.

Andrew approached him, explained what Dr. Murmajee, and later he himself, had come to suspect. Sergeant Inye interrupted briefly to report that he'd found nothing untoward in the hut.

"No, no," said Moi to Andrew at last. "You've got it all wrong, man. I know this sort. Give 'em a bottle of *tembo*

and they can sleep half the bloody day away. The dead
man? As I say, I'm surprised the entire lot of them hasn't
croaked. Place is crawling with germs, rats the size of
zebras. Could have died from a thousand different
things." He raised his wrist, examined the face of his gold
watch.

"An autopsy would—"

"Autopsy?" Eyebrows high. "You must be joking. The
Indian's perfectly happy with cardiac arrest, and he'll say
so on the death certificate. Not to worry, you've done a
smashing job, no doubt. But you run along now. Inye and
I'll finish up here, get the names spelled all proper for the
report. Assuming, that is, that these vermin know how to
spell." He chuckled.

"But if he did die of a drug overdose—"

"What of it? P'rhaps he did. P'rhaps, as you say, he
found something in the trash. Drugs, whatever. What
difference does it make? Man's dead, isn't he?"

That, it seemed to Andrew, was precisely the point.
"But suppose he were poisoned?"

"Poisoned? By one of these others, you mean?" Moi
laughed. "What, so they could obtain all his worldly
goods?"

"An investigation, an autopsy—"

"Look here, Mbutu." Moi draped his arm, great com-
rades, over Andrew's shoulder; Andrew could smell the
inspector's cologne, spicy sweet. "I realize they're Giriyama. Loyalty, et cetera, I can understand that. But,
surely, man, even you can see they're not worth bothering
over. Trash, eh? Riffraff, pure and simple. Suppose one of
them *had* bumped off that geezer in there. Well, where's
the loss? D'you think the Township wants the expense of
a trial for something like this? Besides, what punishment
could a court give any of them that's worse than what
they've already got? Even hanging would be an improvement, eh?" Chuckling, he slapped Andrew lightly on the
shoulder. "No, you let Inye and me take care of this.
That's an order, now."

Andrew was busy all afternoon; it was not until late in the day that he could return to the pit.

"Inspector Moi probably won't like this," said Constable Kobari, tying on his bandana again as the two of them trod down the pathway toward the smoking heaps of garbage.

At mention of the complacent, patronizing Moi, Andrew went rigid. "If you like, you can wait in the car."

"No, sergeant, no. I didn't mean that. Only that he'll be angry. I'd like to see his face, eh? But no, of course, sergeant, we're together on this."

Touched, regretting his peevishness, Andrew nodded. "Yes." He smiled at Kobari's bandana. "We are buckaroos."

Kobari barked with laughter at the English word. "Buckaroos," he said, and laughed again.

The dead man's wife was inside her hut. Posting Kobari outside to keep away the Ngio woman, Andrew called out for, and received, permission to enter.

She sat, her face still empty, legs crossed beneath her *kanga*, on the bare mattress. The child lay beside her, its head on her lap, its large eyes watching Andrew as he squatted down to face the mother.

"Mrs. Ogoyo," he said, "I understand that this is a time of grief for you. But there are some questions that must be answered."

She looked over to him, looked away.

"The *daktari* who examined your husband," Andrew said "feels that his death was caused by the taking of some kind of *dawa*. I believe that you know this to be true."

Again she looked, looked away. "Mathew had no *dawa*," she said, her voice flat.

The phrase had become a litany for these people.

"I believe," said Andrew, "that he did. Or that someone else here did."

Not facing him, she said in a dull monotone. "The other

polisi told us that it was finished. The minister came with some others to take Mathew away."

"It is *not* finished," Andrew said, vexed at this implacable blankness.

And the baby began to cry, let out a shriek, twisted its round face into an ugly mask.

She lifted it, held it to her breasts, rubbed its back. In the same toneless voice, she said, "He has a head fever. It has been getting worse."

The baby wrenched himself in her arms to look back over at Andrew, and wailed again.

Suddenly an ogre, Andrew sat for a clumsy moment amid the hooting and keening. Finally, making reluctant amends, he asked, "Have you taken him to Dr. Sayjit's clinic?"

She stroked the baby's head. "It is too far for me to walk."

The clinic, open at all times, was perhaps five kilometers away. Andrew knew of African women, thirty years older than this one, who could, and often did, walk a hundred kilometers in two days.

"What of your husband?" he asked. "Why did he not take him?"

The baby, slowly calming, sobbed and gasped against her. "He said he would go soon," she told Andrew, and shrugged. "But it was far for him as well."

But no farther than—only a block from—the shops where he bought his *tembo.*

Suddenly the stupidity of all this enraged him. For the first time he spoke in Giriyama, shouting: "Why have a child at all, woman, if you refuse to take care of him?" He stood up quickly, jammed his hands into his pockets: they were trembling. "Bad enough you choose to live your own life in this filth—how dare you bring another into it?"

She had rocked back, away from his assault, face awry. Now she thrust herself forward, her mouth set in a stubborn line. "Women are for having babies."

"Not when they live in a pig sty!" He was sputtering

with fury. At this brainless woman, this doomed child; at the combination of chance and choice that had brought them here (Giriyama, kinsmen); at himself and his shame; at everything.

Over the renewed howls of the baby, Andrew shouted, "If you can't give him the proper care, send him to one of the mission schools. They'll give him food and clothes and a chance to survive. Keep him *here*, and you give him a life even worse than your own."

"*No!*" she said, and wrapped her arms around the child. Her eyes were wide. "You can't take him from me! She said you would try!"

"*Who* said?" Then he knew. "The Ngio woman." He ripped his hands from his pockets, bent quickly toward her. "*What* did she say?"

She was crying now, cowering away from Andrew, clutching the screaming baby with all her strength.

"That if you told us what happened," Andrew snapped, "about the drugs, we would take away your child." He snarled: "*Fool!*"

She flinched, terrified. The baby screeched, great fearful yawps.

Andrew straightened, spun about, took two quick steps, breathing rapidly, raggedly; curdling with self-hate. Warrior, civil servant: terrorizer of feeble-minded women and ailing children.

When, after a few moments, he had got himself under control, his breathing steady, he turned to her. Slowly, deliberately, he said, "No one will force you to give up the baby." He heard the exhaustion in his voice; he felt drained and flimsy. He cleared his throat. "But I must know about this drug."

She sobbed, squeezing the baby closer to her.

"Tell me," Andrew said.

At last, she did.

Andrew stormed from her shack, ignoring a startled Kobari, and stalked to the shack of the Ngios. He slammed the ball of his fist at the side of the entrance-way; the entire structure rattled.

"*Woman*," he bellowed, still in Giriyama. "Get out here!"

Mrs. Ngio appeared at the entrance. She looked at Andrew, made a sour face. "What lies has she been telling you?"

"Not another word," Andrew told her. "I want the bottle of drugs she gave you, and I want the radio."

The woman frowned, opened her mouth to speak.

"*Not a word*," Andrew said. "Get them. Now. Or I'll see that you spend the rest of your life in a prison cell."

An empty threat, but at that moment Andrew sounded extremely convincing.

She ducked back into the shack. Andrew waited. In less than a minute, she returned. She handed over a small plastic bottle filled with white tablets, and a black plastic transistor radio, the size of a small Bible. Andrew glared at her; she stared back, lifted her chin, intractable.

He turned, marched back to the girl's shack, slipped inside. She still sat on the mattress, still held the baby. Not speaking, Andrew set the radio on the earthen floor and slipped back out.

He jerked his head to Kobari. All the way up from the pit's bottom to the Toyota, he remained silent. Getting into the car, he yanked the door savagely shut behind him.

Kobari seated himself behind the wheel. "Sergeant?"

Lips compressed, Andrew shook his head.

Kobari turned on the ignition, backed up the car, turned it around, and set off down the dirt roadway.

When they reached the beach road, Andrew felt the bitter stiffness, the rage, begin to leave him. He took a deep breath, let it slowly out. He held up the bottle. "The dead man found these this morning. Or so he told his wife. She hadn't seen him since dawn, two hours before. She was busy with the baby. He took one of the tablets,

she said. It made him feel very fine, so he took another.
Which of course made him feel finer still, so he took some
more. Ten more, she thinks. Within an hour he was dead.
Vomiting, convulsions . . ." He looked out the window at
the blue indifferent sea. *"Idiot."*

"What are they?"

"Morphine sulphate."

"Why didn't they tell us?"

"The old woman. She told the wife that if we learned
that her husband had used unauthorized *Wazungu*"—
European—"medicine, we would take away her baby."

"But why tell her that?"

"She wanted that bloody radio. The dead man got it in
town a few weeks ago. He spent a good deal of time, it
seems, begging in the neighborhood of the *tembo* shops,
nosing about, making a nuisance of himself. He told his
wife that someone gave it to him. He stole it, more likely.
In any event, the old woman told the wife that she
would keep silent about the *dawa* if the wife gave her
the radio."

"And the wife truly believed we would take the baby?"

"An idiot, like her husband. She and the old woman
washed the body—the old woman's idea, of course—and
then they sent Ngio to call for us."

"So," said Kobari. "It was only an accident then, the
death."

"An accident," Andrew said, and looked out the window. The man's life had been no doubt merely a series of
accidents; why should his death be anything different?

He turned to Kobari. "But it's curious." He rattled the
bottle of pills. "The label on these merely states the
contents—the number of tablets and the dosage for each.
No chemist's name, nothing else. And how did they get
there, in the trash? Why would someone throw them
away?"

Kobari shrugged. "Whoever owned them had no further
use for them."

Andrew shook his head. "No. People—Africans and

Europeans alike—usually keep their medicines long after the illness that requires them is over. As though the medicine were a kind of charm, and keeping it will prevent the illness from returning. Morphine, in particular, is for pain, any sort of pain, and can always be used again. And this was nearly a full bottle before that idiot got to it—if someone needed it for pain, why did he take so few?"

Another shrug from Kobari. "Could we get fingerprints from the bottle?"

"The idiot wiped the bottle off. And the rest of the idiots have all handled it."

"Perhaps if we checked the garbage where it was found."

"The wife doesn't know where he found it."

"Perhaps it was merely thrown away by accident, sergeant. Such things happen."

Andrew nodded. He tapped the plastic bottle against his knee, looked out the window, turned back to Kobari. "Who has died recently? Within the past few weeks." Kobari collected obituaries; he considered, for some obscure reason, that doing so was part of his training as a police officer.

Kobari frowned. "European or African?"

"Both. Asian as well. Tourists, anyone. Natural deaths, I mean, or what appeared to be."

"Well," said Kobari, "there was Bwana Dinsmore, the manager of the fishing club. There was Miss Kaufman, the sister of the old German doctor. That Catholic priest— what was his name?"

"*Baba* Reilly."

"Yes. And Alysha, the wife of Ali the Drunk from the clinic. And Ruth Mbaio, from the Delight. Oh, and that tourist who drowned, a hippie."

"A busy time for deaths," Andrew said.

"The winds have stopped, and the rains have not yet started."

Andrew nodded. He thought for a moment. "I think,"

he said at last, "that we shall have to ask a few people some questions."

Andrew took the bottle of pills from his pocket, leaned forward in his chair, and set the bottle on the coffee table. The man blinked, looked at him, and said, "Where did you get those?"

"Do you know of the Smoke People?"

The man nodded.

"One of them died this morning. Of an overdose of those tablets."

The man said nothing, merely sat back in his chair, waiting.

"You will notice,"Andrew said, "that the label on the bottle contains neither a chemist's nor a doctor's name. Clearly, the tablets were not issued as a prescription. So how could they have come into this man's hands? There were, it seemed to me, three possibilities. First, he simply found them in the trash. Second, he stole them from somewhere. The man's son has been ill, and he had been promising for some time to do something about it. He might have walked to Dr. Sayjit's clinic this morning—he had time to do so—and discovered them lying about somewhere. And pilfered them.

"Third, of course, someone could have given them to him. But if so, it must have been someone who had ready access to such things. And why would such a person give a dangerous drug to a man like this?"

Andrew paused for a moment; the other man shrugged.

"Blackmail occurred to me," said Andrew. "Several weeks ago, a woman died of what seemed to be natural causes. Curiously enough, her husband, I was informed, works in Dr. Sayjit's clinic. At approximately the time she died, the dead man came into possession of a transistor radio. Could he have seen something, I wondered, that enabled him to threaten the husband? To receive from the husband first the radio, and then the drugs?

"But I have since learned that Ali Bey, the husband, has

been in Mombasa for a week, visiting his family. He could not have given the man these drugs today—and it is most likely that the man did take possession of the drugs today, for he seems to have begun taking them at very nearly the moment he obtained them."

Andrew shifted in his chair. "As for theft, the people living with him tried to persuade me that the man had died in his sleep. It is improbable that they would attempt to do so unless they were certain that the man had not come into town this morning: someone might have seen him, and invalidated their story. I enquired at the clinic, and, indeed, the man had not been there.

"So the conclusion seemed inescapable that the man, rooting about in the trash this morning, simply discovered them."

The other was watching Andrew carefully now.

Andrew said, "But why would anyone throw away a nearly full bottle of morphine sulphate?" One by one, he repeated the arguments against such an action that he had earlier given Kobari. "One possibility, however, is that someone had used the morphine to remove someone else, and then, fearing discovery, disposed of the drug. Now the only person in the Township, other than Ali Bey, who has access to these drugs and who has recently suffered the loss of someone close, is you, Dr. Kaufman."

Dr. Kaufman lowered his head and ran a bony hand, freckled with age spots, over his sparse white hair. Andrew waited, glanced around the sitting room. Large but simple, without the usual African gewgaws with which most Europeans cluttered their living space. Dark heavy wooden furniture. A *makouti* roof, thatch, and mangrove pole, high above.

Dr. Kaufman looked up. "It is an interesting story, sergeant." The German accent was only barely noticeable.

Andrew said simply, "A man has died, doctor."

The doctor nodded. "Yes," he said. "Yes." He looked away, lifted the fingertips of his right hand to his temple, closed his eyes. In his late seventies, tall but stooped and frail: his grey shirt drooped from bony shoulders, his grey slacks sagged from bony knees.

He opened his eyes and asked Andrew, "Why did you come here alone?"

"I thought you would talk more freely to only one policeman." The same story he had told Kobari; but Dr. Kaufman was an estimable personage, had lived in the Township since before the European War, was respected, loved even; if Andrew were wrong, it were best the consequences fell only upon him.

Dr. Kaufman said, "You do not have a great deal of proof."

"No," Andrew admitted. "Not yet."

The doctor smiled. Sadly, the deep lines of his face barely deepening. "You are a most intelligent man, sergeant."

Andrew said nothing.

Dr. Kaufman looked around the sitting room, his glance slow and lingering, as though he were committing its contents to memory. Finally his eyes met Andrew's again. "Frieda had cancer," he said. He took a long deep breath. "Hepatic . . . of the liver, you understand? It was inoperable. By the time she told me about the pains, the disease was too far advanced. That was her way, you see. Refusing always to admit to any weakness."

He looked off, remembering; a small smile began. "She. . . ." He shook his head, turned to Andrew, and said briskly, "We flew to Nairobi, we went through all the tests, but it was hopeless. Nothing could be done."

Another deep breath. "She refused painkillers of any kind. She wanted, she said, to maintain her clarity, to experience in its entirety this thing that was happening." He paused, frowned. "No. I make her sound like some kind of Valkyrie. Inhuman. She was not. She believed that this was as valid an experience as any other, and that so long as she were able, she would live it. It was a part of life, she said. It had, and it gave, a meaning. We discussed it. We agreed that when the pain became unbearable, when she asked me to end it for her, I would."

He looked off again for a moment, then returned to Andrew. "She made me promsie to continue, afterward. To go on. We were very close, you see. She knew I would be tempted to end it for myself as well."

He cleared his throat, took another deep breath. "I watched her suffer for three months. I make no excuse, you understand, I only explain. For the last few weeks she could not sleep, could not lift herself from the bed. At night, from my room, I could hear her. Her body clenching. But she never cried out. . . . Finally she told me she was ready. I gave her the morphine tablets to put her under—she had a horror of needles. We had been—what is the phrase?—*rounded up* before the war. We escaped, with some others, from the camp, but the doctors—*doctors*—they had done things to her with needles. . . . And so, when she was asleep, I injected the strychnine. . . ."

Dr. Kaufman stared down at the floor for a very long time. Andrew was silent. At last, not looking up, the doctor said, "I took an oath, you know, quite a long time ago. An oath not to take a life. I violated that oath once, and now it seems I have violated it again." He shook his head. "That poor wretch." He whispered, "*Gott.*"

He looked up suddenly. "I want you to know that I did not throw away that bottle because I feared detection, as you put it. The coroner accepted my death certificate, no autopsy was performed, and what is more natural than morphine in a doctor's office? I threw away the syringe, but I carried the bottle with me for days. I am not sure why. A talisman? A connection, a link. I knew I could not use those tablets for anyone else. But one day, at last, I dropped it into the garbage cannister outside the post office. It was foolish, totally unforgivable—not because of this, not because it brought you here, no, but because of that man. Unforgivable. . . ."

Abruptly, he pulled himself to his feet. "Well, it is over, yes? You will not need your"—he smiled—"manacles? I

will give you no trouble. But if I might be allowed to bring
with me a few small things?"

Andrew knew, all at once, what the doctor intended.
The double violation of the oath overrode the single
promise to the sister.

"No, doctor," he said.

The next morning, the chief called Andrew in. Sitting
behind his deak, his round head and thick shoulders
outlined by the light from the window behind, he held a
sheet of paper in his hands. Andrew sat down.

"I've got the report from the C.I.D." Tapping the paper.
"That man at the municipal dump. According to Moi, the
matter is straightforward, and Murmajee has signed to
cardiac arrest. I'm never altogether certain about Murmajee, you know that, and as for Moi. . . ." He shook his
head, smiling. "I'd like to know if all this sits right with
you. Is that what you think happened?"

A good man, absurdly honest by the standards of this
constabulary, and a great deal more intelligent—astonish-
ingly so at times—than he looked: face like a fist, body all
beef and brawn, slow moving, stolid. And a man who
knew Andrew, gave him more leeway and respect than
most superiors, more than any other Kikuyu ever would.

For the first time in his life, Andrew lied to him. "Yes,"
he said.

One case of euthanasia; another, at the very worst, of
manslaughter; and certain acquittal on each. But for the
rest of his life, long or short, the doctor would have to live
with the chatter that turned to whisper, the stares that
danced away.

Now he had to live, like Andrew, only with himself.
And Andrew had arranged a penance for them both. The
baby of the dead man: the two of them would make
certain that it became, and remained, a healthy child.

Andrew left the chief's office, crossed the squad room,
stepped outside into the bustle of sunshine. In the shade

of the jacaranda, Kobari waited by the Land Cruiser.
Kobari, too, could live with the lie and with himself. And
Andrew had made him swear that if the truth ever came
out, and he were questioned, he would say that he acted
under Andrew's orders. Kobari had sworn, his grin sig-
nalling another lie.

Now Kobari said, "It went all right, then."

Andrew nodded, smiling. It had all gone a great deal
better than anyone might have expected.

"Good," said Kobari, and smiled back.

They got into the car, pulled shut the doors. Kobari slid
the key into the ignition, then turned to Andrew with a
frown. "Only one thing of all this still disturbs me,
sergeant."

"And that is?"

"That radio. I checked the robbery reports, and it
wasn't listed. Where would a man like that get such a
thing?"

Bothersome, true: an unlikely gift for one of the Smoke
People to receive. The ironic truth (or the farcical; or the
tragic; and a truth Andrew had told not even Kobari) was
that its batteries had died a week ago, and none of those
people, none of the four, had known enough to buy new
ones.

"I don't know," Andrew said. "Most likely, we'll never
know."

Kobari nodded, snapped the ignition, rammed the stick
shift forward, and floored the gas pedal.

WILLIAM F. NOLAN

Sungrab

Sherlock Holmes was spitting up.

"Gaaa, gaa," he said, eyes rolling in his leonine skull.

"What's wrong with him now?" I asked Watson.

"A temporary regression to infancy," said the soft-voiced doctor, carefully wiping a bubble of saliva from the great detective's chin.

I scowled, kicking open a flowcab for the office bottle. "How can he regress to what he never *was*?"

"Holmes is equipped with programmed tapes extending back to a womb state. His powers of deductive reasoning must embrace the full spectrum of life." Watson stroked his pale mustache. "I, too, retain memories of a childhood I never actually experienced."

"I think Albin is overdoing things with you robos," I said, pouring myself a solid shot from the bottle.

"You are paying for the services of a master detective," Watson said, whacking Holmes sharply on the right side of the head. "Advanced robotic design is therefore essential."

Holmes blinked rapidly. A thin smile replaced the look of infant blankness. "Ah, my dear Watson," he said, drawing a heavy black pistol from the folds of his Inverness cape and pointing the gun at me. "It seems we have finally bagged our game! The infamous Moriarty is ours!"

I scowled at Watson. "He's still wacko. Tell him who I am before he fires that bloody antique!"

The good doctor leaned close to Holmes. "This is Samuel Space. He is a private investigator, and we are in his office on Mars. He has rented us to work with him."

"Yeah," I nodded. "Fifty solarcreds a day, and look what I get!"

"Stand aside, Watson!" ordered Holmes, keeping the pistol aimed at my chest. "This arch-fiend is a master of disguise, and has cleverly chosen to portray a cheap, shabbily clad private operative of limited intelligence and inferior vocabulary in order to mask his true identity!"

"Shabbily clad!" I snapped. "I bought this zipsuit two weeks ago on Mercury—and the shirt's a pop-cuff self-wash from Allnew York." To Watson: "Better crack him again."

The mustached doctor palm-whacked Holmes once more, this time on the *left* side of his head.

Holmes gulped, slipping the gun back into his cape. He replaced it with a curving deep-bowled antique pipe, into which he tamped a rare blend of mutated Turko-Greek Earthtobacco. He puffed, expelling a cloud of aromatic intensity, regarding me with languid eyes. "I have analysed the fragment of crushed leaf-mold from the riding boot of Lady Wheatshire, and you will be pleased to know, Mr. Space, that I have *solved* the Case of the Missing Claw."

"Hey, wait a sec!" I started to protest, but Holmes silenced me with an upraised hand.

"The jeweled bird we assumed was in the hands of Lord Willard Wheatshire was, in actuality, never in his possession during his tenure at Suffox Hall. In a shameless yet clever act of duplicity, perpetrated by Lady Wheatshire prior to the time of their arrival in Suffox, a fake bird, with the *left* claw removed, was substituted— while the genuine Egyptian Eagle, with the worthless *right* claw missing, was passed to the blind hunchbacked gardener called Fedor, who was, of course, none other than the dastardly Mayfair pederast known as the Earl of Clax."

"Look, I—" But my words were ignored as Holmes' voice rose in triumph: "Ergo—Clax had the Claw—the *left* claw containing, within its taloned grip, the Blood Pearl of the Bonfidinis which was . . ." and he dramatically spaced his words, "never—actually—missing—at—all!"

"Brilliant!" breathed Watson, his mustache trembling. He clapped Holmes on the shoulder. "Absolutely brilliant, old fellow!"

"Except it's the wrong case," I said. "I rented you two wackos to help me solve the Saturn Time-Machine Swindle, remember?"

Watson shrugged, looking at me with sheepish, haggard eyes.

I put the office bottle away. "C'mon," I said, grabbing my classic hat. "I'm takin' you two tin bozos back to Hu Albin's Amazing Automated Crime Clinic and get a refund."

Which is what I did. The next thing I did was vidphone my client on Saturn and admit I couldn't crack the time-machine caper.

You can't win 'em all.

Maybe I'd better tell you a little about myself. I'm an Earth op, working Big Red. I've kicked around the System from Pluto to the Moons of Mercury, but now my base is the big red one, Mars, right here in Bubble City. My office in the Boor Building is a little worn at the edges; it wouldn't cop any design awards. Neither would the cheap fleahut I rent on Redsand Avenue, but it's all I can afford on the limited solarbread I earn. I'm a barely-surviving member of a vanishing breed—what you might call the last of the private eyes. It's a bum's game. Even in its heyday this racket never paid much, but my great-grampa was a private Earthdick back in Old

Los Angeles in the Twentieth Century so I guess it runs in the blood.

But let's get back to the case at hand. . . .

Here I am, half-swacked on Moonjuice, leaving the Happy Hours Alcoholic Emporium after that vidcall to my erstwhile client.

I didn't want to go home because home was a cramped lifeunit full of Martian sandflies and broken dreams—if you'll pardon a poetic reference to personal despair. My last pairmate had walked on me three Marsmonths ago, claiming that our relationship lacked sexual intensity. She was right. I'd used up most of my sexual intensity on a Venusian triplehead during a multi-operational star-dodge tax fraud assignment on Ganymede.

So my unit was empty now—just me and the sandflies—which explains why I was in no big rush to get back there on this particular evening.

I needed a prime brainblast—a full sensory vacation from the lousy detective biz—so I found the nearest Mindmaze, zipped myself into a Tripchair, snapped on the lobe pads, and blasted.

I was deeped, clam-happy, really into it, when an abrupt powerbreak made me surface.

I blinked up at a tall, cat-eyed Earthgirl in a tiger-striped wig. She was poured into a tri-glo slimsuit and knee-high lifeleather bootkins. An absolute knockout.

"I'm sorry I broke your contact," she said, facing my chair, looking very determined, "but I knew you wouldn't be back in your office before morning and I *had* to see you now."

"You could have let me finish my blast," I said, popping my pads and leaving the Tripchair.

"This matter is quite urgent, Mr. Space."

"You know me, but I don't know you."

"Amanda Nightbird," she said. "I shake with the Saints."

"Right," I said. "I've seen you on the vids. How'd you get my name?"

"You were recommended by a friend as a reliable private hop," she said.

"Private *op*," I corrected. "Short for individual operative."

"The term is not familiar," she told me.

"That's because there aren't many of us around anymore."

"Anyhow," she said with impatience, "I know what you do and I want you to do it."

"Do what, Miss Nightbird?"

"Protect. You *do* protect people, don't you? . . . I mean, isn't that part of what you do as a . . . private whatever?"

"Sure," I nodded. "Protection's in my line. Two hundred solarcreds a day, plus expenses. Now, just *who* do I protect?"

"Me," said the girl with a shake of her tiger hair.

"And when do I begin?"

"*Now*," she said, nodding toward the exit. "There's something outside, waiting to kill me!"

She was accurate; it wasn't "someone"—it was "something." A nine-foot multi-armed spider assassin from the Rings of Orion. I was ready for him when he dropped from the roof onto the person he *thought* was Amanda Nightbird.

He got a royal shock: I was wearing Amanda's tiger-striped wig, knee-high lifeleather bootkins and tri-glo slimsuit. Amanda remained inside the building in her skimpies.

I'm trained in seventeen forms of solar combat so when this spider guy landed on my lower back (planning to sink his poison fangs in my neck—or, to be precise, into Amanda's neck) I dipped into a lateral reverse Mercurian half-twist and sent him flying. Before he could regain balance I delivered a neatly-executed double heel snap to his upper mandibles. Hissing, he lunged at me again—but by this time I had my .38 nitrocharge fingergrip Colt-Wesson out and working for me. I re-distributed his atoms, blasting him into a multitude of hairy black pieces. (Universal law: nothing ever dies in the cosmos.)

Then I went back inside and asked Amanda Nightbird why a spider assassin from Orion was trying to kill her.

She wore glitternip on her breasts, and looked so great in her skimpies, with her perfect skin shining in the semi-gloom, that I found it difficult to concentrate on her reply—but it had to do with a risk-debt she'd refused to pay after losing to a rigged Gravgame at Honest Al's Pleasure Palace.

"I know Al," I told her, squeezing her right breast. "I can square it for you."

"He's a crook!" she said with heat. "I wish you wouldn't."

"Square it?"

"No, squeeze my breast. I don't like them pinched or squeezed. My first bedmate did that and it absolutely ruined our pairup. I like them flat-palmed or caressed lightly around the inner aureole."

"Oke," I said, handing over her tiger-striped wig. "But you *do* want me to fix things with Al?"

"Oh, yes, I do," she said as I passed her clothes back to her. "But I *refuse* to pay him a thousand creds when I *know* he manipulated the gravity field on that spinwheel."

"Gotcha," I agreed, watching her slide into her slimsuit.

"There's something else," she said, looking up at me with deep-lashed eyes. "What do you know about the meaning of dreams?"

"I'm an op not a headpsyc," I said. "What kind of dreams?"

"Nightmares. I keep dreaming that frost is everywhere, freezing all life. Over and over lately . . . the same dream. What do you make of it?"

I was watching her tab her bootkins when I realized we were cosmically destined to pairmate.

"I'll have to pass on the meaning of your dreams," I told her. "But I'm convinced we're prime pairmate material. What say?"

Her eyes cat-flashed. "You *are* attractive," she agreed. "But our body-jag will have to wait. I'm due with the Saints—for a shake sesh on the Marble, and you have to square me with Honest Al."

"Ummmmm," I said.

"How much is all this going to cost me?"

"No way to tell," I said. "Depends on what I can do with Al."

"I trust you, Sam." Her voice was a purr as I flat-palmed her right breast. "My future rests with you."

I knew that cosmic destiny could be depended upon. Somewhere in the multi-layered swiss cheese of the universe, in a counter-dimensional reality, we were already body-jagging like crazy.

I looked forward to it.

Honest Al's was located just beyond Mars, on a runt-sized private asteroid called Burton's Rock, which was a quick hop from Bubble City. The Rock got a lot of local action since Gambledens were illegal in B City. I'd been there often enough to know my way around, and I was never dumb enough to buck a spinwheel. I stuck to mag craps. At least you can't rig a set of magnetic dice, so all you had to beat were house odds. Sometimes I got lucky.

You couldn't miss Al's joint; it was set smack into the fat lip of a big radioactive crater. You could see the glow for miles coming in from the dark side of Mars.

Inside, Al's Pleasure Palace was no palace. Al kept the upkeep down and play-profits up; he didn't need high gloss to attract the suckers. I spotted him at a corner drinktable with two fleekers from the Capella System. Al was buttering them up for a big spend. Fleeks have a natural urge for high-stakes action, which Al happily encouraged.

I walked over to his table.

"Samuel!" he beamed. "How jolly to see you again!"

"We need to talk," I said, tight-voiced. "*Alone.*"

The two fleeks looked up at me with lidless orbs.

"Later, Samuel. I'm with friends."

Al was big, maybe three hundred Earthpounds, and his tri-color changesuit didn't flatter his bulk. I put my left thumb against the upper ridge of his bloated neck, applied pressure. He grunted in sudden pain.

"We talk *now*," I said. "You two . . . up!"

The fleeks wavered to their feet; a fleek panics easy. They don't like violence in any form.

"Frap off!" I told them. And they waddled away, their stalk eyes bugged in fear.

I took my thumb out of Al's neck and sat down.

"What'll you have?" asked the drinktable. I ordered a double Irish, no cubes. Al was glaring at me, his wide face flushed and beaded with sweat bubbles.

"I could have you iced for this," he said tightly. His eyes were smoked steel with heat in the center. I grinned at him.

"You're real good at having people iced," I said. "That's why I'm here."

"Huh?" He blinked at me.

"You put out the killword on a Saint, and she came to me. I told her I'd have it canceled."

"You told her wrong, peeper," said Al. "She owes. She won't pay. She dies. One-two-three."

I shook my head slowly. "She was stiffed on a rigged spin, and you know it," I said. "Either you call off the hounds or I bring this seedy joint down around your fat pink ears!"

I sipped my Irish as Al thought that one over.

"You're running a bluff, Sam," he said, but his voice lacked conviction.

I gestured toward a vidphone near the bar. "Try me.

One call to my ole buddy, Solarpolice Captain Shaun
O'Malloy telling him what I know about your sleazy
operation and you're out of biz." I leaned close to Al's
sweating face. "Cancel the word on my client, or I cancel
your whole operation."

Then I sat back and lit a cigar. Al let out a long sigh,
raised a fat hand. One of his boys glided to the table,
giving me a hard lookover. Al snapped out two words:
"Nightbird lives."

The goon nodded and slid back into the crowd.

"Thanks," I said to Al. "That was a real sweet thing to
do."

But Al was still sweating; I wondered why. "Look,
Sam. . . ." His voice was soft. "There's more to this than
wheelmoney. I was under orders. The debt was just a
cover. Take my word and stay clear of her. She's going
down, Sam. One way or another."

I'd never seen Al like this. He was gut-scared.

"Tell me about it," I said. "*All* of it. Who hired you to
kill the girl? And why?"

He looked up at me with agonized eyes. His jowls were
quivering. "I tell you—and I'm dead, Sam. Just like her."

"Nobody has to know you told me anything."

"It's too dangerous. I only said what I did to keep you
out of it."

"No good, Al. I'm in it. Now *spill!*"

His voice went all whispery; I could barely make out
the words: "Amanda knows something she shouldn't . . .
about the Big Lizard."

"Stanton P. Henshaw, the onion magnate?"

Al nodded. "She was hired for one of his bash-parties
on Pluto—with the Saints. They were doing a shake up
there that night and between sessions Amanda wandered
into the gardens next to the main poolhouse. She overheard Henshaw. He was with some galactic highwigs. She
heard them talking."

"About what?"

"Dunno, but something big," Al whispered. "Big

enough for Henshaw to hire me to get a job done on
Amanda Nightbird. I rigged the Gravgame, and after she
lost at the wheel I *let* her find out about the rig. I knew
she'd refuse to pay—which gave me the excuse I needed
to put out the killword. She doesn't know the *real*
reason."

"But if she heard something important enough to scare
the Big Lizard wouldn't she have *told* someone?"

Al's voice became even more intense: "That's just it,
Sam . . . she doesn't *know* she knows what she knows!"

"Run that by me again."

"What she actually overheard has been erased from her
conscious mind. Henshaw deeped her before she left
Pluto—so the words now exist *only* in her subconscious.
But a police data-scan could reveal those words, and the
Lizard wants her dead."

"Then why didn't he kill her himself?"

Al shook his fleshy head. "Couldn't afford the risk.
Everyone knew she was shaking at his place that night.
He had to make sure her death wouldn't tie in to him—
and that's why he contacted *me* for the ice job."

I leaned back, twisting my classic hat in my hands.
"The question is—just *what* did she overhear?"

"I swear you don't want to know," Al said. "Just like *I*
don't want to know. Sure, I'll call off the kill, but it won't
save her. When she walked into that garden she bought
herself a ticket to the boneyard, and you can't save her.
Stay out of it, Sam. Nobody fraps around with the Big
Lizard."

"Just let me worry about that slimy green bastard!"

"But when he finds out I've called in the word . . .
he'll. . . ."

"He won't do anything. We'll nail him first."

Al's thick eyebrows raised. "We?"

"Me and Shaun O'Malloy. The Captain's had a long
line out on Henshaw's scaly hide. My guess is that
whatever's inside Amanda's head will provide the hook
he needs to pull in the Lizard!"

*   *   *

After leaving Al's I booked an express-warper for Jupiter. I had to locate Amanda fast and get her to O'Malloy at Solar HQ in Allnew York. I'd have him run a brain-scan to uncover what she knew.

The police in ten Systems had been after Stanton Henshaw, but—until now—the Big Lizard had been arrest-proof. Sure, every gumshoe in the galaxy knew how crooked he was, knew that his onion empire was just a legit cover for his monumentally corrupt activities, but without hard evidence he was beyond the law's reach. Now, thanks to private operative Samuel T. Space, the Big Boy was about to be netted.

It was a real sweet setup, and I was making it all happen.

When we touched down on the Marble I hailed an airkab for Juketown. I knew Amanda was shaking with the Saints at the Bent Tentacle, an upperclass drinkdive in the heart of town. Most of the hot off-planet acts played there—and the Saints were steaming. Their tri-disc of "Ionized Particle Blues" was numero uno on the star-charts.

At the club they told me she was doing a celeb vidstint as a guest panelist at KRAB, the local Tri-Vid Station. Her appearance was slated as prime PR for the Saints.

The Tri-Vid cameras were still on Amanda as she left the station, so I had to wait until she reached the liftlot outside KRAB before approaching her.

She was startled to see me.

"Sam! What are you doing here? I thought you were squaring me with Honest Al."

"That's done—but it isn't over."

"I don't understand."

An airkab touched down next to us, and I pushed her inside.

"Launchport," I told the kab.

"But I'm due back at the club!"

"Nix on that. We've got to see O'Malloy in Allnew York."

"The solar cop?"

"Yep. He doesn't like private ops, but when I bring you in he's gonna *love* me!"

Her eyes flashed anger. "I have no intention of going to Allnew York with you. I shake tonight at the Tentacle."

"I didn't figure you'd want to go, and I haven't got time to argue, so . . ." I pressed a spot just at the base of Amanda's skull. Her eyes saucered, she let out a small sigh—and slumped loosely against my shoulder.

So far, so good.

When we reached Earth Amanda was totally zonked: I'd slipped her some L-17 on the flight, and I had to *carry* her into Solar HQ. When I located O'Malloy I told him to break out the brain-scan equipment, that we had a prime candidate for a Reading.

He didn't see it that way.

"Space, you're under arrest," he told me, spitting out the words around a cigar the size of a NewTexas fencepost. He was tall and wide and tough—and he seemed to enjoy glaring at people.

I glared back, into his steamed Irish face: "On what charge?"

"Kidnapping," snapped O'Malloy. "You admit you took Miss Nightbird off Jupiter in a disabled condition without her free consent?"

"Sure I admit it, but I brought her directly to you, didn't I?"

"It's not *where* you brought her, it's *how* you brought her! She's still zonked. We can't get a word out of her."

Several other solarcops, equally tough, lounged around the captain's office, giving me the sour eye. The place smelled of stale sweat and cigar smoke. The coolvents were jammed, and the room was windowless.

"The words you want are all locked in her subconscious," I told O'Malloy. "Just do what I *said*, run a mind-scan on her."

"I don't take orders from sleazy, lowlife private snoops," growled the tall Irishman. "I'll decide on a scan—depending on what Miss Nightbird has to say when she norms out."

"I gave her L-17. That's strong stuff. If you wait till she's back to normal we might lose the Big Lizard."

"*We?*" O'Malloy stumped out his massive weed against the side of his nearwood desk and ambled over to me. I was in a holdchair, facing the desk, and he leaned down to cup my chin in a beefy paw. "There's no 'we' in this case, there's only *me!* If the Lizard gets nailed, I nail him."

He uncupped my chin, walked back to his desk and slid into his nearleather swivchair. "Okay, Sammy," he said, "I'll take a chance and play it your way." O'Malloy leaned forward, eyes hard and glittering. "But it better pay off . . . It just *better!*"

I'd never witnessed a scan, so it was all new to me.

The Reading Room was small and white and sterile. Two robos moved inside as we watched the action through a transview-wall. Amanda, still out of it, was webbed into the Bodytable and a faceless robo was attaching brainpads to her skull. A second faceless robo handled the Scanner—a large, floor-to-ceiling console filling one side of the chamber.

"How come we're not allowed inside?" I asked O'Malloy.

"A scan requires isolation," he said. "The isometric electrovibrations would be affected if any other brains were in the room." O'Malloy thumbed a speakswitch. "You can begin."

The lights inside dimmed to black as Amanda's skull began to glow; I could see her brain inside, like Jello in a bowl, pulsing with light.

"Sub-con level achieved," reported the console robo.

"Scan," ordered O'Malloy.

Words flashed in erratic patterns across the console's scan-screen, words deep-buried in Amanda Nightbird's subconscious:

... CAN DO IT? ... YES ... HAVE THE POWER ...
TOW INTO NEW ORBIT ... WITHOUT SUN ...
SYSTEM DIES ...

The words went on, revealing Stanton P. Henshaw's plan as totally monstrous: using a newly developed Moon Machine, the Big Lizard intended to steal our Sun, tow it into a new orbit outside the System, and put its vast solar energy to his own infernal purpose, as fuel for a destructive Device so powerful that Sol itself was needed to power it! With this Device he could control most of the Milky Way!

The words spilled out of Amanda's mind onto the screen as she lay, serene of feature, eyes closed, totally unaware of the incredible data she was giving us.

No wonder Stanton P. Henshaw wanted her dead!

"Now I know what her dreams really meant," I told O'Malloy.

"Dreams?"

"Nightmares about frost being everywhere, freezing all life. . . . With ole Sol towed away things would get damned chilly!"

O'Malloy stared at me shaken. "Can he *do* it, Sam? . . . Can he grab our Sun?"

I nodded. "Sure. Unless he's stopped."

"But how?" O'Malloy slammed a beefy fist against the wall. "If I nab him his lawboys will have him sprung before I can spit! We need to have proof! We need to find out where that Moon Machine of his is stashed!"

"Obviously on a Moon outside our System," I said. "But which?"

"Yeah . . . which?" He scowled. "We need more than some words inside a dame's head to shut down the Lizard!"

"Then I'll get what you need," I promised O'Malloy.

"We know the Lizard has an Onion Palace near Alpha Centauri. I can infiltrate the Palace and get our proof. A plan like this is bound to be fully documented. I'll bring back what you need to nail him."

"Just remember one thing," said the big Irishman. "If you die, the System dies with you."

A commercial starliner got me into the Alpha Centauri System, but I wasn't riding as a paid passenger. I arrived at Henshaw's in a *box*—as one of a houseserve squad of work robos, part of an exchange shipment. His old work robos were to be picked up for restoration, replaced by these new models.

I knew that my robo disguise was flawless, but I was a bit apprehensive as the Froggie Housemom released me from my insulated Pac-crate.

"Name, origin and work specialty," snapped the tall froggie. She was soot-green and stalk-eyed, like all froggies, with the usual spotted stomach and big flat wet eyes. I never liked froggies. They're naturally vicious and anti-social, which is one of the reasons the Big Lizard employed them.

"Speak up!" she demanded.

My bulbeyes blinked at her; a metalspeak altered my voice tone: "Name: Ernesto. Origin: the Earthcoast of Sicily."

"Specialty?"

"I am a faxcab refurbisher," I told her.

She jabbed that info into her punchsheet, nodding her spadeshaped green head.

I was being very clever, since I knew that Henshaw never took the risk of sending his faxfile cabinets out for refurbishing. It was an in-Palace project. The robo I'd replaced in the shipment had been programmed to handle this job—which gave me easy entry to the Lizard's personal files.

And I was fully prepared: my left eye housed a minicam, operated by blinking the bulb on my *right* eye. I could shoot faxphotos as fast as I could blink.

I was grinning behind my faceplate as I walked into

Henshaw's Palace. It took genius to pull off a caper like this.

My kind of genius.

By the end of the first workperiod I'd cased the whole setup: the faxfiles, method of data-storage, location of primary info. I waited until the work shutdown, when all the robos were de-activated, before making my move. The Housemom was offduty, and it was a cinch to slip past the corridor guard.

Inside the faxroom, I did a quick computo-check on primary data and—presto! Jackpot! There it was: Henshaw's full Sungrab plan. I got it all, minicam whirring, and was slotting it back into the proper cab when I heard a slithering sound directly behind me. I spun around, going for the .38 under my chestplate, but I wasn't fast enough. The gun was tongue-snapped from my hand before I could squeeze the trigger. A froggie nightguard faced me, snapping a set of nippers over my wrists.

"Let me go and you're a rich reptile," I told him. "You can retire from this racket."

He watched me with yellow eyes, his tongue flicking against his thin lips. Froggies are incredibly fast with those long sharp tongues of theirs, and I didn't need another demonstration. He wasn't buying the bribe.

"Mom wants to see you," he hissed.

The Housemom's room was as green as she was—a color I never much cared for. U.S. Earthmoney used to be green, back in the Twentieth Century, until the first woman president took office in 1999. She got the Pink Act through Congress and after that money was a lot prettier. Funny, the thoughts that jump through your mind in a state of crisis . . .

"Did you really think I'd be fooled by your clumsy disguise?" the Housemom asked.

"I—don't know what you mean," I said. "It is obvious

that I am a sturdisteel J-4 work robo manufactured for commercial cleanup within the System. My work number is 555563249." I dropped my pants—showing her the number which was stamped into my left buttplate.

She circled me. "And what kind of work robo packs a .38?"

I sighed, having no answer for that one.

In one swift, clawing motion she ripped loose my fake chestplate, revealing pale Earthskin. "Ugh!" she grunted. "How *revolting!*"

"Yeah—well, green scales don't do anything for me, sister!"

And, with that, I reached between my teeth, plucked out the tooth-laser I'd taped to the roof of my mouth, and shot her head off.

She made an ugly green puddle at my feet.

I'd learned something in the faxroom. I'd learned that the Moon Machine wasn't on any moon. Moon stood for Multi Operational Orbit Neutralizer—and the Machine was right smack dab under my nose, in the sub-basement of Henshaw's Palace.

I took a dropchute down there.

Things were getting a bit tight, since the Lizard's plan indicated that he was set to begin his solar tow job any minute now. No time to get back to O'Malloy. I couldn't depend on the cops to stop Stanton P. Henshaw; I'd have to stop him personally.

He was just where I thought he'd be—inside the Machine, at the controls, preparing to launch Operation Sungrab.

Getting in there wasn't easy: I had to gun down three froggies to clear the Machine, then set my .38 at full thrust to cut my way inside. The microblast ripped a hole in the wall of the Machine large enough for me to jump through.

I jumped—taking the onion magnate by surprise. He lunged at me from the control board, an electro-kickstick in his webbed paw. I jerked sideways, but the stick caught me on the upper right shoulder and my arm exploded into pain. The .38 dropped from my numbed fingers as we circled each other.

On the viewscreen I caught a glimpse of our Sun, slowly being sucked into space. It was too late: he was killing the System!

"I am a private operative representing the solar police," I warned Henshaw. "Surrender now, and you won't be hurt."

Henshaw let out a short, barking lizard's laugh. "Your solar system will soon be nothing but so many balls of ice." He kept circling me. "You were exceedingly stupid to come here alone. Did you *really* expect to take me back to Earth?"

"I'll take you back," I promised, and with a brilliantly timed Venusian twist-kick I sent the electrostick spinning from his claw.

They didn't call him the Big Lizard for laughs; he *was* big, over eight feet from the top of his leathery head to the tip of his scaly tail. His daggered teeth, flat-black lizard eyes and hairy green ears were anything but attractive. He wore a tucked-velvet tuxedo, topped by a handsome neckscarf of cross-woven silk which failed to offset his basic grossness. Ugly is ugly—and Stanton P. Henshaw was one ugly lizard.

Henshaw didn't say anything more; his flat eyes glistened with fury as he came at me, claws extended. I dropped to one knee and used the tried-and-true Mercurian headbutt—which sent the big guy reeling back, off-balance and vulnerable to a Saturnian wrist-lock. His eyes bulged as I applied pressure.

"Gotcha!" I said.

I was wrong. A giant onion swung from his neck on a looped chain, and using a free claw he pushed the onion into my face.

I did the natural thing: I burst into tears.

Sobbing, I found myself slammed to the closemarble floor, a wide green lizard's foot on my neck.

"You see," he hissed, "I don't need the help of my froggies in attending to you. In another micromoment your neck will snap like a Plutonian breadstick under my foot!"

And it would have—except for the fact that I was able to grab Henshaw's hanging appendage. I jerked downward with full strength and the Big Lizard let out a howl and staggered back, tail lashing in agony. No reptile I know of, on any planet, likes to have his appendage jerked.

While he howled and hopped I scooped up my .38 and laid the barrel across his skull. Which put him to sleep.

A quick glance at the screen told me ole Sol was being sucked deeper into space—and I had to stop it, fast.

The controls weren't all that tough to figure out, and I was able to reverse the Sun's direction, slowly guiding it back into its proper solar orbit. . . .

Then I locked down the shutoffs and set the Machine at Self-Destruct.

Before it blew Henshaw's Palace into ten billion atomized fragments I was heading back to Allnew York in the onion magnate's personal starhopper.

And strapped into the flyseat next to me, still sleeping like a babe, was the big boy himself.

Sam, I told myself, you're a bloody marvel!

O'Malloy looked terrible when I walked into his office with the Lizard in tow.

The captain was blue; his teeth were chattering and the hairs inside his nose were frozen. A thin film of white frost covered the walls, floor and the top of O'Malloy's desk—and all of the solar dicks in the room looked as bad as he did.

"S-S-S-Sam," he chattered. "G-G-G-Great work!"

"Thanks," I grinned. "I took minicam shots of everything you need to put the Lizard on ice." Then I realized that the term was inappropriate in these circumstances. "Uh . . . look, you'll heat up soon, Cap. I got the Sun back into orbit before I left. Just take a while to thaw things out."

"That's f-f-f-fine," said O'Malloy.

When it was over, with the Lizard locked up and the sun warm in the sky, I took Amanda back to my lifeunit in Bubble City for our body-jag.

We were jagging like crazy when Sherlock Holmes walked in. "How careless of you, my dear Moriarty, leaving your door unlocked. It will doubtless be your last mistake!" He had his pistol out, pointed at me. "Please stand clear of the young woman," he ordered. "And place your hands atop your head."

I hopped from the jumpbed, starkers, hands on head. When a wacky robo with an antique pistol gives me an order I obey it.

"Who is this maniac?" Amanda demanded to know.

"He's from the Hu Albin Amazing Automated Crime Clinic," I told her. "And he thinks I'm a master criminal."

"This is ridiculous," she snorted.

"I've tracked this fiend halfway round the world," Holmes said to Amanda. "Now, at last, he's in my hands!"

"Not quite, old fellow," said a voice behind Holmes. It was Hu Albin, and he was pointing a laser cannon at the great detective. "Now, give me that pistol!"

Holmes turned slowly, let out a long sigh, and handed over the gun. Hu Albin then pressed a button in the robo's neck, and Holmes became motionless.

"Sorry about this, Mr. Space," said Hu Albin. "He's on the fritz again. I'm having him completely rewired."

Amanda and I were standing there, both starkers, staring at Albin. "Get out," I said in a hard tone. "And take that wacked-out tinman with you."

"Of course," nodded Albin, flushing. He pressed another button on the robot, and Holmes meekly padded out, followed by Albin.

I turned to Amanda, but she was dressing. "Hey," I said. "What goes?"

"*I* go!" she snapped. "The jag's over, Sam. Enough is enough. My nerves can't take any more. Your lifestyle is just too erratic."

And she left me. Just like that.

I was alone. Ole Sam, last of the private eyes. Alone again. Well, not quite.

I still had the Martian sandflies.

And a lot of broken dreams.

BARBARA OWENS

A Little Piece of Room

He came out of the red haze that hung like a dirty curtain between the old man and the setting sun.

Seated on the little porch, watching him come, the old man savored the cold itch in the fingers inching down his useless thigh, curling into the heavy boot top and the strap there that held the gun. The closer the boy, the heavier grew the sweet, sour smell of death. Dobey knew it, had always been able to sense it, and had never been wrong about it yet.

Something about Dobey's silent watching made the boy draw up uncertainly by the well. Hunching under his heavy pack, he sent Dobey a wide friendly smile. The old man waited, watching the boy's eyes sweep casually, knowing everything was being catalogued behind them click, click, click—from the dead pickup rusting in the desert sun to the absence of telephone and electric wires, to his own solitary self in the rickety old wheelchair. He saw the boy's measured look at his hand tucked deep inside his boot, and even across the twenty-odd feet between them he caught the quick ugly flicker behind the boy's smile.

The boy cleared his throat. "Uh, sir? Saw your place

from the highway back there and wondered if I could trouble you for some water. Old canteen's just about dry."

He reached back to loosen his pack, suppressing a smile as Dobey's arm tensed visibly at the action. Moving slowly and carefully, the boy unslung a guitar, propping it and the pack against the well platform. He pulled a canteen from his pack and shook it playfully. "Just about a goner. Can you spare a fill?"

East, Dobey thought—that voice don't come from no-place round here. He jerked his head at the well and watched the boy haul up the bucket, drink, fill his canteen, and then empty the bucket over his head, water matting his hair and beard and running down the dusty jeans to steam in puddles at his feet. He laughed, shaking himself like a dog. "Oh, man, I needed that!" Inhaling deeply, he grinned across at Dobey. "You just saved my life, sir, and I thank you. I was about done in for sure."

Dobey waited, letting him play his part. Now he wheeled curiously, as if noticing the remote, desolate setting for the first time.

"Well, I'd say you like your privacy, Mr.—?" The boy paused, waiting. "I'll bet I've walked five or six miles and you're the first living thing I've seen."

Dobey spoke. "What you doin' out here on foot? Break down on the road?"

Responding to an invitation, the boy eased down against the well wall and leaned back with a grateful sigh. "No, sir, not me. I hitch. Thought I had a ride from Phoenix to Needles, but somewhere back up the road there the nice man made me an offer I had to refuse." He grinned wryly.

"Kick you out?"

"Something like that." He sighed again, closing his eyes.

The sun disappeared behind distant mountains and cold blue dusk settled across the desert floor, bringing with it the sounds that brought the desert to life at night. Keeping his eye on the big blond boy slumped against his

well, Dobey carefully drew his hand away from the gun,
letting it rest lightly on his knee, within easy reach. The
first stars gleamed in the pale overhead and when he
looked back from them, the boy was eyeing him with a
flat calculating stare. The smell he carried filled the space
between them, and for the first time in years something in
Dobey came alive, the electric anticipation of combat
coursing through him. It came so quickly and with such
force, it took him by surprise.

"What they call you?" he blurted loudly.

The boy gazed steadily at him. "Mitch," he said finally.
"They call me Mitch. You?"

"I'm Dobey."

"Pleased to meet you, Dobey." Again the practised,
winning smile.

"You one of them college fellas?"

"Was. Gave it up." Then carefully, casually, "Say,
Dobey, I don't want to put you out any, but I wonder
would it be all right if I stayed here tonight? Don't much
like walking the desert at night. I can just throw my
bedroll anywhere."

Dobey watched the innocent blue eyes while his mind
laid things in their proper places. "Gets pretty cold out
here at night. Guess you could sleep in the truck. It don't
run," he added pointedly.

"I know." Mitch grinned. "I noticed that when I came."

They sat silently, and after a time Dobey wheeled
himself inside the one-room shack and closed the door.
He listened until he heard the boy prowling around the
truck, and then came the mellow sounds of the guitar.
Blood racing, Dobey edged against the back wall, facing
the door, gun lying ready in his lap.

For over an hour he watched the moonlit window and
listened to the music. Then, when the music stopped, he
waited for stealthy footsteps on the front porch. Somewhere out in the night rose the threshing animal sounds
of struggle and a high death squeal. Then the footsteps
came. Dobey straightened in his chair.

"Boy?" He spoke softly through the closed door. "You got a gun out there? Less'n you do and can shoot as good as me, you'd best back off while you can. From here I can dump your belly all over the porch. You ever seen a gut-shot man, boy?"

The silence stretched. Dobey's heart hammered thickly in his ears. Then there was a rustle, a snick of metal, and soft steps padded away across the sand. The old man let out his breath with a grunt. He leaned back in his chair, muscles jumping. He felt himself grinning and the taste of acid lay heavy on his tongue. After a long while he napped lightly in his chair.

At the first pink streaks of dawn he rolled to the window. The boy was there, squatting against the well. He was silent, watching, as Dobey wheeled out onto the porch, hand resting just inside his boot. The old man ignored him, squinting out across the scrub, rock, and sand.

"I growed up with guns," Dobey announced to the general area, and spit with satisfaction. "Ain't nobody in these parts better'n me. I forget how many medals they give me during the war."

"Would that be World War Two?" The soft voice was edged with a sneer.

"That's right."

"That's been over thirty years, old man."

"Ain't no worse now than I was then. I shoot some every day and I never miss." He lowered his gaze to meet the boy full on, and Mitch was the first to look away. "There ain't nothin' here worth stealin', boy, less'n it's my gun and you ain't never going to get that."

For the first time Mitch's eyes showed a trace of sincerity. "I don't want your gun, Dobey. I've got no use for guns."

Dobey reached through the open door behind him and drew out a pair of field glasses, training them on the highway and slowly scanning its empty scope.

Mitch straightened slightly. "What're you looking for?"

"Nothin'," Dobey answered shortly. "Same as always. Road don't get much travel."

"Can you see the highway? That must be a good half mile."

"I can see it. See everything that moves on it, and I know most every car. Didn't see any strange one yesterday, like that fella's you rode up with from Phoenix."

Silence. "Yeah?" Mitch said. "That's funny. Maybe he turned off another road after I got out."

Dobey hung the glasses carefully around his neck. "Soon's you wash up and eat, you'll be on your way then." It wasn't a question, and the boy's smile flickered again before he rose slowly and stretched, grinning across the space between them.

"That's right," he said softly. "That's what I'll do."

They ate, Dobey brewing coffee on his camp stove while he watched the boy through the window dig something from his pack and stretch out on the tailgate, facing the shack. "Coffee sure smells good," he called, but Dobey didn't answer.

After eating, Mitch brought his packed gear to the well platform and repeated his performance of the day before. Then he looked across at Dobey in the window. "Want me to draw some up for you before I go?"

"I can manage," Dobey said. He saw Mitch eye the makeshift pulley system rigged between the well and porch, but the boy said nothing. He looked off toward the highway.

"Getting hot already."

"It does that."

Dobey rolled to the doorway, hand close to his knee. Not being a man of emotion, he didn't understand or feel comfortable with the conflicting senses of danger and sudden kinship with this stranger, this boy who stalked him in the night. He wanted him to go.

Mitch was speaking slowly. "Dobey, I'd like to do something for you before I go. In exchange for your hospitality. And to say I'm sorry about last night. I'm not

really—after you've been on the road a while you get—"
He stopped. "Well, I think maybe I can fix your truck. I'm
a pretty fair mechanic." He sounded almost shy.

"Ain't going to do *me* no good if you do," Dobey said
bluntly.

Mitch shot him a bleak look. Then he took one slow
step toward the porch, and in his mind's eye Dobey
watched a rattler coiling quietly in upon itself.

"I'm not going to steal your truck, man!" Dobey's gun
hand twitched, sweat oozed under his arms, but just as
suddenly the tension passed, and Mitch said hesitantly,
"Just trying to apologize for last night."

There was a long silence. Then Dobey surprised himself. "Help yourself, then. They's some tools under the
front seat, but I don't think they'll do you no good."

"I'd like to try."

"All right."

All morning he sat on the porch watching the boy and
the highway, tossing occasional shots at strategically
placed tin cans and rocks. Just before noon Mitch came to
the well, slick and shiny with sweat. He drank deeply.

"I've been watching you shoot. You sure told the truth,
man. You never miss."

"I know it."

"Listen. I can't fix that thing. Needs parts."

"Don't matter, I told you."

Mitch sank down with a sigh. They stayed a while in
suddenly easy silence. Finally Mitch said, "Tell me
something. What're you doing way out here?"

"It suits me."

"Don't get me wrong, but how do you get on—food,
supplies, and things? Who takes care of you?"

Dobey stiffened, glaring across at him. "I take care of
myself!" he snapped. "Always have, always will. Just
'cause my legs is gone don't mean I need a keeper!"

The boy reddened. He looked away from Dobey's
furious face. "I'm sorry, I didn't mean—"

"Aw, hell, there's always somebody after me. Damn

church in town has took me on—preacher comes out once a week to bring me food and shells—and if it ain't too hot, sometimes some of the ladies comes with him, cluckin' round here cleanin' up, emptyin' my slops, tryin' to get me to move into town and civi-ly-za-tion!" He spat disgust into the sand and stopped, surprised. He couldn't remember when he'd made as long a speech.

Mitch was grinning. "Why don't you shoot them? You never miss."

"Don't laugh, boy!" Dobey said, grinning himself. "Once they come out to take me in by force, by God, and I run 'em off with a double barrel. They scattered out of here like a bunch of prairie hens. They give up on me after that."

Mitch shook his head. "You are something. You must be the last original man."

"Yeah, well, the state police still comes around ever' day in one of them helicopters. If I don't give 'em a wave, they set down and come runnin' over to see if a jackrabbit's eat me."

He watched with secret glee as Mitch tensed, absorbing this. After a minute the boy asked casually, "Every day?"

"Yeah. They're checkin' the road anyway for fools lost or broke down, so they take a swing by here."

Mitch glanced up at the sky. "Any special time?"

"Oh, long about noon, give or take," Dobey said, enjoying himself.

"Well," Mitch said quickly, glancing at his watch, "heat's really up. Think I'll grab a bite to eat and maybe take a snooze. All right if I use the truck?"

"Sure. You do that."

Mitch started for it, then stopped. "Don't suppose you've got a radio. Lost mine somewhere. Be nice to have some music."

"Got one of them little transistor jobs, but it's busted."

"Well, I flunked out on the truck. Maybe I can fix your radio."

Dobey reached behind him through the door and tossed

the radio across. He chuckled as he watched Mitch stow all his gear out of sight before he crawled into the cab. Kid took him for a fool. He shook his head, wondering why he was going along with it. When the 'copter hovered overhead some time later, he returned the pilot's wave as usual, keenly aware that Mitch was watching the signal through the sprung truck door.

Late in the afternoon a jackrabbit ventured too close to the shack, and Dobey's shot brought Mitch staggering from the cab. He looked white and sick from heat. Dobey hesitated, seeing the boy and the distance he would have to roll to retrieve the rabbit.

"If you'll bring me over that jack, we'll have rabbit stew for supper, boy."

Wordlessly Mitch plodded into the sand and returned with the dangling, bloody carcass.

"Just lay it down there by the fire and then you back off by the well."

He did, flopping down with a groan. Dobey lowered himself awkwardly off the porch, tipping the chair first one way and then the other, keeping his face toward Mitch and his hand near the gun. At the stone firepit he pulled a hunting knife from his boot, quickly skinned and gutted the jack, and dropped it in the large iron kettle. From one shirt pocket he took an onion, a carrot from another, and with just a pass at cleaning, added them to the pot.

Mitch lay on one side, watching. "Really ready for that rabbit, weren't you?"

As the fire blazed up, Dobey backed away, keeping it between them. "Now you put enough water in to cover it," he said, and soon the rich smell of cooking meat wafted up from the old iron kettle.

They watched each other warily across the fire as the moon rose, laying a strong white light over them. After a while Mitch went to the truck and brought back his guitar. He leaned against the well, fingering it softly. The night air was cool enough to enjoy the heat from the fire.

"That sounds fine," Dobey said finally.

"You like music?"

"Some. Country. I like country."

"Which ones?"

"I dunno. 'Red River Valley,' I guess. I remember that one."

Mitch played it, singing the words as Dobey nodded along. "That's a good one," Dobey said when it was done.

Mitch grinned, putting the guitar aside. "Who the hell are you, Dobey? Where'd you come from?"

"Why you want to know?"

"I admire you. You're what I'd like to be—an original man. I'd like to know about you."

"Ain't nothin' to tell."

"What happened to your legs?"

Later Dobey could never explain how he came to tell this strange boy the story of his life. The night wore on and the stew came and went as he talked—of his boyhood in the Arkansas county orphanage, of running away and bumming around the country, of the army and how he liked it and belonged to it and decided to make it his home, then of the wounds that took him out of it and would keep his nerves deteriorating until his legs became useless. "I was supposed to go back to one of them vet's hospitals when that happened, so they could prop me up somewheres to make baskets the rest of my days."

He told of the gas station he ran out on the highway until he could no longer handle it and how, over protest, he then moved into the old broken-down maintenance shed and spent his days wondering about things, watching the highway with field glasses, and shooting at rocks and cans.

"Just an old cripple, but I get along," he concluded with throat hoarse and dry. "I got my pension. Don't want nothin' else but to be let alone with a little piece of room." He stopped, embarrassed. He'd never told such things to another living soul.

The boy was quiet, gazing into the dying fire. "That is

it, that's really it," he murmured finally, more to himself than Dobey. "A little piece of room." The eyes that met Dobey's were far too old and tired. "There's a lot of us cripples around, old man. You just handle it better than most."

Dobey said nothing. He thought he was on the verge of seeing inside the boy, almost but not quite.

"When you were in the army," Mitch said after a pause, "you ever kill anyone?"

"I did."

"You like it?" The question was soft, so soft the old man almost missed it.

He remembered. The thrill that had no name, the rage, the power, the release. "Yes," he said simply. "I liked it."

Mitch nodded slowly. Their eyes met again and Dobey felt it, the bond that sealed them forever.

"Well," Mitch said, "it's been a long day." He rose and stood looking across at Dobey sitting motionless in his wheelchair. "I'd be glad to help you get that thing back up on the porch."

"I can do it."

"I know you can do it. I'd just be glad to help."

Dobey looked up into the shadowed eyes. "All right."

He watched him come across the sand. He sat stiffly upright as Mitch stepped behind him and wheeled him to the house, tipping the chair easily up onto the old wooden porch. Dobey rolled slowly to face him. The night was suddenly still.

"Okay?" Mitch asked.

"Okay."

Mitch turned and started for the truck.

"Tomorrow," Dobey said, "about noon, when it gets hot"—the boy stopped, waiting—"there's a drywash on the far side of that butte yonder's carved out a kind of lip from the rock. Ain't bad protection, you know, from the sun?"

Mitch's grin came slow in the moonlight. "Thanks. I'll try it. I just about died in that truck today, you old lizard."

Dobey rolled onto his cot and slept the best night's sleep he could remember.

At dawn the boy was waiting by the well. Smiling, he held out a handful of silver rings.

"Know what you need? A ramp. I took these off my pack and if you've got some nails and a length of rope handy, we're going to be in business."

Dobey hawked and spat into the sand. "Out back," he said. "I'll make us some coffee."

They sat side by side on the porch, then Dobey watched while Mitch fashioned a ramp from some old boards. He rigged the rope and rings to the house and porch so Dobey could pull and lower himself with ease. It was so simple and worked so well, Dobey wondered why he'd never thought of it before.

They rested while the temperature climbed. Mitch sighed. "You really had the right idea, you know. A man could be at peace here forever."

Dobey lowered the glasses and squinted toward the highway. "Preacher's comin'," he said.

By the time the dusty old car negotiated the narrow bumpy lane and the preacher stepped out fanning himself with his hat, Mitch was safely down behind the butte in the drywash. Before he left, the preacher complimented Dobey on his fine new ramp, and Dobey said he didn't know why he'd never thought of it before.

That night they ate fresh bacon and beans in the firelight, then Mitch sang and played, beginning and ending with "Red River Valley."

Days passed, and then it had been a week since Dobey had watched a menacing stranger coming down his lane. In daylight he still watched the road and pot-shotted into the desert sands. Mitch rigged some new targets for him and did odd jobs until it came time each day to wait out the heat and the helicopter in the drywash. They met for comfortable moments as if they'd always been together, and at night they sat together before the fire, sometimes for hours in quiet companionship.

On one such night Mitch broke a very long silence by informing Dobey it was time he learned to play the guitar.

"The hell," Dobey said. "Don't know the first thing about it."

"You'll learn. Come on."

Over Dobey's protests he showed the old man how to hold it, and sitting crosslegged before him, patiently took him step by step through the chords for "Red River Valley." The moon rose full and high, and life began and ended all around them in the night, but Dobey, wet with sweat and knotted concentration, plowed doggedly through the motions over and over again. Several times he spat and gave up in disgust, but Mitch coaxed and bullied until, muttering vicious curses, he'd pick it up and try again. At last, with Mitch singing along, he made it through an entire halting, almost recognizable version and lay back in his chair, amazed.

"Well, I'll be damned!" he said, and Mitch fell over laughing.

They sat grinning at each other like a pair of fools. Mitch threw back his head and breathed deeply of the cold night air. "Oh, man!" he said, as if that expressed it all.

"You got any folks, boy?" Dobey asked suddenly.

For a minute Mitch didn't move, but something changed swiftly in the night, something Dobey could almost reach out and touch. When at last the boy lowered his eyes, they didn't match his smiling mouth.

"Sure," he said easily. "Why do you ask?"

"Just wondered. They know where you are?"

The smile tried to die, but Mitch held it steady. "I'm a big boy now, Dobey. I don't have to ask permission."

Dobey knew plainly he should let it alone. "I just figgered if you was my boy—"

"Well, I'm not your boy, old man. I'm not anybody's boy."

The voice was even, but the eyes were slitted, and something tickled at the hairs on the back of Dobey's neck. "You ain't from around here," he pushed on stubbornly.

"No," Mitch said after a pause.

"Back east?"

Slowly Mitch slid away across the sand, putting the fire between them. Again Dobey felt he was watching something cold and deadly coiled to strike. The fingers of his right hand trembled slightly on his knee about the gun.

"Say, I don't aim to pry. You don't have to tell me nothin' you don't want to."

They watched one another over the flickering fire. Mitch was frowning, weighing, his eyes reflecting the distorted dancing of the flames.

"Dobey," he said slowly, "you're the only friend I ever had. You remember what you said the other night? About a little piece of room?" He waited until the old man nodded. "That made a lot of sense to me, made it all fall into place. It's what I've got to have, but I never knew what to call it until now. A little piece of room. To be what you want to be, do what you want to do, and nobody to tell you different. That right?"

"I guess."

"Sure it is. You did it. And I'm going to do it. I come from a long line of successes, Dobey. You know what a success is? It's doing and being the right thing in front of other people. It's country clubs and board meetings, the right marriage and setting a good example. Making the best impression at all times and money—lots and lots and never enough of it, money. You get that from the time you can understand what it is that's expected of you, the last in a long line of successes!" His words hissed across the fire.

"You see," he explained, leaning closer, "there's no room in a long line of successes for anyone who's different, who's crazy enough to want something else. That calls for drastic measures. We've got to whip that misguided someone into shape, get that someone back in line, lean on that someone until he breaks. Crowd him, Dobey, crowd him, crowd him"—he broke off suddenly with a big smile. "You know, here with you this past week, it's the first time in my life I've ever felt good? Relaxed, not tense, you know? Not crowded." He shook his head gently. "I can't take being crowded any more." Eyes glittering, he whispered fiercely, "Don't let anyone take it from you, old man! They'll try. Don't you let anyone into your little piece of room!"

Dobey swallowed drily. "You goin' any place in particular?"

For a minute Mitch stared blankly. Then he shook his head and sat back, laughing. "Man, how'd I get off on that?" As Dobey watched, the wildness in Mitch's face faded. "Oh, I don't know. I'd started out for California. But I sure do like it here."

"Redwoods," Dobey said, anxious to keep the subject changing. "Always thought I'd like to see one of them redwoods."

"Not the ocean?"

"Shoot, I seen oceans."

"Well, my friend, when I get there I'll take a picture of those redwoods and send it to you okay?" As quickly as it came, his former mood was gone.

Dobey smiled. "That'd be fine," he said.

Back inside the cabin he stayed sitting by the window, looking out into the night and wondering what it was that had just taken place. There was no sound or sign of movement from the truck.

He was dozing when a flash of light crossed his eyes. A car turned off the highway, pulled a short way into the lane, and stopped. The lights went out. A minute later a blast of music rolled across the desert floor. Dobey reached for his glasses and trained them on the shadows inside.

After a minute he tossed them aside. "Damn kids!"

The music went on for a long time, cutting through the night air. Dobey was nodding again when he heard the car door slam and the sound of voices. Two figures started toward him, stumbling and giggling down the lane. Music still played inside the car. Dobey rested his hand over his boot.

As they drew closer, he could see one was a girl, and she was protesting in a loud whisper, "Come on, honey, let's go back. I'm scared."

The boy hooted, a ragged adolescent voice. "Aw, he's just a crippled old coot. We'll have a little fun."

Dobey drew back from the window as they stopped a short distance from the porch.

"Hey, old coot!" the boy called out drunkenly. "You got anything to drink in there?"

"Billy," the girl whined, backing toward the well, "you come on now."

He giggled, motioning her to stay. "Hey! We're dry out here! You bringin' it out or do I come in?" He half turned for her approval, doubling over in his glee.

Dobey never saw where Mitch came from. One minute he was nowhere, the next he held the boy's neck tight from behind with one arm while the other hand pressed the long murderous blade across his throat. The young boy's mouth hung open in a silent, stupid howl.

This frozen scene would live in Dobey's mind forever— the girl, the music, the well, the clasped figures in the moonlight, and the little dancing flares off the blue steel blade.

Then he heard Mitch whispering, close behind the boy's right ear, whispering his intent in words that sickened Dobey and sent him crashing and fumbling for the door. For a moment the door held, stuck, then he wrenched it open viciously, hearing something crash to the floor behind him as he shouted from the doorway, "Boy! Stop that! You hear me, boy?"

He stared past the victim's dumb, locked face without seeing it as the face behind it lifted and looked at Dobey with flat colorless eyes. Dobey looked into something he had never seen before: he would never feel such fear again. Breath rattled in his throat, and still the

straining arm did not relax. The young boy's legs began
to sag.

"Put that thing away, I say!" Dobey roared, hand inside
his boot, gripping the gun until he thought his knuckles
would split.

Gently, gracefully, in slow motion, the figures before
him parted, one to sink gagging to his knees in the sand as
the other stepped away, letting his arm fall woodenly to
his side.

"You there!" Dobey rasped to the boy at Mitch's feet,
"you get out of here! Now!"

Without looking up, the boy scuttled crablike across
the sand to the girl, and they both raced wildly to the car.
Mitch's head turned toward them as the motor started,
and he seemed to watch with interest while the wheels
churned furiously in the sand before taking hold. They
both watched it careen away into the dark.

Mitch stood with both hands clenched at his sides,
panting, the knife winking in the light. Dobey waited,
hand clawed around the gun. At last the boy turned
puzzled eyes.

"He was going to—" he began in a high tight voice.

"I thank you for protecting me, boy," Dobey interrupted
harshly, "but I could have handled it myself."

Mitch took several deep shuddering breaths, then sighed
as he bent to sheath the knife inside his boot. He grinned
slyly at this, a ghost of the old. "See? You're not the only
one. I could have—you know—anytime I wanted."

Dobey's clothes were too tight across his chest. "You
got to go," he said.

Mitch smiled, wider, returning to his old self. "But—"

"Yes. They'll be coming."

Mitch looked out toward the highway. "You think so?"

"I know so. Soon's it's light."

"Maybe we can hold them off."

"No. Cain't be that way."

He watched it happen, the control take over, the real-
ization come.

"I guess you're right," Mitch said quietly. He turned toward the truck.

"Wait," Dobey said, reaching back inside. "Take this."

Wordlessly the boy accepted the razor and walked away. When he returned to the well and laid his pack alongside, the beard and long hair were gone, the face was smooth and pleasant and young in the moonlight. He came slowly across the sand and handed Dobey his radio.

"I fixed it." Then he unslung his guitar and laid it gently in Dobey's lap. "This is for you." Dobey made a short choked sound. "No, I want you to have it. To play 'Red River Valley.'"

The old man held out a paper bag. "Here. They's enough food to last a day or so."

"Thank you. Dobey, I've got to have some money."

"I ain't got much, but you're welcome to it all."

Mitch took it and stood gazing down at the old man. "When I get to those redwoods, I'm going to send you a picture." Dobey nodded.

At the well Mitch turned back once more. "I may not make it."

"I know."

He watched him walk away until, even with the glasses, he was just a speck in the distance, fading away finally into the scrub and mesquite and sand.

When the sheriff's car and two state-patrol cars squealed into the lane with the first light of day, Dobey was still sitting on the porch, hands resting lightly on the guitar. The sheriff pulled up at a distance and stuck his red face out of his car door.

"Dobey? You all right?"

At the old man's nod they all came dusting in. The sheriff jumped out.

"Hell, what's going on out here? Ralph Becker's boy come in scared green. Is he gone?"

Dobey nodded, fingers moving silently over the strings.

"Which way?"

"West," Dobey said after a while.

The sheriff fumbled through his pockets and shoved a picture at Dobey. "This him?" Dobey looked and nodded slowly.

"It's him!" The sheriff yelled, and the two patrol cars roared to life. "Get some 'copters in the air!" he shouted as the cars wheeled out and sped off up the lane. Dobey watched the cars out of sight.

"My God, Dobey, what happened?" The sheriff lumbered to the well and pulled up the bucket. He rinsed out his mouth and spat on the ground. "You sure you're okay?"

"You see me," Dobey said.

"Well, you're a lucky one." He sank down heavily beside Dobey on the porch. "You know what that kid done? Killed his own folks out in Massachusetts, one fella in a gas station in Illinois, a fella that picked him up somewhere in Kansas, and we found another'n about ten miles up the road here—the car hid in some brush, fella still in the trunk. And them's just the ones we know about! Looks like he drove the cars until they run out of gas, then ditched 'em. Hell, it's been all over the radio and TV!"

"My radio's been busted."

"Has he got a gun?"

"No," Dobey said slowly. "He's got no use for guns."

"See? This boy's a nut! What you suppose would make a fella do something like that? Well, no matter, we'll get him now. He ain't going to get away." Dobey said nothing.

"Listen, Dobey," the sheriff went on after an uncomfortable sidelong look, "this thing's got the folks in town shook up. I know you ain't going to like this, but the county's decided we just can't let you live out here like this no more. My God, man, you're lucky you ain't cut up in little pieces somewhere!" He waited while Dobey went on fingering the guitar.

"So we're going to have to move you out. Don't give me no trouble, Dobey, this time we're gonna do it. We'll find

you some nice little room in town or maybe down at the
Old Soldiers Home. After this thing we just can't have
you on our conscience no more. It's for your own good.
Dobey, you hearing me?"

"I hear."

"All right." He rose, dusting off his hat against his
thigh. "Hate to do it, hope you know it, Dobey. You get
your things together and we'll be out in the morning to
take you in. You'll be all right till then. Don't worry none
about that boy comin' back—dead or alive, we'll have
him taken care of by nightfall." He waved cheerfully as he
pulled away.

The sun climbed high in the hot white sky. A car slid
by on the highway, melting quickly into shimmering
waves of heat. Dobey squinted into the day.

Finally he reached down inside his boot, lifted out the
long hunting knife. Carefully steadying the guitar against
his lap, he cut each string in two, one by one by one.

MARGARET MARON

Deadhead Coming Down

Funny thing about this CB craze—all these years we trucking men've been going along doing our job, just making a living as best we could, and people in cars didn't pay us much mind after everything got four-laned because they didn't get caught behind us so much going uphill, so they quit cursing us for being on the roads we was paying taxes for too and sort of ignored us for a few years.

Then those big camper vans started messing around with CB radios, tuning in on us, and first thing you know even VWs are running up and down the cloverleafs cluttering up the air with garbage and all of a sudden there's songs about us, calling us culture heroes and exotic knights of the road.

What a crock of bull.

There's not one damn thing exotic about driving a eighteen-wheeler. Next to standing on a assembly line and screwing Bolt A into Hole C like my no-'count brother-in-law, driving a truck's got to be the dullest way under God's red sun to make a living. 'Specially if it's just up and down the eastern seaboard like me.

Maybe it's different driving cross-country, but I work

for this outfit—Eastline Truckers—and brother, they're just that: contract trucking up and down the coastal states. Peaches from Georgia, grapefruit from northern Florida, yams and blueberries from the Carolinas—whatever's in season, we haul it. I-95 to the Delaware Memorial Bridge, up the Jersey Turnpike, across the river and right over to Hunt's Point.

Fruit basket going up, deadhead coming down and if you think that's not boring, think again. Once you're on I-95, it's the same road from Florida to New Jersey. You could pick up a mile stretch in Georgia and stick it down somewhere in Maryland and nobody'd notice the difference. Same motels, same gas stations, same billboards.

There's laws put out by those Keep America Pretty people to try to keep billboards off the interstates, but I'm of two minds about them. You can get awful tired of trees and fields and cows with nothing to break 'em up, but then again, reading the same sign over and over four or five times a week's a real drag, too.

Even those Burma Shave signs they used to have when I was driving with Lucky. We'd laugh our heads off every time they put up new ones, but you can't laugh at the same things more'n once or twice, so we'd make up our own poems. Raunchy ones and funnier'n hell some of 'em.

Those were the good old days, a couple of years after the war. WW Two. I was a hick kid just out of the tobacco fields and Lucky seemed older'n Moses, though now I look back, I reckon he was only about thirty-five. His real name was Henry Driver, but everybody naturally called him Lucky because he got away with things nobody else ever could. During the blackouts, he once drove a load of TNT across the Great Smokies with no headlights. All them twisty mountain roads and just a three-quarter moon. I'd like to see these bragging hotshots around today try that!

Back then it took a real man to truck 'cause them rigs would fight you. Just like horses they were. They knew when you couldn't handle 'em. Today—hellfire! Everything's so automatic and hydraulic, even a ninety-pound woman can do it.

Guess I shouldn't knock it though. I'll be able to keep driving these creampuffs till I'm seventy. Not like Lucky. Hardly a dent and then his luck ran out on a stretch of 301 in Virginia. A blowout near a bridge and the wheel must've got away from him.

Twelve years ago that was and the company'd quit doubling us before that, but I still miss him. Things were never dull driving with Lucky. We was a lot alike. He used to tell me things he never told anybody else. Not just the things a man brags about when he's drinking and slinging bull, but other stuff.

I remember once we were laying over in Philly, him going, me coming down, and he says, "Guess what I saw me today coming through Baltimore? A red-tailed hawk. Right smack in the middle of town!"

Can you feature a tough guy like him getting all excited about seeing a back country bird in town? And telling another guy about it? Well, that's the way it was with me and him.

I was thinking about Lucky last week coming down, and wishing I had him to talk to again. 95 was wall-to-wall vacation traffic. I thumbed my CB and it was full of ratchet jaws trying to sound like they knew what the hell they were saying. It was *Good buddy* this and *Smokey* that and *10-4* on the side, so I cut right out again.

I'd just passed this Hot Shoppe sign when the road commenced to unwind in my head like a moving picture show. I knew that next would come a Howard Johnson and a Holiday Inn and then a white barn and a meadow full of black cows and then a Texaco sign and every single mile all the way back home. I just couldn't take it no more and pulled off at the next cloverleaf.

"For every mile of thruway, there's ten miles on either side going the same way," Lucky used to say and, like

him, I've got this skinny map stuck up over my windshield across the whole width of the cab with I-95
snaking right down the middle. Whenever that old snake
gets to crawling under my skin, I look for a side road
heading south. There's little X's scattered all up and
down my map to keep track of which roads I'd been on
before. I hadn't never been through this particular stretch,
so I had my choice.

Twenty minutes off the interstate's a whole different
country. The road I finally picked was only two lanes, but
wide enough so I wouldn't crowd anybody. Not that there
was much traffic. I almost had the road to myself and I
want to tell you it was as pretty as a postcard, with trees
and bushes growing right to the ditches and patches of
them orangy flowers mixed in.

It was late afternoon, the sun just going down and I was
perking up and feeling good about this road. It was the
kind Lucky used to look for. Everything perfect.

I was coasting down this little hill and around a curve
and suddenly there was a old geezer walking right up the
middle of my lane. I hit the brakes and left rubber, but by
the time I got her stopped and ran back to where he was
laying all crumpled up in orange flowers, I knew he was
a sure goner, so I walked back to my rig, broke on Channel
9 and about ten minutes later, there was a black-
and-white flashing its blue lights and a ambulance with
red ones.

Everybody was awful nice about it. They could see how
I'd braked and swerved across the line. "I tried to miss
him," I said, "but he went and jumped the wrong way."

"It wasn't your fault, so don't you worry," said the
young cop when I'd followed him into town to fill out his
report. "If I warned Mr. Jasper once, I told him a hundred
times he was going to get himself killed out walking like
that and him half deaf."

The old guy's son-in-law was there by that time and he
nodded. "I told Mavis he ought to be in a old folks home
where they'd look after him, but he was dead set against

it and she wouldn't make him. Poor old Pop! Well, at least he didn't suffer."

The way he said it, I guessed he wasn't going to suffer too much himself over the old man's death.

I was free to go by nine o'clock and as I was leaving, the cop happened to say, "How come you were this far off the interstate?"

I explained about how boring it got every now and then and he sort of laughed and said, "I reckon you won't get bored again any time soon."

"I reckon not," I said, remembering how that old guy had scrambled, the way his eyes had bugged when he knew he couldn't get out of the way.

Just west of 95, I stopped at a Exxon station and while they were filling me up, I reached up over the windshield and made another little X on my road map. Seventeen X's now. Two more and I'd tie Lucky.

I pulled out onto 95 right in front of a Datsun that had to stomp on those Mickey Mouse brakes to keep from creaming his stupid self. Even at night it was all still the same—same gas stations, same motels, same billboards.

I don't know. Maybe it's different driving cross-country.

CLARK HOWARD

Last Chance
in
Singapore

He was sipping a gin at the Dutch Club, a week after his return to Singapore, when he heard a soft voice speak to him.

"Hello. It's Alan Modred, isn't it?"

"Hello. Yes." Alan smiled as his eyes swept over her. Twentyish, wet auburn hair, slight overbite, tall, generally slim but a touch heavy in the hips. He dredged his memory without finding her.

"You don't recognize me, do you?" she chided.

"I'm sorry, no."

"I'm Wenifred Travers. Wendy. Jack Travers' daughter."

Alan's jaw dropped in surprise. "My God. You've grown up to be a woman."

"Did you think I'd grow up to be a man?" He felt himself becoming flustered. She had an amused look on her face. "Next you'll be telling me I'm too old to be bounced on your knee."

"I don't know about *that*," he countered with a smile. He took her hand. "How've you been, Wendy? How's Jack?"

Her expression saddened. "Daddy's dead, Alan. Lung cancer, two years ago."

"No. Oh, Wendy." Alan felt a clutch in his chest. Jack Travers had been a good man. "I'm so sorry," he told her.

Wendy nodded. "He was a two-pack-a-day man for thirty years. Every year the doctor told him to quit, but you know Daddy. Eventually it got him." She sighed and shrugged off the memory. "How long have you been back?"

"Just a week."

Wendy leaned toward him a fraction. "Was it terrible, Alan? The Thai prison?"

"It could have been worse," he lied. He wondered how she would react if he showed her the scars where they'd beaten him with a bamboo cane. He imagined she'd swoon. Sheltered young British women probably didn't see much proud flesh. Deciding to change the subject, he bobbed his chin at her wet hair. "Been for a swim?"

"Yes." She put on a half-hearted smile. "My friend Herman is a member here. He's a local rep for Heineken beer. We swim once or twice a week." She tilted her head. "Are you meeting someone?"

"Yes." Alan knew she expected to be told who he was meeting, but he didn't say. The less anyone knew about his activities in Singapore, the better. He directed the conversation back to her. "What made you stay on after Jack's death?" he asked. "You've family in the U.K. haven't you?"

"Not really. Not close, anyway. Singapore has always seemed more like home. Daddy and Mum are both buried here. And I've got a super job at the Jurong Reptile Farm, out near the bird park. There didn't seem much point in going back to England. Anyway, I hate the cold."

A waiter approached and said to Alan, "Excuse me, sir. Mr. van Leuck telephoned to say he was just getting on his way and would be here in a quarter hour."

"Thank you." So much for secrecy, Alan thought. When he turned back to Wendy, she was looking at him curiously.

"Is that Louis van Leuck you're meeting?" There was a hint of accusation in her voice.

"It is." A hint of defensiveness in his.

"Oh, Alan. Must you get involved with that sort when you're just back to make a new start? Louis van Leuck is one of the shadiest characters in Singapore. He's involved in everything from drugs to gun smuggling. To—to—to white slavery."

"Is there still a white-slavery trade?" Alan asked. "I'll have to look into that."

"It's not funny, Alan."

He sighed quietly and fixed her in a steady gaze. "Would you like to know what's *really* not funny?" he asked evenly. "A forty-four-year-old man just back from five years in a Thai prison after being caught transporting jade illegally. That, after having failed at running an import-export business into which he had put his life savings. Before which he had two failed marriages, two *other* failed businesses, and one bankruptcy. At the moment, all he has to show for his life is a bleeding ulcer. *That's* not funny." He shook his head, the momentary hostility gone. "It's all well and good for you to denounce Louis van Leuck as a social undesirable, but the fact is, he's the only person in Singapore willing to talk to me about future employment."

"Yes, but what kind of employment?" She was not about to relent.

"At this point," Alan said flatly, "I can't really be selective, can I?"

Their eyes were locked in a mutually accusing stare when a handsome young Dutchman, his hair wet like Wendy's, walked up to them. Wendy broke the stare to introduce him as Herman Ubbink, the Heineken beer rep she had mentioned earlier. Herman reminded her that they had to meet people for lunch.

"Where can I reach you, Alan?" she wanted to know.

"I haven't found a permanent place yet," he said. It would have been too embarrassing to tell her he had a seedy little room on Serangoon Street in the Little India quarter.

"Please ring me up," Wendy said. "I'm listed."

"Of course."

Alan watched them leave, two vibrant young people with good tans, good posture, good prospects, and all the time in the world ahead of them.

Deep inside, his ulcer began to churn.

Louis van Leuck reminded Alan of Sydney Greenstreet. He wore a white linen shirt with a Nehru collar and sat bent very close to the table so that he could keep an elbow on either side of the plate while he ate. They were in the Swatow Restaurant high up in Centrepoint, an ultramodern, multilevel shopping center to which van Leuck had taken Alan after leaving the Dutch Club. They were eating *dim sum*, a kind of rolling buffet in which trolleys filled with numerous Chinese dishes passed continuously among the tables.

"Try some of that baked tench, my boy," van Leuck prompted. "It's the best fish to come out of China in years."

"I don't have much appetite for fish after eating boiled fish heads every day for five years."

"Try the duck skin, then. It's wrapped around spring onions and cucumbers, coated in black bean sauce. Delicious."

"I'll just have a little boiled chicken and rice," Alan said. "I have a minor stomach problem." Minor. When it wasn't causing him nausea, excruciating cramps, or bleeding.

The food trolleys were being pushed by slim Chinese women wearing *sarong kabayas* slit on one side up to the thigh. They served whichever dishes the patrons indicated they wanted. One of the women had a slight overbite that made Alan think of Wendy Travers. Presumptuous little bitch, he thought. What did she expect him to do, starve? Beg? How simple life always looked to the young.

"Do you have anything for me, Louis?" he finally asked when they were halfway through their second course.

"I wish I did have, my boy," the overweight Dutchman said. "But things are very, very slow right now. There's lots of official pressure about. Election year and all that." He lowered his voice. "If you'd care to get involved with the ah—snow, shall we call it?—I might be able to arrange something. It would mean moving to Manila, of course. I don't fool around with that trade in Singapura—too dangerous. Mandatory death penalty, you know."

Alan shook his head. "I don't care to get into that sort of business." Hadn't he just told Wendy he wasn't in a position to be selective? Now here he was, being exactly that.

"Locally," van Leuck said, "I'm expanding my chain of sexual massage parlors, but I really like to have women managing them—they're so much more reliable, especially Chinese women." He stuffed his mouth with food and talked around it. "I dabble in contraband ivory here, but only on a small scale—not really enough profit there to share. Stolen airline tickets bring in a little. Counterfeit designer purses and other items make a modest amount, despite some really aggressive competition from Malaysia. And then there's my pornography operation: magazines, video tapes, uncensored books. Again, the tight customs controls make that a limited-profits enterprise. I expect things to loosen up by this time next year, however."

"How nice," Alan said. "If I'd known there was a business recession, I would have arranged to stay in prison an extra year."

"That's very funny, my boy," van Leuck said, a bit of orange yam falling to his chin as he spoke. Then his eyes narrowed to slits that could have held matchsticks. "There is one venture currently in the planning stages," he said hesitantly. "It could be a bit out of the ordinary for you, as well as somewhat risky, but the reward would be considerable. I myself am involved only in marketing the project and, ah—shall we say, converting the acquired product. The actual planning and operation is being done by someone else, but I understand he's a man short. I could recommend you, if you like."

"What's the venture?" Alan asked.

"I'm not at liberty to say. That would have to come from the man at the other end, once he approved you."

Alan rubbed his chin, his interest piqued. "Considerable reward, you say?"

"Very?"

"But risky?"

"To some degree."

Alan was silent for a long moment, but finally nodded. "All right, Louis. I'll accept your recommendation, with gratitude."

"Excellent, my boy."

Louis van Leuck smiled and waved over another trolley of food.

That evening, Alan walked slowly up Sago Lane in Chinatown. It was a narrow road, vibrant with streetside activity, sounds, and smells. The fragrance of incense mingled with the smell of frying noodles. Street hawkers chattered among themselves, quieting down and watching as Alan passed to see if he had any interest in their candles, citrus, dry goods, or beansprouts. The cackle of seven Chinese dialects punctuated the night as old women in *samfus* and homemade clogs gossiped in street stalls and tenement entries. Chinese children, spotlessly clean even at play, dashed about, giggling at their simple games.

At the corner of Trengganu, Alan stopped and looked around. A young Chinese woman spoke to him from a doorway. "*Chuang?*" she said, opening her kimono a few inches.

Alan shook his head. "*Bu,*" he replied. The fleeting

thought of going to bed with her made him think for some reason of Wendy. Irritably, he purged his mind of the thought. "*Shu ben shi chang?*" he asked the woman in the doorway. She closed her kimono and pointed down the street. Alan nodded. "*Xie xie ny,*" he said, thanking her.

Walking down to the bookstore he had inquired about, Alan entered. It was a musty little shop, barely four square meters, with no shelves, its books all stacked on several tables as if the owner was prepared to abandon the premises. An old Chinese man in a mandarin coat sat in one corner on an upturned wooden box with a cushion tied to it, smoking through an ivory cigarette holder. He looked sixty, but because Chinese men age so slowly, Alan judged him to be at least seventy-five.

"*Wan an, Fu qin,*" Alan said respectfully. Good evening, Father.

"My humble shop is yours, my son," the old man replied in precise English.

"I seek a gentleman named Dao," Alan said.

The old man shook his head. "You are too late. He is dead. He died from being *jiu.*" Jiu meant very old.

"I was sent here by the *jing ly* named van Leuck," Alan said, referring to the Dutchman as a boss or manager.

"In that case, I am not dead," the old Chinese admitted. He smiled slyly. "I am *jiu,* however, and will probably die shortly, but that need be no concern of yours." He rose and offered his hand. Welcome. I am Dao."

Alan shook hands and followed him into a curtained corner where there were two more box-and-cushion seats and a small table. "*Cha?*" the old man asked. Tea?

"*Boleh.*" Please.

The teapot was set over a burning candle in the well formed by an arrangement of three bricks, keeping it constantly hot without boiling. From a closed wicker basket inside the box on which he sat, Dao removed two beautiful, delicate teacups, each fashioned with symbolic tigers etched in gold, with ruby chips for eyes. Alan, who knew of such things, judged them to be at least one hundred years old. He watched the old Chinese fill them with herbal tea.

The two men sipped their *cha* in silence until the cups were half empty. Then Dao asked, "Do you know the meaning of my name?"

"I believe it means 'knife,' " said Alan.

"Yes. In my youth, when dinosaurs still roamed the earth, I was called Nan Ren Dao. Man of the Knife. An undeserved tribute to a very modest talent. There are those who insist that I could split a swinging pear at fifteen meters. Not being a vain man, I myself never measured the distance. The years, of course, have taken their toll on my eyesight, and my arms have become flaccid and feeble. Fortunately, I have a grandnephew to whom I passed on what little skill I had. He is now the eyes and arms of the man once called Nan Ren Dao. Loyal and respectful young relatives are a blessing to the aged, do you not agree?"

"I do, yes," said Alan. The old man's warning was unmistakable: betray me and my grandnephew will throw a knife into you. Alan heard the shop door open and a moment later a young Chinese woman came around the curtain. She was the same woman who had solicited Alan at the corner.

"My grandnephew's wife," Dao said. "I am happy to know you are not a man who is easily tempted, even after five years of enforced abstinence."

Alan bowed his head an inch. "And I am happy to have passed your test, *Fu qin*. Please tell your grandnephew that it was not easy. His wife is a *mei li funu*."

The young woman suppressed a smile at being called a beautiful lady. As she took her coat from a peg and left, Alan had a fleeting thought of Wendy again. She and the Chinese woman carried the same touch of heaviness in their hips. Why, he wondered, could he not get Wendy out of his mind? Was it desire? It was true, as Dao had said, that he had been away from women for five years.

Plus a week, as a matter of fact, because he still had not had any sex since his release. That fact was a little disturbing to him—he was beginning to wonder if the years in prison, the beatings and other brutalities, the inadequate diet, the occasional sicknesses, the parasites, the constant close exposure to unrelenting dampness during the monsoon seasons had all conspired to make him impotent.

Dao interrupted Alan's brief moment of worry by striking a stick match to light a fresh cigarette in his ivory holder. Then he said, "So. You are interested in joining a modest venture we have planned?"

"Yes."

"Did Herr van Leuck give you any details of the project?"

"No."

"Ah. Well, as I said, it is a modest venture. We are going to rob the Singapore mint."

Alan stared incredulously at the old man. Dao smiled and reached for the teapot.

"More *cha?*" he asked.

The next day, Alan rode one of Singapore's immaculately clean buses out toward Jurong Town, on the western end of the island where the mint was located. From the road along one side of the compound, where he got off the bus to walk, he was able to take a good, leisurely look at it without arousing suspicion.

Actually, there was not all that much to see. It looked a bit like a small prison—unadorned buildings set some distance back from an electrified cyclone fence topped with accordion wire, with gun towers at the corners. Pretty much impregnable, Alan decided, as far as an armed robbery assault was concerned. Their plan, however—he was already thinking of it as partly *his*—did not involve assault or arms. As with drugs, the mere possession of cartridges, much less a weapon in which to use them, carried a mandatory death penalty in Singa-

pore. One had to be a fool to tempt such easily adminis-
tered capital punishment, and Dao was anything but a
fool. No, their plan was devoid of violence—much less
dangerous and considerably less offensive to the Singapore government. They were not even planning to steal
Singapore money, only Malaysian notes printed under
contract by the Singapore mint. That way, Dao reasoned,
if they were caught the Singapore courts might be a little
more lenient.

As for their method, it was quite simple: they were
going to execute the robbery through a tunnel, at night.

As Alan walked along the road, surreptitiously scruti-
nizing the mint, he recalled Dao's words of the previous
night. "The tunnel was already there when the mint was
built above it," the old Chinese had explained. "When
the Japanese occupied Singapore during World War Two,
in addition to the notorious prison camp at Changi on the
eastern end of the island, they also had a smaller camp,
for women, at Boon Lay. Prisoners there were nurses,
nuns, British officers' wives and daughters, unmarried
Occidentals who had been employed in the city at the
time it fell, and a smattering of Eurasian women who
qualified for confinement as a result of their mixed blood.

"These women knew their camp was very close to a
narrow inlet that came in from the south coast of the
island. Many of them had been on family outings around
there in happier times and were quite familiar with the
area. They reasoned that if they could get out of the camp
and reach the inlet, they could, with jewelry many of
them had concealed in their hair, barter with the rural
natives to acquire dugout boats. With those boats they
could sail to any one of the isolated southern islands,
which in those days were not developed at all. There they
intended to live off wild game and fruit, and possibly
cultivate vegetable gardens of some kind. Whatever conditions they encountered, they were unanimously convinced that they would be better off than in their present
circumstances, which were resulting in scurvy, rickets,

dysentery, and numerous other trying physical problems.

"So they set about digging a tunnel. It had to be deep enough to remain undetected for a long period of time, large enough for a person to crawl through on hands and knees, and long enough to take them outside the barbed-wire fence far enough away from the camp to avoid the perimeter sentries. They estimated that it would take them two years to complete it. Work was begun in March, nineteen forty-two.

"By June, nineteen forty-three, the women had progressed beyond the wire and were well on their way through—or shall I say under—the jungle. At that point, however, their Japanese captors closed the camp and moved the entire group to another facility in nearby Sumatra.

"Louis van Leuck learned of the tunnel while visiting London and watching a television show on the BBC called This Is Your Life. It was honoring Brigadier Dame Margot Turner, the former Matron-in-Chief of the Royal Army Nursing Corps. While Dame Margot herself was never in the Boon Lay camp, one of the women who was subsequently with her in the Muntok camp in Sumatra, and who had appeared on the show, had been at Boon Lay earlier, and commented on the tunnel they had dug there.

"Louis van Leuck, whose thinking coincides with my own unfortunate proclivity for felonious endeavors, checked upon his return to Singapore all the land and building records for the area where the Boon Lay camp had been, and where the mint now is, and found no indication that the existence of the tunnel was known. He then took it upon himself to personally explore the acreage in question, in the guise of a botanist studying the island's flora. After several weeks of diligent effort, his initiative was rewarded. He found that the tunnel does, in fact, still exist. Louis has not divulged the location as yet, but I am told that it leads from a point approximately three hundred meters outside the mint compound and terminates directly under what is now the bundling room, where new currency is packaged for shipment."

Dao had gone on to explain to Alan exactly how the robbery would be carried out. There would be no guns, no violence, no contact with any of the mint's nighttime security force. Alan and Dao's grandnephew would negotiate the tunnel and, with tools, battery-operated drills, and duffel bags, wait just below the bundling room. At a predetermined time, Dao and the grandnephew's wife would set off across the road a sequence of spectacular Chinese fireworks, which would have been previously arranged in a wooded area there.

While the mint security guards were distracted by the fireworks display, timed to last at least twenty minutes, Alan and the grandnephew would break through the bundling room floor (ten minutes), fill the duffel bags— six of them, connected by lengths of rope—with all the packaged Malaysian money and other foreign banknotes they could find (five minutes), then drop back into the tunnel, pull the bags in behind them, and crawl back through the tunnel (five minutes). At the tunnel mouth, they would drag the connected bags through, remove them, and cave in that end of the tunnel with a light explosive device they would leave behind, the display fireworks covering the sound.

It was, Alan thought, a plan brilliant in its simplicity— comparatively uninvolved, limited in operation to a very few, able to be carried out in an incredibly short period of time. It had the potential of netting, Dao estimated, ten to fifteen million Malaysian dollars.

Alan had already figured out what his share would be. Say they got twelve million Malay. Louis van Leuck would take ten percent (one million, two) off the top, his fee for conceiving the operation. That would leave ten-point-eight million. Louis would further profit by seeing to the transport and conversion of the currency, buying it from Dao at sixty percent of its face value, about six-and-one-half million. Alan's share of that would be

around one-point-six million Malay. At the current exchange rate of $2.20 Malay to U.S. $1.00, he would have
somewhere in the neighborhood of seven hundred and
forty thousand U.S. dollars.

And that, Alan promised himself, was going to do him
for life. There would be no opening of any business with
this money, no risky speculation trying to make a big
killing, no living it up in the fast lane. Much wiser after
his term in the Thai prison, Alan had modified his wants
and desires to a sensible minimum. Where once he
needed—or at least wanted—tailormade clothes, an expensive car, someplace opulent in which to live, he now
yearned for nothing more than a cozy room, peace and
quiet, comfortable slippers, some books, a television,
medication for his ulcer, and anonymity. The cane beatings had done that to him. The scars on his buttocks and
calves would forever remind him that the simplest things
in life were by far the most valuable.

This venture, Alan was certain, was his very last
chance for a decent existence. Probably his last chance for
anything in life. There was no question in his mind that
he had to take the chance even though the prospect of
doing it terrified him.

Walking away from the area of the mint compound, Alan
encountered a directional sign that read JURONG BIRD
PARK. He remembered Wendy Travers saying she worked
at a reptile farm near there. Without debating it, he
decided to go see her. She was more or less constantly on
his mind, and he didn't know why or what to do about it.
Perhaps seeing her again would give him a clue.

The farm was a walled area much smaller than he had
imagined. Inside the walls were two exhibition structures
in which some species of reptiles were on display behind
glass. In two exterior areas, others were kept behind fine
grille-wire in ground cages with corrugated roofs. Upon
inquiry, Alan was directed to one of the cages, where he
found Wendy, in safari clothes, holding and stroking a

fire-hose-sized snake which hung down to the ground and appeared to be at least seven or eight meters long. Alan stared incredulously until Wendy noticed him.

"Alan! I'm so glad to see you!" Her overbite smile lighted up a freshly scrubbed face.

"I'm not sure I can say the same," Alan told her. "I expected to find you behind a typewriter, not a snake."

She smiled. "No boring typewriters for me, Alan. I'm assistant to Professor Angus Ferguson, one of the world's foremost authorities on reptiles. He's written several field guides on reptilia and amphibia. You can come a little closer, Alan—they can't get out."

Hesitantly, Alan moved up to the cage grille. "Aren't you afraid that thing might strike?" he asked, regarding the long blue-and-brown-patterned snake with unconcealed revulsion.

Wendy shook her head. "This is a non-venomous species," she explained. "It's called a *python reticulatus*, or reticulated python. It has teeth instead of fangs. Killing of its prey is effected by constriction. This one is quite docile. Would you like to hold him?"

"No," Alan said.

"He's really a dear, Alan. Absolutely loves human warmth and stroking. We call him Apollo because he's so beautiful. He *is* a bit spoiled, however."

Wendy put the python on the ground and came out of the cage. Alan had to steel himself not to flinch when she casually took his arm with hands that had just cuddled Apollo.

"What made you decide to come see me?" she asked.

"I was in the area," he replied vaguely.

"Oh. Well, I'm glad anyway. I'm off in half an hour. If you haven't a car, you can ride back to the city with me. I might even cook for you this evening if you encourage me a little."

He touched one of her hands, forgetting about Apollo. "You've always been a very sweet girl, Wendy."

She smiled sadly. "That's what Daddy used to call me, remember? His sweet girl."

"Yes, I do," he said.

When her shift was over, Wendy led him to a BMW with a right-hand drive, and they started for the city. On the way, they drove past the mint compound and Alan could not help staring at it. Wendy noticed his preoccupation with curiosity but did not comment.

She lived in a small apartment at the back of a garden complex off Orchard Link. It was bi-level, secluded, and had a tiny private patio and garden. "This is lovely," Alan told her.

"A lot of things were Mum's," she said, gesturing toward the furnishings. "Or Daddy's. That's his leather chair there, remember? Why don't you sit in it while I fix you a gin?"

Wendy had a drink with him while they reminisced a bit, then left him with a second gin while she went off to the kitchen. "Do you still like those outrageous omelets with all sorts of things in them that you and Daddy used to wolf down?" she asked.

"Yes, but they no longer like me," he called back. "I've a bit of a stomach problem—just eggs-and-cheese will do fine."

"You're easy," she said. "I may keep you."

It was not a cool Singapore evening, but it was tolerable enough for them to eat on the tiny patio and enjoy the little garden, which she had lit with Chinese lanterns. As they ate, she said, "Listen, Alan, forgive me, but I'm still troubled about your contact with Louis van Leuck. A man of your intelligence and capabilities shouldn't have to go over to the shady side to earn a living. I've been thinking. You remember my friend Herman Ubbink you met at the Dutch Club? Well, Heineken is transferring him to London next month. He has a friend he plays squash with, Steven Howard, who's head of marketing for *Time*. Steven's giving Herman a big going-away bash and there'll be all sorts of Singapore business types there. Why don't you come with me and I'll introduce you around. We can say you've just moved back here from South America or someplace and are looking for a niche. I'm almost sure someone would ask you to come around and talk. What do you think?"

Alan smiled fondly at her across the table. "I think you're 'a sweet girl' to be so concerned about my future. I appreciate it and I'm touched by it. It's been a long spell since anyone gave more than passing interest to my well-being. But I must tell you, dear Wendy, that I think you're being naive. Suppose someone at the party *was* interested? How long do you think that interest would last when I had to provide references for the last five years? Or when they ran a local credit check on me and learned of the two failed businesses and the bankruptcy? Or even worse, applied for a work permit for me and a police check showed I was extradited from here to Bangkok to face jade-smuggling charges for which I was subsequently sent to prison?" Reaching over, he put his hand on hers. "I know you mean well, Wendy, but it simply wouldn't work. I've got only one last chance here in Singapore and that's with Louis van Leuck."

Wendy fought back tears and abruptly came around the table and sat on his lap, as she had done as a child. She pressed her face against him and he felt wet eyelashes on his neck. "I'm just so afraid for you," she said in a strained voice. "It hasn't been that long since I lost Daddy. Now I've found you, Alan, and I don't want to lose you, too."

"I know." Alan patted her head, again as if she were still the little girl he remembered—all the while realizing by the heat and shape of her body against his that she was not.

She felt the heat, too, felt everything, and whispered, "Let's go in, Alan."

He slept very soundly for the first hour after they made love. Wendy hadn't blanched at the sight of his horrible scars, had in fact kissed them in her passion, and his self-consciousness about his age, his physical condition, the fear of impotency had all vanished in the indulgences of their lovemaking.

Then it started to rain, a heavy monsoon deluge that threatened to tear shutters off, and he dreamed briefly about the Thai prison before coming awake and sitting bolt upright in a sheet of sweat. He was not cold but he was trembling. Wendy cradled his head against her.

"You're afraid, aren't you?" she asked.

"Yes. God, yes."

"Tell me what of."

Alan swallowed as much fear as he could and replied, "The tunnel. I'm afraid of the tunnel."

Then, in the darkness, his face pressed to the softness of her, he told her about the plan to rob the mint. About the hundred-meter tunnel he and Dao's grandnephew would have to crawl through. And about a punishment in the Thai prison called "the trench."

"It was like a grave," he said. "A deep, earthen grave with narrow walls. They tied your arms to your sides, tied your ankles together, and put you in a burlap shroud up to your throat. Then they lowered you into the trench on your back. A wooden plank was lowered above you until it almost touched your face. It was held in place by four ropes tied to stakes at the corners of the trench. With the board in place, dirt was shoveled in by other prisoners. While you lay there helpless, you heard shovelfuls of dirt hitting the plank just over your face. Some of the dirt trickled down each side. Slowly the daylight disappeared and you were buried alive."

Alan pushed his sweating face harder against her, as if her flesh could erase the memory. "I was put in the trench four times," he told her. "Each time I though I would lose my mind. Or suffocate. But the bastards always got me out in time. They had it down to a science. A few died in the trench, but not many."

"The tunnel under the mint reminds you of the trench,"
Wendy said.

"Yes. How did you know?"

"Daddy," she told him. "He was a prisoner during the
war. Years later he was still having associated nightmares
and depression and such. You're afraid you can't make it
through the tunnel, aren't you?"

"Yes. The thought of crawling through that long, narrow, dark hole—" Alan shook his head desperately. "It
terrifies me."

"Then don't do it," Wendy said. "Say you can't."

"They wouldn't let me. I know all the particulars of the
plan now. After all, I did ask to be let in. Anyway, even if
they did let me back out, if anything went wrong when
they pulled the job they'd never believe I wasn't somehow
responsible. No, I'm afraid I'll have to stay in."

"Drop out of sight, then," Wendy pleaded. "Move in
here with me. They'd never find you."

Alan shook his head. "That would be prison all over
again. I'd never be able to go out on the streets for fear one
of van Leuck's people would see me." He took a deep
breath. "I'm just going to have to steel myself for it, that's
all. I'm going to have to get through it."

In the darkness, Wendy whispered, "Maybe we can
think of something."

"Sure," Alan said. His tone told her he didn't for a
moment believe it.

The robbery was scheduled for Tuesday night, just before
the Wednesday shipment of banknotes to Malaysia.

Alan still had his room in the Indian quarter even
though he had been staying with Wendy most of the time.
He returned to the room only to get messages. She had
gone with him once and found the place disgusting.
"This is awful," she said. "You're so fastidious, just like
Daddy was—I don't see how you can stand it."

"I shouldn't have to stand it much longer," he said.

Wendy wasn't with him on the weekend when he got

the message that Dao wanted to see him. In the bookstore, the old Chinese told him when the robbery was scheduled. On Monday night, Alan shared the information with Wendy.

"The fireworks are being put into place tonight. Dao and I will go to van Leuck's house in the morning and he'll show us on a map where the tunnel entrance is. It's supposedly well grown over with brush and vines, very difficult to find, but easily accessible once one knows where to look. I won't be able to stay with you tonight, Wendy. I'll have to be where Dao can reach me in case there's a last-minute change of plans."

"I understand," said Wendy. "Where does van Leuck live, anyway?"

"Upper Thomson Road. Why?"

She shrugged. "I just wondered where a person like that would live. One always wonders about people like van Leuck. They're morbidly fascinating, like some of our reptiles at the farm. The venomous ones."

"I imagine Louis can be venomous, all right," Alan agreed. "Especially if anyone crossed him."

"You still don't think there's a chance they'd let you pull out?"

He shook his head. "It's too far along now." He took both her hands. "I don't know what I'd have done without you this past week. Gone mad, most likely."

When Alan and Dao arrived at van Leuck's house the following morning, they were surprised to find a police car, an ambulance, and a plain, unmarked panel truck there ahead of them.

"We have trouble," Dao said. He instructed his grandnephew, who was chauffering them, to keep driving and park around the corner. Then he sent the young man back on foot to investigate. The grandnephew returned within five minutes, an expression of shock on his face.

"Mr. van Leuck is dead, Great-uncle," he said. "A most

tragic occurrence. A python somehow got into his house last night, wrapped its body around Mr. van Leuck's head and face, and smothered him. The panel truck you saw in front is from the reptile farm. They sent two keepers to capture the snake. Alas, for the unfortunate Mr. van Leuck it is too late."

"As it also is for us," Dao said quietly. "Take us back to my shop."

The three men rode in silence back to Chinatown. Only when they arrived did Alan ask the obvious question.

"Will you try to find the tunnel yourself, *Fu qin?*"

"I think not," the old man said. "The snake was a sign. It came out of the jungle to tell us that the tunnel belongs to the jungle, not to us. Perhaps the snakes now use the tunnel for their home. In any event, I think we will listen to the snake."

Alan saw a look of enormous relief come over the face of Dao's grandnephew. So, he thought, I was not the only one terrified of that hole.

"It shall be as you wish," Alan told Dao.

He shook hands with the old Chinese and left. On South Bridge, he caught a taxi and rode up to Serangoon where he had his cheap little room. Wendy was waiting in her BMW out front.

"I have your things," she said. His canvas bag was in the back seat." And I settled your bill. Let's get away from this filthy place."

Alan got in beside her. She drove away, calm and unruffled as if she had not committed murder.

"Was it Apollo?" Alan asked.

"Yes. I told you, didn't I, he likes human warmth?"

"Yes, I recall you saying that." Alan's mouth was suddenly dry. "Well, what now?" he asked as casually as he could manage.

"You'll come live with me," Wendy said. "You can have Daddy's chair. I'll be your little girl. Just like I was his."

Alan stared at her without blinking.

"All right?" she asked.

Wrapped its body around Mr. van Leuck's head and face—

"Of course," Alan agreed. "Whatever you say."

Inside, his ulcer reminded him it was still there.

JAMES HOLDING

The Treasure of Pachacamac

W hen he found his notebook was missing, Professor
Felipe de la Vega knew they intended to do more than rob
him. Before, he had suspected that they might steal his
few personally owned antiquities and go away—back to
Panama City, perhaps, where unscrupulous buyers for
genuine but illegally exported pre-Columbian Peruvian
artifacts undoubtedly lurked. But when he returned
home from his morning archeology lectures at San Marcos
University and saw that his thick black book of hand-
written notes was gone—that's when he first seriously
knew they meant to kill him.

The Professor was a hook-nosed slender man, below
medium height, with a dark brown skin and calm black
eyes. He looked more Indian than Spanish, and maybe he
was. For who could say, after all these generations, how
well his ancestral Inca strain had withstood the weaken-
ing infusion of conquistador blood?

He stared at the empty space on the book shelf in his
study where the notebook had been. He felt first surprised, then angry, then affronted, and finally, more
powerfully than any of these, he felt a deep sense of
shame for his cousin, Luis. After all, Luis was his only

195

relative, the son of that Aunt Luisa, his father's sister, who had run away from Lima to marry the itinerant bullfighter many years ago. Had the bullfighter ever married Aunt Luisa? Perhaps not. But here was Luis, at all events.

Seeing that his notebook was gone, the Professor thought: this is unexpected, to say the least. And it was very clear to him that they were after far bigger game than he had first suspected. It was clear, too, that somewhere in the course of playing this game they would find it necessary to eliminate him.

They had arrived from Panama, they said, aboard a rusty, leaking tub that berthed in Callao Harbor. And at first, when they appeared at his little house in Lima, the Professor was quite glad to see them. It was just as darkness descended on the city and the illuminated cross atop Cerro San Christobal began to glow in the gloom. The professor made them welcome. He was pleased to have their company, for at best he was a lonely man.

The name Felipe de la Vega was widely known in scholarly circles. Was he not the holder of the Bolivar Chair in Inca Studies at the University? Was he not, at thirty-five, already the nation's outstanding authority on Peruvian history, which really meant Peruvian archeology? Yes, true. But though he had a thousand academic acquaintances, he had no close friends. Even the students to whom he delivered his lectures at San Marcos thought him unfriendly, deceived perhaps by the remote, brooding set of his dark features. He had no wife, no family. In consequence, a visit from his cousin and a friend of his cousin introduced variety into the Professor's austere life.

Certainly the two visitors were different from the Professor. One was his cousin, Luis, and the other was a man his cousin called Ramón, a large, quiet man with small, sharp eyes and almost no lips at all. He spoke a heavily accented Spanish in short bursts like machine-gun fire, and treated Luis as though he were nothing but a puddle of muddy water to spit in.

The man Ramón wore an American-made suit of light blue cloth, with a double-breasted jacket which he seemed reluctant to shed, even in Lima's baking heat. His breath smelled as though he had some decayed teeth.

The Professor insisted that they stay with him, eagerly offering them his spare bedroom. They accepted with alacrity, dropped their cheap fiber suitcases there, and proceeded to make themselves at home in the Professor's house.

"Ah, Felipe," Luis said, "it is good to be here with you. It is so calm here. So peaceful. So safe."

"And I am extremely glad to see you, Luis," Professor de la Vega said sincerely. He did not know what to say to the man called Ramón.

Ramón was looking about the room, the Professor's study, in which they sat. It was lined on one side with books, but was mainly remarkable for the untidy collection of Peruvian antiquities which crowded it. Book shelves, table tops, even the walls held mementos of various important digs the Professor had supervised. There were Nasca and Mochica vases, Cat-God figurines from the Chavín culture, molded black-ware pottery of the Chimú Empire, weavings from the Paracas peninsula, polychrome eating plates of the Inca, copper surgical instruments, animal statuettes, a star-pointed stone war-club. Ramón looked at them carefully with his small sharp eyes.

"What's all that junk?" he said finally. "Worth anything?"

"It is not junk," the Professor said politely. "It is on such articles as these, dug from our earth, that the whole body of Peruvian history is based." He thought perhaps he should deliver to Ramón the first lecture in his Peruvian History course.

"I mean money," Ramón said. "Is it worth anything?"

"Yes," the Professor said. "Undoubtedly. But these objects mean more to me than money."

Luis said eagerly to Ramón, "Cousin Felipe is a famous

archeologist. The antiquities in this room alone are worth thousands of sols de oro."

Ramón looked at Luis, his eyes suddenly bright. "Thousands?" he asked in his staccato fashion.

"This is museum stuff," Luis said. "Very valuable. The University lets Felipe keep an item or so from each of his discoveries. Just as a souvenir. You know?"

"This is worth money to museums? This junk?"

"Yes," Luis said.

All right, Professor de la Vega thought. Let it be that way. No use trying to tell the man called Ramón about Peruvian history.

But he was wrong, as it turned out. For Luis said to Ramón, "Cousin Felipe has been working for years, trying to trace one particular batch of antiquities. An enormous treasure."

"Treasure?" The word seemed the only one Ramón understood.

"Assuredly." Luis paused. Ramón sucked on his almost invisible lips. Luis went on, "My cousin, Felipe, knows more about it than anyone in Peru." There was a quality of family pride in Luis' statement. At least, that's what the Professor took it to be. Luis said to him in a wheedling voice, "Come on, Cousin, tell Ramón about the Treasure of Pachacamac."

The Professor, whose spirits had been somewhat dampened by his guests' commercial viewpoint on antiquities, nevertheless revived quickly at Luis' invitation to tell of Pachacamac. His eyes kindled. He had suddenly the look of a man who is about to discuss the dream of his lifetime, as indeed he was. "Are you sure your friend is interested in Pachacamac?" he asked in a last flicker of courtesy to Ramón.

Ramón answered for himself. "Certainly. Tell me."

The Professor took a deep breath. "Well," he began, "when the Spaniards under Pizarro came to Peru in 1532, and conquered it, the Indian monarch Atahualpa, who was the Lord-Inca, was captured and held for ransom at

Cajamarca. His ransom was to be—surely you have heard
the famous legend—? enough gold and silver to fill a
room twenty-five feet long and fifteen feet wide as high as
a mark on the walls that even a tall man could not reach."

"You're joking," Ramón said.

"No, no, it is true," Luis said. "Even I know that."

Ramón looked at Luis as though Luis were *taquia,*
llama dung.

"They filled it not once but three times, that room," the
Professor said proudly, feeling the tug of his Inca heritage.
"In six months' time. Twice with silver, once with gold."

The man called Ramón was impressed.

The Professor went on, "Messengers were sent to all
parts of the Lord-Inca's lands, requesting that gold and
silver be collected to pay his ransom, and sent to Cajamarca at once. On such a treasure-gathering expedition,
Hernando Pizarro, the brother of Francisco, the Con-
querer himself, came to Pachacamac."

"Where's this Pachacamac?" Ramón interrupted.

"Twenty-five miles south of here," said the Professor.
"Hernando Pizarro found Pachacamac running over with
gold and silver. For it was an ancient holy city, dedicated
before our history began to Pachacamac, the fearsome
Earth-God, the Creator-God. And the God Pachacamac,
from an inner room in the citadel, delivered through his
priests and his virgins many predictions and oracles to
the people, and recieved great wealth from them in
return. And when the Inca conquered the city, it became
a center of Sun-God worship, with priests and virgins of
the Sun to serve it, and its wealth increased many times
over."

"Get to the point," Ramón said impatiently.

"I am there," the Professor said with dignity. "Hernando Pizarro caused to be gathered together gold and
silver to the extent of a hundred llama loads at Pachacamac, and started this great treasure train off towards
Cajamarca under escort of several Inca chieftains."

"Where's Cajamarca?" Ramón asked.

"A hundred miles north of here," the Professor said. "So what happened?"

"The treasure train started out from Pachacamac. At an unknown point in the journey the Inca chieftains in charge of the train received a message from Cajamarca by runner. The message stated that their monarch, the royal and divine prisoner Atahualpa, the Lord-Inca with ransom for whom their llamas were laden, had been treacherously strangled by the Spaniards." The Professor paused.

"Here's the best part, Ramón," Luis said. "Coming now."

"The Treasure of Pachacamac never reached Cajamarca," the Professor finished. "It disappeared from the Inca road and from history at that exact moment. No one knows what happened to it—to the chieftains, or the llamas, or the gold and silver."

"In the form of coin?" Ramón asked, with one of his machine-gun bursts. "Or in junk like this?" His eyes went around the study.

"Imagine," the Professor said reverently, caught up in his dream, "such artistic miracles as delicately modeled human figures of pure gold, many of them life-size. And images of llamas, fish, and birds, also in natural size, cast in pure, radiant silver, the metal called by the Incas 'tears of the Moon.' And imagine, too, if you can, the dazzling beauty of trees and plants and flowers, daintily mimicked in precious metal by the Inca goldsmiths!"

"What's the use?" Ramón said. "The stuff is gone."

Luis threw a curious look at his cousin Felipe, "Maybe not, Ramón," he said. "To find out what happened to the Treasure of Pachacamac is what the Professor has been trying to do for many years. And he has made good progress." Luis' voice turned sly. "He himself told me so."

The Professor started. "What are you saying, Luis?" he asked sharply. "You are wrong. Certainly I have been working on the problem of the Treasure's disappearance.

What a glorious thing it would be for Peru to unearth those fabulous art objects and place them in our museums for all to see and take pride in! How thrilling to use them as the springboard from which to leap joyously into new realms of knowledge about our ancestors!" When aroused the Professor tended to express himself a trifle flamboyantly. "But after twelve years of studying old documents and of personal exploration inland from all points along the old Inca road, I still do not know where the Treasure of Pachacamac is to be found."

"Not exactly, perhaps," Luis said. "But you know where it is *not* to be found. You have narrowed down the possibilities, have you not? So you told me in your letters."

The man called Ramón was following this conversation closely.

My cousin, thought the Professor, may merely be proud of me and my work. It is true that I have eliminated many possibilities. And it is true that I have narrowed the area of search. He said aloud to Luis, "I have there—" he gestured towards his book shelves—"a whole book full of painfully accumulated notes which prove only one thing: where the Treasure is *not* to be found. All else is rank speculation."

"In your last letter to me, Cousin," Luis said smoothly, his eyes on Ramón, "you mentioned that you thought you were now quite close to the secret."

"I may indeed have said such a foolish thing, Luis. But it is man's nature to boast about a dream, and one must forgive him. After all, this is a dream I have held all my life—to discover for Peru the ancient Treasure of Pachacamac."

They left it then, but the Professor slept uneasily that night. He thought perhaps Luis was more like the bullfighter than like gentle Aunt Luisa. When he awoke once, in the night, he heard the rumble of voices from the spare bedroom, and smelled cigarette smoke.

In the morning he left them sleeping and went off to his

morning classes at the University. It occurred to him that he might make inquiries at the police station about his two guests, who were too tense, and somehow too oddly assorted not to be running from something. But a cousin was a cousin, he thought—even Luis made a family relationship, the only one he had. So he delivered his lectures and went to his house for luncheon, avoiding the police station.

No one else was in the house. He stepped into his study to secure his before-luncheon cigar. It was then he saw that his notebook was missing from its place. The Professor was affronted. He felt that his dream of finding the lost treasure of Peru, of helping to increase his country's meager knowledge of its own past, had been tarnished and made cheap, somehow, by contact with the grasping avarice that so plainly motivated the man called Ramón— and also, yes, to his shame, his cousin Luis. The Professor felt a slow and ancient anger rising inside him.

He went out and climbed into his covered jeep, which stood at the curb before his house in the Plaza. The University supplied the jeep for him to use in his archeological rambles along the waterless desolation of the Peruvian coastal desert. He put the car in gear and drove slowly down past the University, and around the square toward the new skyscraper, and as expected, he soon distinguished his two house guests, huddled obliviously on a bench under a tree, examining his black notebook with feverish eagerness. He did not stop, but continued around the Plaza to his own house again, parked the jeep as before, and went in. The anger in him now was hot and burning.

He prepared luncheon for them. But first, he descended to the tiny cellar of his house and rooted out two eight-inch images of Inca priests which he had bought once, long ago, to use in a lecture class. They were not genuine antiquities. They were replicas of two originals in the National Museum, done in cheap materials for the tourist trade.

He set them on a bench and sprayed them all over with aluminum paint from a pressure can, covering the dark, earthen surfaces with a film of shimmering silver. When the paint had dried for a few minutes, he carried the figures out to the jeep and deposited them in a burlap bag under the tarpaulin which covered his battered archeological tools in the back of the jeep. This burlap bag was a kind of exploring kit, containing food, water canteen, and a few utensils, always ready for use on any desert expedition.

When Luis and the man called Ramón returned from their conference on the bench across the Plaza, the Professor greeted them cheerfully. All through luncheon he was cheerful, talking with animation, but he could not draw his guests into conversation. They seemed distraught.

After they had eaten, he said to the man called Ramón, "Where did you go this morning?"

"For a walk," Ramón replied.

"Yes," said the Professor, "I can see you got very warm." He looked at the sweat stains on Ramón's blue jacket.

"This damnable sun can boil the brains in your head," Ramón said.

The Professor nodded. "Lima is hot in March, but they say that exercise can increase one's resistance to the heat.

"Exercise!" Ramón said bitterly. "It would kill me!"

"That is why I suggest it," the Professor said quietly.

Ramón's lips were not visible at all. His small sharp eyes turned cold. "What do you mean by that?" he said.

"Nothing, Ramón," Luis said quickly. "He was joking. Weren't you, Cousin Felipe?"

"No," the Professor said.

"I didn't think so," Ramón said. He rose from his chair, clenched his big fist, and moved quietly towards the Professor.

"Wait," said the Professor, "how would you like to know where the Treasure of Pachacamac is?"

Ramón said nothing, but he stopped moving.

The Professor said, "You have stolen my notebook and read it. True?"

Luis said evenly, "We were just curious, Cousin. We glanced through your notebook, yes, but we meant no harm. You yourself said it would not reveal the secret of the Treasure's whereabouts."

"But you didn't quite believe me, did you?" the Professor went on. "Now, having read the notes, you think I lied. And now, for my part, I know that you and your friend are thieves and rascals."

The man called Ramón sneered. "You know a lot, don't you? But only one thing interests me. You know where to find that Treasure. I know it. I feel it. I am sure. Because your notebook admits it, at the end. You have narrowed down the possibilities until there is only one left."

The Professor watched the big man calmly, his eyes glinting, waiting for the inevitable question. It came. "Where is Cunti-suyu, Professor?"

The Professor laughed. "Do you think that I, Dr. Felipe de Ayala de la Vega, with Inca blood running in my veins, would reveal where the treasure lies to such as you— even if I knew?" He went quickly towards the door that led from the dining room to his study. "I shall, instead, telephone the police and report two thieves in my house!"

The man called Ramón moved swiftly. The Professor was then privileged to see why he had not discarded his jacket, even in the heat. Ramón's hand dived under the double-breasted coat and came out holding a large revolver. "Wait, Professor," he said. The Professor halted at the door. Ramón regarded him a moment in silence. Luis made no move.

Finally, Ramón said harshly, "The hell with this. I'll shoot him now. We can find the place by ourselves."

Luis spoke urgently. "Don't shoot him yet, Ramón—we cannot find the place without him. Would he write the name in his book if it were a well-known place? No. It is probably a pile of crumbled bricks in the desert, known only to him. No. Ramón, we could not find it alone."

"It is near Pachacamac," Ramón insisted. "The notebook says so."

"Have you ever been into the desert?" Luis asked.

Ramón considered. Then with the gun still pointed at the Professor, he walked past him to the study and ripped the telephone wires out of the wall. "Let us not call the police. Please, Professor," he said, "por favor." It was an insult, the way he said it. Then he came over to the Professor and struck him expertly above the ear with the gun barrel. As blackness descended upon him, the Professor thought with wry amusement, I am like the Lord-Inca—held for ransom.

It was dark when the Professor came to his senses. A jolting told him he was in a moving vehicle. Of course. The jeep. He nodded his head, pleased that he had anticipated their actions accurately. But the nod made his head pound like a skin drum.

He was in the back of the jeep, half reclining on the hard seat, half sprawled on the tarpaulin that covered his tools and burlap kit bag. They must have slung him in like a sack of wheat, after dark, when no curious eyes around the Plaza near his house could have seen them. He felt a quick thrust of satisfaction when his questing hand told him that the tarpaulin and what it covered had not been disturbed.

Ramón was driving the jeep. Luis sat beside him. Ramón said, "You'd better know what you're talking about."

"I know, all right," Luis said, like a small boy boasting to a big one. "We're in Miraflores now—a suburb. We'll be on the coast highway in a few minutes, and then head for Pachacamac."

"So we'll head for Pachacamac. But where is Cunti-suyu?"

Luis faltered, "I don't know."

"We need the Indian," Ramón growled. The Professor realized with surprise that Ramón was referring to him. "Read me that last entry again," Ramón said.

Luis leaned forward under the dashboard light and read from the Professor's notebook: " 'If it is to be my happy fate to discover for Peru the lost Treasure of Pachacamac, I shall not achieve it, it is now obvious, by further researches along the northern segment of the treasure train's projected route to Cajamarca. Rather, I am now convinced, must I pursue my search with greater diligence in Cunti-suyu, near Pachacamac.' "

The Professor smiled at the grandiose style of the notes. "That's it," he said aloud. "Cunti-suyu—near Pachaca-mac."

"Oh." There was relief in Ramón's voice as he swiveled his head on his thick neck to look at the Professor. "You're with us again, are you? Good thing. We need you. We're all going on an archeological expedition together." His spirits were rising by the moment. "Isn't that cozy?"

"Even a blind llama," said the Professor sententiously, "occasionally finds the path."

"So the first thing," Ramón said, "is tell me where Cunti-suyu is."

The Professor smiled. He did not tell them that Cunti-suyu was the Inca name by which the entire southwest quarter of the ancient Inca world was designated—a vast territory of mountains and desert littoral extending from Cuzco to the sea, and from modern Lima southward to the Chilean border. He said, "Cunti-suyu is a pile of Inca ruins in the desert between here and Pachacamac."

"I told you," Luis said.

"Shut up," Ramón said. Driving with one hand, he brought the revolver out from under his coat and lifted it so that the Professor, in the back seat, could see it. Jovially, he said, "So you tell me where to turn off, Indian. Right? To keep your health."

The Professor injected resignation into his voice. "I will tell you," he said.

They were now on the wide coastal highway. They bowled along in the jeep. To his right the Professor could dimly see white, curling breakers rolling in from the Pacific. Off to his left the Andes loomed out of the desert like parched bones.

At his direction they turned from the paved highway some miles farther on, pointing the jeep's nose gallantly into the desert and towards the distant mountains. There was no road. There were no trees. There was no brush or moss or lichen. There was nothing except a dry and stony desolation, lying forlorn in the starlight on all sides of them, from the sea to the towering cordilleras ahead.

The jeep jounced, and rolled and jolted. But it drilled steadily eastward over the shale-like rocks and sandy earth, trailing a cloud of dust behind it that was visible even in the darkness. The man called Ramón drove with care, and at a snail's pace, following a route the Professor pointed out to him.

At Ramón's request, and encouraged by another flourish of the gun, the Professor explained his reasoning to them as they bounced along. "To me it is logical," he said, "that when the Inca chieftains in charge of the treasure caravan received the message that their Lord-Inca was dead and had no more need of ransom, they turned off the route to Cajamarca immediately, and ran for concealment with all speed. Where could they run but into the desert? The sea was on one side of them, the desert on the other. And it is equally logical that they must direct their flight towards the nearest settlement, where they could find sympathetic countrymen willing to help them conceal themselves and the treasure from the Spaniards."

"Quite a trick," Ramón said, "to hide a hundred llamas."

"Easily done," said the Professor. "They would merely add them to the village's own herd. Like hiding leaves in a forest."

"And the treasure?"

"In the storehouse, perhaps, covered with grain. Or in the village cistern, under muddy water. They had to find a town, in any event. You agree?"

"How the hell do I know?" Ramón said. "You're the expert."

Luis spoke to the Professor without shame. "You think Cunti-suyu might have been the town, Cousin Felipe?"

"Do not call me Cousin," the Professor said. "It offends me." He sighed. "How many scores of ruins have I investigated! And always, nothing. But yes, it is possible—it could have been Cunti-suyu."

He saw in his mind the "Cunti-suyu" he was taking them to—a nameless ruined village of the Incas, archeologically barren, that he had himself discovered and explored years ago. And the Professor thought acidly: what credulous fools these are! The greatest scholars of the world, including Felipe de Ayala de la Vega, have been searching in vain for the Treasure of Pachacamac for four hundred years and more—and these children think that they can find it in a single night!

"How far yet?" Ramón asked.

The Professor looked about him. The desert had merged into mountains. The jeep was laboring uphill, slipping and skidding in a dry streambed. The Professor estimated they had come twenty miles from the coastal highway. He recognized a mound of rocks. "We are there," he said. "Cunti-suyu lies at the head of this arroyo. Go forward another hundred yards, then stop."

When the jeep pulled to a halt, the high shapes of rocks and surging mountains, and the low shapes of crumbling walls, loomed around it. Luis and the man called Ramón alighted. It was very still. And no longer hot, but growing chilly.

Ramón left the headlights burning. In their glow he glanced at his watch. "Almost four," he said. "The sun will rise soon." He reached an arm into the back of the jeep and hauled the Professor out. "You stay with me,

Indian," he said, grinning. "We don't want you withdraw-
ing unexpectedly from the expedition."

He forced the Professor to sit beside him on a rock near
the jeep, keeping a muscular hand on his arm. Luis sat on
Ramón's other side and they waited for daylight.

After ten minutes of silence the Professor said, "It
would be pleasant to have coffee."

Luis laughed nervously. "He wants coffee, Ramón. Did
you hear him? Coffee!"

"Why not?" the Professor said. "Wouldn't you like
some? To take away the dawn chill?"

"Shut up," Ramón said viciously. The Professor could
tell that the idea of coffee appealed to him.

"I have coffee in the jeep," he said. "Shall I make
some?"

Ramón looked closely at him. "Go ahead," he said. He
released the Professor's arm, but pulled out the gun and
trained it on him. "Go ahead and get it."

The Professor walked over to the jeep and lifted the
burlap bag from under the tarpaulin. He then went back
to the others. "Here it is," he said, and took coffee-making
materials from the sack. He balanced the chipped coffee
pot on two stones, set a lighted can of Sterno beneath it,
poured in water from his canteen, then added coffee.
While they waited for the water to boil, Ramón said
suddenly, "What else is in that bag?"

"Food," the Professor said. He showed them several
cans of peaches and tomatoes from the bag, and put them
back. "And we are fortunate this bag was in the jeep.
Without water and food, a man can die here in the desert
country in a single day. Did you know that?"

They said nothing. When the coffee was ready, the
Professor poured some into a plastic cup from the bag.
"This is the only cup," he explained. "I shall try the
coffee."

"No," Ramón said, "*I'll* try it." His arrogance extended
even to priority in coffee drinking.

"As you like," the Professor said. He held the cup of

hot liquid towards Ramón. Then he flipped it, with a shoveling motion, so the scalding coffee flew from the cup into the face of Ramón, and some burning drops sailed beyond to splatter Luis.

Both men cried out. The Professor seized the burlap bag at his side and leaped away in the darkness. Ramón's gun cracked—a sound of intolerable loudness above the desert. He is impulsive, thought the Professor who had heard the song of the passing bullet close to his ear—he will soon realize how foolish it is to shoot me. And in truth, the gun did not speak again.

As he ran, turning sharply to the right around a squat upthrust of rock, the Professor groped in the burlap sack and found the two Inca images he had placed there. Was it only thirteen hours ago? Scrambling and dodging among loose shale and shards of ancient masonry, he could hear someone running after him. He came to a large, box-shaped rock that might once have served as an altar or an anvil.

He recognized it, crouched behind it, scooped up a handful of dust from the ground, and rubbed it thickly on the silver-painted images. Then he disposed of them by tossing them, one at a time, into a blackness that yawned below him.

When he let himself be caught a minute later, feigning a turned ankle, it was Luis who shouted triumphantly to the man called Ramón, "I have him! He is here, Ramón! And he tried to take our food and water with him!" Luis spoke as indignantly as though the contents of the bag were truly his.

A rosy glow appeared above the mountains and objects began to take clear shape as night withdrew. Luis led the Professor back to the jeep, where Ramón still sat on his rock, a handkerchief held to his scalded face. Around the handkerchief his eye glared at the Professor. "Indian," he said tightly, although sucking on his lips with pain, "that was good coffee."

Apologetically, the Professor said, "I would have withdrawn from your expedition successfully, but I turned my ankle."

"A pity," Ramón said. The gun was still in his hand. He pointed it towards the Professor. "Tell me, Indian," he said, "where, in this village of Cunti-suyu, was the storehouse of grain? And where, also, the cistern?" His small sharp eyes regarded the Professor coldly.

"I will show you," the Professor said.

"You will tell me," said the big man.

"Very well. Look for the storehouse below. That way." He pointed. "The cistern should be above us. That way. Let us go."

"Thank you, Indian." Ramón smiled around his crumpled handkerchief. "Your ankle pains you?"

"Not greatly, no."

"You can walk on it without difficulty now?"

"Certainly."

"See how far you can walk on this," the man called Ramón said. He placed the muzzle of the gun against the calf of the Professor's right leg and pulled the trigger.

For an instant Professor de la Vega felt nothing. Then he knew agony, his senses blurred, and he thought he might faint. He fell to the ground. The wetness of fast-flowing blood soaked his trouser leg in a twinkling.

Ramón laughed and put away the gun. He said to Luis, in good humor, "Now, if we want him again, we have him. He is hitched to the ground." He wiped his coffee-burned eye and restored the handkerchief to his pocket.

They went away and left him. The Professor was dimly conscious of it through his pain. In the swelling light of daybreak they walked down the dry streambed. The fools.

Lying beside the jeep, the Professor saw that his abandoned coffee pot was within reach of his right hand. He fought down arising nausea, struggled to a sitting position, and dumped the still warm coffee grounds from the pot into his hands. Then he raised the cloth of his trousers from his wound and watched, for a moment, the blood welling from the small blue mouth in his leg.

Inca blood, he thought light-headedly, looks like any other. It did not seem to him that the bullet had harmed the bone of his leg, drilling merely through the muscles of his calf. But the bleeding was bad.

In a fog of pain he placed the coffee grounds on the wound, forcing them into the hole the bullet had made when it entered his calf, and stopping the exit-hole. If coffee grounds can halt the bleeding of machete cuts, he thought, perhaps they will do the same for bullet holes; and the grounds must be almost sterile, having just been boiled. He tied his handkerchief tightly around the wound to keep the coffee grounds in place. Then he drew down his blood-soaked trouser leg to hide the bandage, and lay back on the ground.

He heard the man called Luis talking with Ramón as they returned—or was it his cousin Luis talking with the man called Ramón? He was confused. But he knew they had found nothing—not even an old storehouse.

When they paused near his recumbent body, the Professor pretended unconsciousness. Through his eyelashes he saw Ramón look down at him. Ramón had lost his lips again and his face was black with anger. He drew back a foot and kicked the Professor heavily in the side.

"Wake up, Indian," he said, "we shall need you soon, I think." They went off together then towards the cistern, which they now believed would prove to be as non-existent as the storehouse.

The Professor lay still, trying to hold his straying senses together. His leg throbbed; but he felt no more blood dripping from it. Above him, in the deep hot sky over the mountains, wheeled a large black bird. He smiled a little at that, and thought, not yet—you must be patient, bird. He gathered his strength.

Suddenly, a shouting began, off to his right. His smile broadened, and his cheekbones caught a new highlight from the upward hastening sun. For he knew what the shouting meant, almost as though he had been there to see. Luis and Ramón had found the cistern. And they had seen the heart-stopping flash of Inca "silver" in the dusty rubble of the cistern floor.

In a moment running footsteps approached him. He heard Luis crooning like a madman as he scrabbled in the back of the jeep. "We have found it! It is ours! The Treasure has revealed itself! Where, in the name of God, is a rope?"

Heedlessly, he tossed the Professor's tools out of the jeep, some of them falling on the Professor's inert body. Soon he found a coil of rope and ran frantically off again, carrying the rope and—the Professor noted with amusement—a long-handled shovel.

Painfully, then, the moment Luis was out of sight, Professor de la Vega raised himself to his feet, using the rusty crowbar that had fallen across his chest as a staff. Once up, he stood for an instant, breathed deeply, and rested some weight on his injured leg. And although his dark skin paled to gray, and waves of weakness assailed him, he knew he would be able to bear the pain. Now, at last, he thought, I shall humble myself no more to the man called Ramón; and Luis, my cousin, must share with him the punishment. There is no other way.

He limped as quietly as he could in the direction Luis had taken. The crowbar was under his armpit, now, a serviceable crutch. He had not far to go. When he came in sight of the altar rock which stood on the lip of the cistern, he saw that Luis had tied the rope around the rock and that the rope's free end, by which they had made their descent into the pit, trailed downward into the cistern. Two voices, shrill with excitement, came up to him.

The Professor now abandoned caution. He stumped to the altar rock, ignoring stoically the agony in his leg. Standing behind the rock, he reached around it and quietly took the trailing rope in his hand. He jerked it once, savagely, and it came arcing up from the cistern to collapse like a long, back-broken serpent on the ground beside him. Then he stepped from behind the rock and looked down into the cistern, an impressive relic of the ancient irrigation system that once had been the lifeblood of this arid Indian marca.

The reservoir was thirty feet deep. Its steep, smooth walls were unclimbable and formed of monolithic blocks of stone so cunningly shaped and fitted by the Incas long ago that the mortarless joints between them would admit not even a knife-blade. And standing upon the rubble of centuries at the cistern's bottom were Luis and the man called Ramón, each with a small, aluminum-painted image in his hand. They stood motionless, their heads lifted towards him, as still as images themselves, arrested by the Professor's voice above them.

"Have you found the Treasure of Pachacamac?" the Professor said, leaning on his crowbar.

They looked up blankly, stupidly, at the spot where their rope had hung and now hung no longer—their only avenue of escape from this smooth-walled prison, contrived for storing water half a millennium ago.

"Those images are tourist bait," the Professor said. "Not worth a dozen sols. I painted them—and planted them—myself."

He saw understanding rock them like a blow. Ramón reacted first—his hand dived for his gun in the hidden holster, but when he got it out and fired, the Professor stood safe behind the altar rock on the cistern's rim.

His face made gaunt by pain, and the anger in him again, the Professor said, "You called me Indian, Ramón. I am Indian. And proud to be. And I therefore leave you to the mercies of the Indian's ancient god, the sun."

"Wait, Cousin," Luis called out frantically. "We are trapped here, without the rope. We cannot get out. We will die!"

"It is possible," the Professor said politely.

"You'll die, too," Ramón said. "I have the keys to the jeep and you cannot walk to Lima."

"But I have food and the water canteen," the Professor replied. "Especially, the water canteen. These are good to have, don't you agree? And besides, I keep a spare set of keys to the jeep in my supply sack."

The man called Ramón was silent. He stared at the rock behind which the Professor was sheltered, then grimly down at the gun in his hand.

"You may welcome that before long," the Professor remarked.

Luis dropped the false silver statue on the ground and held up his hands towards the Professor. "I did not want to harm you, Cousin," he said. "It was the Treasure. All your life you have searched for it. And I believed from your letters you had found it."

"Of course, Luis," the Professor said. "It was the Treasure of Pachacamac. And see what a thoughtful cousin I am. I leave you with this treasure. Perhaps all you need to win it is to dig with the shovel. The Treasure could be there beneath your feet—as well as anywhere."

"Yes," said Luis in a hopeless and frightened tone.

"Professor de la Vega," said the man called Ramón, "you are a man of principle. You are not without scruples. You have taught us the lesson you wished to teach us. Now let us out."

"No. I am an Indian, remember. And it is well-known that Indians have a deep sense of justice. Guard the Treasure for me until my return, will you?"

"You aren't truly going to leave us here?" Luis pleaded.

"I have no choice, Luis. I must get this leg of mine to a doctor. And I must report to the authorities without delay. The police are very strict with men who plot to steal Peru's antiquities, you know."

"Please, Cousin," Luis said, sobbing now. "We do not want the Treasure of Pachacamac."

"Ah," the Professor said. "You are undoubtedly telling me the truth at last." He paused. "I shall return tomorrow evening—or perhaps the evening after tomorrow. With the police. Meanwhile, you may pass the time quite pleasantly—digging for the Treasure of Pachacamac."

"Professor," said the man called Ramón, "if you are truly leaving us here, permit us to have a little of the water in the canteen." There was no longer any arrogance in his voice.

"No," said the Professor. "I shall need the water myself. Did I tell you I was wounded? I may have fever. But while I am away, perhaps it will rain and you will be refreshed that way."

"Rain?" queried Ramón with a flicker of hope.

"Yes," said the Professor. "Rain. We need it very badly. Do you realize that not a drop of rain has fallen here on the desert littoral for fifteen years?" He laughed. "I am going now. Goodbye. The sun will soon be high and will drink up the shade in your cistern."

"No, no!" Luis screamed. "Do not leave us to die in the sun!"

"You will die," said the Professor politely, "but you will not be alone." He looked upward to the mountain peaks and saw the large black bird still circling in the deep sky.

Then, Professor de la Vega set the crowbar under his arm and turned away. Behind him, in the Inca cistern, the two men were suddenly quiet as they felt the heat of the day begin.

JEAN DARLING

The Matchstick Hut

A shimmering blanket of heat lay heavily over Monrovia that day late in the month of March 1957 when the *Siren Call* tied up to off-load cargo. As was his habit in each port, the Captain gave three of his hands shore leave—this time for ten hours, from 10 A.M. to 8 P.M., and Macker Malloy was one of the three.

After leaving the ship he paused to watch camera-laden Americans stream down the gangways of the gaily pennanted *Bergensfjiord* to have their pictures taken with dusky bare-breasted girls grouped here and there along the quay. In the shade cast by customs shed and warehouse walls, souvenir sellers knelt beside cloths spread with ebony carvings and thorny, shellacked blowfish with bulging eyes and tiny open mouths. Pile after pile of red and white bags of Purina Feed, as indigenous to Africa as the mosquito, could be seen through gaping warehouse doors.

Farther along the quay, musicians accompanied animated haystacks who were advertising the straw dances to be held somewhere or other late in the afternoon while, near the water side, a snake charmer posed for a Yankee dollar with his pet's head in his mouth. Men in bright-colored shirts offered tours in antique taxis or on foot; each was better than the other, louder than the other, cheaper than the other.

Leaving the dock area behind, Macker Malloy headed along the dusty road into the capital city of Liberia through swarms of insects buzzing on the still air. Like a giant hand, pressing the old beachcomber hat down on his head, the sun squeezed sweat out of him as though he were an overripe fruit. Macker mopped his face with a handkerchief, and taking off his jacket he finger-hooked it over his shoulder. What he needed was a long cool drink in a cool dark bar.

The city itself was alive with strolling couples. Each had a string of Liberian children in tow who teased for oranges being sold at every street corner, peeled and piled on the cement in pyramids of four. As the tall fair-haired Irishman passed, the little orange sellers giggled shyly behind slender long-fingered hands. These girls, like all the other women in town, were covered from neck to ankle in brilliant floral cotton, and their heads were wound in similar cloth. But for all the activity, all the to-ing and fro-ing, there was no place to go.

Macker had walked from one end of the main drag to the other without seeing a single establishment open for business except for one general store at the far end of town and the hotel. He retraced his steps to the hotel but there too a CLOSED sign sealed the glass door to the bar despite the fact he could see Americans from the cruise ship crowded around every table.

On being questioned, the desk clerk told Macker it was Sunday, and on Sunday the bar was open only to residents. While speaking, the man had opened the register and produced a pen. "That will be ten dollahs, sah!" His smile was wide and white. Macker shook his head and went back out into the glaring heat. By this time he would have settled for a glass of water or a pyramid of peeled oranges, but the thought of the bout of galloping yab-yabs that would follow dismissed any idea of buying oranges from the little gigglers. If worst came to worst he always could return to the *Siren Call*, but that would be the end of his shore leave. He decided to try the general store at the end of town.

Several people were waiting in line ahead of him, white as well as black. Macker wished the shopkeeper would get the lead out and not chat with each customer. It reminded him of home where everybody's personal affairs had to be discussed at length before a sale could be rung up. He almost had decided to vault the counter and grab one of the bottles of soda pop lined along the shelf behind the shopkeeper, when a man gathered up his purchases and turned to go.

"Well, I'll be damned! Macker Malloy!" the man exclaimed, stopping dead in his tracks. "What in hell are you doing in this kip?"

"It can't be—Sergeant-Major Toomey!" Malloy put a hand on Toomey's arm as though to make sure he was real. "Is it truly yourself, Shay Toomey?"

The two men stood laughing at each other, shaking their heads and laughing some more.

"Come on, you old gurrier, I'll buy you a drink." Shay Toomey crossed the street and led the way along a sidewalk that sprouted pavement at intervals to a low building. At the back of a deep stoep two large shop windows framed a door on which QUANTITY SURVEYOR had been painted. "Will you do the honors?" Shay asked, standing to one side while Macker opened the door into a dingy office empty of furniture except for a table, a camp bed, and an ancient safe with its door sagging open. A map of Africa was thumbtacked on one wall and a single light bulb dangled from the ceiling along with a number of flypaper ribbons black with victims.

"So what brings you down this way?" Toomey dropped his purchases on the camp bed behind the table that was covered from one edge to the other with a rambling monstrosity built of matchsticks. "Six boxes, that's all

he'll give me at a time. But he did give me a pot of glue!''
His tone was triumphant.

"You building this—whatever it is?''

"Now I am. Turn on the fan, why don't you? The switch
is over there by the door.'' Macker obliged and the fan,
perched on a high shelf wedged in a corner, began to wag
back and forth. "Come on through, the fridge is in here.''
The room beyond held another camp bed, a sink, a
kerosene stove, and an old-fashioned tin bathtub filled
with water and bottles of beer. A small fan perched on a
chair rippled the water. "The fridge,'' Shay said, reaching
in for two bottles of beer. "Wrap yourself around that.''

And so they sat drinking beer and reminiscing about all
the grand times they had shared in Italy while serving
with the British Eighth Army during World War II. When
the sun brinked to begin its long journey down to the
horizon, they switched to whiskey and subjects more
current, like just exactly what set of circumstances had
dropped both of them in Monrovia.

With Macker, boredom had been the catalyst that sent
him to sea. "I get back to Ireland to see the wife every
three, four months for a few days. That's enough.''

Shay nodded, his face creased with drunken understanding. "I suppose you're wondering how I came to bed
down in this little paradise on earth.''

"I wouldn't say it was because you liked it, but I'd
guess you're probably making money.'' Macker got another bottle of beer to chase down the whiskey. "How did
you get into surveying?''

"Like it? Here? You must be joking. Why even the
President—you saw that big white yacht when you came
in to port this morning?'' Malloy nodded. "That's where
Tubman lives and he's the President, so that should give
you an idea.'' He slopped whiskey into their glasses.
"Slainte!'' he said.

"Slainte!'' Macker echoed the Gaelic toast.

"As for making money, I haven't seen any in so long
I've forgotten what it looks like.''

"Come off it, no one can live without money. What about the matches and stuff you bought at the shop? That took money."

Toomey shook his head. "It's all on the house, so it is. Let me show you something," he said, fumbling three large white pebbles from his pocket. He handed them to his friend who set down his glass and studied each one carefully, his pulse rising.

"Diamonds," he breathed. "Uncut diamonds."

"They are o'course." Shay snatched the stones and dropped them back in his shirt pocket.

"Is that the lot? Only the three?"

Toomey ignored the questions. "I'll begin—at the beginning. Me?—I survey nothing. Willie Schultz surveys." He was very drunk by now, and his words slurred together. "Poor old Willis Schultz." He groped for the bottle, and it tipped. Macker caught it before its contents spilled onto the floor.

"Steady, lad," Macker said, dividing the remainder between the two glasses.

"Thanks, mate.—I was on this ship coming up from Cape Town. One of those deals you hang around a port asking till you find a captain who'll carry you for a pound a day. Well, we stopped here to take on cargo. It's Firestone Rubber land, you know. Would you believe nobody's paid till all the sap's in. If the workers are paid they won't work again till the money's gone. And you know the dames? They carry little bundles of cloth to wear in town—it's illegal to go bare-breasted within the city limits. God, civilization is dirty-minded." His head fell forward and he drowsed over his glass. Macker shook him.

"Wake up!" He slapped Toomey's cheeks. "Wake up!"

"Huh!—huh?" Shay waved him away. "What do you want?"

"You were telling me about the diamonds and if you have any more."

"Oh. No, I wasn't—hadn't got there yet—so the ship

tied up and I came ashore and got drunk. It wasn't Sunday, so I got drunk and ended up in the cop shop. Willie Shultz got me out, but by then it was too late—my ship had sailed o'course, so Willie took me in." He wiped his hand over his face. "That matchstick Banshee hut out there's Willie's. He started it, says he, so's he wouldn't go bonkers waiting for the chance to escape."

"Escape from what?"

"He was building some kind of a church, says he, but I just put on matches till the table was covered, and then I started another layer. Now it's so big it has to be put down on the floor. I don't know how, but it has to be so."

"You'd best give over playing with toys and get out of here—"

"Don't be a fool, mate, I can't. I'm a prisoner watched twenty-four hours a day."

"Go 'way with that. I didn't see anyone watching you when we walked from the shop."

"Sorry, lad." Toomey lurched out the back door to a hut at the end of the high-walled yard. When he came back he seemed almost sober. "Come on. I want to show you something." He went to the safe and took out a Hershey Bar carton. The inside bottom was covered with a thin layer of white pebbles like the ones in his pocket. "There you are. A present fit for the Aga Khan's birthday."

"You just leave all those diamonds in an unlocked safe?" Macker's voice was hoarse with desire. "Where did you get them?" he breathed, pouring a half-dozen stones from one hand to the other, his eyes glittering with avarice.

"Willie said they came from Sierra Leone. I don't know how he came to have them, but it was illegal, that much I do know."

"How do you come to have them? Did Schultz just leave you minding the shop?"

Shay Toomey shook his head. "Willie died," he said after a pause. "The reason I have them is because Willie couldn't take them with him.—He couldn't take them with him," he repeated, laughing until the tears ran down his cheeks. "Hey, that's a good one. Willie couldn't take them with him and I can't take them with me." Suddenly he was serious.

"So why the hell don't you stop moaning about being watched and walk to the quay and climb on the first ship that sails? That's what I'd do. What do you want to bet I could tip that lot in my pockets and walk out that door and board the *Siren Call*—"

"Ah, it's not boarding the ship," Shay interrupted. "I can do that. Sure I can walk out that door and board any ship I fancy but—that's the operative word 'but.' *I* can go—*but* without the diamonds. And unless I can take every one of those dirty-looking bits of glass with me, I'm not going—it's as simple as that.

"Look, I'll show you. If I go this way"—he moved over to the map of Africa and waved his hand in a 180-degree arc around the western coast of Liberia—"I'm in trouble with DeBeers."

"DeBeers?"

"The South African diamond cartel. They check the source of every uncut gem stone offered for sale anywhere in the world in this year of our Lord 1957. That's how the market is controlled. If I went that way and tried to sell even one stone it would be confiscated and I'd be locked up for a month of Sundays. Hell, if they saw this lot, they'd throw away the key! You can't blame them, really. If they weren't careful, man, they'd be robbed blind. Illegal stones flooding the market would bring down prices.

"Now, if I go this way"—he punched Sierra Leone with a fingertip balled from years of nail biting—"I'm dead. The authorities there know all about Willie's diamonds, so just one step over the border—" He shot himself in the temple with his finger. "Stealing their diamonds can be a capital offense."

"So why don't you travel across Africa to the East Coast? There you could get a boat or, better still, a plane.

With the kind of money that lot would bring you could live like a king for the rest of—"

"East Africa or West, what difference would that make to DeBeers? DeBeers' octopus is all over the world, can't you get that through your stupid head? A polished stone ready to be set as jewelry? No problem. It's uncut ones that mean trouble. Here the stones are safe—it's neutral territory."

"You say you've got no money. Who pays for this place, the stuff you get at the shop, the booze?"

"I don't know—whoever paid for Willie, of course. Some guerilla leader hoping to overthrow one of these shaky African states, I guess. And when *whoever* takes over *wherever*, he'll probably put the stones on the market claiming to have found a new small dig and use the money to consolidate his position."

Shay picked up a match from a pile at the edge of the table. "It's best to burn the stuff off, then spread a thin bit of glue along the side and press it into place. There. Can't do this for long though, it's too high. Makes my arms tired."

He built in silence for a while as Macker squatted on the end of the bed, the Hershey Bar carton on his knees, examining first one stone and then another, the need to possess them growing within him like a mushroom in a rain forest.

"Why would anyone like that feed you and Willie? Wouldn't it be simpler to have you deported or eliminated?" Malloy asked, glancing up.

"They can't deport me, they're not Liberians—at least, I don't think they are." Shay rubbed his hands across his mouth. "Whoever pays the bills gets his kicks watching a white man wallow in sweat and greed. It's a good way to pass time while keeping the loot on ice—let the sucker dream his alcoholic dreams before snuffing him like a candle. What do you know, I'm getting to be a golden-tongued Irishman!"

He paused, gazing at a small blob of glue glowing amber

in the light. "What I'm waiting for is Southern Africa to blow up politically, then perhaps the DeBeers stranglehold will be broken. If at the same time whoever's keeping tabs on me relaxes his vigilance, maybe I can get out with both the stones and my skin intact."

"And nobody's ever tried to rob you?" Malloy sat the box on the bed.

"Ah, no. I'm safe as houses if I stay within the boundary lines—from here to the shop and back, and across the street to the pub. But one step out of line and some big black yokes with high-powered rifles are waiting to pick me off. They're not only to keep me in, you know, they're to keep stealers out. Hell, I need another beer." He moved into the other room with his friend close behind.

As he bent over the tub, Macker's hand rose and cracked down on the back of his neck. The move was made without conscious premeditation. It was as though the hand, recognizing opportunity, acted with a mind of its own. Down it chopped and Toomey's upper body splashed into the water threatening to drag the tub over on its side. Macker steadied it while holding his friend's head under the water until the bubbles stopped rising. Then the fair-haired Irishman carefully eased the body to the floor.

An hour and a half later Shay Toomey was buried beside a similar mound in the high-walled back yard and the diamonds were all tucked away in the money belt Macker Malloy girded himself with, rich or poor. He shrugged on his jacket and looked around to make sure nothing had been forgotten. The tub was full of water, the little fan buzzing away, the floor had been mopped dry. On the bed lay clothes and pillows bundled into a satisfactory "sleeper" covered with a blanket.

The Hershey box, back in the safe, contained ordinary pebbles that Malloy had gathered while digging the grave.

He checked his watch—6:40. Time to make for the ship, he thought, running his hand over the matchstick monstrosity. He was filled with scorn that anyone could have been stupid enough to waste his life playing with a useless toy. If Shay Toomey couldn't have got away with the diamonds, he should have cut and run. Freedom was the most valuable thing in the world to Macker. Sure he'd try to make off with the stones, but if it wasn't in the cards, no one would catch him wasting time gluing matchsticks together.

For the benefit of anyone who might be watching, he paused on the stoep calling goodbyes to Shay, and promises to stop by the next time the *Siren Call* was in port. "Okay, I'll call your mother. No, I won't forget—soon as I get home. See you," he shouted, and hat on the back of his head, thumbs hooked in his belt, Malloy strolled toward the harbor. No one on earth would ever guess a king's ransom in diamonds encircled his waist, not even the riflemen who had put the wind up Shay Toomey—if there were any. More probably the heat had worked on his friend's mind, the heat and booze.

As he walked, Malloy made plans. He would stay with the ship until the end of this run, then a couple of quick backroom sales in London would buy him passage on the Queen Elizabeth II. He'd like a world cruise, being waited on hand and foot. And he'd be smart—he'd sell the rest of the stones one at a time in a port here, a port there—that way he'd be safe as houses. Not even DeBeers would worry about an odd uncut diamond, he reassured himself as he neared the general store, closed now and padlocked. Except for a group of Americans a hundred yards away who were on their way back to the *Bergensfjiord*, the street was empty. He quickened his pace—he would feel less conspicuous in their midst. Not that he put any faith in Shay Toomey's blatherings about being constantly watched.

Malloy was almost past the shop now, past the limit his friend had put on his right to stay alive. Just one more step would prove Toomey a liar or a fool—or both.

But Malloy never made that step.

Twenty feet in front of him a huge black man, cradling a rifle in the crook of his arm, stepped into his path.

Beyond, he could see the Americans small in the distance compared with the giant blocking his way. If he could reach them he'd be home and dry, he thought, his heart pounding. No gunman would fire willy-nilly into a group of passengers from the first real cruise ship to call at Monrovia. So smile at the man, wave your hand, now turn around like a good boy and take one—two—three steps toward the survey office, spin around, and run like hell for the tourists.

Suiting actions to thoughts, Malloy's long legs ate up the distance between himself and the Americans, the black man politely having stepped to one side. Mid-stride, Macker stopped dead in his tracks. Then, whirling around, he raced back toward Shay's place. A shout or two from the curious Americans dwindled as he ran. The sudden reversal of Malloy's flight had been caused by a single sentence spoken by the rifleman as he passed.

"Just beyond the hotel, man, I'll kill you," he said, swinging the rifle up into position.

On nearing the office, Malloy saw that a second rifleman was barring his passage in that direction, putting paid to any notion he might have had about ducking around the side of a house and doubling back to the quay. For a moment Macker stood looking from one man to the other. Then, shrugging, he went inside. He had been caught in the same trap that had caught Sergeant-Major Toomey who lay dead beside the man he had murdered for a double fistful of uncut diamonds.

Malloy wondered how the riflemen had known Shay Toomey was dead. It must have been the digging, he decided. That was where he had made his mistake. He should have left the body under the blanket instead of pillows. Burying him had been a bad mistake. Burying him had taken too much time. If he had left at 5:30 or 6:00—but that wouldn't have helped either. The *Siren Call* wasn't due to sail until 8:00. The gunmen would have hunted him down on the ship.

Malloy switched on the light. He crossed to the camp

bed and picked up a box of matches. One after the other he struck them, then blew them out. He took off his coat, swatted mosquitos, made a mental note to buy new ribbons of flypaper first thing next morning. Macker glued a few matches here and there along the top of the edifice, all the time thinking—thinking—trying to find some way out—with the diamonds—of course.

After a few minutes his arms grew tired. Shay Toomey was right, the damned thing was too high. He went into the next room for a bottle of beer, then decided against it. Better get back to the matchsticks, he told himself. Keep busy, that's the answer. His mind had to be clear to figure out a way to scarper with the diamonds, and it wouldn't be if he allowed himself to fall into the bottle the way Toomey had. He had to keep busy if he didn't want to go nuts.

Besides, if he seemed to accept captivity, there was a possibility he might find out the reason for this weird setup, find out whether it—whatever it was—were political or some kind of "private" caper. If he seemed a weakling, perhaps the watchers would grow lax.

Malloy tried pushing the matchstick monstrosity to the edge of the table. There was an ominous crackling sound and some matches crumbled off one side. It was too fragile to be moved even if there had been several people to help him. But if he were to keep a clear head it would be easy to work on.

Macker Malloy took a not too clean handkerchief from his jacket pocket and went outside. He strode boldly along the street with the handkerchief held aloft. One step past the general store the rifleman appeared. Macker went up to him. He spoke. The man nodded. Macker returned to the house to wait.

Ten minutes later four tall black men walked in the door. The one holding the gun stood beside Macker Malloy as two others, one at each end, held up the table while the fourth man sawed off the table's legs. That done, the matchstick Banshee hut was lowered carefully to the floor.

JOYCE HARRINGTON

Night Crawlers

Oh, he's laughing at me again. Can you hear him, little ones? Haw, haw, haw. Thinks he's so funny."

Mirabelle squatted beside the long wooden box and unhooked the wire mesh screen that covered it. Gently she raised the lid and propped it back against the cellar wall.

"Why don't you get married, that's what he said. Past time you got married. You and Catfish Charlie would make a good pair. And then he laughed like a loony. Big joke. He's still laughing. Can you hear him, little ones?"

Mirabelle cried fat clumsy tears that dripped off her chin and plopped into the rich peaty earth in the long wooden box. She drummed rhythmically with large-knuckled fingers on one side of the box.

"Oh, I told him, though. I could of got married, I said. Years ago. I could of married Roger Sprouse. He wanted to marry me. And do you know what he said, little ones? He said Roger Sprouse must of been half blind as well as half witted. And if he wasn't, then he must of been after the money."

Mirabelle's drumming soothed her and she stopped crying. Small clods of earth in the box began to shift delicately. Three or four glistening pink cylinders emerged from dark burrows. They wavered upright, momentarily blinded in the dim cellar light. Then together they hunched and wriggled toward the source of the compelling thrum. Mirabelle stopped drumming and picked up the longest worm. The others tumbled about in a tangled directionless heap.

"There you are, little one," Mirabelle crooned. "Aren't you a pretty little one? You'll never laugh at me, will you? Maybe I will marry Catfish Charlie. He wouldn't think it was so funny if I did. Roger Sprouse wasn't good enough for *his* daughter. Nobody was good enough for Lewis MacMaster's daughter or Lewis MacMaster's money."

Mirabelle MacMaster cradled the worm gently in her strong hands. Its long reddish-pink body coiled and undulated, seeking escape from the imprisoning fingers. Mirabelle tenderly wound the worm around her third finger left hand and admired the effect. She thought of the day twenty years ago when she'd told her father of Roger Sprouse's intentions. Roger had been a bit leery of speaking for himself and wanted Mirabelle to elope with him. Now she wished she had. But at the time she simply couldn't run off and leave her crippled father alone in the big old house on the hill overlooking the river. So she'd told him. She could still hear the scornful words.

"Roger Sprouse? That little runt? Why, girl, he's a foot shorter than you. And besides he's nobody. No job, no money, no family. Face it Mirabelle. You're a great big homely soft-hearted booby. And if you think Roger Sprouse is attracted by anything more than my disability money, well, you're dumber than I thought. You just wait, girl. The right fellow will come along. Just be patient. Roger Sprouse, hah!"

He'd laughed then, an ugly derisive laugh. And he'd been laughing at her for twenty years. Because, of course, no other fellow had ever come along after she sadly told Roger she couldn't marry him. Roger had left the valley and she never heard from him. She did occasionally hear rumors that he was working the oilfields in Texas or trapping in Alaska. But never once did he write to her.

Mirabelle sighed and uncoiled the worm from her

finger. She placed it gently back in the long box. The other worms had burrowed back into the crumbly earth and now this one did the same.

"Feed time, little ones." She rose achingly to her feet, her legs cramped and tingling from squatting so long beside the worm box. Mirabelle MacMaster stood six foot three in her worn sneakers, but lost a few inches to the discouraged stoop of her shoulders. She wore a shapeless home-made cotton smock and no stockings. It was hard to find ready-made clothes to fit. She was a heavy woman, but not fat, and her arms and legs seemed to grow out of the smock like the limbs of a smooth, patient beast. Her face hung round and high in the cellar gloom, a full moon shining down on the row of worm boxes. Her features resembled a blurred lunar landscape—a craggy jutting nose, round heavy chin, dark eyes set deep in bony craters. Her long brown hair, threaded with gray, was pulled back and carelessly braided into a lopsided wad at the back of her head.

"Feed time, little ones. And then I'll have to go and feed *him*." She sloped dejectedly to a sawhorse table under the high cellar window where she kept the feed cans, an assortment of tools, and the polystyrene container of worms that were scoured and ready for sale to the fishermen who tried for catfish and bass in the muddy brown river that curled through the valley. Mirabelle's worms were famous in the valley for being fresh, lively, and long-lived.

From the row of old coffee cans on the table she selected one, removed the lid, and sniffed. It was a mixture of cornmeal, coffee grounds, and brown sugar.

"Smells good, little ones. Nice and fresh and sweet."

As she filled a coarse mesh strainer with the cornmeal mixture, she listened for sounds of activity from above. He'll be finished with the evening paper soon, she thought. He'll be rolling through the house soon, yelling for his supper. It was a thing he did every evening. For that matter, yelling was a thing she did every evening. It was a thing they did to each other, and neither one of them could stop doing it. It was the way the long hateful days ended.

Every evening after Mirabelle got him up from his afternoon nap and settled in his wheelchair with the evening paper and a light whiskey and water, and the table set, and supper simmering on the stove, she would go down to the cellar and tend to the worms. And there she would stay until he yelled for her to come up. If he didn't yell, she wouldn't come up. Once she stayed down there all night because he wouldn't yell. She'd slept on the dirt floor next to the row of worm boxes, and he'd had to spend the night in his wheelchair. At least, that's what he said. The supper had burned to a sticky black mess and Mirabelle had to throw her best stew pot away. But it was worth it to let him know that she was her own person and had something more to do in life besides care for him. After that he yelled for her to come up. Every night.

Mirabelle shook and tapped the strainer over each worm box so that the black earth was covered with a light sprinkling of the cornmeal mixture. Then with a rake she mixed the feed gently and thoroughly through the dirt until none remained on top. In each box she felt the soil and crumbled it between her fingers to make sure it was damp enough, but not too damp.

Before she had finished with the sixth and last box, she heard the faint rumble overhead. The wheelchair was moving from the front parlor into the hall. She heard the floorboards creak. She heard the wheels trundle down the uncarpeted hall. Now he was passing through the dining room, in one door, the wheels muffled by the worn carpet, out the other door and into the kitchen.

Mirabelle paused in her raking of the last box, and her eyes followed the path of the wheelchair over her head. Into the kitchen now, so close she could hear the rubber squeaking on the slick linoleum. Any minute now he would yell. Mirabelle held her breath and peered up the cellar stairs to where she knew he was lurking on the other side of the cellar door.

At last it came. "Mirabelle! Hey, down there! How about some supper? Mirabelle, you gonna stay down there all night?"

Satisfied, she called back, "Coming, Pa." And went back to raking the feed into the last box. She took her time about it, muttering to the worms that popped up as she turned the earth over. "I'd like to put some of you into his supper. That's what. That would be a good joke on him. See if he laughs at that. Worms in his supper. Supper's ready, Pa. Worm soup tonight. Come and get it."

She finished raking and then went round to all the boxes checking to be sure the screens were tightly hooked so that no worms could escape to burrow into the dirt floor of the cellar. She stood back to admire the neat row of boxes. Six in a row, she thought, filled with hundreds of shiny healthy night crawlers munching away at their tasty supper. Just like six coffins in a row with worms busy inside.

Mirabelle turned and trudged up the cellar steps.

"You're a good cook, Mirabelle. I have to give you that. Not much to look at, but a good cook."

The old man scraped away at the last speck of gravy on his plate with a crust of bread. He crammed the bread into his thin-lipped mouth and his jaws chomped noisily up and down.

Mirabelle picked daintily at her food and thought of the worms below. Hundreds of tiny jaws chomping up and down at their cornmeal supper.

She said, "Thank you, Pa."

There came a scratching at the screen door leading from the kitchen to the back porch.

"Must be your beau. Ask him in, Mirabelle. Give him a piece of your chocolate cake, and maybe he'll pop the question. Cut me a piece while you're at it."

Mirabelle cut a piece of cake and placed it before the old man.

"It's only Charlie come for some worms."

"Just what I mean, girl. You got old Catfish hooked. Better not let this one get away. Haw, haw."

"You're plain loony, Pa." Mirabelle rose from the scarred table and left the shabby dining room. Through the immense old-fashioned kitchen she went, past the black iron stove for which she chopped and stacked wood, all the way through to the back door.

"Hello, Charlie."

"Evenin', Miss Mirabelle. I come for some worms."

Mirabelle held the door open for him, and the tall gaunt figure sidled into the house. No one knew how old Catfish Charlie was or where he came from. He lived in a one-room shack down near the bend in the river. Had lived there as long as anyone could remember. He always looked the same, a little bit like a catfish with his long turned-down mouth and his straggly mustache and round stubbled chin. Somewhere along the way the mustache and stubble had turned gray. Summer and winter he always wore the same old greasy knitted wool cap, so no one knew if his hair had turned gray, or even if he had any.

Charlie was the best fisherman on the river, but he only bothered to catch enough to fry for his supper and a few over to sell for tobacco and bait money. Between times he did odd jobs around town—shoveling snow in the winter, cleaning leaves out of gutters and rain spouts in the fall.

"I could use about a dollar's worth," he said in a soft whisper.

"Come on down cellar, Charlie."

Mirabelle opened the cellar door and started down the rickety steps.

The old man's voice rasped at them from the dining room.

"You mind your p's and q's down there, Catfish. Don't you go taking no liberties with my little girl. Else I'll take my shotgun after you. Haw, haw, haw."

Charlie froze at the top of the cellar steps. Mirabelle turned and saw the fright in his faded blue eyes.

"Don't pay him no mind, Charlie. He's just teasing."

Still Charlie hesitated at the top of the stairs, shifting from one foot to the other, getting ready to bolt if the wheelchair started rumbling toward the kitchen.

"Come on, Charlie. I got some real good wigglers. Saved 'em special for you. Besides, he ain't even got no shot-gun."

"You sure?"

"Sure, I'm sure."

"Well, all right then."

Charlie followed her, trembling, down into the cellar.

While Mirabelle dipped into the styrene container, counting out worms and packing them into an old cottage-cheese carton, Charlie paced nervously up and down the row of worm boxes.

"I heard something, Miss Mirabelle."

"Did you now, Charlie."

"I heard something and I'm gonna tell it to you."

"I'm listening." Mirabelle knew that Charlie couldn't be rushed, that whatever he had to tell would come out as long as she didn't ask him any questions.

"I heard it down at the store. I was down there gettin' some cut plug." Charlie had stopped his pacing and was peering intently at the floor.

"Reminds me I have to get in some Mason jars. Got to get those tomatoes put up before they rot on the vine."

"I heard them say it," Charlie told the floor, wagging his head in wonderment. "They said Roger Sprouse was back in town. Drove in yesterday noon, they said. On the stroke of twelve. In a big Cadillac car. Staying at the hotel, they said. Gave a big party last night at the Red Rooster Club. Bought beer for everybody. They was all talking about it down at the store."

If Charlie had not been regarding the floor so intently, he might have seen a tremor pass through the body of the large woman at the work table. It passed quickly and

Mirabelle clamped the lid on the carton of wriggling worms.

"That a fact, Charlie," she said. "Here's your worms."

Charlie probed inside the bulging pockets of his ragged windbreaker and brought out a wadded dollar bill.

"That ain't all, Miss Mirabelle," he continued, for the first time looking directly at her face. "I seen him. I seen him today at the gas station. He was gettin' gas in his car. Boy, that's some car."

Mirabelle's eyes were flat and expressionless in her round face.

"You seen him," she prompted.

"I seen him, and he said—he said I was to tell you—I was to say, 'Roger Sprouse has seen the world and he's back home to stay.' Yes, that's the way he said it, Miss Mirabelle." Charlie nodded his head vigorously.

"Well, thanks for the message, Charlie. Let me know how you do with these worms. I put a few extras in."

Mirabelle handed him the carton and pocketed the crumpled bill. She plodded heavily up the stairs. Charlie tiptoed behind her. Before he could ease himself out the back door, the old man wheeled into the kitchen and fixed him with a penetrating leer.

"You been a mighty long time down cellar with her, Catfish. You just lucky I ain't got my shotgun handy."

Charlie swallowed a mangled protest and leaped out the back door. As he skittered away into the night, the old man's mocking laughter reverberated through the kitchen.

"Did you see him jump, Mirabelle? Haw, haw, haw. Funniest thing I seen since tadpoles."

"He's my best customer, Pa."

"Want to go to bed now." The harsh voice crumpled into a tired whine. "My legs's been painin' me something awful."

Mirabelle turned the wheelchair and pushed it out of the kitchen and through the house to the small room just off the front porch that had been her father's bedroom ever since the accident that had crippled him for life.

There she undressed him and lifted him from the chair
to the bed. He was a tall old man, taller than Mirabelle, or
would be if he stood up. The years in the wheelchair had
left him scrawny and pale.

Lewis MacMaster had been a railroad man, working the
freight trains up and down the hills and valleys, sometimes as far as Chicago. When Mirabelle was fourteen
years old, there'd been a derailment. Her father had been
pinned beneath an overturned gondola. After six months
in a hospital where no amount of operations or therapy
could get him on his feet again, Lewis MacMaster came
back to the valley with a disability settlement and a
monthly pension check.

There were those in the town who said that Lewis
MacMaster's frail pretty wife died because he was too
miserly to spend any of his disability money on doctors
or medicine for her. There were others who said that she
simply wore herself to death taking care of her crippled
husband. Whichever it was, Lena MacMaster quietly quit
living in the winter of the year following Lewis' accident.
Young Mirabelle took over in her place.

The years passed and Mirabelle, tall and strong to begin
with, grew even stronger caring for her invalid father.
And as Lewis' dependence on Mirabelle settled into a
routine, he grew even more miserly and cantankerous.
From his secret hoard he doled money out in stingy
allotments to cover their daily necessities. He never gave
Mirabelle a dime for any fripperies that a young girl might
take pleasure in.

When Mirabelle was eighteen she started growing a
vegetable garden and set up a roadside stand. With the
money she earned from her first sale of squash and
cucumbers, she went into town and bought herself a box
of face powder, a lipstick, and an eyebrow pencil. When
she appeared at dinner that evening, all bright and gay
and clown-faced, Lewis MacMaster laughed. His ridicule
did more to squelch the timid girl inside the elephantine
body than if he had stormed and scowled and forbidden

paint and powder. Mirabelle ran off to wash her face, and hid her cosmetics in the back of her dresser drawer. They were still there.

Mirabelle still grew vegetables, but only for their own table. Over the years she'd tried other money-making schemes, always to the accompaniment of her father's scornful laughter. She sold jam and preserves; she baked pies; she made fragrant lavender-scented soap. But although each of these ventures brought her a small income and she had a tidy emergency fund put by in the People's Bank, none of them satisfied the yawning hollow within that other people filled with ambition or children.

Until she started worm farming. She'd gone fishing one day, just to get away from the house for a while, and met Catfish Charlie down by the river. Side by side they'd fished off the rotten pier at the foot of MacMaster's hill. Mirabelle was using fat earthworms she'd dug from her garden. Charlie had an assortment of grasshoppers, small skinny worms, and bread balls. For an hour or so neither one of them said a word, but Mirabelle pulled in several bluegill and a fair-sized bass. Charlie pulled in exactly nothing and was looking pretty glum.

At last he whispered, "Mind if I try one of them worms?"

"Help yourself," said Mirabelle.

Charlie looked happier as he began to fill his gunny sack with bluegill and a particularly ugly catfish.

As he baited his hook with Mirabelle's last worm he muttered, "Ol' Roy Goff ain't sellin' night crawlers no more. He give it up."

So Mirabelle took the notion and went to see old Roy Goff. He told her all about worm breeding and how he couldn't keep it up since his arthritis had got so bad, and how since he quit nobody was selling any good bait in the valley. Mirabelle went home with the breeding boxes stacked in the rear of the pickup and a new idea. This was about five years after Roger Sprouse had left the valley.

It was along about this time that Mirabelle saw an apparition. She was twenty-five years old, and although the garden and the chores around the house, and her father, and her newly acquired worm business kept her busy throughout the day, she often had trouble sleeping at night. This particular night she was sitting by her open window watching the shift of clouds against the face of the moon and wondering if things would ever be different for her, although she had no idea of how she wanted them to be different. Her room was dark behind her and the night was bright outside.

She sat, wide-awake but motionless, watching the moon disappear into the belly of a stately black cloud and waiting for it to come out on the other side. She was thinking that she might as well go to bed as soon as the moon reappeared when she saw a flicker of white moving slowly down by the edge of her tomato patch.

She turned quietly in her chair until she could take in the whole of her garden, the tangled underbrush beyond it, and the pine-covered hillside behind the house. She saw a tall column of luminous white swaying past the staked rows of tomato vines, lurching away from the house and toward the path leading on up the hill. The cloud passed away from the moon, and by its light she saw that the spectral apparition had bristly gray hair and was wearing bedroom slippers and a nightshirt. It was her father. Walking. Using a discarded stake for a walking stick. Having a hard time of it, but walking.

Mirabelle knew there was only one thing in the world that could get her father on his feet. She stopped long enough to cover her own pale nightgown with a dark coat and tie up her sneakers. Then she followed. She crept past the garden and into the low brambles, choosing her way carefully. Ahead she could hear her father's stumbling footsteps.

She followed swiftly and quietly, hugging the edge of the path, ready to fade into the dark pines at the first sign of his return. But he didn't return. On he went, and on and on. Up the hill and around to its northern side, the side away from the house, the town, and the river. At last Mirabelle came to a clearing bathed in moonlight.

She crouched behind one of the boulders that studded this side of the hill and scanned the space before her. At the far side of the clearing there was a dark jumble that might have been boulders or scrub. At one side of this mass she saw the tall white figure moving back and forth. He seemed to be pulling at something. Suddenly part of the hillside seemed to move with a scraping, crackling noise. She saw her father straighten and glance round the clearing. She felt rather than saw the look of greed and cunning on his face. Then a light appeared in his hand and he disappeared into the face of the hill.

Mirabelle waited. The light in the clearing waxed and waned as more clouds marched across the path of the moon. Mirabelle thought about what she had seen. Her father could walk. She'd given ten years of her life and lost her only chance of getting married, all for nothing. Mirabelle was not surprised. She blamed herself for being a fool.

After perhaps fifteen minutes the gaunt white figure reappeared and again the scraping, crackling sound echoed through the clearing. Her father staggered off down the hill, passing within a few yards of Mirabelle's hiding place.

Mirabelle stayed in the clearing the rest of the night. Sometimes she drowsed propped up against the boulder, sometimes she watched the moon drifting down the sky until at last it set. She pondered what it all meant and what she could do about it.

When the sun rose, she crossed the clearing. What she had taken in the moonlight for a pile of rocks or a thick growth of scrub turned out to be a cleverly intertwined screen of dead twigs and branches. Looking quite natural, this heap of tangled deadwood moved easily when she tugged at one end. Again the scraping, crackling sound filled the clearing. Behind the screen lay a hole in the hillside, a small cave roofed with rock. It could only be entered on hands and knees.

Mirabelle hunkered down and peered into the hole, but the light only penetrated a short way. She couldn't see the end of it or whatever there was in the cave that drew Lewis MacMaster to it in the middle of the night. But she had a pretty good idea.

She crawled into the cave, moving like a great black bear into its den. The light failed immediately, blocked out by her own bulk. She crawled on for about five or six feet in total darkness, feeling first that the floor of the cave was tilting down and then again that it was climbing up the inside of the hill and she might come out on top. The roof of the cave scraped against her back and its sides pressed in against her shoulders. Soon she could only progress by inching forward on her stomach.

The walls of the cave grew narrower. Mirabelle thought she might get stuck. Wouldn't that be a good laugh on him? He'd have to send out a search party and the whole world would know about his treasure cave. No, he wouldn't let anyone know where his money was, not even to save her life. Maybe the next time he came up here he would find his way blocked by her lifeless body and he'd have to wait until she rotted away before he could get at his hoard. Either way, Mirabelle didn't care. She struggled on, scraping her elbows on the rough floor. At one point she tried to inch backward but found it nearly impossible, so she went on.

At last she came to a place where her groping hands met nothing but space. The floor fell away abruptly and her fingertips couldn't reach bottom. The sides of the cave flared away from her shoulders, and on reaching upward she found that the roof soared off into blackness. She drew her knees up and sat at the edge of the void. Glancing back over her shoulder she saw a tiny glimmer of daylight at the entrance to the cave. It was not enough to light the abyss before her, but it would serve as a beacon for her return.

Cautiously she lowered her feet into the pit. She felt absurd and foolish when her feet immediately encountered solid rock. She lowered her heavy body into the pit and, squatting on her heels, she duck-walked her way around the perimeter of the cavern, patting the walls and the floor as she went. Searching. When she found the strongbox on a small ledge against the wall, she sat down in darkness and held it in her lap. This was the thing that had stunted her life, yet she didn't know what to do with it.

She felt no animosity toward the box. She wasn't even interested in finding out what was inside it. In the blackness of the cavern she sat holding the box in her lap and feeling an odd kind of strength flow through her. It wasn't physical. Mirabelle knew all about physical strength. One of the few things she had to be proud of was the strength of her outsized body. This was different.

After a while Mirabelle lay the box back on its ledge and crept back to the narrow tunnel leading to daylight. She burrowed back through the tunnel, the way out seeming much shorter than the way in. She was dressed and in the kitchen frying grits long before her father began yelling for her to come and help him to get out of bed.

Mirabelle continued to live in the big old house on the hill and to care for her father. But after the discovery of the strongbox her nursing was tainted with small meannesses. Her father retaliated with ridicule and scornful laughter. And increased miserliness. And the hoard in the strongbox grew. Each month, when Lewis MacMaster received his pension check in the mail, he would endorse it and send Mirabelle to the bank to cash it. On her return he would count over every nickel, dime, and dollar of it, and spread it out temptingly on his bedside table. By morning it would be gone, and Mirabelle knew that during the night he had made a pilgrimage to his cave. When Mirabelle needed money to do their meager marketing, she would mention it to him in the evening, and in the morning a few bills would appear on the table.

Only once in all those years did Mirabelle return to the clearing in the woods. She didn't enter the cave, but sat on a boulder near its camouflaged entrance. Like a brooding stone guardian she sat for several hours, until at length she rose, shaking her head and muttering to herself, and went home.

On the night that Catfish Charlie told her of the return of Roger Sprouse, Mirabelle felt a resurgence of that peculiar strength she'd felt long ago in the cave holding the money box in her lap. As she massaged her father's wasted legs before tucking him in for the night she said, "Got to go to the store tomorrow. Need some Mason jars and some sugar."

The old man grunted. "Get me a wedge of that store cheese. I got a yen for some of that cheese."

Mirabelle adjusted his nightshirt and covered him with the threadbare blanket.

"Good night, Pa," she said, avoiding his greedy black eyes.

She went upstairs to her room, but didn't go to bed. Instead she settled herself in a chair by the window as she used to sit when she was young and when restlessness possessed her nights. Patiently she waited through the hours with no moon to light her vigil. About two in the morning she saw the old man slide past the tomato vines. At the edge of the garden, before plunging into the underbrush, he flicked on his light.

Mirabelle followed. Out of the house and around the garden plot. Into the brush and up the hillside, with the tiny light in her father's hand bobbing before her, drawing her like a magnet. Sometimes she lost sight of it, and the pine woods closed in dank and mysterious. But always it reappeared, beckoning her on, sending her light-footed and silent through the moonless night.

By the time she reached the clearing, the deadwood screen had already been thrust aside and her father had disappeared into the cave. She crept up to the cave mouth and listened. Inside she could hear a faint scrabbling. It continued for a few minutes. Then it stopped. Mirabelle judged that her father had reached the secret inner chamber. Certainly he would spend some time there counting his money, fingering the bills that meant more to him than life and health and his only daughter's happiness. Very well. Let him spend the rest of his life with the thing he loved most.

The boulder that Mirabelle had sat and brooded on all of one summer afternoon lay at one side of the cave mouth, just where the deadwood screen came to rest when it was in place. With all her considerable strength, the strength given to her by the years of lifting the old man into and out of his chair and bed, she pushed the huge rock. The rock resisted. Left behind by a retreating glacier, it would not be moved by mere mortal strength. But Mirabelle's heart was ice, too. Chill hatred knotted her stomach and tensed the muscles of her thighs.

She put her shoulder to the rock, closed her eyes, and with all the might of her years of servitude and humiliation, she pushed. The rock groaned and gave way. Slowly at first, then with increased momentum, it tumbled out of its bed and down the slight incline to the cave mouth. There it came to rest, hard, just as Mirabelle had planned it.

She felt all around the edges where the boulder, larger than the mouth of the cave, met the opening. She could feel no chink. Air and light were cut off, and escape. She rested against the boulder, breathing rapidly, picturing the old man within engrossed in the contents of his money box. Beyond that she would not imagine.

Before she left the clearing, she dragged the pile of dead brush across the front of the cave, leaving the scene almost the way it had always looked. She crossed the clearing sedately, at her usual pace, and entered the woods. But before she had gone very far, she felt the urge to run, to leap, to dance in wild fleering circles.

The dark pines gloomed down on her grotesque cavorting, but Mirabelle was beyond fear of the dark forest and the things that inhabited the dark. She had left all that behind in the cave on the hill, along with hate and pain and impotent tears. If anyone had seen her dancing down the hill that night, whirling and leaping, crouching and springing, they would have thought her possessed.

She reached the house, breathless from her exertions. Once the door was closed, cold practicality reasserted itself. Somehow, she would have to produce an explanation for her father's disappearance. To be sure, very few people ever saw her father, but sooner or later someone would inquire. So sooner or later, she would have to have an answer. Better sooner than later, she thought.

She sat down at the kitchen table with a glass of Lewis MacMaster's whiskey, and considered possibilities. But the only possibility that presented itself, where the lack of a body would not be an overwhelming difficulty, was the river.

"The river," Mirabelle breathed and drained off the last of the whiskey.

"The river," she murmured as she stalked through the darkened house to her father's room.

"Down by the riverside," she sang as she trundled her father's wheelchair out onto the front porch. She sat down in the wheelchair and practiced a few times, rolling it back and forth along the porch, to gain the touch of steering it. Then she was ready. She sent the chair swooping down the board ramp that she had placed over half of the porch steps to allow her father to roll up and down and give him the freedom of the yard. Then down the path to the road, across the dirt road and on down the hill on the other side. The chair moved easily, although the ride was bumpy.

She allowed the chair to increase its speed, pumping

away at the wheels with her elbows flapping like giant wings.

"Wheee!" she cried into the black night. And "Wheee-oooeee!" as the chair hurtled down the hillside toward the river. She felt the tall grass come up between her feet and flatten under the passage of the runaway chair. At the foot of the hill the chair slowed and Mirabelle guided it, peering into the darkness, until she found the old pier sticking out into the river. The river was high, almost at flood stage, and she could hear it rushing past, lapping at the pier.

She bumped the chair up onto the pier and rode it slowly out into the hungry river. Before she reached the end of the pier Mirabelle dismounted. Then she pushed the chair, as she had pushed it for so many years with her father in it, to the end of the pier—and right over the edge into the dark water. Then she waded downstream until she reached a rocky outcrop that led back up from the river to the road. She climbed this, went home, and crawled into bed.

In the morning she got up at her usual time and made breakfast as she usually did. When breakfast was ready, she went into her father's room and looked at his empty rumpled bed. Then she went out of the house and walked all around it, poked around the garden, and even went a short way into the woods. All the places where a man in a wheelchair could go without too much difficulty. Her face wore a puzzled frown.

After a while she got into the pickup and drove to town, straight to the Sheriff's office on the second floor of the People's Bank Building.

She came right to the point. "Pa's gone," she said to Sheriff Rickett hulking behind his desk in his two-by-four office lined with Wanted posters.

"Where's he gone to?"

"Don't know. Can you come out and help me look for him?"

Mirabelle explained how she had put him to bed the

night before and had gone to bed herself; how she got up in the morning and made breakfast and how he wasn't in his bed when she went to get him; and how she'd looked all over the house and grounds and couldn't find him.

"He's just plain not there," she said. "Wheelchair's gone, too."

Less than a year away from retirement, Sheriff Rickett believed in comforting the womenfolk and not telling them too much of anything lest they get hysterical. He'd seen a lot of hysterical women in his lifetime, and they made him uneasy.

"Well, Mirabelle," he said. "Suppose you go on back out to the house and I'll get up a search party and be out in about an hour. Chances are he'll be settin' on the front porch by the time you get back there."

"Maybe so," said Mirabelle.

The search party consisted of Theo Curtis who ran a drive-in movie out on the main highway and held a part-time job as guard at the People's Bank. He dreamed of daring bank robberies that he would foil through his quick thinking and bravery, and often served as Sheriff Rickett's unofficial deputy. The B movies that he watched night after night inspired his prosaic days.

The Sheriff and Theo Curtis searched the house from top to bottom, examining closets and cubbyholes and sneezing their way through the attic where the dust of forty years lay undisturbed. In the cellar Theo became excited by the worm boxes and wanted to turn them all out to see if a body was concealed in one of them. He was convinced that someone, Mirabelle or persons unknown, had murdered the old man.

"An old geezer like that just don't up and disappear, Sheriff. I'll bet she done it. Them boxes look mighty suspicious."

"Suppose you just take this rake handle, Theo, and poke around in them boxes. And if you find anything besides worms you let me know. I'm gonna take a look around outside."

Mirabelle sat on the front porch and waited while the Sheriff searched the grounds. He was joined by a disappointed Theo, and they spread farther afield into the woods and down to the dirt road. It was Theo who discovered the wheel ruts and the flattened grass.

"Ho, Sheriff!" he called. "Lookit this." Sheriff Rickett ran ponderously down the slope. Mirabelle came off the porch and followed the track of her wild night ride.

"Goin' on down to the river, looks like," exclaimed Theo, eager to make the most of this major clue. "Somebody dumped him in the river. Sure thing."

"Take it easy, Theo. All we got here is wheel tracks. No sign of anything else. Suppose we see where they go."

Down on the muddy river bank the wheel tracks were even more pronounced, but where there should have been footprints if someone had been pushing the chair, there was nothing. Out on the pier there were parallel lines of dried mud that petered out before they reached the end of the pier.

Theo volunteered to dive and the Sheriff didn't stop him. Stripped to his undershorts and with the undersea exploits of 007 firmly in mind, Theo Curtis plunged into the swirling brown water. He came up spluttering about four yards downstream from where he went in. The Sheriff watched from the pier and Mirabelle waited patiently on the bank. With difficulty Theo swam back to the pier and hung on gasping to one of its rotting supports.

"That current. It's really something. I'll try one more time."

Theo submerged again, stayed down for a few moments, and came up close to the pier. He swam for the ancient ladder and hauled himself up shivering.

"Chair's down there all right." He shook water out of his ears. "Stuck in the mud or something. No sign of the old man. With that current he would be halfway to Cincinnati by now."

Back at the house, Sheriff Rickett questioned Mirabelle about her father. She answered briefly and seemed wrapped in thought.

How was his health lately?

Not too good.

Did he seem moody?

No more than usual.

How old was he?

Seventy-two come October.

Could he move the wheelchair by himself?

Yes.

Could he get into it by himself?

Sometimes. If he felt like it.

Did he have financial problems?

She didn't know.

"But, Sheriff," she said, "you know how peculiar Pa was about his money. After he lost the use of his legs and Ma died, it was the only thing he had left."

"I know, Mirabelle." He hoped she wasn't going to turn hysterical on him. "I only have to ask for the record. I'm going to write it down as an accident. Temporarily. You understand, it may have been suicide, but we don't know. It won't do him or you any good for that to get around. Well," he hitched up his belt and put on his hat. "Guess we'll be getting along. You understand, if the body comes ashore, you'll have to come down and identify it." His voice trailed off. "Goodbye now. You need anything, just come and see me."

In the car going back to town, Theo Curtis bubbled with excitement and theories.

"She could of done it, Sheriff. She's strong enough. Did you see those arms of hers? She could of snapped his neck like a toothpick and dumped him in the river. What do you think?"

"Not unless she could fly, Theo. No. If Mirabelle MacMaster was ever gonna kill that mean old buzzard, she'd of done it twenty years ago. And I wouldn't of blamed her one bit."

After the Sheriff and Theo left, Mirabelle went up to her room. She put on a clean smock and brushed out her hair. It hung below her waist in kinky billows from having been braided so long. She tied it back with a red ribbon the way she used to do twenty years ago.

She rummaged in the back of her dresser drawer and brought out the face powder and lipstick, hidden away but not forgotten. She patted a light sprinkling of powder on her face, just enough to tone down her freckles and soften the creases around her eyes. The lipstick was dry and hard and would only leave the faintest of pink smudges on her lips. It was enough. She decided that her thick black brows didn't need any penciling.

Then she went downstairs to start supper. She stoked up the old black stove. She stuffed a chicken and put it in to roast. She made a pie with blueberries from her garden.

While the pie was baking, she sat on the front porch and waited.

About four o'clock she saw a dust cloud down the road coming from the direction of town. She sat stiffly on the top porch step until she saw that it was only Willie Bateman in his jeep delivering the evening paper. She got up and went inside to take the pie out of the oven.

She set the pie to cool and was basting the chicken when she heard the car door slam. Toe-tapping footsteps sounded on the porch and a loud rat-tat on the door.

"Mirabelle, honey! Are ya home? Hey, Mirabelle! It's me. I came to take you for a ride."

Mirabelle closed the oven and put down her basting spoon. She heard the door creak open and the sharp heal-and-toeing come into the house.

"Where you hidin' at, Mirabelle? Ne'mind. I'll find you. You can't get away from me that easy this time."

Roger Sprouse stood in the kitchen doorway looking dandy in a plaid jacket and dark blue pants. He held a

Stetson hat in one hand and a box of chocolates in the other. His shoes were shiny and had thick soles and even thicker heels. Even so he was still a head shorter than Mirabelle; he was still skinny and bowlegged. But he was there.

Mirabelle grinned, for the first time in twenty years. "I fixed chicken and blueberry pie," she said.

"M-m-m. I thought something in here smelled pretty good. We got time for a little spin first? I want to show you off to my new car."

"Whyever not," said Mirabelle.

Mirabelle was dazzled by the long lemon-yellow convertible that crouched next to her rusty old pickup in the yard. She couldn't know whether it was this year's model or ten years old. It was powerful and bright. And obviously expensive. And obviously Roger had done well.

Roger drove fast, up and down hills, along the river road, over to the highway and back again. Mirabelle untied her hair ribbon and let her hair blow wild and free.

On the way back Roger slowed down and began to talk seriously. "I was sure sorry to hear about your pa, Mirabelle. But to tell the honest truth, if it hadn't of happened I wouldn't of come out to see you. I was gonna wait till you came into town to say my piece."

Mirabelle nodded and smiled.

"I was gonna catch you at the store or at the bank or at the post office. And I was gonna take you over to the hotel and give you a restaurant meal and tell you all about my travels, about the jobs I done and the places I seen and the women I almost got hooked up with, but didn't. And then I was gonna tell you how wherever I went I never stopped thinkin' about you, and wonderin' what it would of been like if you'd come away with me that time. And then I was gonna ask you to come away with me this time, and we'd go off to Mexico or California or wherever we liked."

"Well, now we don't have to go away," said Mirabelle shyly.

"Ain't it the truth."

Roger moved into Mirabelle's house, but occupied the old man's bedroom downstairs until they were married two months later. Mirabelle insisted on observing the proprieties to that extent, but felt it was extravagant for Roger to pay for a hotel room when there were rooms to spare in the old house on the hill. Besides, he was eating all his meals at the house, and over those meals he spoke enthusiastically of the improvements they would make in the place and what a valuable piece of property it was.

"First of all, we'll get that kitchen fixed up. Think what you could do, Mirabelle, with an electric range and a big freezer and a dishwashing machine. And then we'll get the whole place painted, inside and out. Why, I don't think it's seen a touch of a paintbrush since the day it was built."

Mirabelle was enchanted and agreed to everything. He brought her expensive presents—perfume and earrings and fancy nightgowns which she wore to please him but felt silly wearing. He forbade her to continue in the worm business.

"Roger Sprouse's lady don't have to mess around with no worms," he said. "And that's what you are, Mirabelle. A lady."

Mirabelle was astonished and amused by marriage. If that's what it's all about, she thought, I wonder why I felt so mumpish all those years. But she liked having Roger around the house, even though his great plans didn't seem to materialize and he did nothing about finding a job. He spent a lot of time at the Red Rooster Club where Mirabelle felt conspicuous and out of place.

Whenever she asked him about his plans he would say, "I got something cooking, Mirabelle. I got a terrific deal cooking. In the meantime we're doing okay. Right? Ain't we having fun?"

And Mirabelle agreed. For the first time in her life she was having fun.

About six months after Roger moved in, Mirabelle

happened to be on the front porch when Willie Bateman's jeep drove up and Roger swung down from the passenger side with the evening paper under his arm. It was a cold lowering day with a north wind whipping around the hill and chopping the river into sharp little wavelets. Roger wore only his bright plaid jacket against the chill. He shivered into the house and Mirabelle followed, wondering.

"Where's the car?" she asked.

"Traded it in on a new model," Roger answered. "I'll pick it up in a day or so."

The new model never appeared, and Roger took to driving the old pickup into town.

A few days later Mirabelle asked Roger for some housekeeping money. He'd given her money from time to time, but mostly she'd been using her emergency bank account to buy groceries and keep Roger in beer. She hated asking him for money; it was too much like the way she'd had to ask her father. But her bank account was almost wiped out. It never occurred to her to go to the cave in the hillside.

Roger cleared his throat, rattled his newspaper, and asked, "Whatever happened to the old man's money? Did he use it all up?"

"No," said Mirabelle, feeling suddenly homely and stupid.

"Well, don't you have it now?"

"No."

"Why not? You're his only relative, ain't you?"

"Yes."

"Well, then. You inherit. It's that simple."

"I guess so." Mirabelle felt that her voice would dry up if she had to answer any more questions about the money. But Roger pressed on.

"You didn't let any lawyers get their hooks into it, did you? You couldn't be that dumb."

Mirabelle looked at him with flat dumb eyes.

In the days that followed, Roger prowled the house. She could hear him in the attic, ripping up floorboards. He tore the backs out of closets looking for secret hiding places. He progressed through the bedrooms on the second floor. He completely destroyed the little room off the front porch where her father had lain for so many wasted nights. She sat in the kitchen while the destruction raged and said nothing.

At last he came to her, mean and hungry, and held her by her long hair.

"You know where it is, don't you?"

"Yes."

"Why won't you tell me?"

"Didn't know you wanted it so bad."

"Well, you're gonna tell now, ain't you?" He twisted the long hank of hair until her neck was bent across the back of the chair she sat in.

"Can't." Her dark eyes stared up at him out of their hollow craters.

"Dammit, woman! Don't be such a fool. Why do you think I married you? It sure wasn't your pretty face."

"Can't tell you. But I can show you," Mirabelle whispered.

"When?" he demanded.

"Tomorrow. Tomorrow I'll take you there."

The next morning Mirabelle got up early and braided her hair. She put on an old smock and tied up her sneakers.

"Better bring a flashlight," she said as she buttoned up her old black coat. "You'll need it."

She led Roger past the shriveled tomato vines, through the bare frozen underbrush, and up the hill into the dark winter pines. She crossed the clearing and wrenched the pile of branches away from the front of the cave.

"You'll have to help me with that rock. I can't do it by myself."

"Why, Mirabelle, honey." Roger was all smiles now. "Is that why you never touched the old man's money?

'Cause you couldn't move that little-bitty rock by yourself? Who put it there, anyway? Did you and the old man
think this up between you? And you couldn't trust your
own ever-lovin' husband to help you out?"

"I'm trusting you now, ain't I? If you want the money,
you'll have to push the rock."

Roger laid his shoulder to the rock and Mirabelle did
the same, wondering what she would do if a skeletal hand
emerged pointing an accusing finger at her. She hoped the
old man had chosen to die in the inner chamber, comforting himself with his strongbox to the very end. The
rock teetered and crunched against the side of the hill,
and slowly, slowly ground away from the mouth of the
cave.

A dank underground smell arose from the opening in
the hillside. Roger didn't seem to notice it. There was
nothing in the entrance as far back as Mirabelle could see.
Aside from a few scratches on the rock face such as might
have been made with the butt end of a useless flashlight
hammering in the dark.

"In there?" Roger asked, looking a little unhappy.

Mirabelle nodded. "All the way back. There's a tunnel
and a sort of room at the end. That's where the strongbox
is."

Roger hesitated. "How much is there?"

Mirabelle shrugged. "Don't know. He never told me."

"In town they said he must have put away thousands.
They said he never touched the disability money and
saved most of his pension."

"Could be true. All I know is we lived on beans and
sidemeat most of the time. And what I grew in the garden.
You figure it out."

Roger's spirits rose and he flashed her his happy grin.
"Mirabelle, honey, I'm sorry for all those things I said.
I'll go in and get that money and then we'll have us a
riproaring good time. We'll go to Mexico and live like
kings. Okay?"

"Suits me."

Roger switched on his flashlight and plunged into the tunnel. Mirabelle waited long enough for the soles of his shoes to disappear into the darkness of the cave. Then she started pushing on the rock. This time it was harder for her. This time she had only disappointment and chagrin to help her move mountains. But she had not as far to go.

The rock slid slowly and inexorably into position. It sealed the cave as if it had never been moved, and Mirabelle pressed her heaving body against it, whispering, "You were right, Pa. You were right. If only you hadn't of been so mean about it."

Mirabelle went home and spent the rest of the day cleaning and repairing her worm boxes. She filled them with fresh black earth and peat moss and mixed up a new batch of feed. She would dig the worms at night in the garden. Spring would soon be here and by May or June she would need all the money she could earn. Let them talk about her in the town. Let them say, "Poor dumb Mirabelle Sprouse couldn't hold her man." Let them say, "That Roger Sprouse, wasn't he something? Blew into town and blew right out again. Went off to Mexico or somewhere and never knew he was a daddy-to-be. Or maybe he did. Maybe that's why he skedaddled. Haw, haw, haw."

Mirabelle didn't care. She would have her worms and she would have her child. She would grow a garden and sell tomatoes and squash and cucumbers. And on summer nights she would sit in the clearing on the hillside and watch the clouds drift across the face of the moon.

STEPHANIE KAY BENDEL
The Woman in the Shadows

Alan Warrington's death was officially recorded as a suicide. The date and time of death were listed as Sunday, February 20, at 9:20 in the morning. If, however, I were asked to testify under oath, I should have to say that Alan died at the hand of another, and that he probably died sometime on Saturday the nineteenth, no matter what the medical examiner's evidence showed.

On the other hand, Elyssa Warrington's death was never recorded and never will be, despite the fact that it was witnessed by at least a dozen people. It seems that in death, as in life, poor Elyssa was doomed to go unnoticed.

But I am getting ahead of myself. My story actually begins about a week earlier, on the day of our arrival at Casa Mendez. The place was originally a private villa built by Señor Enrico Mendez some forty years ago to celebrate the occasion of his marriage to his third—and very young—wife. The villa sat on a small hill overlooking the ocean about twenty miles out of San Juan. One approached by way of a long palm-shaded drive that led to the front door, where the driveway circled a lovely marble fountain surrounded by scarlet geraniums. Bougainvillea climbed the walls on either side of the wide-

arched entrance and potted palms graced the cool marble
floors inside.

The villa was enormous, surely no less than fifty rooms
in three stories that enclosed a large courtyard. There
were also two atriums, each with fountains and rock
gardens. I remember thinking on the day of my arrival
that Señor Mendez must have loved his young wife very
much to have constructed such a lovely and luxurious
home for her. His admiration was not misplaced, as I
came to learn, for Señora Mendez—I think her first name
was Estellita, but I am not certain—was a woman of
unusual mettle.

After twenty years of apparently happy—though
childless—marriage, a series of financial setbacks forced
Enrico Mendez to sell his plantation for a small portion of
its worth. Brokenhearted and already in failing health—
he must have been in his seventies by then—he died not
long afterward, and Señora Mendez, who was not yet
forty, found herself the mistress of an opulent oceanside
villa without the necessary income to maintain the place.
Seemingly faced with the choice of either selling the
home she loved dearly or letting it fall into ruin, this
resourceful woman hit upon a solution. She would con-
vert Casa Mendez into a small private hotel that catered
exclusively to the wealthy and particularly to the handicapped wealthy.

An intelligent, energetic, capable woman, Señora Mendez soon transformed her home into a hotel of no small
reputation. Although it was never advertised, several of
my wealthiest patients had described it to me in glowing
terms.

*"I tell you, Dr. Harwell, two weeks at Casa Mendez did
more for me than your operation."*

*"I really don't think I need this medicine any more, Dr.
Harwell. Since I've been to Casa Mendez, I've felt remarkably better."*

At first such remarks tended to irritate me. After all,
they implied that my medical knowledge took second

place to that of a woman who had never so much as looked at a textbook in physiology. But I am objective enough, I think, for soon I found myself unable to deny that my patients did improve with a stay at Casa Mendez. Nervous conditions, arthritis, general malaise, gastrointestinal sensitivities—all were allayed by a visit to Señora Mendez's hotel. I found myself curious about the place, but the opportunity to visit there did not present itself until last February.

My good friend Adrian Christopher had been an artist for many years before a tumor on the optic nerve caused him to go blind. It is to his credit that the loss of his sight did not deter him from his art. Rather, he went from painting in oils to creating clay figures he molded by hand. I've watched him work, his long slender fingers moving deftly over the clay, pressing and scraping, his sightless eyes riveted on a fixed spot in space as though he were looking into another dimension at the finished model of his creation.

Christopher had had a lingering case of bronchitis that winter. Much to my frustration, conventional treatment with antibiotics seemed only to ease the condition, not cure it.

"What you need, my friend," I said finally, "is warmer weather. I'm afraid you may be coughing and hacking until spring."

Adrian smiled at me. He is a tall man, and exceedingly lean, and even when he smiles there is an air of solemnity about him. "Rather than waiting for warm weather to come to me, perhaps I shall pursue it," he said. "What would you think of a trip to the Caribbean?"

"An excellent idea," I replied. "Probably the best thing you could do for yourself."

"I was hoping I could do it for you, too," he said. "Traveling is so much easier for me when I have a friend along. What do you say?"

I hesitated. I hadn't had a vacation in a couple of years, and I *had* recently taken on a partner to reduce my case load. Some time off was not impossible to arrange. And when Christopher said he had just found out that Casa Mendez had a suite available due to a last-minute cancellation, I was sold. My curiosity about the place would at long last be satisfied.

We arrived late in the afternoon of Saturday, the twelfth of February. Señora Mendez herself saw us up to the third floor on a lovely elevator that was finished in rosewood and brass. A tiny woman with a still-youthful waistline and snapping black eyes, she seemed a bundle of controlled energy. "The individual rooms are on the second floor," she said. "All the suites are here on the third. The view is better." We stepped off the elevator, and she led us to the second door on the left and opened it.

We found ourselves in an airy sitting room with marble floors and a glass wall that had sliders opening onto a balcony that overlooked the ocean. I stepped out onto the balcony, which was surrounded by a white-painted wrought-iron railing that had been designed to look as though there were clusters of grapes hanging from it. I saw that the balcony ran the length of our suite, and that a similar balcony edged the other suites on the third floor. Below me was a bricked terrace on which stood several tables with white and yellow sun umbrellas. From the terrace a steep stairway led down to a white sand beach.

I stepped back into the sitting room. Señora Mendez was saying, "Dinner is at eight in the main dining room. If there is anything you need in the meanwhile, I will be most happy to see to it."

Adrian bowed. "You are most gracious, Señora Mendez. I know that we shall enjoy our stay."

She smiled and left us.

"Your choice of rooms, old man," Adrian said after she'd departed. "Which decor do you prefer? It makes no difference to me, of course." I glanced at the two bedrooms, one on either side of the sitting room. Both were tastefully done, one in pale blue and white, the other in an icy green. I chose the green.

Dinner was a delight. The main dining room was huge, with walls of a rose-colored stucco and pink marble floors. I noticed lovely carved wooden railings along the walls, designed to aid those who were no longer sure on their feet. "I've never seen so much marble in my life," I said, as I described the room to Adrian. "Even the ramps for wheelchairs are made of it."

"I've heard that Enrico Mendez imported not only all of the marble in the house from Italy, but all of the workmen as well," Adrian remarked. "He is said to have spared no expense in its construction."

"I believe it. I count seven crystal chandeliers in this room alone, and every table has a large arrangement of fresh flowers."

He nodded and sniffed. "Gardenias and jasmine among them."

The dining room was filled with an assortment of people. Wealth was obvious in the quality of dress and the amount of jewelry displayed. Not all the guests were past middle age, I noticed. There were several children. At least two wore cumbersome braces on their legs, one was blind, and one was obviously recovering from brain surgery. Yet the atmosphere in the dining room was decidedly unhospitallike. Those with handicaps were treated with a matter-of-fact efficiency. I sensed an optimistic air as if to say, "The worst is over. Now let's get on with recovery."

We were seated next to an elderly gentleman in a wheelchair. He was a distinguished-looking man, with a silvery beard and mustache and intelligent blue eyes. He introduced himself as Bernard Warrington. He indicated a frail-looking young man to his left. "My son, Alan."

Alan Warrington reached across the table to shake hands with us. He was blond and very pale and in general gave the impression of having been ill for a long time. Though he looked to be only in his early twenties, his hair was thinning and even his pale brows and lashes seemed scant. I wondered whether he was in the beginning stages of alopecia or perhaps had been subjected to chemotherapy. His handshake was not a strong one, and I suspected that it was Alan and not his father who had come to Casa Mendez seeking better health.

Mr. Warrington explained that he was in banking and for a while the conversation revolved around current trends in interest rates, foreign trade, and the stability of the dollar. I noticed that Alan took little part in the discussion, and at one point in the evening as he reached for his teacup, his hand trembled noticeably. I found myself pitying the boy, for his father was obviously a strong-willed, self-made man whom Alan could not hope to emulate. Yet, too, I noticed a tenderness about the old man whenever he looked at or spoke of his son. I suspected the boy had been sickly all his life.

As dinner ended, a broad-shouldered valet appeared and wheeled Mr. Warrington out of the dining room. Alan stood up and, as he made a move to follow, he staggered.

I rose. "Are you all right?" I asked. "I'm a doctor. If I can be of any assistance—"

He shook his blond head. "Thank you, but I'll be fine. Sometimes when I stand up too quickly, I feel a bit faint, but it passes. It's nothing."

I watched him leave the dining room. I remember thinking that whatever was wrong with Alan Warrington, it was very serious indeed.

Adrian and I returned to our suite to find a small native sculpture of a woman and child on the coffee table. There was also a note from Señora Mendez.

"Dear Mr. Christopher," I read out loud, "I thought you would appreciate the loan of this piece. It was done by a local artist." The note was signed "E.M."

I picked up the sculpture and exclaimed in delight. "It's lovely! Look, Adrian!"

I was always making such inappropriate remarks, for it was easy to forget that Adrian was blind. But he seemed not to notice and reached for the piece. "Marvelous!" he breathed as his fingers explored every detail of the work. "Look, Gordon, the artist has given the woman slightly bowed legs. In the past, that particular trait was not uncommon among the natives because of dietary deficiencies. Nice detail!"

I marveled then—as I have often done—at how little Adrian misses even though he is sightless. I left him admiring the statue and went for a walk along the beach. I had eaten rather too much for dinner and I knew that if I did not take a little exercise I should be miserable trying to sleep, even though our long flight had left me more tired than usual.

The evening was deliciously beautiful. The sun had set a while ago, but little threads of rose-colored clouds still showed above the horizon to the west. A warm breeze filtered through the palms as I walked through the soft sand, listening to the gentle slapping of the waves on the shore. The floodlights from the back of the hotel shone down upon the beach for some distance. I walked along the water until the floodlights were behind me and the nearly full moon cast shadows among the trees.

I was thinking how peaceful this place was and how I finally understood the healing powers of Casa Mendez when I heard singing. I paused beside a grove of palms and saw one of the most enchanting sights I've ever witnessed.

A young woman was dancing barefoot in the moonlight near the water's edge, singing softly to herself. Her loose peasant blouse had slipped off one shoulder, and she picked up her long, full skirt to keep the edges from getting wet. On her wrist were a number of jangling bracelets that glinted in the moonlight. Long, dark curls cascaded down her neck and bounced as she turned. I heard her giggle with delight as a wave suddenly slapped against her legs. She twirled, her arms extended as if she were dancing with an invisible partner.

Then she saw me and stopped. "Oh!"

I smiled and stepped out from the trees. "I'm sorry if I startled you," I said. "Don't stop, please. I enjoyed your dancing very much."

In the moonlight I saw the flash of her smile. "You liked it? Really?"

"Oh, yes. But aren't you afraid of being out here alone at night?"

She bit her lip. "I'm not supposed to be out here," she admitted. "But it was such a lovely night that I couldn't stay in. You understand, don't you?" She laughed. "But of course you do! You couldn't stay in, either!"

I found myself laughing with her. Now that she was closer to me, I saw that she was truly beautiful. Long dark lashes framed her eyes and cast shadows on her cheekbones. And she appeared to be even younger than I had thought—perhaps in her late teens.

"Are you a guest at the hotel?" I asked.

She nodded.

"May I see you safely back, then? I'm staying there, too. My name is Doctor Harwell."

"How do you do, Dr. Harwell. I shall be delighted to have you accompany me, but first I have to find my shoes—they're around here somewhere!" I heard a low melodic chuckle as she looked around the beach. "Here they are!"

Holding her slippers in one hand and lifting her skirts with the other, she walked along beside me, humming softly, her bracelets clinking.

As we approached the lighted area of the beach, she tugged at my arm. "Tell you what," she said mischievously, "why don't you go into the bar and get a couple of piña coladas and bring them out here and we'll sit and drink them on the far end of the terrace where no one can see us."

I looked at her in amazement. "My dear! I think you're rather young—I mean—" I found myself sputtering in discomfort. In fact, the girl was young enough to be my granddaughter.

She laughed. Then she sobered. "I'm sorry. I didn't mean to upset you. It's just that—I've never had a drink—not with anyone, that is. I've sneaked some of father's liquor when I was alone, but that's not the same as enjoying a drink with a friend, is it?"

I was strangely touched that she called me a friend. We'd met only minutes before. And yet, I felt she truly meant it—that she trusted me for some reason.

"I—I don't even know your name," I stammered.

She laughed again. "Oh, I'm sorry! It's Elyssa. Elyssa Warrington."

"Warrington? As in Bernard and Alan? What a coincidence! I had dinner with them this evening!"

She nodded. "I know."

"It's too bad you weren't there. You would have livened things up at the table."

She looked down at her bare feet. "I'm not allowed to eat in the dining room."

I stared at her. "But why not?"

"They're ashamed of me. Actually, I'm never supposed to leave the suite, but I do. I sneak out! Do you think I'm terrible?" She laughed and tilted her head sideways. A curl fell across her cheek and she brushed it aside.

"I don't think you're terrible," I said. "I think you're charming. But I really can't believe anyone's ashamed of you!"

She looked out toward the water. "But they are. It's very hard to be always locked up."

"Surely that's an exaggeration!" I exclaimed.

She shook her head and her curls bounced. "No. Even at home, I'm never allowed to leave the house. The only reason I'm here at all is that Alan has to see a new doctor in San Juan, and they couldn't very well leave me at home."

"But you must go to school!"

She shook her head again. "Never! I'd love to, but they won't let me."

I found myself doubting this incredible story. Surely

Bernard Warrington was a level-headed, decent man. The idea that he would lock up this lovely child and refuse to educate her was preposterous. Was this young woman given to fantasies?

"You're well-spoken," I objected. "You must have had some education. A tutor at home?"

"No. They wouldn't even let me have that! What I know I've learned from Alan and from watching and listening to Father and the servants."

I drew a deep breath. "If what you say is true, there must be a reason."

As she looked up at me, a soft breeze riffled the palm above us and a shadow fell across her face. "I told you. They're ashamed of me."

"But—"

She turned and glanced at the third floor of the hotel. "I'd better go before they discover I'm out here." And with that, she darted across the empty terrace and into a small dark doorway I hadn't even noticed earlier. As the jangling of her bracelets faded, I felt oddly alone.

Back in our suite, I found Adrian reading, his fingertips flying lightly across the pages of his book. "Did you have a pleasant walk?" he asked as I came in.

"A pleasant walk," I said, "but a most disturbing encounter." I told him about Elyssa and what she had said about the way her family treated her.

"I should be very surprised if what she said is true," Adrian replied. "My impression of Bernard Warrington is that he is a very decent and fair man. I can't imagine him abusing a child so."

"Yet, it happens. And sometimes in the best of families. You know that as well as I do. The thing is, now that I'm aware of the girl being kept prisoner, so to speak, I feel responsible. I ought to do something, but I don't know what."

Adrian nodded. "And it would be doubly difficult because neither we nor the Warringtons live here. I should imagine the local officials would be very reluctant to get involved."

He was silent a moment, then said, "Gordon, you know teenage girls are notoriously imaginative. You really can't do or say anything until you are sure she's not making all this up."

My friend was right, of course. My first obligation was to determine the truth of the matter and that meant observing the situation for a little while at least.

I did not sleep well that night. I dreamed of a gypsy girl who danced on the beach in the moonlight, her bracelets jangling in rhythm to her steps. Suddenly a dozen policemen came running across the sand and grabbed the girl, pulling her away despite her screams. "No! No! Please don't lock me up anymore! Please!"

I awoke in a cold sweat and a great sense of depression washed over me. I saw by the luminous dial on my clock that it was about four in the morning. Out the window, the first light of day was just beginning to crack across the sky. I lay back upon my pillow and tried to fall asleep again when I heard someone say, "No, please! Don't lock me up anymore!"

I shook myself to make sure I was awake. The voice was coming from the other side of the wall, and I recognized it as Elyssa Warrington's. The Warrington suite must be next to ours, I realized. Feeling not at all ashamed of myself, I pressed my ear to the wall and listened.

"You were out last night! You *know* you can't go out!" That was the voice of Bernard Warrington.

"I didn't do anything wrong! I just went for a walk on the beach!"

"What if someone saw you? Do you realize the damage you could do to Alan?"

There was a momentary silence, then the girl said, "No one saw me. You don't have to worry about your precious Alan!"

"Just the same, it must not happen again!"

"Do you know what it's like to be locked up all the

time? Never to be able to speak to other people?" The girl's voice was rising. "I didn't ask to be born, and I've done nothing to deserve this!"

Bernard Warrington's voice softened. "I know you haven't, and I regret having to do this to you. But you know I must."

The girl began to cry then. Her sobs were alarmingly close to my ear. I imagined that her bed was against the other side of the wall from mine.

I couldn't sleep after that, so I dressed and went for an early-morning walk on the beach. No one was about yet, and the silence was broken only by the wash of the incoming tide and a half-dozen gulls squawking at a pair of pelicans who were gliding low above the water, ready to scoop up any tasty tidbits that the tide brought in.

I found the spot where Elyssa had danced, and I stood watching the waves creep up gradually to wash away every trace of her. It gave me an eerie feeling, as though Nature itself were conspiring with the girl's family to erase her existence.

It bothered me a little that Elyssa had lied about meeting me. Not that I didn't understand why she had lied. Her father's anger was formidable. What worried me was how easy it would have been to believe her, had I not known the truth. And what if she had lied to me as well? What *was* the truth?

It was nearly seven by the time I walked back to the hotel. Several of the guests were having breakfast served on the terrace, and I found Adrian among them savoring a cup of coffee.

"Ah, there you are," he said cheerfully as I walked up—his ability to identify people by their footsteps always amazes me. "I was just going to order some breakfast. Will you join me?"

I shook my head. "I can't eat." I told him then about the conversation I had overheard.

Adrian listened in silence and bit his lip when I had finished. "I don't know what to tell you, Gordon. You must realize that you don't have what the authorities would call proof of wrongdoing. The father might easily say the girl is being punished for something or other—I understand they call such confinement being 'grounded.' It seems to be quite a common method of discipline. Then too, even if the girl's story is true, it's entirely possible that she would deny everything if confronted—simply out of fear of her father.''

I knew he was right, of course, but I couldn't imagine what evidence I could obtain that would convince the authorities a horrible injustice was being done to a young human being.

I let Adrian persuade me to have some toast and fruit—fresh pineapple and bananas—and just as we were finishing up, I saw Bernard and Alan Warrington take a table on the other side of the terrace. Alan looked tired. His father looked worried. They spoke very little, and as soon as they were through eating, the two of them went back indoors, apparently to their rooms.

I found myself watching the Warrington suite most of the day, in case Elyssa decided to slip out again, or in case I should hear or see something that might help her, but nothing out of the ordinary occurred. I listened at my bedroom wall again, but I could hear no conversation. It was not likely that I would, I realized, for I really could only hear what was said in Elyssa's bedroom, and most conversation in the suite would be taking place in the sitting room.

By late afternoon I gave up. Adrian was napping—his bronchitis left him chronically tired—so I went down to the bar and ordered myself a scotch. I carried it into the courtyard and found myself a comfortable-looking wicker chair that afforded me a view of the rock garden and man-made waterfall that stood in the center of the court-yard. After a few minutes, Señora Mendez appeared.

"Ah, Dr. Harwell! At last we have a chance to get to know each other! Many of my clients have spoken favor-ably of you."

"Really?" I said. "From what they've said to me, they seem to think your hotel is far better for their health than my treatments."

She laughed. It was a pleasant warm laugh. "Ah, no doubt, people can be tactless! But take no offense—you do what you do well, and I, too, do my job well. The difference is, you treat the body, and I treat the spirit. Together, I suspect we could heal anything." She laughed again.

I shook my head. "Unfortunately, there are still diseases that no one can conquer. And suffering—" I thought suddenly of Elyssa and asked, "Do the Warringtons come here often?"

Sadness came into Señora Mendez's eyes. "Yes, from time to time. The boy sees specialists in San Juan, and it is difficult for the Warringtons to stay in the city. Here they have more privacy—few questions are asked."

I hesitated. "I met the daughter last night—Elyssa—a lovely girl. I think it strange that she stays in their suite all the time."

The woman's expression turned to wariness. "Dr. Harwell, my clients sometimes confide in me, and I'm proud that they trust me so much. At the same time, you realize I cannot divulge their personal secrets any more than you can speak about your patients. I will say only this: Leave the girl alone. Tell no one you have seen her. It is for the best."

"How can you say that?" I sputtered. "Best for a young girl to be locked away from the world—a prisoner in her own home?"

"You do not understand and I cannot explain. The Warringtons are good and decent people caught in a tragedy not of their making. Do not interfere, I beg you. You will only make things worse." She stood up and walked away quickly, and I was left with a growing feeling that I was the only sane person in a crazy world.

Adrian was awake and dressing for dinner when I returned to the suite. I told him of my conversation with

Señora Mendez, and he frowned. "Señora Mendez is a wise woman. Her advice is generally sound. Perhaps you should heed it."

"How can you say that?" I exploded. "A helpless girl is being made a victim and everyone seems to want to deny her very existence! Now, you, too! She's real! Don't you believe me? I spoke with her, walked with her! She's real, and she's in pain!"

"Oh, she's real, I don't deny that. I, too, spoke with her."

"*What*? When?"

"A short time ago, while you were downstairs. I woke up and decided to sit out on the balcony for a little while. As you know, the Warringtons' balcony adjoins ours. I was enjoying the ocean air when suddenly something ran up my arm and I heard a soft giggle behind me.

" 'Don't be afraid,' a young woman's voice said. 'It was only a chameleon—they're quite harmless.'

"She introduced herself to me then, and we reached over the balcony rails to shake hands. She told me that she had enjoyed meeting you last night—she seems to think you're quite wonderful. We spoke only for a moment or two, and then she said, 'Someone's coming! I have to go now.' I heard the sliders opening and footsteps on the balcony, and then she was gone."

"But you met her!" I exclaimed. "You must realize now that she's a nice young girl who has every right to a normal life! It's wrong to keep her locked up, and you and I must do something about it!"

Adrian was silent for a long while.

"Well, don't you agree?" I asked impatiently.

"It may not be as simple as that," he said slowly. "If what I suspect is true, you cannot help her."

I nearly shouted. "What are you talking about? What is it you suspect?"

He sighed and shook his head. "I shouldn't speak until I'm certain." He turned his attention to his cuff links.

I put my hands to my temples. "Curiouser and curiouser! I'm beginning to think I've somehow fallen down a rabbit hole!"

I half expected Adrian to laugh at my bewilderment and explain himself, but he didn't. His face grew very serious, and he said nothing more.

During the next two days I saw little of any of the Warringtons. Alan and his father appeared for breakfast in the dining room and shortly thereafter drove off in a limousine along with the nurse, presumably to visit Alan's doctor. The broad-shouldered valet remained behind—I assumed he was to keep an eye on the girl. I half expected Elyssa to take advantage of being left with only one watchdog and somehow escape from the Warrington suite, but she did not. Both nights, shortly before midnight, I walked the shoreline, but the beach was empty. On Wednesday night, however, I was returning to the hotel in disappointment when Elyssa stepped out from the shadow of a palm tree.

"Oh, it's you, Dr. Harwell. Hello." Her voice was filled with sadness.

"Are you all right, child?"

"As well as I can be."

"Is there anything I can do to help you?"

She shook her head, her curls flying. "I'm afraid no one can help me. I'll never be free until they're dead."

"Don't say such things!" I said, alarmed.

"It's true!"

"It doesn't need to be! I'll help you. Somehow, we'll get you free."

"How little you understand!" To my dismay, she began to cry.

"But I want to understand! You must explain what is going on."

"They hate me! They're ashamed of me, and they have been, ever since I was born. They say that's when Alan's troubles began, and that it's all my fault."

"Well, how can that be? You were just a baby! You

couldn't cause any trouble! What else happened at that time?"

She sniffed. "Mother died. Alan took her death hard. He was only five at the time, and it affected his mind. He's been seeing doctors ever since."

"What exactly is Alan's problem?" I prodded. "Perhaps I can recommend—"

She shook her head. "You can't help. Alan's seen doctors all over the world. He's just not a very strong person. He's been in mental institutions, you know. After a while he gets better and they let him out, but before long, he can't cope again. Don't think I don't feel sorry for him—I do. But it still isn't fair the way they treat me!"

"I agree. And there must be *something* I can do!"

She looked up and I saw her tears glistening in the moonlight. "If only there were!" She stood up. "I have to go now. They'll miss me before long." She blew me a kiss and darted into the shadows.

On Thursday morning, when I came down to the dining room, I saw that Bernard Warrington was having breakfast alone. As Adrian had opted to sleep late, I was also eating alone, and I ventured to ask Mr. Warrington whether I could join him. "Of course, Dr. Harwell. Please sit down." We spoke of the weather and the stock market, of government bonds and foreign currency prices, but Bernard Warrington's heart didn't seem to be in the conversation. He looked worried. I surmised that whatever Alan's doctors had said, it wasn't good. Yet, I felt I had to press on for Elyssa's sake. Over our second cup of coffee, I said gently, "Oh, by the way, I met your daughter."

The effect on the man was electric. His hand began to tremble so violently that he nearly spilled his coffee. There was a long silence as he struggled to regain his composure. Then he said, "I have no daughter."

"But—Elyssa—" I sputtered.

"I do not wish to discuss Elyssa, Dr. Harwell. I suggest you mind your own business." And with that, he jerked his chair back and wheeled himself out of the dining room.

I was flabbergasted. Was there no end to this madness? Couldn't I reason with anyone?

A short while later, I saw Alan at the newsstand near the main desk. It was now or never, I told myself. *Someone* had to have *some* feeling for the girl. "Mr. Warrington," I said as I approached, "Do you remember me—Dr. Harwell?"

He gave me the ghost of a smile. "Of course, Doctor. How are you?"

"I, quite frankly, am disturbed. I met your sister—"

But I got no further. Alan Warrington's face went white. "Elyssa? She's been out? Father didn't tell me—oh, my god!" He began to perspire heavily and his whole body trembled. "Excuse me," he whispered. Then he turned and headed for the elevator.

I returned to our suite, where Adrian was again examining the small sculpture Señora Mendez had lent him. "This really is exquisite," he murmured as his fingers detected every nuance of the piece.

"Well, some things in this life are not so exquisite," I grumbled. "Some things are plain crazy!" I told him how I had tried to approach the two Warrington men, and how futile my efforts had been. He simply nodded and said nothing.

"I've been trying to figure out some rational explanation for all this," I said, "and I've come up with two possibilities."

"Yes?"

"The first is that Mrs. Warrington died giving birth to Elyssa and both men have somehow concluded that Elyssa was responsible for her death. And because little Alan took his mother's death so hard that he developed emotional problems, Elyssa has been blamed for his troubles as well. Consequently, as incredible as it seems, they have made her a nonperson, simply refusing to recognize that she exists, as punishment for her 'crime.'"

Adrian nodded. "It's possible. Stranger things have happened. And your other theory?"

"My other theory is based on the fact that when I mentioned Elyssa to Mr. Warrington, the first thing he said was, 'I have no daughter.' And what struck me about that was my conviction that he was telling the truth! Now, it may be that he has denied her for so long he truly believes he has no daughter. Or—it may be that Mrs. Warrington was unfaithful to him—that Elyssa was her daughter but not his. That might explain the remarkable difference in coloring between Alan and the girl, even though there is a definite facial resemblance. If Elyssa is indeed not Warrington's child, I can understand—though I don't condone—his trying to deny her existence."

Adrian said nothing. "Well?" I asked. "What do you think?"

"You may be right."

"But you don't believe it. Why don't you tell me what your theory is?"

He shook his head. "My idea is a bit preposterous. If I'm wrong, it's better I say nothing."

"*Damn!*" I fumed. "Everyone around here seems to know something I don't! I—"

I stopped. There were voices coming from the adjoining suite. I hurried into my room and lay down on the bed, my ear to the wall. Adrian followed me.

"I *will* not have it! You deliberately disobeyed me!" This was Bernard Warrington's voice.

"I didn't do anything wrong! I only went for a walk. I said hello to some people! What's so terrible about that?"

"What is so terrible is what you've done to Alan! He's so weak, he can hardly stand! Your behavior is killing him!"

"I don't care! Do you hear me? *I don't care!*" The girl was screaming now. "All you're concerned about is Alan! Whenever you have to choose between us, you always choose him! And I'm all alone!"

I was momentarily shocked to hear her once again

express so little emotion at the thought of her brother's demise. I couldn't help but think how like a small child's her reasoning was. But that was to be expected. They had not educated her, not allowed her to mature—she couldn't be sympathetic to anyone else's problems when no one had ever shown concern for hers.

She spoke again: "He's so weak and sickly, maybe he'd be better off dead!"

"Don't you *ever* say that!" Bernard Warrington's voice struck a strange note. Through the wall I heard a moan. Then I heard Alan say, "What's going on here? *What have you done?*"

"I didn't do anything! He was yelling at me and his face got all red, and he put his hands to his head—"

Then Alan was shouting, "Nurse! Nurse!"

I looked at Adrian. "I've got to go over there. I think Mr. Warrington's had a stroke."

A moment later, I knocked at the door of the Warringtons' suite. The valet opened it and looked at me. "I heard a commotion," I said. "I'm a doctor. If I can help—" I was quickly ushered into the bedroom, where Bernard Warrington lay unconscious. He did not look good. The nurse was on the phone, calling for an ambulance. Alan was standing beside the bed, holding his father's hand. "You can't die, you can't!" he murmured. I looked around but saw no sign of Elyssa. The Warrington suite was considerably larger than the one Adrian and I had, and I figured someone had hustled Elyssa into one of the other bedrooms when I knocked at the door.

There wasn't much I could do for Bernard Warrington besides make sure his airway was unobstructed and that he was kept warm until the ambulance came. It was apparent the stroke was a serious one and that if he survived, he faced several months or even years of recovery.

Alan looked terrible. He was perspiring heavily and I feared he was going into shock. Gently I led him to a chair in the corner of the room and wrapped him in a blanket.

"Right now, the best thing you can do for your father is take care of yourself," I said.

He nodded and seemed to shrink into the chair. I took his pulse—it was rapid and thready—and I noticed a large ragged scar across his wrist. I'd seen scars like that before on people who had attempted suicide. I worried that if Mr. Warrington died, the shock of his death might be more than Alan could deal with.

The ambulance and the paramedics arrived in short order and whisked Mr. Warrington off to the hospital. Alan insisted on going along, and the nurse accompanied him. The valet ushered me out of the suite rather abruptly and locked the doors behind me. I found myself in the hall, wondering about the girl. She must be frightened, I thought. Her father might well be dying—and she would probably be blamed for that, along with everything else. I considered knocking at the door and asking to see her, but I was sure the valet would refuse to let me back in.

As I debated what to do, Señora Mendez stepped off the elevator and walked up to me.

"I only just heard," she said. "How is he?"

"It doesn't look good," I replied. "They've taken him to the hospital. Alan and the nurse went along, but the girl's been left behind, and she's frightened, I'm sure—"

Señora Mendez looked at me for a moment, then she took my arm and led me away. "I beg you, Doctor, leave the girl alone. She will be all right. I will see to it."

By this time we were at the door to my suite and, feeling rather like a chastened schoolboy, I could do nothing but agree. Adrian turned his head when I came in. "What happened?"

I told him. "I fear the old man won't make it," I said. "All the signs are bad."

The next morning—Friday—we heard that Bernard Warrington was in a coma in critical condition. I didn't see Alan or the nurse around the hotel, so I assumed that they were staying at the hospital. I saw no sign of Elyssa or the valet, either.

That evening, I was asked to be a fourth at bridge and the game didn't break up until after midnight. I was waiting for the elevator when Señora Mendez approached, her face grim. "I have just had bad news, Doctor Harwell. Señor Warrington passed away a short while ago."

"Oh!" I exclaimed. "Poor Elyssa!"

She looked at me sternly. "You must not concern yourself about the girl. It is Alan who is in danger. Without his father, he may not survive."

I remembered how sickly the boy had looked the last time I'd seen him and I realized she was right. "His doctors," I said. "Someone should alert them."

"I have just been on the phone with them. Unfortunately, they feel Alan needs to be hospitalized, and he has always resisted that. His father was the only one who could convince him to sign the commitment papers."

I looked at her. "If you think I can help, I'll be happy to speak to the boy."

"Thank you, Doctor. Perhaps it will be necessary."

Once again I couldn't sleep. The clock on my bureau read 1:20 when I heard voices on the other side of the wall.

"You killed him!" Alan's voice was angry, but not strong.

"I *didn't* kill him! We were arguing, yes, but I couldn't help it if he had a stroke! It's not my fault!"

"I can't stand you! You've brought nothing but misery to us!"

"You haven't exactly made my life a bed of roses, Alan. But that's going to change now, isn't it?"

"What do you mean?"

"Without Father, you're not strong enough to control me! I'm going to be free! I'm going to live like everyone else!"

"You can't! You mustn't!"

"Try to stop me!"

"You'll kill me—you can't do this!"

"If my freedom kills you, dear Alan, then so be it!"

I admit I didn't understand all the nuances of the conversation. Why Alan should be so frightened at the prospect of his sister living a normal life was beyond me. And once again I found myself feeling chilled by Elyssa's attitude. She seemed not at all sad at the loss of her father. And she showed no compassion for Alan's distress.

It was no consolation to realize that her outlook was probably normal considering the abnormal way she'd been raised. Children who have been abused are often lacking in compassion. And their very insensitivity is nothing more than a defense against their own pain. But someone would have to teach Elyssa all the things she had not been taught during her curious childhood.

In the morning I learned that an autopsy was being performed on the elder Warrington, as is usual in cases of sudden death. The body would not be released for at least another day, which meant the rest of the Warrington party could not leave immediately. I promised myself to speak to Alan at the first opportunity, suggesting therapy for Elyssa.

But my good intentions were not to be carried out. Alan did not leave the Warrington suite at all on Saturday, and on Sunday Adrian and I were at breakfast in the dining room when to my astonishment, Elyssa entered. In the full light of day, her beauty was startling. She wore rather too much makeup for early morning, but I have noticed that many young women do. Her pale blue silk shirtwaist and ivory slippers were the essence of femininity. Her hair hung loose in the rather touseled look that was so popular just then. Gold hoop earrings matched her wide gold bracelet. Altogether, she was a remarkably lovely girl, and heads turned as she walked across the room to take a table by the window.

I got up and walked over to her. "Elyssa," I said, "I heard about your father. I'm sorry."

She looked up at me and smiled. "Thank you. But you

needn't be sorry. These things turn out for the best. Father was quite old, and his heart was not strong.''

Again I was stunned at her lack of feeling and had to remind myself that she had never been taught appropriateness of remark or emotion.

"How is Alan taking it?" I asked.

"Oh!" She waved her hand. "You know Alan! Goes to pieces over every little thing!''

I was speechless. What could I say to a remark like that? I began to worry that the emotional damage done to her was beyond repair. Perhaps she would never have feelings for others.

"It's Miss Warrington, isn't it?" Adrian's voice came over my shoulder. He extended his hand and Elyssa grasped it, smiling. Adrian took her hand in both of his and held it tenderly, fingering it as he would a work of art. "Our meeting the other day was so brief," he said. "I'm glad to be able to see you again—so to speak.''

Elyssa laughed. "And I'm delighted to see you again, Mr. Christopher. I've heard you're an artist. I'd love to discuss your work with you sometime.''

Adrian nodded. "I would enjoy that very much. Perhaps soon." He left us then, and I said to Elyssa, "I must speak with Alan.''

"That won't be possible.''

"Why not?" I asked, surprised.

"Alan's gone." She bent over her menu and studied it with interest. "Oh, my! I think I'll have French toast with strawberries. Sounds scrumptious, doesn't it?''

I was dismissed. I went back to Adrian and found I had no appetite. "Something is terribly wrong," I said. "The girl is a deficient personality, as might be expected from her isolation and social deprivation, but there's something else—I can't put my finger on it. My God! I get the chills when she speaks! And I'm really worried about the boy.''

Adrian shook his head. "I'm afraid it may be already too late for him.''

"What does that mean?"

But before he could answer me, the waiter came to take
our order, and then a middle-aged woman approached
our table and introduced herself as a devotee of Adrian's
earlier works. Adrian, ever gracious, invited her to join
us, and I realized I would have to wait to learn what was
on my friend's mind.

As we were finishing our coffee, I saw that Elyssa had
gotten up and was walking out of the dining room. I went
after her.

"I must talk to Alan," I said again as I caught up with
her.

"I already told you—you can't!" She entered the elevator and I followed her.

"Where has he gone? I'll get a message to him."

"Why is everyone always interested in Alan?" she
cried impatiently.

"I'm interested in you, too," I said in what I hoped was
a soothing voice. "But I must talk to Alan."

She stared at me for several moments.

"At least let me speak to Alan's nurse."

"I've dismissed her," she said simply. "Wilson, too. I
don't need them."

"But Alan does," I said.

She didn't reply. The elevator doors opened and she
stepped out. I went after her. She took a key from her
pocket and unlocked the door to the Warrington suite.

"Look, I promise to help you be as free as you like. All
I ask is a few minutes with Alan. He must go into the
hospital."

She turned in the doorway and looked me in the eye.
"No. No more hospitals. Not ever!"

"Don't you want him to get well?" I knew it was the
wrong thing to say as soon as the words escaped my lips.
But I wasn't prepared for what she said next: "Alan can't
get well. He's dead."

"What—what happened?"

"Nothing happened. He simply died. He was tired of

living. That's all." She stepped into the suite and made a move to close the door in my face, but I was too fast for her. I pressed forward and forced my way in.

"I don't believe you! Where's his body? I want to see it."

"No one will ever find it," she said simply. "What difference does it make?"

"Difference?" My mind was beginning to whirl. "Elyssa, child, you can't simply dispose of a body! The authorities have to be notified, no matter how Alan died. I will call them if you won't."

"You mustn't!"

"I *have* to!"

"But if they can't find Alan, will they put me in jail?" There was a plaintive—even childlike—note in her voice.

"I'm sure they won't," I said. "You need help, Elyssa. After all you've been through, you need a doctor more than—"

"I'm *not* going to a hospital!" Her eyes filled with panic. "They lock you up! I want to be *free!*"

And before I could stop her, she darted into one of the bedrooms and locked the door.

"Elyssa!" I pounded on the door. "There's no reason to be frightened. I'll help you."

I heard the sliders in the bedroom open onto the balcony, and I suddenly knew what she was going to do. I rushed to the sliders in the sitting room, but I wasn't fast enough. I caught a glimpse of blue silk disappearing over the wrought iron railing. There were screams from below.

As fast as my legs would carry me, I ran down the fire stairs and out onto the terrace. Quite a crowd had gathered. "Let me through! I'm a doctor!" I shouted, puffing.

As people moved back, I hesitated to look directly at Elyssa, but I saw the blue dress. One ivory slipper lay off to the side near a wide gold bracelet. Then Elyssa tried to move, and her hair fell off. The touseled black curls lay on the terrace and cradled a bloodied head of thinning blond hair. I grasped one wrist and saw a wide ragged scar.

"It's a man!" a woman in the crowd screamed.

And indeed the body I was examining was male, but the soul that looked out at me through those blue eyes was female.

"I . . . had as much right . . . to a body as . . . he did," she gasped. Then she went limp and her pulse disappeared.

I closed her eyes and removed my jacket and placed it over her face.

"You knew, didn't you?" I asked Adrian later that day.

"I was pretty sure at breakfast this morning," he replied. "The bone structure of her hand was identical to Alan's, save for the false fingernails, of course. Chance of that in siblings other than identical twins is remote. There was a remarkable similarity in their gaits, too."

I shook my head. "I still find it hard to believe. She seemed so real."

"She *was* real. There are plenty of cases of multiple personalities on record, and quite a few in which the personalities are of opposite genders."

"She killed Alan, didn't she?"

"In a way. As she got stronger, he got weaker. But I don't think she was an evil person. To her it seemed a matter of survival. Her only crime was that she wanted to exist."

"What a strange life the two of them led!" I said sadly.

Adrian nodded.

A month or so later, he gave me a small clay figure he'd modeled. It was of a young woman in a peasant blouse and full skirt. Her long hair was touseled and she wore several bracelets under which, with a magnifying glass, it was possible to see the end of a ragged scar. Her arms were extended as if embracing an imaginary lover, and the expression on her face was one of childlike joy.

"I call it 'The woman in the shadows,' " Adrian said.

It is one of my most treasured possessions.

AMANDA CROSS

Tania's No Where

My name is Leighton Fansler. I have long wanted to publish some of the cases of my aunt, Kate Fansler, who, while never a private investigator in any professional sense—she certainly never had a license nor was she paid—took on, like Sherlock Holmes and Peter Wimsey, many interesting cases. She has been adamant until now about her refusal to let me tell the stories of any of her cases, and no one can be more adamant than Kate Fansler. I finally got her to admit, however, that this case was an exception. All those intimately concerned with it are now dead, and no harm could be done to anyone in the telling of it. Indeed, she mused, it might be of help to some.

What was clear to Kate at the very beginning of the case was that by the time Tania Finship was sixty-two, and almost the oldest member of the faculty in her department or anywhere else, she had become beloved. After her disappearance, it became clear that, in the opinion of her colleagues and students, she had not known this. She had done her job efficiently, curtly, honorably, and without notable tact, and had undoubtedly considered, if she reflected on the matter at all, that the outrage and anger she heard from students who had not done well in her courses represented the general opinion. As is, alas, so often the case among human beings, who tend, whatever their profession, to substitute tardy regret for timely expressions of appreciation, Tania Finship was gone before anyone had told her that they loved her.

If she was dead, there was no evidence to say so. Had her husband wished to claim her savings and remarry, he would have been hardput to do so before the statutory seven years. As it was, he mourned her, having always loved her and made his affection clear, if unspoken. She may have kept her professorship through tenure, as many disgruntled younger professors had been heard to mutter, but she kept her marriage because it suited them both: in the United States in those years one did not stay married unless one chose. Her children, grown and moved away, had come East when she disappeared, and finally returned to the West Coast, keeping in close touch with their father. As to her savings, all she and Tom, her husband, owned they had owned jointly. It was already his, but, as he often made clear after the disappearance, sharing it once again with her was his only, his fervent wish.

No one could imagine what had become of her. The police were as puzzled as the F.B.I. and the C.I.A., who had entered the case on the thinnest of suspicions that she had been part of a spy ring. Her parents had been Marxists and Trotskyites in the twenties and thirties, and one never knew for sure that they had not become Stalinists and planted Tania for future spying at birth. Unlikely, but the C.I.A. is nothing if not expert at the unlikely. She might have waited all those years, until her children were grown, and then taken off with her ill-gotten information. What information a professor of Russian literature could have acquired in a blameless life was at best unclear, at worst nonsense. Still, she did read and speak Russian, and what is more she had been clearly heard to say critical things about the United States government. Anything might be suspected of someone as profoundly antinuclear and antiwar as Tania.

"Which," as Fred Manson said to Kate Fansler, "is just the problem. The C.I.A. has got this ridiculous bee in their bonnet, but the result is everyone has just decided she's in Russia and stopped looking—everyone who had the ghost of a chance of finding her, that is. And the students are getting restless. They've heard her hold forth, and they're perfectly sure leaving this country or even her penthouse for more than a few hours was the last thing she wanted. If Tania had ever had any wanderlust, she had long since lost it, or so the students and her husband reported. The point is, can you help us? I've heard a lot about you."

"What do you think happened?" Kate asked.

Fred Manson heaved a great sigh. "I try not to think," he said. "The fact is, Tania was a bit of a burden in the department; conscientious, heavens yes, and hardworking, and highly intelligent. But she had taken to cultivating a crusty manner that was as hard on her colleagues as it was on her students. You want an example? All right; at a meeting of the curriculum committee some weeks ago, when we were discussing next year's catalog, I had to report that some man who had promised to teach the survey course next year was now refusing to do so. Tania was in charge of survey courses, and was considerably annoyed, as anyone would be at that news that late. What she said was: 'Couldn't we just tell him to go pee up a rope?' "

"I see what you mean," Kate said. "You're not suggesting that the man in question heard about it and abducted her?"

"I'm not suggesting anything; certainly not that. But it's hard enough to run a language department. They're the worst kind: for some reason those who teach languages become ornery from the moment they learn about inflected nouns, without having them talk nothing but mayhem, kidnaping, and worse. Find out what happened to her, please, for the sake of the academic world and my sanity. The department has discretionary funds, and the university will help, all on the q.t., of course. The university position is that she needed an emergency operation and doesn't want anyone to know. They may have to admit a scandal, but not before it's absolutely necessary."

"I should think," Kate said, "that the feelings of the university were not anyone's prime concern. They certainly wouldn't be mine. You've checked the hospitals?"

"Everything has been checked," Fred Manson said. "Everything. When my mother used to lose things, she always said they had disappeared into thin air. Of course, they always turned up fifteen minutes later. If there's one thing I can't stand, it's cliches enacting themselves. Tania's no where, God damn it, no where."

"I'll think about it," Kate said. "I'll let you know my decision in a few days. Meanwhile, may I talk to Tania's husband? Will he see me?"

"I'll damn well make sure he'll see you," Fred Manson said. Kate could not but reflect that, chancy as the Chair's disposition clearly was, this disappearance had done nothing to improve it. Could Tania have simply decided to vanish for the sheer joy of ruining Fred Manson's life and temper? Or could the husband, however devoted he was reported to be, have also inspired such retribution?

One hour with Tom Finship proved that supposition as unsubstantial as all the others had been. He greeted Kate in the penthouse on Riverside Drive he had long shared with his vanished wife. They had bought it many years ago, for a now (given the state of New York City real estate) ridiculously low sum. As their penthouse had risen in value, they had always talked of selling it and buying a house in the country where their gardening joys might really have scope. But the moment had never arrived. The terraces on the penthouse were large, and while Kate Fansler could scarcely tell a lilac from a rhododendron, there was no question even to her ignorant eye that this was an extraordinary rooftop garden. "The house in the country never quite worked out," Tom said when they were once again seated on the terrace after the tour. Kate, looking over the Hudson River to New Jersey and sipping the ice tea with which Tom had served them, did not try to hide her scrutiny of Tania's husband from him. He was in that state of calm which follows upon terrible news, but also in the state where talk is necessary and all but ceaseless. Kate, glad to serve as an audience to one who would be helped simply by talking, also needed to learn all he could tell her, which was the story of their lives.

"We would have had to trade this"—his arm swept to indicate the whole terrace with its rich plant life—"for a small apartment and a house, and somehow the whole thing never fell into place. God knows we had great offers for this place, but when we looked at the small apartments we could by then afford we began to feel cramped, cabined, cribbed, and confined, as Hamlet said, before we had even tried it out. And with a house in the country, Tania would have been there only weekends and in the summer. So we just kept talking about it. Now, without her—" He did not complete the sentence.

"It was Macbeth," Kate said. "Hamlet talked about being bound in a nutshell. When did you retire?"

"Five years ago," Tom said. "I was a professor at City College, and I just couldn't take it any more, teaching remedial English and being mugged in the parking lot. A lot of us took early retirement when the system, in order to get rid of us, made it especially attractive. And it wasn't really the remedial English and the parking lot, it was just that I'd been at the same game too long. As you can see, I've even forgotten my Shakespeare—not that I'd taught him since open admissions."

"Have you enjoyed the retirement, until this came along?"

"Moderately. The days pass. I like working around the house. I have a few investments, and they need looking after. I've always wanted to write a novel, but having all day isn't particularly conducive to creation, or so I've found. Funny thing, though, I discovered I really liked cooking. Tania always said she had the oldest kitchen boy

in town. We had people in a lot, for dinner, drinks out
here. It was a good life. Regular. It doesn't make any
sense."

"What do you mean by 'regular'?"

"Every day was just like every other. Well, not exactly,
of course. The days Tania taught were different from the
days when she didn't teach. We joked: if Tania's teaching
Chekhov, it must be Tuesday. And then every afternoon,
when she'd come back from the university—she taught in
the morning and advised from one to three—or just when
the hour came round, on the days she didn't teach, she'd
take her walk. Down Riverside Drive, across Seventy-
second Street to Broadway, down Broadway to
Fifty-ninth, and across to Fifth Avenue. Then she'd turn
and come back, without the carrots."

"Carrots?"

"For the horses, the ones that pull the carriages through
the park. For tourists, I suppose. Tania loved to offer them
a carrot each, brightening their lives. It's funny how it
began, really." Tom seemed lost in thought.

"How?" Kate urged him.

"She was crossing Fifty-ninth one day, she told me—
going somewhere, not on her exercise walk—and a little
girl got out of one of the carriages she was riding in with
her family, to have her picture taken with the horse, and
she tried to feed the horse a carrot, holding it upright, by
its end. Of course, the horse took her hand with the carrot
and the girl dropped it, screaming. To the rescue, Tania.
She showed the girl how to hold her hand flat with the
carrot on it, and calmed her down, although, Tania said,
she couldn't convince the child to try again. That's what
put the idea of carrots for the horses in Tania's mind.
Also, it gave her a destination for her walk and made it
possible for her to say she walked almost three miles
every day—warding off osteoporosis, and other dangers
of aging."

Tom fell into a sort of trance, staring out over the
Hudson River. "I've been thinking," he finally said, "how

we work so hard to avoid the dangers of old age, now that we live so long, and then, suddenly, we're gone."

"There's no real evidence she's 'gone,' " Kate said.

"I can't believe she wouldn't have let me know, if she was able to. Something terrible must have happened."

"You've been married a long time then," Kate said, not making it a question.

"We were married in the war. We both finished graduate school, and then the children were born. Tania taught all through those years; we needed the money. It was a busy life, but a good one. The children keep calling," he added, reminded of them. "I've gotten to dread the phone calls. 'No news, Pop?' And I always have to say, 'No news.' She can't just have disappeared into thin air," he concluded in an unconscious echo of Fred Manson.

"What have the police done?" Kate asked, more to have something to ask him than because she needed to be told. The police had put Tania on their Missing Persons computer, and had made inquiries—perfunctory, Kate felt sure. There had been no ransom notes, no signs at all. Either she was dead—though in that case where was the body?—or she had chosen to vanish. The police admitted that, in the case of aging wives, this was unlikely. Amnesia? Possibly. But the hospitals had received no one of that sort, nor had the shelters for the homeless. Weren't there a lot of homeless women on the streets? God knows there were, and one could hardly question all of them, though most of them were well enough known in their neighborhoods. Still, no one was likely to report a new bag lady. The police shrugged, officially and metaphorically. Call them when there was a body.

After a while, Kate ran out of questions and Tom fell into silence. She left him finally with sympathetic reassurances, but without much hope on either side.

Later that week, Kate called Fred Manson and told him that frankly she didn't think there was much she could do. Just for the hell of it, she had walked Tania's exercise route, but no inspiration followed. It was a rainy day, and there were not many horse carriages lined up—just a few across from the Plaza, the horses, under their blankets, looking sad, and the drivers, under their raincoats, looking sullen.

Fred Manson was not in the best of humors when Kate reached him, and he told her, far from tactfully, that she had been their last hope but not, as far as he was concerned, a very likely one. He'd been told she had a reputation as a detective, but in his view detectives had their being exclusively between the covers of books highly suspect as to quality. Only Dostoyevsky had been able to write intelligently of crime, and he showed you the murder taking place—no nonsense about clues. Kate wanted to say she vaguely remembered a detective in that novel, but resisted the impulse.

"Well," Manson said, "I'll have to hire a substitute for her in the fall if she isn't back by the end of this semester. I've got an assistant professor filling in her classes, but it's hardly fair to anyone. Do let me know," he added unkindly, "if you're inspired with any knowledge of her whereabouts. I certainly hope she returns, but I don't mind telling you, it's the uncertainty that's killing us all." And that was the end of the story as far as anyone knew.

Then, just about at the end of that semester, Tania called Fred Manson and said she was back, she'd just been away a while, and she'd be teaching and everything as usual in the fall semester. Naturally, Fred wanted to know where she'd been and how she was, but she wouldn't say much, just that she was back and that it was good to see Tom, who was glad to have her back, the children were also relieved, and they could all now forget the whole thing and enjoy their summer.

Except, Tania added, Fred ought to call Kate Fansler and thank her, and apologize for being such a prick (obviously Tania's language hadn't been changed by her absence), because it was due to Kate she was back. She

was never, Tania announced, going to say another word
about it, but she didn't think Fred ought to have sneered
at Kate as a detective. Kate didn't identify with criminals,
like the detective in Dostoyevsky and other deep types,
but she was damn good and Fred might as well say so.
Fred did write Kate a rather gracious letter, and that was
that for a long while. It was only many years later, when
Kate told me about Tania, that I learned the part of the
story nobody else had ever been told.

Tania and Tom were both killed in a car crash years
after Tania had retired, and it was when Kate heard that
she finally told me the whole story. Kate doesn't often fall
into a reminiscent, story telling vein, but she did that day.

Kate said it was the most patient, foot-slogging work
she'd ever done. I like this case because I think only Kate
could have solved it. Policemen and tough-guy detectives
don't bother with cases where they haven't got a body and
a bellyful of hate in at least five suspects. That's what
made this the perfect Fansler case. At least, pointing that
out was how I got Kate to let me publish it.

Somehow, Kate kept finding herself across from the
Plaza, studying the horse-drawn carriages. She seemed to
have developed a new consciousness of the things; they
stopped being a familiar background and moved into the
foreground of her awareness. Many years before, she and
Reed, when they were newly met, had hired a carriage
and tried to imitate the proper romantic attitudes connected with them. They had ended up dissolved in
laughter, at their own antics and the prattle of the driver,
who took them for newlyweds and tourists, pointing out
features of Central Park that Kate had known since birth.
The ride had cost five dollars, which indicated how long
ago that had been. The notices on the carriages Kate
observed informed the romantic and unwary that the
price was seventeen dollars for the first quarter hour.
Despite these prices, business was good, to judge from the
number of carriages lined up, especially on the weekends.

On a warm spring weekday afternoon Kate hired one. The driver was a young girl in a top hat, her blonde hair seeming to pour out below it to the middle of her back. Kate had approached the girl because she looked some-how easier than the male drivers to induce into conver-sation as opposed to barker talk. Her other attraction was that she had tacked onto the front of her carriage a neat placard announcing that she took American Express cards. The combination of the girl's attractiveness and Kate's lack of cash confirmed the matter.

"I'm not a tourist," Kate said, when they had turned off into the park at Sixth Avenue. "I really wanted to ask you about driving these things. It looks like every child's dream. Do most of the drivers like horses? Do they always drive the same horse?"

"Even tourists ask that," the girl said, smiling to make the words pleasant. "Some of us do, some of us don't, to both questions. Mostly we drive the same horse, but if we aren't going to be out, someone else takes over, on a weekend, say. I always try to drive this horse; her name, though you might never guess, is Nellie. She's one of the few mares; mostly they're geldings."

"Do any of you own your horses?"

"Not many any more. You writing a book or some-thing?"

"Not even 'or something,' " Kate said. "I've just got interested."

"Why don't I give you the usual spiel without your having to ask the questions; would that help?" Kate laughed, sitting back, enjoying the slower pace and the sound of the hoofs on the road. The park was closed to cars in the afternoon, and the forsythia was out. Kate couldn't think why she hadn't done this before. Because, she guessed, one thought of it only as a couple or family thing, while it was (though she saw not a single other carriage with only one person in it) an ideal solitary experience. Kate asked for the "usual spiel."

"We all keep our horses in the same stable," the girl

began. "The carriages, too. There's a good bit of turnover in drivers. As I said, we like horses—or if we don't we pretend to. It would never do to be mean to a horse in the public eye, and we're always in the public eye. That last was not part of the usual spiel, as I'm sure you've guessed. There are rules regulating the treatment of the horses. On the hottest days in summer, they can't stay out too long, and they have to have water, and blankets in the winter. People worry a lot more about the horses than the drivers. I don't usually say that, either."

"There's a novel by Aldous Huxley," Kate said, "in which some animal lovers take an ill-treated horse away from the man who works it, and as a result the man starves to death together with his family. Nobody notices that."

"You a professor or something?"

"Do only professors read?" Kate asked.

"Nobody ever mentioned a book to me before—at least, not a book like that. In the summer when there are more carriages to go out, we get some guys from college as drivers. They don't last very long, but they've read a book. Probably some of the customers are readers, but they don't have books on their minds. You'd be surprised what goes on in these carriages sometimes, particularly at night—I mean, people make out anywhere. I like a little privacy myself, but it all goes with the territory, I guess. Anything else I can tell you? This trip's going to cost you already."

Kate agreed to return, and watched the driver pull out her charge card machine and then write out Kate's charges. Kate signed the slip, adding a generous tip. "Thanks a heap," the young woman said; "any time."

"Do many people feed the horses carrots?" Kate asked as an afterthought, pocketing her receipt.

"A lot. Occasional children, though mostly they don't know how, and old ladies who are pretty regular about it. People used to feed the horses sugar, which was bad for them, although they loved it, of course. But the new diet mania in America has helped horses. Most people don't seem to have lumps of sugar any more; it's more carrots now, much better for the horses."

Kate thanked her again. "It's been a pleasure meeting you," she said. "I may be back." And she was the next day, and the day after that.

Kate got into the way of coming almost every afternoon with carrots for the horses, and sometimes an apple. After a while, she began to distinguish between the horses and to recognize the drivers, who tolerated her and even greeted her, a not untypical female animal lover of the sort they found familiar. But this one distinguished herself by occasionally hiring a carriage and taking a ride—not often, but often enough to keep hopes and tolerance high. The regular carrot ladies never rode.

Kate, of course, could come only in the afternoon, and not every day. Unlike amateur detectives, whether the effete upperclass English variety or the tough American kind, Kate had a full-time job. I've never really understood what a professor does who teaches only four to six hours a week, though Kate tried to explain it to me once. There are committee meetings and office hours and the need to go on writing and publishing and presenting papers at conferences. That spring, though, Kate devoted a lot of time to horse-drawn carriages. She's an animal lover, like all the Fanslers—I sometimes think it's all she and I share with the rest of the family—and she became quite fond of the horses after a couple of weeks.

There was one driver she noticed, indeed everyone noticed, who worked almost every day, including weekends, and who stood out because he dressed up for the part. He looked exactly like a cabbie from a Sherlock Holmes movie. He wore a black suit, a white tie and shirt, and a top hat. You almost expected someone to get into his carriage, hit the roof (there wasn't any roof, of course) with his cane, and say, "Victoria Station, driver, and hurry."

Kate took a ride with him one day. This was not as easy

as it sounds, because you couldn't just pick out the carriage and driver you wanted. They lined up in order, and you had to take the next one. Kate thought free enterprise would have been better demonstrated if the customers were allowed to choose their carriages; certainly the competition would have spruced up the carriages and done something for the drivers' appearance; most of them wore old pants and T-shirts, which is what made the elegant man so noticeable. He probably would have had all the customers if the customers had had the choice.

But one day, when Kate came and began her offer of carrots to the horses, the "Edwardian" driver, as she had come to think of him, was third in line. So she sauntered along, feeding and greeting the horses, and chatting with the drivers, until her man was first. Then she hired him.

His spiel turned out to be as unusual as his costume. He began by wishing her goodday and asking if she had any place she especially wanted to see. When Kate said no, just around the park, the driver asked if she would prefer that he talked or kept silent. "And if I keep silent, ma'am," the driver said with, Kate was amused to notice, just the hint of a cockney accent—one expected him to say "Right you are Gov'ner," but of course he didn't— "I'll still be here to answer questions, if any."

"I'd rather hear what you have to say," Kate said.

"Righto, ma'am," he said, turning sideways in his seat so that he could talk to Kate and at the same time keep an eye on the road and the horse. "This is the carousel. Been here over seventy-five years; they give the horses a bit of paint every so often, and change the tunes. Fifty years ago they still had rings you caught as you went by, silver rings but one gold, and if you got the gold they gave you a free ride." The man seemed to embrace all the park as he spoke of it, as though it were his creation; certainly it was his special pride.

"How long have you been driving a carriage?" Kate asked.

"Oh, most of my life, ma'am, one way or another. I was driving in the park before they ever closed it to cars. I remember when people were married at the Plaza and they would have a horse-drawn carriage ready to start them on their honeymoon. There were fewer of us in those days, and a different type, ma'am, if you take my meaning. I sometimes try to imagine what New York was like when there were only horse-drawn vehicles about."

"It probably smelled of horse manure and not carbon monoxide," Kate said, sitting back and enjoying herself as the description of the passing park scene continued. She didn't interrupt with any more questions; she mused. Wherever Kate is, if she's into musing, she muses. I like to think of her riding around the park on that spring day.

In the end, Kate paid the driver with cash; he did not have a charge-card notice on his carriage and she had come equipped with enough cash. "I like the way you drive," Kate said. "Is there a time I can come when I'll be fairly certain of getting you?"

"This is a good day," he said. I think it was a Tuesday. "If you come about the same time you did today, we ought to connect. Sometimes business is brisker than other times, so you might miss me, or you might have to wait. The other drivers are all good chaps," he added.

"I'm sure they are," Kate said. "I like your top hat and your line of patter, and your spruced-up carriage. Maybe I'll try again."

And she did try again, a week later. The spring semester was coming to a close, and Kate had to all but walk out on a meeting to get to Central Park South in plenty of time. It was not a particularly fine day, and the Edwardian driver was fourth from the head of the line. Kate sat on a bench with the other drivers—those were the only benches on that block—and corrected term papers while she was waiting. To her astonishment, she looked up to see "her" driver pulling his horse out of the rank of waiting carriages and driving off. Kate leapt into the carriage at the head of the line: "Follow that carriage!" she said to the driver.

"What? The horse-drawn one?"

"Yes. Hurry!"

"I can't follow him, lady. He's off back to the stables. I can't take no customers there."

"For a hundred dollars?"

"I might make an exception," he said, whipping up the horse. "But I want to see it."

Kate leaned forward and handed him three twenties. She'd really learned about cash and horse-drawn carriages. This was no moment for American Express, even if it had been the blonde young lady. "Here's sixty. You'll get the other forty when we're there."

But, as it happened, they soon caught up with Kate's Edwardian driver, who pulled over and acknowledged defeat, more with a gesture than anything. Cars started honking, Kate handed her driver the other forty, thanked him, got into the other carriage and said: "Back to the park, my good man."

The man had to go around the block to Sixth Avenue and head toward the park. Kate waited until they were through the traffic and back on the park road. Then, "Why did you take off like that?" she asked.

"It was the papers you were correcting, waiting for me. They rang a bell, somehow. Suddenly, I remembered having heard about you and knew who you were. They hired you, I guess."

"I wouldn't say 'hired,' " Kate said. "I haven't promised anything. I can forget I ever rode in a carriage. I've forgotten less forgettable things."

"After all your trouble?"

"No trouble; a pleasure, in fact. And I remembered the gold rings. My brothers used to brag about knowing how to get them. They were already gone in my day. Is this the life you want really, from now on? And of course, there's Tom."

"What made you guess?"

"Lots of things. His quoting Macbeth mainly, though he thought it was Hamlet. Hamlet may really have been closer: 'I could be bounded in a nutshell, and count myself a king of infinite space, were it not that I have bad dreams.' Was that it, or was it Macbeth: 'cribbed, cabined, confined'?"

"You mean you understand?"

"Lord, yes. But most of us don't have a dream to step into; we don't have a job to go to."

"I got to know this old man who drove. Met him when I was feeding the horses. I've always loved horses, not racehorses or riding horses or herding horses, but horses that pull carriages. He wanted to quit, and I offered him enough for his carriage and horse really to tempt him, if he could get them for me and the right to keep them where he did, to live where he did, right close to the stables. He said at first he couldn't manage it, but in the end he did. I was offering to exchange my escape for his and I knew it would work if I was patient."

"Is that his suit?"

"No. This outfit is all mine. He was a much smaller man, wizened and disillusioned about the carriages working the park these days."

"What about Tom? The worry it's been to him?"

"He's been worried, but I bet he's also felt alive; something to think about, to plan beyond. It's brought a change to his life, too; it was getting too predictable. As to the department—"

"I know," Kate said, "they can all pee up one rope. When will you decide about going back? Not that I want to rush you."

"Once more around the park; on me."

And so they rode around in silence. The evening was drawing in. "You mean I have a real choice?" the driver said, looking back at her, and when Kate nodded turned around and continued driving in silence. Until they were leaving the park:

"Mine has been such an orderly life," Tania said. "I

married when my mother and everyone else thought I should. Not that it wasn't a good marriage. We had children at the right time; they were good children. I guess working was the only unusual thing I did, and of course I became a language teacher, which was okay for a woman. Somehow, except when I was very young, there wasn't time for a dream, for an adventure. Suddenly, this seemed the perfect thing. A carriage, a horse, an outfit."

"You weren't afraid of being recognized?"

"Not in this outfit. People see what they expect to see. And I've always had a deep voice and a flat chest. Very good legs, though," Tania added.

When they pulled up at the curb on Central Park South, Kate said: "I get off here. I understand more than you'll ever know about how you felt. You decide it the way you want. I shan't say a word to anyone. And I won't bother you with any more rides if you decide to stay with your carriages and horses. But if you decide to go back, just call your Chair, dear Fred Manson, and announce your return next semester. 'Never apologize, never explain.' A good Victorian piece of advice."

As you know, Tania decided to return. And from that day to this, no one ever knew where she'd been and no one ever guessed. They were all glad to see her back—Tom, and the students, and even her colleagues—so she found out she was loved. Maybe that made her return more rewarding.

JANWILLEM VAN DE WETERING
The Jughead File

T ext of a police file used as study material in a detective course at the Police Academy of Kyoto:

A report drawn up by Inspector Third Class Saito Masanobu, Crime Squad, Municipal Police, Kyoto
                                                   Kyoto, 20 April 1979

Alerted by a telephone call made by Kogawa Sujuru, I visited a house, 7-3-5 Kawabata, this morning at ten o'clock. At the house, on the second and upper story, in a room at the rear, I found the lifeless body of a woman, Washino Maiko, 64 years old. Dr. Obata's report, stating the cause of death and a description of the woman's remains, is attached. Several garbage bags, made of grey plastic, had been cut open and tacked to the paper sliding doors and windows in order to block the flow of air. I found a small gas cylinder in the room, of the type that will fuel a cook-stove. The cylinder's faucet was open and its contents had escaped. Mrs. Washino lay on her bed on the straw floor-boards. Her arms were crossed on her chest.

The only other inhabitant of the house, Kogawa Sujuru, a forty-year-old man, told me: "It must have happened during the night. I had been drinking last night and slept deeply. I live downstairs and always spread my bed in the lower front room. When I woke I smelled gas and saw that the small cylinder that feeds gas to the kitchen stove had been removed. I ran upstairs to call Mrs. Washino. She adopted me as her son five years ago and she owns this house. I opened the door to her bedroom but staggered back because of the gas escaping into the corridor. I saw her in her bed, covered my mouth and nose with a cloth, rushed in, and opened the windows. I then called the police. Mrs. Washino suffered from depressions and often talked about suicide."

Kogawa is an artist, a painter, self-employed. I interrogated him in his studio, the rear room on the lower floor. He said: "I feel guilty. Mrs. Washino has never married and is quite well off. People from the neighborhood call her 'Mrs.' but that isn't really correct. It was most kind of her to be willing to adopt this humble person, a struggling artist, as her son. Thanks to her, I no longer have to sell my drawings and paintings in the street. Since Mrs. Washino accepted me as her official son, she made me comfortable here and paid all my expenses. I have been unworthy of her many gifts. I should at least have tried to cheer her up. Now I inherit all her possessions and cannot repay her many favors."

As both circumstances and the doctor's findings indicate that Washino Maiko died voluntarily and by her own hand, I conclude suicide.

A report drawn up by Inspector First Class Saito Masanobu, Crime Squad, Municipal Police, Kyoto

Kyoto, 3 May 1983

Alerted by a telephone call made by Miss Ozaki Jumoko, I visited a house, 7-3-5 Kawabata, at nine-thirty this morning. Miss Ozaki, a charwoman employed by Kogawa Sujuru, the well known artist, took me to the lifeless body of the owner of the house. It hung from a beam in the studio, the room at the rear on the first floor. Dr. Obata's report, stating the cause of death and a description of Kogawa's remains, is attached. I also attach a lengthy letter I found pinned to the kimono the corpse was wearing. After having ascertained that the handwriting was the same as that on various documents found in the house, and in view of the doctor's report and the circumstances I observed, I conclude suicide.

Letter written by Kogawa Sujuru directed to Inspector Saito Masanobu

Kyoto, May 2, 1983

Friend and Devil who pursues me:

You will doubtless remember what I told you when you visited here on the occasion of my adopted mother's untimely and unnatural death. You suspected that I was lying. My lies were convincing enough as I had wrapped them around the truth. My adopted mother died, four years ago, because she choked on poisonous gas and you interrogated me at length. I saw that your ears stand out rather and therefore called you "jughead"—not aloud, of course. The physical flaw that makes you look rather comical impressed me deeply.

You wanted to learn the truth. Did you ever hear the Buddhist tale about the onion? I refer to the comparison here because before you asked me all your questions, you said that you subscribe to the Zen Sect of the Buddhist faith. You treated me politely, even with some kindness, perhaps out of habit but also, it seemed to me, to make me drop my defenses. I own a small statue of Bodhidharma, the first Zen master, who came from India a long time ago. You admired that impressive work of art. I said that I had been given the little sculpture depicting the fat, angry-looking patriarch by my father. My father had in turn received it from the Zen master, Gota, the recently deceased teacher who was in charge of the Northern Temple.

Gota often talked about the onion. When we peel an onion, one layer after another comes off until finally only emptiness is left—just as the Buddhist training gradually peels off the ego so that we can enter the great void. You wanted to peel my onion, tear off my lies that, as a scaly hull, cover up my truth. For even I, I dare to presume, have the divine core, the silence that we all share in the end.

You sat there so strongly and quietly, like a monk in deep meditation. You wore a dark western-style suit of good

quality, tailor-made perhaps, a white shirt, and a narrow
tie. You had folded your legs, your head stood straight on
your shoulders, and your torso rested squarely on my poor
wornout floor. I felt that you didn't believe any of my filthy
fabrications, but I made them up anyway, so that you could
write them into your report. The death of my stepmother
was framed within those lies as a suicide that could not be
disputed. I said I was sorry so that my innocence might be
clear. Anyone who breaks the law is careful when the
police face him in his own quarters. You were my enemy,
a devil ready to drag me into hell.

A jugheaded devil?

A physical aberration increases the humanity of your
appearance. I beg your pardon—I'm not saying that you're
physically handicapped, like me. Did you mention in your
report that I have a hunchback and squint terribly?

I don't think you did, although the information could be
relevant. To what? To murder. Surely you noticed that my
stepmother was hunchbacked, too, and squinted behind
her thick glasses. Some people thought Mrs. Washino was
my mother long before she officially adopted me. In reality,
our similarities must be due to an interesting twist of fate.

Can I tell you something about my life? Even you, an
intelligent and well trained police officer, may learn
something about the way human relations come about.

My mother died shortly after my birth. My father was
ashamed that his son was a crippled horror but he
couldn't avoid raising his own child. He designed kimo-
nos for a well known store here in town. After my
mother's death, he got up early every morning and visited
Zen master Gota. I think my father wanted to know what
he had misdone in order to deserve a son like me. Surely
my handicaps and my mother's untimely death are consequences of mistakes he had made in previous lives.
Master Gota devised some riddles that my father was
supposed to solve and advised lengthy meditations so
that my father could reach his deeper mind.

My father always had little luck. Now he couldn't even

rest after his long hours of work, for which he was never properly paid. I wonder now if master Gota's efforts were very helpful. He heaped more questions on my father's basic query: why does a well meaning man have to suffer in his everyday existence? Zen riddles make little sense— they can't be solved logically and tend to drive the disciple crazy.

Stop the express train from Osaka. Have you ever heard of that Zen riddle? Isn't it rather a cruel command? My father must have thought so, for one day he was found dead on the railroad track. I think he was waiting for Buddha, thinking maybe the Holy One would show himself as a train. The corpse was mangled but I recognized his remains as those of my father. I was fourteen years old then.

The stop-the-train riddle interested me profoundly. Half my being originates in my father's genes—I am the continuation of all of his inquiry. I burn incense in front of his photograph now, but it would be better if I could find an answer to his question.

Stop the train from Osaka. How often didn't I stand on the track on the spot where the hill rises and one can see the ancient Tojy Pagoda on one side and the modern Grand Hotel on the other, a symbol of western civilization that has moved us so far forward in time. Time—that has to be the answer to the riddle, time that doesn't exist, but my father wouldn't see that. He still believed that he had to hurry somewhere, but master Gota wanted him to stop himself. He didn't suggest that my father should try to flag down a rushing train.

Shouldn't Zen masters be equipped with some psychological insight? Are such lofty souls allowed to push the silly under a train? I think master Gota was sorry, for he sent his head monk to take me to the temple. For two years I was given board and lodging at the monastery, went to school during the days and spent the evenings with the monks in meditation. They made me get up early so that I could sit quietly in the mornings, too, and whenever I dozed off they beat me with a stick. Afterward

I had to bow down to show my appreciation. Beating seems to be part of a proper education. There was an article in the paper the other day, praising the president of a company manufacturing luxury cars. He had beaten a student laborer with a wrench because the young fellow hadn't properly fastened a bolt.

The head monk was an aristocrat. Every time you visited me, you reminded me of him. You wore your tailor-made suit like he wore his robe. It's fashionable in the Zen temples to always wear the same robe, so that outside people can see how little money the monks are spending on themselves. When the fabric tears with age, the monks patch the holes. The head monk spent much time and trouble continuously repairing his robe, and it was a work of art, a most subtle combination of bits of cloth in all possible shades of blue and black. I often painted him, although he refused to model for me. Master Gota would say I wasted my time whenever he saw me busy with my brushes. He would confiscate my paintbox, but I got pocket money from the monks so that I could save up and keep replacing my supplies. When high school was over, I escaped from the temple and began to wander about. For many years I slept under bridges and tried to sell my work in the streets.

I was alone and hated everyone around me. Cripples learn how to hide their feelings, however. The other homeless bums abused me and kept stealing my money. I dreamed about revenge. Perhaps my hatred kept me alive in those days. Street-people die easily enough. They lie down somewhere, embrace themselves, sigh a few times, and die in their sleep. But I still needed life and was strengthened by my fury. I dreamed that I broke the posts that hold up the famous old buildings of our city or that I burned down City Hall. I exploded temples and caused huge holes in busy streets. In reality I behaved pretty well and made nice pictures, showing cute toddlers playing in gardens or darling kittens adorned with shiny bells dangling from velvet collars. The kittens are fat and happy, not at all like the starved creatures people dump in temple gardens thinking that Buddha will take care of them. Buddha never sees them, but the kittens' screams bother the monks, who drown them in the temple pond.

Did you grasp any of this when you stared into my squinting eyes, when you inquired how Mrs. Washino had met her end? I believe you did. I do squint rather badly, as you surely noticed. Passersby often laugh at me. "Don't you get bored with the view of your own nose?" more than one has asked. The way your ears jut out amused me, too. I wanted to ask, "How is it you don't get blown away when the typhoon descends on the city?"

How did my stepmother and I meet? You asked me that and I supplied you with some of the required information. I said that I rented a room in the old lady's house and that she liked me more and more, and then took me to City Hall one day to have me inscribed as her lawful son.

As her son, I was heir and her death would be of material benefit to me. So I manipulated her into death. Ungrateful, right? I am now allowed to fill in the remainder of the pertinent information?

I was showing my work in the streets and slept under a bridge, the Godjo Bridge it was at that time, by far the worst shelter the city offers—there are drafts even when the wind dies down and the rats are bigger and more aggressive than anywhere else. The bums are worse, too—drunken muggers and toothless old hags creaking with filth.

I had just started portraying the Buddhist holy men— Bodhidharma leering over his scraggly moustache, the ancient master Hakuin falling apart with age, the retarded Ananda, Buddha's first disciple who always repeated his teacher's words and was therefore called Parrot. Tourists often come to Kyoto because they think that our temples emit a heavenly radiance and holy pictures make suitable souvenirs to bring or show the folks back home. One day I made a fair amount of money and couldn't resist the temptation to buy myself new clothes. I suddenly looked so neat that I didn't dare to go back to my bridge. I wandered about aimlessly until I saw a well kept house in an alley of the Eastern Quarter. There was a sign on the wall, *Room for Rent*.

That was the beginning of the big change. Mrs. Washino opened the door and permitted me to come in. I hadn't been in a proper home for so long that I felt ill at ease. I had to restrain myself for I wanted to grin—Mrs. Washino was hunchbacked, too, and also squinted horribly. We couldn't look straight at each other and had to hang over somewhat to counterbalance the weight of our misshapen backs. The rent she offered was reasonable enough and I said I would take the room. She thought it was strange that I wanted to move in at once, but I had everything with me—my rags in a bag and my work in a wooden cylinder. I thought she might refuse and quickly counted out some notes. She nodded in acceptance. There's something indecently alluring about cash openly displayed.

I wasn't decent, either. Mrs. Washino often came to chat and would offer tea but I always insisted on drinking rice wine. Under the bridges I had become accustomed to alcohol. Fiery rice wine warms the bones and can be inspiring at times. I kept painting holy men and needed to be somewhat drunk in order to get their expressions right. But not too drunk. It was only later that I became really addicted.

Mrs. Washino liked to chatter, and her choice of subjects was rather monotonous. She usually discussed death and ways to die. She often watched TV stuff in which noble gentlemen and ladies of long ago get themselves into trouble and are forced to take their own lives. We would talk of various deadly poisons, knife and sword thrusts in belly or neck, swallowing broken glass, suffocation by hanging, jumping off cliffs, walking into the sea, and other methods. I suggested gas, for she kept gas in her home. I understood, of course, that she discussed her own death even as she forced all sorts of depressed friends and acquaintances she didn't have into her tales. She didn't know anyone at all.

I would paint until noon and spend the afternoons in the streets. One day she asked me how I made my money. I told her the truth and she shuffled out of the room without saying anything. She didn't even bow. Later that day she came back and accused me of shameless begging. She said I would have to go. I could stay until the end of the month, but not a day longer, for a person who squats on the pavement waiting for passersby to hand out money was not the type of tenant who was welcome in a nice lady's home.

"If I'm not welcome, I won't stay a moment longer," I said curtly and began to pack my belongings. Mrs. Washino said she wasn't evicting me but she knew a shed where I could possibly stay. I left angrily and slept under the bridge again. The next day she found me in the street, selling near the Imperial Palace gates. She told me she had been looking for me for hours. She cried and apologized and so I moved in again.

She wasn't a bad woman, you will say, although she might possibly be a little proud and generally limited in her outlook. I agree, with some hesitation. Human motivations aren't always easy to grasp. We looked alike and she may have considered me to be her own continuation. Then again, perhaps she wanted to have me in her power or saw a chance to gain honor through me. I'm not an untalented artist. Haven't I proved my worth since then? My *Cranes on a Rainy Evening* won a prize last year and *Kyoto Art* regularly shows reproductions of my work, followed by lengthy articles in which the experts sing my praise. *Kyoto Art* is the best art magazine in the country, some say. Mrs. Washino would have been proud of me if she were still alive.

When I returned here from my night under the bridge, she and I had a long and serious conversation. I need pay no more rent if I promised not to sell my work in the streets any more. From that day on, she paid for my paint and brushes and brought me all my meals. I was to produce a fair number of paintings and find an agent who could introduce me to the galleries and arrange exhibitions. I did my best and within a year or so my work became known.

Can you imagine what it's like to be attached by a leash

to an old woman's claw? Certainly I could paint under favorable conditions, but I had lost my free will. I fought back by drinking more than before and regularly invited other artists I'd met through my agent to help me empty the jug. I became quarrelsome and encouraged her when she got into her death talk again. Whenever I sold a painting I kept quiet, but I made sure that all my disappointments were fully discussed. The subject of suicide cropped up more and more often and I insisted on the providential use of gas.

The cylinder with cooking gas belongs in the kitchen but was found in her bedroom when you came to inquire about my stepmother's death. Who carried it up? She didn't ask me to lug that heavy object up the stairs, but one evening I thought the time had come, and was proved right.

Isn't it amazing how roles sometimes revert? At first she could control me at will but gradually I became the driving factor. My stepmother committed suicide. She unscrewed the faucet after she had pinned the plastic garbage bags on the frames of her doors and windows. I only carried the cylinder up. To assist in a suicide is illegal, but hard to prove.

As her only heir I became a suspect, but the truth is that I didn't need what she left me. A week after Mrs. Washino's death, my first big exhibition opened and I knew that I would sell. My hunch wasn't unfounded. My name had been mentioned in the right circles for a while.

So why did I help her make up her mind? I think I did that to wipe out my own past. I wanted to be rid of the disgusting beggar I had been for so long, and Mrs. Washino was the only one who had known him well. Perhaps my misdeed was also caused by the dreams of revenge I experienced under the bridges. Had I finally found someone who was even weaker than me? Or did I long for the beautiful young women I couldn't bring into the house because my stepmother's possessive jealousy barred them from my life? Did I intend to free myself once and for all? Or was it her negative talk getting on my nerves too much?

It's hard to know oneself. You saw me as a potential

murderer and kept coming back from time to time. Very clever of you. As a policeman, you certainly knew your duty. You couldn't prove my guilt, but you suspected that I wasn't quite done as yet and stayed in touch in order to prevent further upheavals. You wanted me to know that the State had her eye on me, isn't that right, Inspector? Isn't it your task to protect society? Or were you interested in my case, like Zen master Gota once was when he made me sit in his temple where the monks were beating me? Every one of your visits inflicted severe pain on my soul. Your soft polite voice hit me like a whip. Your gaze burned into the very depth of my being. You are a devil employed by the judges of hell. Doesn't Buddhism claim that only development matters and that pain is the best teacher? Isn't that truth so convincing that we enjoy reading in the paper that a student laborer in a motor-car factory has been beaten by his highest boss with a wrench?

I see you now, with your jugheaded face. If you had normal ears, you wouldn't have impressed me. Unblemished truth-bearers can dazzle us too much. Master Gota suffered from the disease of Parkinson and his trembling hand underlined everything he was trying to show me. Why does Bodhidharma's image fascinate me? Because that great teacher made use of a fat body and a grumpy face and because he slowed himself down by always displaying a nasty temper. The stylized Buddha images mean nothing to me. What do they display but inimitable perfection?

You haven't visited me for a while, but I know that you can drop in any minute now. Your visits were always unexpected and I was never able to prepare myself properly.

I assume that you will read this letter in my studio. Look about you, please. Do you see my latest work? The portraits of the ballet dancer Netsuku? Yes, that's right—on all my sketches the poor girl squints. Netsuku is known for her beautiful eyes that contemplate infinity with their luscious radiance, but in my portraits she shortsightedly peers at the tip of her nose. That failure made me buy the rope that will strangle me. I did keep trying for days on end, I've always been good at drawing eyes but I must have lost that ability for good. If you check my chest of drawers, you will find hundreds of scraps of paper on which I tried to depict Netsuku's eyes. What shows, as you will see, is my step-mother's unhappy squint.

The end of the road. Suicide is always inspired by despair. My father jumped against the thundering engine of the Osaka Express, Mrs. Washino opened up a faucet. I'll be kicking a stool in a minute. When one does that, there has been the choice of the only way out. I can only guess at what went on in the minds of my father and stepmother, and in my own mind the process is not too clear, either. Should I have confessed my crime? What would you have done? A confession alone does not stand up in court, but if together we had collected some proof my guilt could never have been washed away.

Do I realize now that I must punish myself by cutting short a most promising career? In a way I need to thank you, terrible devil who never gives in, for you destroyed my revenge. By visiting me from painful moment to moment you made me peel my own onion of ignorance. I'm not done yet—there are still tear-drawing skins that need to be ripped away, but does any process ever come to an end? Is the end of death no more than a new beginning? I will meet my stepmother again, in another form and under fresh circumstances, for if there was no connection between us, this present life has certainly tied us together.

I hear the monks sing chant again when they began their morning's meditation and a new day:

I myself see where I failed before.

Is there no end to the greed, rage, folly that brought about my birth and determined the place of a fresh start?

I confess my ignorant mistakes now, so that I can keep moving forward.

You'll have to cut me loose, put me down, and write your report. I'm sorry I cause you trouble. Meanwhile, thanks to you, I float away and am finally rid of your infernal but benificent meddling.

About the Contributors

STEPHANIE KAY BENDEL is the author of *Making Crime Pay: a Practical Guide to Mystery Writing* and *A Scream Away* (as Andrea Harris). Her short stories have appeared in *Ellery Queen's Mystery Magazine* (as Hilary Stevens) and in *Alfred Hitchcock's Mystery Magazine*. After residing in New England for fifteen years, Stephanie recently moved to Boulder, Colorado, with her husband and two children.

AMANDA CROSS'S first novel, published in 1964, won her a Mystery Writers of America Scroll. To date, she has published eight novels; "Tania's No Where" was her first story. It appeared in *Ellery Queen's Mystery Magazine*. When she isn't writing, Amanda is an Avalon Foundation Professor in the Humanities at Columbia University.

JEAN DARLING was born in Santa Monica, California, and began her acting career in films and on Broadway at the age of six months. For five years, "Baby" Jean enjoyed worldwide renown as the leading lady of the *Our Gang* comedies. In the years since then, she has appeared in Vaudeville and on TV and radio, in addition to her stage and movie experience.

Jean's mystery/horror short stories have appeared in such American publications as *Ellery Queen's Mystery Magazine, Alfred Hitchcock's Mystery Magazine, Whispers, Fantasy Book,* and *Night Cry.* Her work has also been published in Ireland, where she has resided since 1967 with her husband and son.

LILLIAN DE LA TORRE was born in New York City on March 15, 1902. Educated in the East, she holds degrees from Columbia (M.A. 1927) and Harvard (M.A. 1933), with a recent doctorate in Humane Letters from Colorado College (1987). Lillian married George S. McCue, a college professor, in 1932. She began her "Dr. Sam: Johnson" historical mystery short story series in 1942, adding to it over the years for a total of thirty-one, now collected into four paperback volumes in the International Polygonics Limited Library of Crime Classics. Meanwhile, she has found time to produce a number of books in various fields: true crime, cookery, girls' books, and several plays. Her hobbies are amateur acting and choral singing.

JOE GORES was born in Rochester, Minnesota. He received degrees in English literature from Notre Dame and Stanford, and spent twelve years as a private detective in San Francisco. He is a past president of Mystery Writers of America (1986) and has won three of their Edgar Awards (first novel, short story, teleplay). His eighth novel, *Wind Time, Wolf Time,* is due from Putnam in 1988; he is working on the movie version of his seventh, Edgar-nominated *Come Morning.* He has also written a massive fact book, *Marine Salvage,* some one hundred short stories and articles, and has edited two anthologies. *Hammett* was filmed by Francis Coppola; *Interface* is under option by director Walter Hill. Gores has written seven commissioned screenplays and twenty-four hours of television for such popular shows as "Kojak," "Magnum, P.I.," "Mike Hammer," and "Remington Steele." He and his wife, Dori, live in Marin

County, California. Their son, Tim, works in music videos in Los Angeles, and their daughter, Gillian, is a student in Italian at New York University.

JOYCE HARRINGTON's first short story, "The Purple Shroud" (*Ellery Queen's Mystery Magazine*), won the Mystery Writers of America Edgar Allan Poe Award. That was in 1972. Since then, she has gone on to write many short stories and three novels. Her latest novel, *Dreemz of the Night* (St. Martin's Press), is a gritty tale of the murder of a New York City subway graffiti artist. Three of her later stories have been nominated for Edgars. The story in this volume is one of them. Harrington lives in Manhattan and has served on the MWA Board of Directors as secretary, treasurer, and executive vice president. She is currently working on a new novel.

EDWARD D. HOCH was born in 1930 in Rochester, New York. He is a past president of Mystery Writers of America and author of more than seven hundred published short stories, mainly in the mystery field. He has appeared in every issue of *Ellery Queen's Mystery Magazine* since May 1973. Among his thirty-one books are a half dozen novels, several collections of short stories, and more than fifteen anthologies, including the annual *Year's Best Mystery & Suspense Stories*. Hoch resides in Rochester with his wife, Patricia.

JAMES HOLDING, after graduation from Yale and a year spent traveling in Europe, joined the advertising agency BBDO, Inc., as a copywriter in its Pittsburgh Office. Thirty years later, as a copy chief and vice president, he retired from the advertising business to try his hand at writing fiction. Since then, he has traveled widely and has used some of the faraway places he visited as settings for many of his mystery stories and children's books. Currently, Holding lives with his wife on Siesta Key in Sarasota, Florida.

CLARK HOWARD has been writing for thirty years, full time for fifteen. He is an Edgar winner and won the first two *Ellery Queen's Mystery Magazine* Readers' Awards. Since 1980, his short stories have been selected every year for an award or nomination for a writing honor. He is also the author of eighteen novels.

MARGARET MARON's short stories have appeared in such magazines as *Alfred Hitchcock's Mystery Magazine, Mike Shayne Mystery Magazine, Redbook, McCall's,* and *Reader's Digest,* and have been reprinted in various anthologies here and abroad. Now at work on her seventh novel to feature Lt. Sigrid Harald, NYPD (*Death in Blue Folders, The Right Jack*), she presently lives on the family farm in central North Carolina.

BARBARA OWENS holds a degree in theater and originally aspired toward a career in acting until, fortunately, she fell in with the wrong crowd and turned to writing instead. Her story "The Cloud Beneath the Eaves" received the Mystery Writers of America's Edgar for 1978. Her work has also appeared in science fiction magazines, and a treatment of her story "The New Man" aired as the premiere episode of the syndicated TV series "Tales From the Darkside." "A Little Piece of Room" originally appeared in *Ellery Queen's Mystery Magazine* in December 1979.

HELENE JUAREZ PHIPPS' first short story, "The Dog That Only Barked at Anglos," was published in *Texas Quarterly* and later in the Mystery Writers of America anthology *Copcade.* She won the Southern California MWA prize for "Running Lovers," which was later published in *Ellery Queen's Mystery Magazine.* In addition to her short stories, Helene has written articles about Mexican artists and authored a cookbook, *Authentic Mexican Cooking* (Simon & Schuster, 1985). She resides in California, where she is the statewide coordinator for the California Democratic Council.

WILLIAM F. NOLAN has operated a miniature railroad for children, raced sports cars, acted in motion pictures, painted outdoor murals, served as a book reviewer for the *Los Angeles Times,* edited a score of books and magazines, plotted Mickey Mouse adventures for Walt Disney, taught creative writing at Bowling Green State University—and has sold novels, short fiction, essays, articles, and verse to 100 publications, from *Playboy* to *Alfred Hitchcock's Mystery Magazine.* Nolan's work has been selected for more than 150 anthologies. As a biographer, he has written books on Ernest Hemingway, Dashiell Hammett, John Huston, and Steve McQueen. He has also written a critical history of *Black Mask* magazine.

HERBERT RESNICOW's first book, *The Gold Solution,* published in 1983, was nominated for an Edgar and was quickly followed by three other Gold books, six books of the Crossword series, *Murder at the Super Bowl* (with Fran Tarkenton), the first of the Sports series, and *The Dead Room,* first of the Business series. He recently completed *Bean Ball* (with Tom Seaver), the second in the Sports series, and is presently working on *The Gold Gamble* and *The Whodunit,* a series of critical essays.

His hobbies are weight lifting, loudspeaker design, music, theater, ballet, and reading. Resnicow lives in a suburb of New York with his wife, Melly. They have four children.

WALTER SATTERTHWAIT has lived throughout the United States, in Greece, and in Kenya. He has published two books with Dell, *Cocaine Blues* and *The Aegean Affair.* His most recent novel, *Wall of Glass,* a mystery set in Santa Fe, New Mexico, was published in February of 1988 by St. Martin's Press. Mr. Satterthwait, currently in transit, would like to extend his gratitude to Cathleen Jordan and Lois Adams of *Alfred Hitchcock's Mystery Magazine.*

JANWILLEM VAN DE WETERING, a native of Rotterdam, the Netherlands, began writing at the age of forty; at forty-five he moved to America. His writings include *The Empty Mirror*, *The Sergeant's Cat* (most recent volume in the Amsterdam Cop Series), *Inspector Saito's Small Satori*, and several children's books. He contributes to *Ellery Queen's* and *Alfred Hitchcock's* magazines, writes reviews for the *New York Times*, and enjoys, with his landscaping wife, the miracles of the wild Maine cost.